The Tiger's Eye
New & Selected Stories

Gladys Swan

Gladys Swan (signature)

SERVING HOUSE BOOKS

The Tiger's Eye: New & Selected Stories

Copyright © 2011 Gladys Swan

ISBN: 978-0-9826921-8-9

Cover art by Gladys Swan

Author photo by Gerik Parmele, Columbia, MO *Tribune*

Serving House Books logo by Barry Lereng Wilmont

Published by Serving House Books
Copenhagen and Florham Park, NJ

www.servinghousebooks.com

First Serving House Books Edition 2011

For Madison and Erika

Also by Gladys Swan

Novels

Carnival for the Gods
Ghost Dance: A Play of Voices
The World of Carnival (selections)

Short Fiction

On the Edge of the Desert
Of Memory and Desire
Do You Believe in Cabeza de Vaca?
A Visit to Strangers
News from the Volcano
A Garden Amid Fires

The author would like to acknowledge the presses that originally published her books and the publications in which they have appeared.

On the Edge of the Desert, Illinois Short Fiction Series :

"Flight," *Virginia Quaterly Review*, Finalist, Emily Clark Balch
   Competition; Honor Roll, *Best American Short Stories*.
"Losing Game," *The Interior Country: Stories of the Modern West*.
"The Wayward Path."

Of Memory and Desire, Louisiana State University Press:

"Lucinda," *Ohio Review* , *Best of the West II*, and *Ohio Review, New &*
   Selected—30th Anniversary Issue.
"Getting an Education,"*Mid-American Review* and *Voiceless Cry: An*
   Anthology of Stories from Women Around the World. (Serbia)

Do You Believe in Cabeza de Vaca? University of Missouri Press:

"Painting the Town"
"Do you Believe in Cabeza de Vaca?" *Kenyon Review*.
"The Turkish March" *Ohio Review*.
"The Old Hotel," *Manoa* and *Best of the West IV*.
"Dreaming Crow," *Green Mountains Review* and *Birds in the Hand,*
   Poetry and Fiction about Birds.

A Visit to Strangers, University of Missouri Press:

"The Demon of Forgetfulness," *Ohio Review*.
"The Blind Musician," *New Letters*.

"The Afternoon of the Pterodactyl," *Prairie Schooner*, Lawrence Foundation Award.
"Venus Rising"

News from the Volcano, University of Missouri Press:

"News from the Volcano," *Green Mountains Review; Walking the Twilight, II : Stories by Western Women Writers; World Wide Writers (England), Times of Sorrow, Times of Grace: Writing by Women of the Great Plains/High Plains.*

A Garden Amid Fires. BkMk Press:

"The Death of the Cat," *Manoa*.
"The Orange Bird" and "Uncle Lazarus," *Sewanee Review*.
"Exiles," *The Literary Review*.

Uncollected stories:

"The Tiger's Eye," *Writer's Forum* and *Paraspheres: Fabulist and New Wave Fabulist Fiction.*

"The Darkness Hawk, *Chariton Review*.

"Spirit over Water" and "The House on the Lake," *Sewanee Review*.

Gladys Swan is both a writer and a visual artist. She has published two novels, *Carnival for the Gods* in the Vintage Contemporaries Series, and *Ghost Dance: A Play of Voices*, nominated by LSU Press for the PEN Faulkner and PEN West awards. *A Garden Amid Fires* is the most recent of her six collections of short fiction. Her fiction, poetry, and essays have appeared regularly in the *Sewanee Review* and other literary magazines. She has received a Lilly Endowment Open Fellowship and a Fulbright Fellowship to Yugoslavia, as well as a Lawrence Foundation Award for fiction and a Tate Prize for poetry.

Contents

Preface

The stories in this book have been selected from the six previous collections of short fiction I have published, as well as from recent work. They represent what I've written in that genre over the past four decades. Though I've made various ventures into the novel, as well as poetry and the essay, I find that I cannot do without the short story—it is such a beautiful form. I love the challenges it presents in dealing with characters and situations that light upon the cusp of the moment and which must be handled with an eye to economy and unity of effect. As with many writers, I began writing stories out of a love for the fairy tales, legends, and other works of fantasy that seized hold of my imagination as a child and continued to shape my sensibility.

When I was thirteen and in the eighth grade, our spelling teacher, actually our P.E. teacher, told us to write a story using that week's spelling words. She read mine to the class. It was, as I recall, a story about a man trying to break a horse and who kept getting bucked off. (I had yet to discover "The Strawberry Roan" with its wonderful conclusion.) This was the pivotal incident that convinced me that I wanted to be a writer. How extraordinary are the springs of action! My small triumph spurred me to put together a collection of stories, which my father, after bragging about me to his friends, actually sent to Simon & Schuster. (Not only children are subject to illusion. Perhaps I was supposed to be a genius.) When the printed rejection came, with a box marked at the side of a question as to what should be done with the manuscript, I was too disheartened and embarrassed to arrange for its return.

But for some unknown reason I continued to write. During the summer after my first year of high school, my wonderful English teacher, Ella Snodgrass, who also wanted to write and was taking a course from *Writers' Digest*, very kindly gave me the lessons after she was finished with them. According to them, there were three classes of stories: pulp fiction; slick magazine fiction; and something called "off-trail" stories. I decided immediately that the last were what I wanted to write. I tried one—with a surprise ending. It was rather a contrived affair.

In college, my Introduction to Fiction class was a revelation. I discovered the stories of Chekhov, Hawthorne, Faulker and Joyce, Flanner O'Conner, Eudora Welty and Katherine Anne Porter. I learned that there was a level to language beyond its literal sense and entered a territory of rich ambiguity, symbolic depth, and irony--a territory I call home.

I had no idea what I was doing or trying to do in my early efforts to emulate the writers I admired. I knew only that I wanted the sense of rightness, of integrity I found in their work, even though my efforts fell so abysmally short. Nor did it help that my own experience seemed so insignificant I hardly knew what to write about. I wrote two stories a year, laboring over them, taking them through version after version. Fortunately, most of those wooden results were never published. Some few I returned to later with greater clarity of vision; these I rewrote and was able to publish. All of this took a good many years. Except for a six-week class in creative writing, taught in summer school by a visiting professor trying for a little extra cash, I had had no real training in the craft. I learned by reading and the practice of writing. I didn't know any other writers.

Until my first book was published, my only reader was my husband, and those editors who kept sending back my work. Almost always with a paperclip holding it together--a dead giveaway of its history. One of the worst things one could do, it seemed, was to announce to an editor that a piece of work had previously been rejected. That meant a great deal of retyping and lost time. I seized upon the expedient of typing the first and last couple of pages and ironing the rest, in order to send it forth in its pristine condition. When my first two stories were published in the *Colorado Quarterly* and the *Virginia Quarterly Review*, a finalist in the Emily Clark Balch

Competition, I felt I'd made a beginning, but it was another five years before I could publish another. My first collection of stories was published in the Illinois Short Fiction Series in 1979, when I was forty-five. Nearly all of the stories in the book had been making the rounds for eight or ten years. Only half of them had appeared in literary journals. During that time I had no notion of who my audience might be, if indeed there was one.

Since a collection such as this is a kind of retrospective, it has offered me a chance to look back at the seventy-odd stories I have written and see what has taken my attention. I see that a number of my stories deal with characters who stand at the edge of or outside the social order, wrestling with their various predicaments, trying to find a place for themselves, a way to live. I can see that two major questions have occupied me: what is meant by "experience"? and what kind of knowledge can be apprehended through the imagination? For me, the mystery of character has deepened over time and the possibilities of the imagination have kept expanding. I am glad to know I have been occupied by questions that will always remain open to investigation and discovery, and I hope that I've been true to the impulse that has kept me on the path.

•

I wish to express my gratitude to the editors who have published my work and given me their generous support, particularly, George Core, Alex Blackburn, Wayne Dodd, David Lazar, Bob Stewart, Robert Shepard, Beverly Jarrett, Ben Furnish, and Walter Cummins. I am grateful for gift of time and space at the residencies I have held at the Vermont Studio Center, Yaddo, the Chateau de Lavigny, the Fundación Valparaíso, the Wurlitzer Foundation, the Martha's Vineyard Writers' Residency, and the Norton Island Residency. My thanks and appreciation go to the various colleagues and friends, whose encouragement, advice and good offices have made it possible for me to continue: Thomas E. Kennedy, Dale Kushner, Leslie Ullman, Phyllis Barber, Pamela Painter, W.D. Wetherell, Fred Chappell, Gordon Weaver, Kelly Cherry, Baron Wormser, Laura Bornholdt, Monique Salzmann,

Alice Friman, Herbert Lust II, Kay Bonetti, Philip Parotti, Marie Harris, Roberta Bienvenu, Ed Weyhing, Marly Swick, Trudy Lewis, and Craig Barrow. No doubt others deserve to be included in the list, among them, some wonderful readers.

I am grateful to my family for their forebearance and good humor during those years when my preoccupation caused me to burn pots on the stove and put strange things into the refrigerator. And finally, I must acknowledge the great debt I owe to my late husband, Richard Swan, who, for over half a century, read everything I wrote and responded to it not only with sensitivity, critical acuity, and honesty, but also with great-hearted generosity.

A voice, her own and yet her sister's spoke the dream words. Our heart must have its shadows, self scrutiny's harsh working light / destroys the darkness where life sends out is roots. Deeper, always darker.

Melissa Zink

Losing Game

Turn the things out of a man's pockets and take their testimony: a soft brown leather billfold worn to limpness without ever having been made fat with prosperity, home of a few snapshots, Social Security card, driver's license, expired; a gadget combining pocket-knife, corkscrew, and can opener; a book of matches; a pocket comb with teeth broken out; the stub of a pencil; an old pocket watch with the staff gone, around the house for years lying broken—his father's and now his, therefore a piece of inheritance; a letter, the last his father had written, the address more than five years old; two quarters, three dimes, and four pennies. His belongings—down to the lint in his pockets. Uneasy from the lightness of his jacket, he stood, missing something, as though he weren't all there. They dumped the stuff on the desk and let it sit in a little heap while they dug out a few facts—to hold against him, he supposed—to clinch the evidence of what they'd found on him.

Name? Jason Hummer. He'd have lied if his things hadn't been such a dead giveaway, his principle being never to tell the truth if it gave somebody a hold over you. But he wasn't sure the lie would make that much difference. Another name, another man? Jake Hemphill, suppose. He saw a school janitor sweeping slow, eyes wedded to wastepaper and wads of chewing gum. John Harding: solid sort—bust a man in the crockery for making eyes at his wife; good provider. Junius Holloway: banker, pillar of the church, a power in the town; storm cloud by day, pillar of smoke by night. Jay Hay: playboy—white convertible, leopard-skin seat covers; a creature of speed and spring and back-seat quick-hand. Nope, for better or worse, he was stuck with himself.

Age? Twenty-eight. Hair, brown; eyes, brown. Distinguishing

marks and characteristics? None. No visible scars, birthmarks, carbuncles, tics, tattoos, hardly even a mole of any size or interest. True, he was looking a bit shaggy and unkempt.

Occupation? That was a tough one. He had been either too many things or too few to add up to something you could write in the space on a printed form. Not that he hadn't been occupied. Handyman, he said. He'd done enough of carpentry, wiring, plumbing, to qualify. He couldn't make out what the deputy wrote down. Bum, maybe. Vagabond, derelict, good-for-nothing. Vagrant. At the moment, nothing else could be his occupation.

Fingerprints. Right thumb, right hand. Left thumb, left hand. No two sets alike, it occurred to him—like snowflakes. He stared at the mark of his uniqueness. A man was his fingerprint.

The deputy beckoned him down the corridor to the lockup, held open the door of the cell and then shut him in with a clash of iron reverberating, working down his spine. Bunk, chair, open toilet—the comforts of home. He sat down on the bunk, his nostrils hit by the smell of disinfectant, powerful, yet somehow impure, as though tainted by the corpse of whatever it killed. For just beneath the overbearing smell another odor leaked in, faint but pervasive, a presence almost that could not be drowned out. The residue of occupancy, an odor of staleness, like dirty socks or dried sweat, but more like something that, deprived of light and air, had taken its last breath and given up the ghost.

Well, here I am, he thought, as if he had reached a destination. And the other, where was he? Probably carted off to a hospital somewhere—the man who had fallen among ruffians. And he saw the fellow again, a vivid presence. He was red—face red, hands red. A figure sitting on the curb of the street, dabbing at his face with a handkerchief—covered with paint, or so it looked. But then, it had flashed through his mind, why would anybody be covered with red paint? Blood, he thought, just as quickly—that's blood. And he was close enough now to see that the face was streaming with blood, and the hands and arms. The handkerchief that the fellow kept dabbing in a slow unhurried way was itself red, a piece of bright rag held up to the flow.

"My God, fella, what happened to you?" he said.

"Some guys jumped me. Beat me up. Six of 'em."

Nothing like a fair fight. "You can't sit here. Where do you live? Want me to call somebody?"

"Better call the cops."

He didn't much want to call the police. As with doctors and lawyers and hospital personnel and public officials in general, he was content to live and let live. But the case seemed pressing. He crossed the street to the pay phone and put in one of his dimes. If he'd had any sense, he'd have quietly disappeared after doing his little duty. But the fellow was beaten up pretty bad. By the time he got back, he had passed out and was lying on the street. So he stayed till the cops came. He told them what he knew, while a few bystanders milled around, soaking up the scene and waiting till the ambulance came with a fine wail of the siren. They would have to start asking him questions. Once they got on the trail, they kept it up till they had him treed: no job, no money, no place to go. So they hauled him in. Did they suspect him of having beaten up the fellow himself? He explained that he'd come to town trying to locate a relative. Looking for somebody to leech onto, he could hear them thinking; yeah, we know all about it. Actually, he had already been to the town from where his father had sent the letter but hadn't found him.   They hauled him in.

"Say, man, what'd they grab you for?"

He looked over to the shape leaning against the bars of the cell across the corridor. "For being plain damn dumb."

"Join the club. Never trust a buddy. Remember that—rule of life. Don't even let a guy smoke in here. What a fleabag."

Here he was—among those nameless others who had bequeathed their presence, a part of that brotherhood that had stood, on the wrong side of a barred window. The walls bore the marks of their presence. Names and dates, notches to mark off the days, drawings of women with extraordinary breasts and thighs like columns and explicit crotches—goddesses of waiting and boredom. Obscenities, doodles, scribblings, even a bit of verse carefully boxed in. The pencil had smudged a little, blurring some of the words, but he could make them out:

The five cards in the cradle
Are the five cards dealt by fate
You're in a game of poker
And luck is an inside straight.

Except for a few dirty limericks, he hadn't been much for verse since the fifth grade, when Mrs. Pennuel had made them memorize it and recite it to the class. But it was mostly high-minded and instructive and never stooped to anything so low as a poker game:

Build thee more stately mansions,
O my soul, as the swift seasons roll,

he dredged up from somewhere, unable for the life of him to think of the next line—what you did when you found a place you liked, if you ever did, that was clean and livable and not too high in the upkeep. He had not gotten things too well by heart, having lost all interest in scholarship when the teachers quit reading stories out loud and letting the kids draw pictures with crayons. His mother had spent a lot of words and useless grief trying to shame him with the fact that she had always been at the top of her class in school. With slightly more effect, she used to sit with her sewing to keep an eye on him while he struggled through his homework and would thump him on the head with her thimble when she saw his attention lag. Maybe if she had thumped him harder, the thought occurred to him, circumstances would have thumped him less; for he'd maybe have learned whatever it was that was supposed to do him some good. He read on, squinting to make out the words:

Sometimes a pair is winner,
Sometimes a flush is not,
And you'll lose all your singles
If losing is your lot.

Good grief, he thought—sure for a moment that his father must have stood in that self-same cell. It could have been his voice speaking, except for the rhyme. Whoever it was must have fared just as badly at poker. A descendant of Wild Bill Hickok? Like his father? Was there something at the marrow of things, he wondered, that made a pair of aces and a pair of eights unlucky? Something you'd get shot in the back for holding? . . . At least James Butler Hickok was the sort of man you could feel bad about getting it. Which he'd started doing about the time he was nine years old. Yes indeed. Drama of the Old West, Part I:

THE TRUE SON OF WILD BILL HICKOK
or
Ladies, If You Have a Love-child, Lie a Little
Scene:

Salida, Colorado, on the banks of the old Arkansas.
White frame house with pillars holding up the front porch. A swing on that porch. The noise of that swing as it goes back and forth, not a squeak exactly, but a low-toned rake, a comfortable sort of noise. Himself on the porch swing, listening:

> *I tell you, boy, there was no finer man than Wild Bill. Handsome and brave . . . .*

The old man, his grandfather, talking—in his eighties now, come down to Salida, Colorado, to fret out his last years—a straight-backed, hawk-nosed old man, impatient of old age.

> *When I was grown up some, I went round to all the men I could find who'd known him when he was marshal in Abilene and Hays City. See, looka here, this is his picture.*

The boy looks at the picture, studies it:

> *He looks kina mean with that mustache.*

His grandfather takes the picture, holds it out in front of him, can't hold it steady because his hands shake.

> *No, boy, he wasn't mean, nor wild. They called him Wild Bill, only he wasn't mean nor ornery, not like the ruffians he was trying to take a little law and order to in them wild cow towns. He never killed a man but in self-defense.*

The boy looks at the picture again to make sure.
His grandfather: Once three men set upon him at the same time
     and he shot his way out alive. You had to defend yourself in those
     days. Still do. (Little sharp laugh.) And you remember that—the
     manly art of self-defense. (Gives the boy a little friendly poke in the chest.)
     And remember what you came from. Remember now that when Jack
     McCall shot him in the back not all his blood ran onto the ground.
     The blood that is flowing in your veins, just like the blood flowing in
     mine, is the blood of Wild Bill Hickok . . . .
The old man holding him by a look, as though he were hypnotizing him.
          ENTER *a thin, long-faced, bony woman.*

*Wild Bill Poppycock, you mean. That's the only stuff
flowing around here. No blood neither—just hot wind.*

*They look up. His mother, having entered upon the scene unnoticed, stands
in front of them, arms akimbo.*
*His grandfather: What do you mean, daughter, coming sneaking up that-
a-way? And what do you know about what I'm saying to the boy?*
*His mother: You ain't no more descended from Wild Bill Hickok than
I am. I know all about that: Well, I s'pose your ma had to have
somebody to lay it on to—ha! Well, she picked one all right. To take
the edge off the disgrace.*
*The old man stands up, red in the face, the veins in his forehead looking
as though they will burst. The boy looks at his mother, then at his grandfather. His stomach hurts the way it did when he ate too much candy
and junk at the carnival.*
*His grandfather: Shame. How dare you say a thing like that to me? And
here in front of the boy . . .*
*His mother: And shame on you, filling up his head with lies and tales—
all kind of nonsense. Hard enough time I got as it is pounding some
sense into him. What's going to happen to him in the world, the
kind of stuff you're loading him up with.*
His grandfather (under his breath): Bitch.
*His mother: What? Yes, well, I know how it is. You never liked me from
the beginning. Thought I wasn't good enough for that precious son of
yours. Well, you don't have to like me much longer—that's how it is.*
*Words flying back and forth as the lights fade, carrying both his grandfather
and mother into the darkness. A single spotlight lingers momentarily on
him, held for questioning:*

*??????? GRANDSON OF A NOTORIOUS LIAR   AND SON OF A
BITCH ???????*

●

They brought him a tray of food, recalling to him that he
hadn't eaten yet that day.

"Don't look too close at them beans," the fellow across the
corridor told him. "You might see something move."

25

"Well, I'm needing a little red meat."

"Haw, well, it'll put hair on your chest."

The beans were hard and sapless like they'd had to be unstuck from the bottom of the pot. There were potatoes and something else swimming around in the gravy. He ate it all, wiped round the plate with a piece of bread, and sat back content, though he knew that the flavors would keep him company the rest of the night. True, he'd eaten worse, but not much worse.

●

But his mother had to be wrong. For if his father didn't bear Wild Bill's blood, he certainly shared his fatality at poker. Not that there was any other resemblance between Wild Bill and his father, a slim, middling sort of man who'd lost most of his hair and gone slack in the gut by the time he was thirty and could only spend the rest of his life getting balder and slacker. The only thing he'd managed to hold onto was a knot of worry above his nose. For the things that belonged to him had a way of deserting him and the rest had a way of going against him. Penniless relatives and stray cats turned up at the door, starving hungry and howling for food; and small-time hoods smelled him out for a little protection money like rats after crumbs. Otherwise he might have done decently enough with the bar he ran there in Salida, Colorado, though his wife never liked to mention what it was that bought the victuals and paid the bills. She'd have been better pleased if he'd run a grocery or even a feed store or traveled around selling some gadget that lightened your chores.

When he thought of his father, he could sometimes hear his voice and remember something of his general shape; but he could but dimly see his face. Nor could he put his impressions together to form a picture of the man. Specifically he remembered the three signs of his father's presence those evenings he was home and it came time for the kids to go to bed. He and his sister would be making a ruckus, chasing each other around the house, teasing and throwing pillows. His father would clear his throat. That was the announcement that they'd better quit horsing around and do what they were told. Nobody would pay any heed. Next his father would rattle his newspaper. They'd keep on. But when he started knocking the ashes out of his pipe, they'd tear upstairs. He didn't know why. He didn't know what his father would have done if they hadn't. Perhaps they knew by instinct that they oughtn't face him with the crisis. For it was his mother that always gave them a hiding. She kept a switch and she knew how to use it.

So that what happened afterwards didn't fit in at all, and nobody could say what it was that got into his father the night of the poker game. He wasn't what you'd call a gambling man. Two or three times a month he'd play a game of nickel ante, his one diversion. So there was nothing new in that. It was true that Avery was a stranger in town, and maybe a sharp stranger, though he couldn't picture it. More than likely, Avery simply fell into something. But if he were actually looking for a way to make his fortune, Fate led him to the right place. Even so, that still didn't account for his father. Maybe his father didn't know what was happening to him, found himself in so deep he couldn't get out. Or maybe he'd thought he could track down the luck that was always giving him the slip. Or maybe he'd picked up the cards as though the next day didn't matter because he didn't want to think about the next day.

Or maybe it was just a kind of fatality. Maybe the moment you were born, somewhere else was born the man who'd do you the dirty—the Jack McCall who'd shoot you down: like the yolk and the white of an egg. No matter how far away he was, something must be that beckoned a man's destroyer. Then the thought came to him, How about if you created him? It was a puzzle.

In any case, he didn't know what had gone on in the back room of the bar. The only part of the drama he knew about came after the game, and perhaps that was the only part that mattered. Drama of the Old West, Part II:

THE ERRING SON OF WILD BILL HICKOCK
or
When the Chips Are Down, Boys, Never Let a Female Get the Drop on You

Darkness. He wakes to find voices rising up, piercing sleep like knives. He is in bed. He lies listening:

27

You're crazy. Drunk or plain crazy. Keeping me up till all hours,
worried to death you'd got yourself killed or something worse.
And now you come telling me you've lost the place. You're drunk
or crazy.

He strains to catch the answering voice, his father's—low but not blurred.
Yes, lost it.

His mother: You mean . . . you mean you'd gamble away our living? You'd
risk that.

His father: Risked it and lost it.

His mother: Fine, oh that's fine, and what are we supposed to do now?
Turn us out into the street. And what do you want—me to walk
the street now? I'd prob'ly get us a better living than you ever got.

His father: Hush up, Ella, you'll wake the kids.

His mother: Don't you be telling me when to shut my mouth. I don't care
if I wake the dead. You snake in the grass, you crawling, low-
bellied, lying . . . sneaking . . . I could kill you for this. Oh, I could
kill you.

He gets up out bed and quietly sips downstairs to the doorway of the
living room. He blinks in the light.

His father: You never liked the place anyway.

His mother: Oh, so that's how it is. She doesn't like it, so the hell with
it. So now what are you going to do, you yellow-bellied, slack-
gutted flea-brain?

His father: I don't know yet.

His mother turns, rushes to the little cupboard just to the side of the
fireplace and takes out the Colt Peacemaker his grand-father swore had
belonged to Wild Bill Hickok himself.
Get out. Get out.

His father: Don't wave that thing around—it's loaded.

He rushes in, throws himself down, and clings to his father's knees.

His mother: What are you doing up? Get yourself out of here.
This is nothing to do with you. Go on, get, before I take the
switch to you.

His father: Put that goddam thing away. But then I s'pose you want my
blood too. Don't worry, I'm leaving in the morning.

His mother: We can get along without you—all you've ever done around
here. Well, all I'm saying is you'd better get your traps and haul your

dead ass out of here by noon and not a minute past.
His mother turns and goes out of the room, throws down a blanket and pil-
low into the middle of the floor.

> *Now get on out. If you want to sleep, you can sleep on the front*
> *porch ... (then noticing him). And you get on up to bed.*

He goes back up to bed and lies there in the dark. He can't close his eyes.
He lies there holding up the darkness with his eyeballs. Suppose his
father could take hold of that Colt and go after the fellow who'd done
him in. Then there wouldn't be any more trouble. But there is a question.
He slides out of bed, opens the window, and climbs out onto the roof and
shinnies down the pillar. His father lies curled up in the porch swing, his
head turned toward the back. He squats down beside him.

> *Pa, what happened, Pa? Did he cheat you?*

His father turns over, peers at him in the dark.

> *Did he cheat you, Pa?*

His father leans over.

> *No, boy, he won it fair and square. (A long pause.) Sometimes you ...*
> *There's something ... and you got to ...*

The light goes on inside the house. The sound of steps.

> *His father: Quick, now, get on back to bed before your ma catches*
> *you out here.*

Scene ii:

Carrying his suitcase down the sidewalk of the empty street at half past
noon, his father rides out of town for the last time—on the Greyhound.

It was a night without peace. He'd just dropped off to sleep when the door of the cell next to his clashed shut on a pair of drunks they'd hauled in from somewhere. One got sick all over the floor and the other kept yelling for somebody to come and clean it up. Nobody came. The smell was enough to unlatch his innards, and though he tried to escape into sleep, the smell kept pulling him back.

They let him out the next morning after breakfast.

Sunlight took him by surprise, so accustomed had he become to the glare of artificial light, which had its own kind of dimness. But when his eyes were used to the sunlight and he'd filled his lungs with air, he felt good all of a sudden, as though air and sun alone were cause for celebration. Which direction now—north, south, east, west? He had one more place to look before he called it quits and moved on. He was almost afraid to look further, afraid the old man was dead or else lying in an alley somewhere curled up next to an empty bottle of rotgut. The one place he still had to look was the fairgrounds. He'd come upon an old fellow in a grocery store/ filling station who seemed to know everything that had happened in those parts for the last seventy-five years and who'd told him he thought—yep, name sounds familiar—he knew a Hummer out at the fairgrounds working in the carnival. And if it were his father, what sort of thing would he be doing there?

Jason waited till nearly dark before he set out to answer the question, walking along the highway out to the fairgrounds, where all the cars were headed, a lot of them jammed full of teenagers in a hurry. He found it pleasant walking while the evening dimmed down to the last streaks of sunset fading behind the hills. The air was cool with the lateness of summer, suggesting what would come: the kids starting back to school; the carnival packing up, the rides being taken down in great chunks of metal; the empty grounds left for the wind to pick at scraps of paper.

But there ahead, the sky was all livened up with strings and circles of lights, though it wasn't dark enough yet for them to stand out sharply. As he approached, he thought he smelled hot dogs. Food—and it smelled good. Since he wasn't about to pay for a ticket, he walked around till he found a place where he could slip into the carnival itself, in between the trucks that held the generating equipment.

He came in near where the ferris wheel was in motion to the grind and putt of the motor below. There were people on it, though not many, the empty seats rattling as they swung back and forth. Two girls flew shrieking past, clinging to each other as they went flying up, then down to catch the lights of the town in their laps. It might be, he considered, taking up possibilities, that his father was selling tickets for one of the rides or maybe peddling popcorn or candied apples, though he couldn't feature it.

30

He threaded his way through a crowd that was beginning to thicken up with ranchers and town folks with all their kids. Little kids yammering and pulling at the big folks to take them on the rides or buy them popcorn, and solemn staring-eyed babies kept up past their bedtime. He had to work his way around a bunch of the older kids laughing and talking, arms knotted, not looking out where they were going. A few of the gray-headed and thickset had plumped themselves down at the bingo game—a row of bottoms along a bench. The caller, with a voice that twanged like catgut, stood in the middle by a table piled up with lamps and waffle irons and sets of glasses and ashtrays on stands and black ceramic panthers, and called out the numbers.

Not at the ferris wheel or the bingo game, nor as a barker for the freak show, where the man with the rubber neck and the amazing man-woman were on display. Nor did he find him with the girlie show, where the girls stood out on the platform with set faces, like plaster casts, not giving anything away for nothing.

He paused a moment by the merry-go-round and breathed in the smell of hot dogs and popcorn and listened to the calliope and watched scenes of Indian maidens and swans, sailboats and islands with palm trees flash by. He'd wandered here and there without seeing anybody that bore the slightest resemblance to his father, but then he couldn't be sure he would recognize him after all these years. And the question occurred to him, What would he do if he did see him? All the time he had been looking, the question had never crossed his mind; only now when there was a real chance of finding him. For now he was convinced that his father would be working one of the booths. His father ought to know something about games of chance.

For the crowd it was a question of whether to throw darts at balloons or balls at weighted dummies, or toss rings around knife handles, or nickels at little squares; whether to pick a number that might come up at the spin of the wheel or place a coin on a horse in a miniature race—so as to win one of the great bright pink or blue pandas on the shelves or a cigarette lighter, pocketknife, or watch that glittered under the lights, but more likely one of the glass ashtrays hidden under the counter. He watched a young fellow

31

throwing balls, three tosses for a quarter, while a girl waited for him to win one of the giant stuffed pandas for her. He had a pile of quarters on the counter and was determined to do it.

When Jason looked their way, the operators caught his eye, shouted to him to try his luck. "You wanna play, mister? You win some of these, eh?" The slang hammered out in a foreign accent made him pause to look at the face: high cheekbones, red hair cruelly dyed. But it was the voice that got him—hard beyond the hardness of things, but keen-edged with the sharper's interest in getting around them. She was turned sharper just like a man. A great screeching racket met his ears before he saw that the next booth was filled with cages of parakeets. "Come on, mister, ya get de boid." The flash of a gold tooth came with the laugh. Jason couldn't imagine his father among the sharpers, a crew that seemed to have come from an alien place, if not a foreign country.

Then he saw him, or at least he saw a man that could have started out as his father: an old man, nearly bald, wearing blue jeans and a checkered flannel shirt. The hair he had left was a shaggy fringe of gray above his ears and around his skull, and his belly was such that he had to belt his pants below it, two skinny little legs taking him the rest of the way to the ground. His care was half a dozen Shetland ponies rigged up to a wheel to make them walk in a circle and saddled up for children to ride. He lifted up the children and set them in the saddles and guided their feet into the stirrups and set the little animals to plodding around in a ring. The ride over, he lifted the children down and turned them loose. Then he went around to the ponies in turn, patting each on the head, giving each a bite of the apple he'd taken out of the pocket of the coat lying across the railing. Then he hoisted up a new set of children. But he had no eyes for the children, nor for their folks, who stood smiling and calling and waving to the tots in the ring. He had to get done with them to have his turn with the ponies.

As Jason watched, it came to him quite without premeditation that he would never go up to his father, even if he were positive it was he, and make himself known. For his father was no more linked to the past that included him than was one of the horses: he was a man alone, without wife or child or any other kin. It seemed that

32

he might as well have forsaken humankind altogether and gone to the wilderness to live among mavericks, listening to coyotes and following the track of the wild mustang. But he had affection for the little horses, stroking their heads, giving each a bite of apple, a lump of sugar.

Uncertain for a moment where he ought to head, Jason stepped back into the crowd and drifted on past to the end of the midway. So this is what it all adds up to, he thought, turning to walk down the other side. Losing game or ace in the hole? The manly art of self-defense? He had a mental image of his father taking up the pack of cards and tossing them into the air, as though casting them into the teeth of fate, in that moment of risking everything and losing everything—to win back himself. He stopped for a moment, feeling slightly dizzy, the way he had felt that morning when he came out of jail. He wanted to laugh and he could have wept, and he could not tell an old ache from a new sort of awe, now that he had come and received his father's blessing: "You're all on your lonesome, boy. You're all on your own."

The Wayward Path

Soon as she saw what it was, she ducked down the side street and came home the back way. Somebody was moving in. She could spy out through the torn place in the lace curtain and see furniture coming out of the dark opening in the great orange ark that filled up the street. A sofa appeared, walking down the ramp, two legs at either end, rearing up to mount the steps. Two chests, gaping in the middle where the drawers went, lumbered down the walk. A sleek table sauntered by. Came a fat chair and a three-headed lamp. Furniture marching in to take possession of the house: Miss Bessie Stephaney's house.

—Think of it, Bessie— Sibyl Gunther said, —strangers. Coming to take over your house. You have to keep a sharp eye, Bessie— For sometimes you could look out and catch them— strangers coming in close, to where they hadn't been before. And if they didn't see you, you were one look ahead. Bessie wouldn't know a thing about it. Instead Miss Bessie was saying, "I'm going to bid six spades." She could see her plain as day, sitting across from her: round face with two pink spots of rouge on the cheeks and the shine on her forehead coming from her good humor over her cards. She always went set, too, trying to push her luck. Letty Turner was bringing round mocha tarts, and Bessie would insist on having some. "I'll take just the teeniest piece of that, they look so good." She couldn't turn down a sweet any more than a child could. "Now Bessie," Letty was saying, "you know that's not good for you." Then her jaw went stubborn, as usual: "This little piece won't hurt me a bit." And they had to let her have her way . . . .

She would have to spy out again to discover who it was that would be coming up the walk and going past the front stoop and into the rooms, making floors creak where nobody had set foot these many years. She couldn't recollect how many. Trouble was, time buckled up like an accordion and ten years got pleated into one. 'Twas hard to sort things out. Old Mrs. Bice had had it—Bessie's sister—and then the house went to her feeble-witted daughter, Sarah? or maybe Clara. Clarissa? But they put her away, packed up her life all in one basket and took her where they take people out of your ever hearing of them again. Then the house sat empty under the rain and snow, tangled up in lawyers. She'd seen how things went with it, letting an eye trail over it now and then, watched how the vines and creepers twined up along the porch, choking the posts, and how the weeds made a wilderness of the yard, saw how stones put out the windows one by one and how the weather beat it down, stripping off the paint.

Mercy, she hadn't even put away her things. She took off her cap and her brown jacket and put the gunny sack up on the table to have a look at the morning's collection. One good bottle, a skinny blue one with gold on the label. She could have had all the whiskey bottles she wanted, people throwing them left and right in the alleys and lots, but they didn't count—ugly brown things. —They couldn't find your poems, Bessie— She'd done everything just pat, so it must be she hadn't wanted anybody to find them. Sly, she could be sly . . . . A piece of red paper, some packing cord, a piece of metal, heavy—she couldn't say what it was, but it had a good solid roundness to it and not a bit of rust—two little boxes, good and sturdy, the right size for buttons and pins, half a dozen magazines with the covers torn off, a rhinestone earring—she held it up to let the light play on it—and a pencil with the eraser used down. And, ah, she'd nearly forgotten. Reached down into the pocket of her jacket for the Canadian penny; bent toward the light to look at the date. 1917. A good old one, too.

Through the torn place in the curtain she saw that outside things were still coming: beds and mattresses, boxes and more boxes. Then she saw who would be her neighbor. A woman stood in the yard holding two little girls by the hand. Children in the house. And there'd be a man, too, no doubt, coming directly. The house, bright with new paint, had been waiting for them. One morning, after she'd come back from her rounds, made early before the trash men came, she saw ladders leaning up against the house and men on the roof, ripping and hammering. There never was such a racket. Then they tore off the trim from the porch and took down the rotting pillars and built it all back up again. Painters came with brushes and buckets. An old man with a sickle took out after the weeds . . . . She'd have to keep a watch: somebody would be coming.

   —It was knowing she was going to lose her toes that made her do it— Sibyl Gunther thought. It would have been too strange, parting company with something that was you, never knowing when you might have to let go of something else. Bessie had left a note telling how she wanted everything done, down to being buried in her transformation. She'd never even let on she was going bald. (Letty Turner went to a beauty shop twenty miles away to have her hair dyed, but all the girls knew she did it and let her go right on pretending.) They found her in the bathroom, with the gas heater turned on. She'd put a rug underneath her so she'd be comfortable.

   She put the bottle up on the shelf with the others, so many there was hardly room. But she hadn't a blue bottle. There was a piece of amethystine glass, a jar she'd found in the cemetery, and a china vase fished up out of the sea near the Virgin Islands from when the slaves had rebelled and thrown in all the dishes. The sea had fingered it and twisted it out of shape. Perfume bottles, medicine bottles, too, of all sizes—they were the easiest to find. —The man will be coming directly—Sibyl Gunther said. —In the mornings I'll scoot out before he ever sets eyes on me— He'd be going out to work, all neat and proper in a suit and carrying a briefcase, maybe. —Dust— she said, and blew the dust off the china vase, which she prized. Dust on everything. She ran a finger down the side of a green wine bottle. —You may as well go out collecting dust— she said. —That's what it comes down to—

   A man and a woman and children in the house. She'd never go near them, no indeed, never set foot in the door. She'd not gone to call on her neighbors for more years than she could remember. Couldn't even tell you their names any more, save for the Russoms across the street, who'd kept on in the neighborhood, waiting to see which would go to ruin first, them or it. One by one the houses had gone down. The big white one with the leaded glass windows where the mayor used to live. —John Corbett, I never saw such a man for joking. Not a serious bone in your body— She saw a huge lively man with a red face and a great meaty palm to shake you by the hand, to thump you on the back with. The porch was falling apart on the dark brick that used to be Jesse Ormsby's. —Matilda should see it now. Listen to her and you'd have thought 'twasn't a fit place for humans to live. But then nothing suited Matilda, she was so uppity up. Tried to run everybody—ran Jesse—would have run the bank, too, if they'd let her— The gray frame with the pillars, where the Snyders used to live. —Clarence a lawyer and having no better sense than to get tangled up with a trollop like that. Julia went where? To her folks in California, most likely, after she left him— They were all the big houses: carved up into apartments now.

Sometimes she looked into the open doorways as she went past and saw the children's toys lying in a clutter of bent and broken things and spied a woman who'd gone thick in the middle and flabby, dressed in shorts, hair up in curlers, working the vacuum over the rug and looking like something had gone bad right under her nose but she had to go on smelling it. And she walked past quick as she could before the stink of diapers or whatever disagreeable thing frying in the kitchen could choke her. Once in a while she'd say a word to one of the children scrabbling in the dirt out in front. The little ones looked at her with solemn faces, all eyes, like owls. One of them had burst into tears when she was trying to be friendly with him, so she didn't stop very often. —It's the looks of me— she said. Folks took her for a man more often than not, dressed as she was in her corduroy pants and jacket and cap, her hair cropped off short.

She wouldn't talk to anybody if she didn't want to. "You're a proud woman, Sibyl Gunther," she head John Corbett say to her, and remembered how her toes felt when she had danced with him once. —Well, John, you were right. I was proud at the beginning and I've been proud ever since— There she'd caught him. Ha!—just in time to see the man going up the walk, a tall fellow with dark hair and an easy stride. —I'll scoot out in the morning before you— she said —but you'll never measure the length of my pride— She'd come to town with her head high in those days, newly married, on the arm of the town's fire chief. And led the waltz at the firehouse and been invited to all the parties and gone out to the roadhouses to play at the roulette tables. For Edward was a man to gamble. — Liked to throw your money around, Edward— Generous and fun-loving, a man for a good time, a sporting man. Blessed too much with good looks, mind you. The cleft in the chin was what did it with the women. —You always liked the best of everything, Edward. Good whiskey and a good cigar—

It was the sheriff knocking at the door that night late in the winter. She couldn't make out what he wanted, he looked so hangdog and wouldn't come straight to the point. Warrant for his arrest? Edward? He must be crazy. Bootlegging. She hadn't known a thing about it except that all sorts of people were doing it. Some said it was a frame-up to put off the revenue men. They said all the bigwigs in town were in on it. And they made Edward come to trial and sent him off to prison. She never saw him after that, the stranger she had married. Alone, with the child, money all but gone. . . . The only thing she had left of him was a rug made from the head and pelt of a polar bear he'd shot on a hunting trip up in Alaska. And she could see that fierce white shadow moving over the whiteness, unseen, hunting perhaps, white fangs ready—but hunted too.

—So there it was, John Corbett. You kept on talking to me, but what about the others?— Gave her a job, he did, in the city hall. And didn't that set the tongues a-wagging. She got to help take the census one year. Worked at the polls for the Democratic party during the elections. John saw to all that, till he ran for the state legislature and lost by six votes. Chewed over the bitterness of it till he died —So that was the one thing left I had to keep hold of, John—my pride— It was hard on Neva growing up with the disgrace on the tongues of the town. And she couldn't live down having a father in the penitentiary. Wanted to go around with the high school boys that cruised around in their cars. Wanted to be popular. Wanted to run with the best in the pack, just like her father. —That was the trouble, Neva. Letting all the boys into your pants— She went off to college, too, for boys with faster cars.

And who remembered all that now? People coming and going in the town, dying off and being born. The Reverend Warren Kemble was gone too and she wouldn't know the present minister if she saw him.

Reverend Kemble had sat in her living room, had come by a time or two even after she'd quit the First Presbyterian. He had sat on the sofa with an aura of disapproval around his head like a cloud of gnats. She'd left a missing place in his church. He liked his church full, the pews all packed close and the hymns sung out in good round tones. Let people sit there looking at their neighbors and they'd keep each other out of mischief. Such was the power of religion. But she wasn't going to sit there under the eye of anybody. And what harm did he think it likely she might do— lay a curse on the cattle and afflict the babies with the milk sick? But the Reverend Kemble didn't come back after a time. And the town let her alone . . .

. . . let her alone except when the mailman brought her the tax notices twice a year. When she saw the envelope in her mailbox, she was all in aquiver till she'd opened the envelope to see whether or not they'd raised her taxes. And even when she stood in the assessor's office to get her receipt, she trembled lest a voice speak out, "And how is it they missed you in the last assessment?"

The town came to her once a year at Christmastime with a basket of canned goods, a plucked turkey nesting on the top, and Mr. Toby Sheets on the doorstep, nose red with cold, stamping the snow off his boots, taking time off from the gas company to head up the Good Cheer Fund. "Hello there. Merry Christmas. Look what we got for you." "Ah," she got to say, "that's very nice of you to remember an old woman," talking to him as though she were talking on the telephone. But all the time he was standing there, she looked him in the eye to see what he was thinking and what he might be about to run off and tell to somebody else. She ate turkey for a week after.

—They're all done now— she said. She watched the men put their dollies and mats inside the truck and get into the cab. Slowly and with a grinding roar, the great orange truck moved up the street. Inside the house they would be unpacking all the boxes, putting things away in the cupboards and closets. And there'd be more things. —Oh, you'll be surprised all the things that pile up over the years. They'll sit in the attic and the basement— Sometimes you didn't even know what you had . . . till one day you'd come across it and it'd be a new discovery. Sometimes you tried to sort things out and throw some away. Oh, but it was hard. She found things in the trash that people tried to throw away and brought them home—valuable things, too. She had drawers of calendar pictures and buttons and old Christmas cards and ribbons and coins and scraps of cloth and bits of lace—some things so old they were worth money. —It's seeing what you've collected is the main thing— she said. Sometimes people didn't know what they were keeping and what they were throwing away.

And so she had gone her way, and the town didn't say anything when she got up early and put on her mannish clothes and took her gunny sack and a stick to keep off the dogs and went along the alleys rummaging through the boxes and barrels. She was careful not to let anybody see her if she could help it.

For she had secrets. She had awakened one morning to the strangeness of things. First she discovered she could talk to her cat. Alone, they had things to say to one another. She had understood when the cat came to her asking where she ought to have her kittens. --Why, puss, I'll get you a box. You needn't worry— The cat felt better, she could tell right away. When the kittens were born and were lying in the box, little blind grubs with the mother cat purring warmly over them, it seemed to her that when she went back to the things she was used to, they were all strange. Even the birds, when she thought of flying, of lifting wings in flight. Or plants, with their invisible factories making food of sunbeams. Some days she would go out to the vacant lot next to hers to spy on the dark life in the grass, the little plants and insects that had their unknown connections, some breathing in life while others breathed it out.

And whenever she thought, bits of the strangeness came to her. And she grew strange to herself. --I won't talk to anybody I don't want to-- she said. Lots of people you talked to it was like plugging into a switchboard and picking up the receiver, giving out your hellos, how-are-yous. Then when you were through, you pulled out the wire and put down the receiver. But when she reached down, she found invisible filaments or tendrils that could go from one eye, one core to another and would have remained past all separations. And deep in her imagination she found the thought of another man she might have loved, or perhaps a woman. She had her secrets, all right, and she had to keep on her toes for fear she might be found out.

--Why here I am, not doing a blessed thing-- she said. Now the neighbors were inside she could go out to the vacant lot and see what had been blown or thrown into it--maybe a scrap of wood for the stove. She was stooping down in the weeds when she heard the children coming. Squatting down, peering out through the grasses, she saw the two little girls swinging their arms, heading right for the vacant lot. They ran into its wildness and went roaming through the weeds and bushes, bending over now and then, looking the way she looked for things. For, as she watched, that was in her memory now, the way she'd gone hunting for things as a child and found treasures--a bit of tree bark to be rubbed against the pavement till it was the right shape to sail in a puddle, a piece of colored glass that made the houses and the weather green or brown, shells and pebbles, an unknown part from an unknown machine. . . . They'd come upon her directly if she did not get up and flee into her house; but memory held her fast.

"Annie, come look. Look what I found," she heard one of the little girls say.

And thinking she'd see what it was too, she stood up. Both little girls gave a shriek.

"Oh, I didn't mean to scare you," she said, trembling. She should have thought.

"I found a bird's nest," the bigger girl said, breathlessly. "It fell out of that tree up there and it's still got a little piece of shell in it." She was breathing very fast and it looked as though her heart was pounding in her chest.

"Are you a witch?" the smaller girl said.

"Hush, Annie," the older one said, nudging her sister. "That isn't nice."

But Annie paid no attention and waited for her answer.

She laughed. "Just old, my dear." Even the laugh sounded strange in her ear. Not laughter—a cackle. Perhaps the child heard that. "When you live a long time, you get wrinkles in your face."

"Do you live there?" the older girl asked, pointing to her house.

41

"Yes, that's my house. And do you know what's in it?"

"What?"

"Many, many things. A conch shell you can hear the sea with. And money from the Sandwich Islands. And two little dogs that move when you put them close. And a picture of my old boxer that could do tricks—" It came out all wrong when she said it. She could tell by the look in their eyes.

Then the little one started running and the other took out after her. "She is too a witch, she is too a witch," she heard the little one yell.

That night the town came to her and stood in a ring about her. She could not see the faces, though in the flicker of the torches she could pick out here and there a forehead, a cheek, an eye, and then a ring of eyes. A figure detached itself from the crowd and started to parade back and forth, doing a little shimmy now and then. Neva, she cried, what are you doing here? Then the faces became those she recognized. Letty Turner and Matilda Ormsby. She caught sight of the sheriff, Phil Goodwin. And there was the Reverend Kemble. Ah, she said, and even you, John Corbett, for she could pick him out hiding in the crowd. She looked down and saw that even the children were there. And while she watched, one of the children picked up a stone and threw it. It came straight at her, and before she knew it, the stones came flying, thick as snowflakes. And the stones became a wall.

Flight

An empty belly is all it takes to bring a man to grief—his own and somebody else's. At the moment, he could call that wisdom—or, at least, part of wisdom. Another part of wisdom newly come to Orlie Benedict was that even when your belly was full, your grief, yours and somebody else's, did not necessarily depart. It clung to you like glue, as though it had a craving for company. The source of his particular trouble was a mere table length away. Just Nevermind—he hadn't been able to coax a name out of him—sat opposite, tearing apart a piece of bread, eating wolfishly. Orlie watched him wipe up the last streak of egg yolk on his plate and stuff the bread into his mouth. Gaunt face, several days' growth of beard along the jaw, circles beneath the eyes like bruises. He turned his eyes away—it was too much like staring into somebody's window—and put together thoughts of escape. Let us flee, said the fly. Let us fly, said the flea. Let us get the hell out of here, said Orlie Benedict to himself.

He glanced down to make sure. Yep, he had it, lying across his knees even, sticking out on both sides, handy to reach in case he wanted it—the rifle he'd never let go of, the rifle he'd met him with, when unluckily he'd come wandering up the road. Casually, Orlie moved his chair back and reached down for his guitar. They made interesting partners in misery, at any rate, he with his guitar, Gauntface with his smoke-pole. But he felt better with his guitar in his hands. He'd picked up a guitar along about the time he was eight or nine and hadn't ever really put it down. Without it, he felt naked. Moving his fingers over the strings was a way of thinking, putting things into a shape and working them out before they slipped away. Right now he had a few to go.

Gaunt Partner in Misery, now that he had cleaned up the

43

food on his plate, sat in relative calm, knuckles bent around the mug of coffee, as though he were warming his hands. "Can't recollect the last time I put food in my mouth," he said almost sociably.

"It can be hard on a man," Orlie said, having listened more than once to his guts growl. He tried out a couple of chords and sang:

> I'll eat when I'm hungry, I'll drink when I'm dry
> If the wandering don't kill me, I'll live till I die.

If Gaunt Partner had anything to do with it, it might be sooner rather than later. Hard on a man for sure.

"Funny thing," Gaunt Partner said. "I don't hardly know where I'm at." He looked around the room, then shook his head, as though he had come into a strange world—thinking he had awakened but finding himself in a nightmare. And no wonder. The place was a shambles: dishes, cans, and bottles swept from the shelves and lying broken on the floor; curtains ripped from the windows; papers, shoes, magazines thrown helter-skelter. And Orlie'd walked right up and into the middle of it, had opened up the door to a whirlwind. He strummed up a little tempest on the guitar. Then he backed up for a bit of melody, lighthearted, just as he had been, walking up the road, almost drifting through the quiet of the summer afternoon toward the peace of that farm in the late sun.

First thing he'd noticed as he came round the bend was an old pump under a shade tree, with a flop-eared hound curled up next to it. He looked over the barn—red once, paint flaked down to the bare boards. He liked barns—they had character, more than houses sometimes, almost as much as people. Some so clean and red and sharp they made you whistle—so fine and big the house that stood next to one was put to shame; others all gray and tumbledown, as though weather and neglect had got the best of them and it was only a question of time until they caved in. This was a barn on the way down, a little seedy, but the house was still trying, the paint recent enough to give it some credit. Nothing fancy, but perhaps you could ask a meal from it, in return for a little work, and a place to put up for the night.

He caught sight of a man out back behind the chicken house and went on past the house to say "Hi there," and wangle a meal. Then he stopped, was stopped rather—brought up sharp, the breath snatched out of him. His eye had gone on ahead and his thought had lagged behind. A lot of chicken feathers, he noticed. Then he saw what he had been seeing: chickens strewn around the yard, lying with that particular limpness that gave him to know their necks had been wrung. Who'd do that? he wondered, sickened by the slaughter. What kind of nut?

Transfixed by the sight, he hadn't gotten from the question to the thought of what he'd do next when Gaunt Partner came up with his rifle. "You ain't gonna get her," he told him, jerking the gun up. "Man, I don't want her," Orlie said, backing off, ready to get out of there in one hell of a hurry. "Just you wait. You get on in there," he said, waving the gun in the direction of the back door. "Look, fella, I didn't mean any harm. . . I was just passing through." "You're not about to go and bring the rest of 'em down on me." He's kidding, Orlie thought in disbelief. Been seeing too many bad Westerns. But it was clear he meant it. They went into the house. There was no arguing with a crazy man.

He hadn't been surprised to find the chaos of the house inside. Well, it figures, he thought simply, when he walked in, though he had no idea what had brought it all on.

"Sit down," he was told. He sat. It seemed as though he must have sat for a long time, long enough for the room to make him feel a little crazy himself. It made him jerk his shoulder every once in a while, twist in the chair. He found himself mentally returning cans to shelves, straightening the bent curtain rod and putting the curtains back up, sweeping up the broken glass. It was nerve-wracking to do nothing: for a time he was driven to making patterns out of the fragments of broken glass on the floor in front of him, staring at them until they came together in some way. Then almost gratefully, he found his attention absorbed by his hunger, that familiar reminder of his physical life.

"Mind if we have a bite to eat?" he ventured.

"There's food," Gaunt Partner told him, without apparent interest, bent over in a chair, gun across his knees, absorbed in whatever whirled in his head. Orlie's presence seemed to make little difference to him.

And though it had brought him into trouble in the first place, he was again grateful for his hunger. It gave him something to do. So he'd pawed around in the wreckage, found bread, not fresh, but edible, found eggs in the refrigerator, discovered the coffee can. The coffee, black and bitter though it would be, boiled on top of the stove, reassured him, the fragrance reminding him that somewhere calm and the simple routine of the evening meal existed. He had brought the two plates of food to the table and they'd broken bread together.

It might be, Orlie considered, that the food had had an influence for the better. He didn't mind his face so much now— it was looking halfway human. Some of the wildness had gone out of it, leaving behind a look of great weariness, as of spent force. Rather a young face, Orlie saw with surprise, the face of someone he could know. But the impression left when Gaunt Partner stood up. "Where did I . . . what's happened here?" Then he flashed around. "Where's Molly?"

"Steady, man," Orlie said, reminded of his danger. He had no idea who Molly was, but it seemed he had her to thank for some of his trouble. In his imagination he had run out the door and down the road. What to do. He tried to hatch an idea. Maybe he could do it the way they were always doing it in the movies. "You got anything to drink?" he wanted to know.

But Gaunt Partner wasn't paying him any mind, going on about Molly and where was she—the frenzy returning, if it had ever abated. Frantically, Orlie was rummaging through shelves and cupboards. Just my luck if he's so square he never takes a drop, he thought. Good sober lad—just tears things to pieces. He hadn't seen any broken whiskey bottles—a bad sign, or maybe a good one. If he had one, where would he keep it? As Gaunt Partner ranted on, he could have wept and raged himself. One more minute, he thought, and there'll be two of us. Under the sink, next to the potatoes, he found a bottle. Great day. He jerked off the top and took a swallow. Here's to you, friend, he said silently. The life you save may be mine.

Seizing an unbroken tumbler, he poured it over half full of whiskey, ran in a little water from the tap, and carried it over to the table. Should he or shouldn't he have a drop to hold himself together? Wisdom was tugging at his sleeve: what did he want to go and muddle his head for? But Lord, he wanted a drink! It seemed to him that he had soaked up in a single day all the wisdom he could possibly hold, so he allowed himself a dollop.

"Come on," he said, encouraging Gaunt Partner back to the chair. "A little of this will take you to the moon without wings." Gaunt Partner sat down with a moan, collapsed rather, like a sack of potatoes.

He must have been raving around quite a while, Orlie decided. How many hours, days? Strange to think of anybody doing it for very much time. He looked like he couldn't have a whole lot of raving left. But it might be that once he got caught up in the storm, his craziness had given him a queer sort of strength. Surely he'd have to sleep sometime. The whiskey might help him along. Get him drunk enough and he'd pass out. At least it couldn't make him any wilder than he was already. Or so he hoped.

Picking up his guitar again, he sang

Rack falls the Daddy-o
There's whiskey in the jar.

Gaunt Partner sat neglecting the glass, leaning his head in his hands. "Gone," he moaned.

Looked like he and the wife had come to a parting of the ways.

Maybe she'd just packed up and taken off—that's what'd happened to his brother. Came home and found a chair to sit on and a bunch of clothes hangers in the closet and the cat meowing to be fed. He tried to get the feeling of departure, thought of the chair sitting there in the empty room. But he had no real experience. Even with his folks. He'd been born when they were old, and he couldn't grab hold of a distinct impression separating the time he'd had them from the time he hadn't. But he had learned some words

The longest train I ever did see
Was a hundred coaches long
And the only woman I ever did love
Was on that train and gone.

There was a long silence, after which Gaunt Partner raised his head and sat up. Orlie took a swallow of the liquor by way of encouragement. But Gaunt Partner might as well have had blinders on, for all the good it did.

"I can't believe it," he said slowly. "I think it and I can't believe it." There was a long pause. "She had yellow hair," he said.

He'd sung about all kinds of hair and eyes. Black was the color of somebody's true love's hair. And somebody had dreamed of a girl with light brown hair. And somebody else had thought it over and found brown eyes so beautiful he'd never love blue eyes again. When you fell in love, even if it was only for half a week, you were ready to go on about the girl's hair and her eyes and her cheeks and her lips. Yellow hair was all right too. He could say that much. And he knew a little of things breaking up with a certain amount of regret. Not that his experience had been great.

Once I had a yellow-haired gal
Once I had a yellow-haired gal
   Things've gone wrong with my yellow-haired gal
   What has become of my yellow-haired gal?

Yellow o my yellow o my yellow-haired gal
She's long gone, my yellow-haired gal.
Yellow o my yellow o my yellow-haired gal
Yellow yellow yellow, yellow yellow yellow,

he sang, carried away by the pure sound of it.

Yellow yellow yellow
Sad and sorry fellow
She's done come and
   sad o sad o sad o

48

She's done come and
mad o mad o mad o

oooooooooooooo

She's done come and gone.

There, he thought, delivered of song, that'll do for a jilting
or a divorce. She smashes all the crockery and he—then he thought
about the chickens. But who does that?

"Goddam it! What do you know about it?" Gaunt Partner
said, bringing his fist down on the table so that the plates jumped
and the tumbler of whiskey spilled all over.

"I'm sorry," he said, taken down. Gaunt Partner had turned
away from him. He'd missed the boat, that was clear, but he didn't
know how. He waited.

"She's dead," Gaunt Partner said. His back held considerable
dignity.

"How did it happen?" he asked, thinking, I don't even have
the right . . . .

But Gaunt Partner, becoming more lucid, seemed to be hit
by the impact of things standing in the harsh light of greater clarity.
"Good Lord," he said, standing up. "What's happened? I don't know
where I been." He walked up and down the room, in front of the oil
burner and past the doorway from which could be seen the brown
painted chest of drawers and the bright squares of the quilt on the
brass bed, then around by the sink where a faucet dripped, perhaps
examining the damage done or maybe just seeing how the familiar
had shifted and shown him strangeness. "Who . . . did . . . all this?"
he said, holding out his hands.

Orlie let it ride. He'd know soon enough, know maybe more
than he could use.

"And who the hell are you?" Gaunt Partner demanded, as
though it had just now occurred to him that he didn't know.

"Orlie Benedict," he said, with a shrug—as though that
answered anything. What else should he say? The fellow you told
to get on in here. Tune picker. Wanderer. He shrugged again. Your

49

partner in misery—one way or another he had been stuck with that.

But Gaunt Partner seemed to have lost interest in the question. "I don't know where I been . . . " he muttered, as though he were struggling to find his way back to a beginning. "Funny thing, you know," he said. "You think you know where you are . . . and then you don't. Like I fell off a cliff."

He probably didn't remember about the chickens, Orlie thought.

Didn't even know he was doing it, most likely. And what was he going to think of it when he found out? But that would wait. It was just part of the aftermath, of the full ugliness of misery working itself out. Gaunt Partner had come back to himself and there was not a thing for him. Wife dead. Ruins at his feet. What was he, Orlie Benedict, supposed to do about it? Where were his friends, anyway, and his folks? Probably ran them all off. Once they started running, it wasn't likely they'd care to come back. Not that he could blame them. To run had certainly been his own first impulse—which only proved that most people had more brains in their feet than anywhere else.

"I don't know where I been," Gaunt Partner said. "And I don't know where I've come."

It seemed like a natural time for a man to pour himself a drink and dive to the bottom of the glass. Orlie reached for the tumbler, poured out another round.

"And I don't give a shit," Gaunt Partner said, as a sort of conclusion. Then he took up his rifle and sat there sighting along the barrel. Was he going to take a gun to his troubles? Orlie wondered. Shoot them away? Suppose one could. . ... He took his guitar again, from where he'd laid it across his knees, and sang:

> Oh, I'm gonna chase that wild, wild wind
> I'm gonna catch that rover
> Oh, I'm gonna chase that wild, wild wind
> Till he gives back my lover.

Gaunt Partner set the gun down for a minute and looked at him as though waiting to hear something he could tell him.

Oh, you'll never catch that wild, wild wind
You'll never catch that rover
What he takes away, he never gives back
The wind that blows you over.

He spat with disgust and raised his gun. "Shoot it," he said.

"Won't do any good," Orlie said.

"Shoot the whole goddam world."

"There's a power . . . " Orlie began. But his words were lost in a blast that went ripping through the front window.

"Careful, man, you want to kill somebody?"

Gaunt Partner looked at him with haunted eyes.

Orlie's heart thumped in his chest like a wild thing butting against the bars of a cage. And his fear spoke to him with a thought: It's him. He's the one who's killed her and now he's going to kill me. What else had he been ranting about when Orlie came up? From the midst of his fear, he spoke: "It won't bring her back," he said.

Gaunt Partner stared at him for a long moment. Then he set the gun down, leaned his head in his hands, and wept.

Orlie sat for a moment, letting his heart calm down. Death had brushed by his ear so close he had felt the whirr of its wings. Then suddenly he thought, I can go now. As soon as he knew that, knew it with a sense of release, the urgency seemed to diminish. He wasn't ready to go yet.

There's a power, he thought again. You sing a tune, by a mountain, maybe, and when your tune is done, the mountain is still there—it hasn't changed any and doesn't show a trace. Nothing is changed except maybe yourself for singing, and if anybody else happens to hear you, maybe something happens to them, but it was nothing you could know for sure. But what did that have to do with anything?

He let his fingers wander over the strings of the guitar as he tried to find out. It was a struggle—finding out. He had to wrestle to get the right note and the right word. To get them, he had to work till the spirit of the thing he was yearning toward and the music met. And sometimes he didn't know what thing it was he groped for in the dark. If he got to it, it was like making a cup out of his hands and catching something for a moment—and for that moment he became the music—but pretty soon the spirit splashed through, flowing on past. That was the power—the thing one could never wear out. Then he thought, If you could get it all in one tune, or even a dozen, it wouldn't be worth having. There seemed to be a comfort in that almost, that nobody could ever get it all, that the force was real, not some poor thin stuff he could wear out if he set his mind to it.

It's the same power, he thought suddenly. Gaunt Partner had had to look at one side of it, and he'd been looking at the other. He thought he saw now how they were joined.

Orlie glanced over at him. He was sitting quietly now, gazing out through the broken window. In the still light sky a crescent moon was visible. "You all right?" Orlie said. But the other did not turn nor answer.

I can go now, he was reminded. But still he wasn't ready. Gaunt Partner had gone out of his mind and now he had come back. He wanted a word—what was it?—he had known once and that still flickered somewhere in the back of his head. He worried around till he found it. It was a case of fugue—a flight from what was too much to bear. Fugue. Odd that the word should also be a flight of music. Then he thought, I'll take a little flight of my own. It took him awhile to get it. Then he sang:

> Loss of love,
> Loss of memory—
> Flight from the void
> Flight into the whirlwind.
>
> Flight from the void
> Flight into the whirlwind.
> Memory of loss
> Memory of love.

When he had finished, he saw that Gaunt Partner had his head tilted back, asleep. Not a matter for whiskey after all. Now it was time to go, to take flight himself. But still he didn't move. He sat looking into the face relaxed in sleep and found again something familiar—human. Maybe he'd get a better sleep if he were stretched out on the bed. Putting his arm around his chest, he half carried him to the bed. Though he muttered, perhaps in protest, he did not wake. Orlie untied his shoes and slipped them off, then unloosened his belt. He stood there for a moment watching him sleep. He had done, for the time being, all that he could.

The Tiger's Eye

Cocky little devil, you'd have said, seeing him walk along—jaunty stride, arms in full swing, like a kid who imagines himself at the head of a parade. Maroon jacket, gray slacks, white bucks—who does he think he is? Retired, living out his days on Social Security. You'd think he was on his way to be bank president. "Just look at him now," Mrs. Margolis says aloud, seeing him bend over and snap off one of her carnations to put in his buttonhole, as if it grew there for his special benefit. Ought to give him a piece of my mind, she thinks, so I ought—Walter Lawrence, who thieves her flowers. Before she lifts the window, he catches her eye. He has waited for her as she stands there behind the lace curtain, a bulky shadow, and he waves, nice as you please, and smiles.

Before she had directed her will to raise up the window, off he goes with the carnation in his lapel. Tomorrow a rose, very likely—a red rose for passion; a white, for purity, depending on the urge of his inner being. And she had provided, will provide—for he is partial to roses.

Tomorrow, he thinks, it will be a rose. A rose, a rose; a rose is a rose, by any other name smelling as sweet. My luv's like . . . a rose, a rose—his thought goes in time with his step.

And Mrs. Margolis, letting drop the curtain, wonders if she should take the scissors to the flower bed, bring all her prizes indoors. It's not worth the effort, she decides, turning away, while he continues down the street oblivious. A strange man, maybe a little cracked. For rather than come to tea with her, he goes every day to visit the zoo, where he would much rather talk to the tiger. Imagine. And with a flourish of indignation she goes on to straighten and dust her bric-a-brac.

54

A brief pause for the delight of the flower, and Lawrence resumes his walk and his worry, frowning and oblivious, all his thought for the tiger. For the tiger seems to be ailing lately, has a keeper he has taken a violent dislike to. Afraid the keeper has it in for him. And Lawrence has been concerned about him.

As he cuts across Chalmers Street on his way to the bus—jaywalking, making a car stop for him, the driver swearing—reaches the curb, misses seeing Jake Henderson wave to him from the barbershop, he finds himself turned loose among a variety of impressions welling up from the past. He remembers the first time he saw the tiger:

It was almost as though a knife went through his heart: the splendor of the beast—a white Bengal tiger. The magnificent line of the body, the carriage of the head, the rippling muscles of the shoulder and flank as it moved on strong padded feet, the grace, the power—daggers of black marking the silvery terror and beauty. The spectacle left him breathless.

"You are overwhelming," he said aloud.

And he thought, though he could not be certain, he heard the voice of the tiger speaking to him. Somewhere the words formed, whether in his head or outside, but certainly they were not his own.

"You better believe it," the tiger said.

When he looked around, he saw only a small girl with her mother in front of the tiger's cage. "Big, big kitty," the little girl said. And they moved on to look at the panther. But he stood rooted to the spot.

•

He boards the bus on Washington Street. Sometimes when the weather is fine and he is in the mood, he walks part way to the zoo. But not today. He sits by the window and lets the street slide past, lets slide past the fretful and changeable fantasies of the city—what it wants or thinks it wants, its materializing hopes, its graying and deteriorating failures. Now a Chinese restaurant dedicated to the best of Szechuan; next to it a loan company with a heavy mortgage on the possible. Now a whole new tower of high-rise apartments

55

thrusting up; now a row of buildings seemingly abandoned, windows broken out, boarded up—eyeless and waiting like pensioners, but whether for the ball of the wrecker or the scaffolding of the restorer, it is impossible to say. Impossible to know what energy is working underground that in the next moment will rise and tear out a piece of the past and whip up something new in its place or else gather itself to renovate, renew, restore. He thinks how he has seen the city, even his suburb, change and change again—something always materializing, something always in the works. Some of the streets he hardly recognizes when he thinks of what they have been. A new bank on the corner of Welby and Long, he notices. More banks everywhere. And fast food places. Someone, somewhere is always hungry for something. It is as though he steps into the midst of a different life every time he boards the bus. But even so, it has always been there at the end of the ride—the tiger he has come to see.

After his first visit, it was a long while before he came back to see the tiger, he remembers, and by then he had very nearly lost the original impression. He was beaten down with overwork, tense with strain. And things had become increasingly difficult—a euphemism for intolerable—between him and his third wife, Angela. Perhaps what had happened with his career had done in his marriage as well—it is hard to say. But just when his years of service and what had been praised as top-notch work for his company, a trust management firm, had brought him to the point of a major promotion, he had been passed over. They brought in a young hot-shot to manage the division. And left him in a corner to rot. And he had felt pained and empty, as though one of his vital organs had been cut away.

For some reason, he thought of going to the zoo. He thought it might soothe his nerves, the presence of animals. He left the house after a flare-up with Angela, words of their latest quarrel flaming in his ears.

He found the tiger curled up in the corner of the cage. At first, he thought it was asleep, but he saw that the tiger regarded him with half-closed eyes. Then the tiger spoke to him again.

"I'm bored," the tiger said.

"Did you speak?" Lawrence said aloud.

"Certainly," said the tiger. "Who else?" And gave a great yawn that revealed the wonderfully honed ivory of his fangs. "I'm dismally, outrageously, overwhelmingly bored."

"So am I," Lawrence said, realizing that he had just been given the word to describe his true condition. "I'm bored to death." And with that, he seemed to reach all the way down to where the juices had stopped flowing.

"It's bad enough just lying here with nothing to do," the tiger said. "Oh, I know, we're supposed to be educational—let people see firsthand the many wonders and splendors of nature. Sounds good," the tiger said, "but what does it come down to? Continual harassment. Make the big tiger roar, make him get up. Run a stick along the cage. Throw a paper wad. And the lack of privacy. When I had a mate—how eager they were to see us do it in public. Disgusting . . . "

The tiger picked himself up and paced round the cage— once, twice. "The circles of boredom," he said.

Yes, it was true, Lawrence thought. Boredom goes in circles, ever narrowing, funneling downward—just like the inferno. What were his days? Talking to stuffed shirts whose lives were spent in back-biting and ass-kissing, company officials who snarled and glared and tried to plant you with the blame for the way the world was run. He was weary of figures and percentages and rules—he was weary of himself, the smell of himself, which was as rank as the tiger's cage.

"It's true, he said, with a sudden rush of sympathy. "I know just what you mean."

As though this note of sympathy had struck a real chord with the tiger, he began suddenly to speak of the jungle. It was as though he were creating a poem—the poem of his existence: the richness of birds, the sudden flashes of brilliance through the leaves, bursts of color—like a vision half-glimpsed. The chatter and play of monkeys, the flight of the swift-footed gazelles, the sudden trumpeting of the ponderous elephants. Lawrence could see it all, as though a tropical paradise had suddenly sprung into existence at the center of the city, graced with palms and parrots.

A sudden clang of iron against iron, the echo reverberating

down the spine, and both he and the tiger were snatched abruptly from the space they had been inhabiting, the vision broken, and planted once again within and outside the cage.

"Mealtime anyway," the tiger said, with resignation. "It's the one thing I look forward to."

"Shall I go?" Lawrence asked, in deference to the tiger's privacy. The keepers entered the cage.

"No, not at all," said the tiger, moving off to a discreet distance. "I enjoy the company. Only it isn't pretty. I hope you're not squeamish."

He took up a chunk of raw meat and chewed thoughtfully. "If I were home where I belonged," he said, as though he had once again caught a brief glimpse of the jungle, "I'd be doing things for myself. Ah, the hunt—nothing like it to get your blood up." He tore away a strip of meat from a carcass and gave a little growl of pleasure that reminded Lawrence of what he had felt on first seeing the tiger.

He had almost allowed the impression to dim. Some shape of horror was about to coalesce in his mind.

"Well, you got to eat," the tiger said, "with or without knife and fork."

He caught a sudden image of himself leaping savagely on his bit of chicken. He hadn't been brought to that yet, Lawrence thought—fortunately.

"But in the bush," the tiger said, licking a scrap from his lips, "What's a little death?"

•

The tiger seemingly had no better luck with the female of the species than he had had. By the time Lawrence saw him again, his third marriage had ended up on the rocks, with considerable animosity on both sides.

"I suppose it was my fault mostly," he found himself admitting to the tiger. "She was young, volatile—liked a good time, excitement. I just didn't have it in my any more."

"I know what you mean," the tiger said. "They gave me a mate—as lovely a creature as ever walked, but we just didn't get on."

"When Angela wanted to go out on the town, I was ready to

58

sit down with a quiet scotch and a little soft music."

"Changeable, willful disposition," the tiger said. "Chances were when I came to her, she'd turn away and growl. She was never in the mood, even when nature was on my side. And if we did get together—" he paused, "she wasn't pleased then either—if you know what I mean."

"I can't say that was my problem," Lawrence said. "There were times when she was insatiable."

"You can't win," the tiger said. "Fortunately, once the cubs came, they separated us. I've been alone since—I count my blessings."

"I've never really understood women," Lawrence said. "I think I've done badly by all of them. With the first, I was tough when I should have been tender; with the second, indulgent when I ought to have been firm. I could deny her nothing—she had such a sweet way of rubbing against me when she wanted something. When she pulled out, I had a stack of bills a foot high. Women and money. . ."

"Mine was just one of those bad-tempered cats," the tiger said. "I did everything to please her but stand on my head."

"Angela was gorgeous from behind. I loved to watch her walk away—the delicious little bounce, the lovely curves. And then when you turned her over . . . There were compensations in that marriage."

"I'm well rid of her," the tiger said. "To be alone is to be happy."

"I'm alone now too," Lawrence said, wondering if he agreed with the tiger. "There is," he said, "the sense of loss."

•

And so it's been over the years, Lawrence is thinking as he heads down the tree-lined avenue towards the entrance of the zoo. For a time he used to visit the tiger once a week or so; now with his retirement he comes every day. They are used to him now. The keepers greet him familiarly, and no one thinks anything of it when he stands in front of the tiger's cage talking to him long into the afternoon. He hurries now.

Arriving at the cage, he sees immediately that the tiger is in a bad mood. Even after he inquires softly how the tiger is getting along, tries to soothe him with his voice, the tiger paces, flicking his tail, not to be appeased.

"He's out to get me," the tiger says. "I know he is."

"I admit he's a nasty-looking type," Lawrence says. Something in his face he disliked right away. A sort of meanness. Skimpy. Nothing of a chin. Mealy complexion. Snub nose. Nothing generous in the mouth—tight, thin-lipped. Human—he had the shape, but all the light had gone out. "But maybe—" he begins, then stops himself. It would be an insult to suggest that the tiger might be exaggerating. And besides, he doesn't know what it is to have to live with the man.

"For one thing, he's afraid of me," the tiger says. "I can smell his fear."

"Why do you think? Any special reason?"

"Look at his hand sometime," the tiger says. "He's been mauled—I'm sure of it."

"Why is he here?" Lawrence wants to know. "There are other jobs, other parts of the zoo."

"Not for him, there's not—if you know what I mean."

"I think I do. I've come across those types."

"He'd love to use that whip. He's just itching to use his gun. It makes me nervous—just look at him now."

The keeper moves toward the cage, opens it and steps inside with his companion. Something dark and furtive in his look. The fear is there, but something else: the hatred that is part of the fear.

"All right, move off—" The two keepers are in the cage. One with the food—the other to keep an eye out.

The tiger paces nervously back and forth.

"Easy does it," Lawrence says. "Keep calm, my boy. Just take it easy."

"He'll be sorry if he don't," the new keeper says. "I can tell he don't like me . . ."

"Come on, Harry," the other says. "You're making trouble. He's never bothered anybody since I've been here."

"Well, I don't trust the brutes. All cats are treacherous. As

60

soon kill you as look at you."

Alone in his cage again, the tiger sits picking at his food. "I think he's putting something in it," he says. "I think he's trying to poison me."

"Why would he do that?" Lawrence says, horrified, wondering if the tiger is suffering from some deeper malady, something infecting his imagination.

"A world of people has passed in front of my cage," the tiger says, "and a number have come inside. And I think there are some who have a grudge. They carry it inside them all their lives, and they want only to bring vileness and chaos wherever they go. They carry it like a worm eating their insides or like a fire glowing in the dark, and it feeds and feeds until it grows into a huge . . . "

"Tiger, tiger burning bright," Lawrence says, without thinking.

"What was that?"

"Nothing," he says, embarrassed. "A poem I once knew."

But the tiger insists that he repeat it from start to finish. When he ends, the tiger lets out a great roar of rage and pain that seems to shake the ground with its violence.

"I shouldn't have done that," Lawrence tells himself guiltily. But whether the tiger was protesting his existence or all the more passionately affirming it, he is not able to say.

•

Before he was laid up with a bout of 'flu that kept him from his visits, Lawrence had spent a good deal of thought and effort on the tiger's condition, but to no avail. The director of the zoo, a Mr. Ferris, was sympathetic, but Lawrence knew that he regarded him as a crank—harmless, but a crank. He had suggested as politely as he could that the vet ought to have a look at the tiger. The director explained that animals frequently get a bit off their feed and just as spontaneously recover. Lawrence tried to explain the tiger's dislike of the keeper. He held back the tiger's impression that the man was out to get him. The director explained patiently that he had a limited staff. Turnover was a headache. Funds from the city were limited. Hard to get qualified people. As it was, he had a harrowing schedule trying to get all the animals fed, their cages cleaned. They could not take into account all the eccentricities and little quirks of temperament you found in a zoo full of animals. "After all," the director concluded, "we can't disrupt a whole zoo for the sake of one discontented tiger."

"And yet what do we run things for?" Lawrence wondered afterwards. At times, it seemed to him, only for the sake of running them. How many mornings he had rushed to work, to be on time to do nothing. And a powerful discontent seized him, something large and vague and cloudy that had to do with the inherent stupidity of things. Or so it seemed when he was in that frame of mind.

The tiger at least had a more immediate object for his rage: "I could tear him limb from limb—I could . . ."

"You're getting all worked up."

"I know. I must be wretched company," the tiger said, apologetically. "There's no danger. I wouldn't lay a claw on him. He's just looking for an excuse. But I won't give it to him. Now he's trying to weaken me. I turned up my nose at the food, so now he gives me scarcely enough to satisfy an alley cat."

"I went to the director," Lawrence said. "But it didn't do any good."

"No, I don't imagine. It would be lovely to be out of all this," he said, looking around the bars.

"You're not getting . . ."

"Despondent? No, no, not at all," the tiger protested. "I'll rage till the last. I did make it out once though. Escaped—think of that. Four days of freedom before they found me."

"Really? What did you do?"

"Had a couple of excellent meals of squirrel in the park," the tiger said, "and a rather simple-minded little pug that came sniffing in my direction. But that was a minor thing."

He waited.

"It was a real adventure. I became part of the dreams of the city. For it has dreams, you know. Restless dreams, unquiet dreams, dreams of violence and madness. Nightmares. I was among them. In the shadows lurking. Stalking prey."

"You frighten me," Lawrence said.

"And you're not frightened without me?" the tiger asked, with what appeared almost a smile. "But that wasn't all," the tiger continued. "I was part of its other dreams too—in the park among the flowers. Dreams of gaiety and rest. Looked at the statues of swans and maidens and generals on horseback—those all are dreams too, made solid, fashioned into statues. Though, I must say, with limited interest. I stalked and leapt—I made grand leaps, as though I were in the jungle again." A spark seemed to animate the tiger momentarily. "It was a great joy."

"Yes, I can imagine," Lawrence said and felt a touch of lightheartedness.

"A rare moment," the tiger said. He flopped down and put his head on his paws. He seemed quite weary. "Sing something to me," he said.

Lawrence rummaged for a moment among the tunes that had been gathering rust and forgetfulness in his mind—a few hymns from childhood, fragments of old popular tunes, some chestnuts from the classics—thin pickings. Ah, he thought, with sudden inspiration, and struck into "On the Road to Mandalay," thinking it might put some heart into the tiger, remind him of happier days in the jungle.

"I don't mean to interrupt," the tiger said, after the second line, "but could you pick something quieter, a little more soothing?"

He looked at the tiger for a long moment. How many years it had been—that they'd been friends, he thought. It hadn't occurred to him before to give a particular definition to his relations with the tiger. But yes, they'd been friends.

"Sweet and low," he sang, "Sweet and low. Wind of the Western sea . . ."

"That's very pleasant," the tiger said.

Lawrence had had a fine tenor voice in his youth and now, quite as though his singing had brought it to life again, the notes came through clear and pure.

People paused to listen, and he went on singing till he saw that the tiger was asleep.

Mrs. Margolis looks out to see which is in the greatest danger this morning, her carnations or her roses. This time she is quite certain she will have a word with the man, in revenge at least for his refusal to come and have tea with her. All for the sake of a tiger. Indeed! But as she gazes out, the man, her prey, flies right past, and there is something in his look, in his stony, concentrated unseeing that leaves her in wonder. He has the look of a man struck by lightning.

And indeed it is true. He is disturbed. Even the return of morning with the light of gathering rationality has not diminished the sense of the momentous. For in the middle of the night the tiger came to him.

Had come—it was too bizarre to stand the inspection of the mind. But what other words could describe the visitation? The tiger had come—unless he could say simply that he had gone out of his mind. But perhaps . . . What can he say? He is in the greatest perplexity.

When he arrives at the zoo, he goes straight to the cage, but the tiger is gone. A terrible weakness seizes him at the knees. He knows the worst. But even so, he goes in search of the keeper—the one—whom he finds watering the elephants.

"Yep, dead all right," the keeper tells him. "Had an attack in the middle of the night and we had to shoot it. Vet's done a report on him. He couldn't recover."

The man is perfectly matter-of-fact, though Lawrence thinks he detects a certain satisfaction in his voice. At any rate, he is spared some sort of lugubrious sympathy.

"Didn't even get up when I came in to shoot it," the keeper says. "He was in a bad way."

I'll bet he roared though, Lawrence thinks. He must have roared. "Well, thank you," he says, turning away, allowing the keeper his triumph, if that is what he had. Perhaps he had wanted to kill it, whether he knew it or not—in his fear, his hatred of what the tiger was. But that, he thinks, is neither here nor there.

So it was gone—the silvery splendor, the black daggers. But—he straightens up, walks slowly back to the entrance—it had visited him before it left. And he had looked at it, looked deeply into its burning eye.

Lucinda

The night before, Alex had come, arriving sometime after midnight. Pilar sat up in bed, first hearing the car door slam, then the sound of the key in the lock. She slipped out of bed without turning on the light, hoping not to wake Lucinda, who lay in a warm curl beside her, her small chest rising and falling with her breath. When Alex was gone, Lucinda slept in his place.

"You are here," she said going into the living room, blinking against the light. He had thrown his windbreaker across the chair and was sitting on the couch, taking off his tennis shoes, grunting, and groaning like an old man.

"I'm beat. All the fucking trucks on the highway. Crowd a man. Have to take up the whole goddam road. Oh, God, I am fucking tired."

"Do you want me to rub your back?" she asked.

He worked his shoulders around—heavy, muscled shoulders. "Thanks," he said. "But I'm too goddam tired to stay up for it. Just got to get me some shut-eye." He heaved himself off the couch and into the bedroom, Lucinda's room.

Pilar stood in the doorway, watching him take off his shirt and undo his belt. He looked fat and tan, as though he'd soaked up all the sun he could find out there on the Coast, put some of it on his shoulders and the rest on his belly. He was a burly man, thick, carrying a load at the middle. Too much food, too much beer, Pilar thought as she gazed at him. Now he was there—back. She did not know exactly where he'd been and what he'd done—that is, what he had brought back with him, what she was supposed to do with it.

"You gonna just stand there?" Alex wanted to know. "Look, kid, you ain't getting nothing out of me tonight. Right now I'm no

65

more good than a spavined horse." He flopped heavily onto the bed, made it groan.

She turned out the light and went back to Lucinda. When she slipped under the covers, Lucinda turned over, murmured something in her sleep and nuzzled against her. Pilar touched her on the shoulder, not enough to wake her, and lay in the dark for a moment, taking in the warm, sweet scent of her childhood.

Alex was home—for how long this time? It was his way, to come in like a change of weather, like a cloud of dust on the desert, or a cloudburst that sends the rivers roaring through the arroyos. Without warning. And when he came, it was always different, and when he left something changed with him. She lay in the dark wondering why this was, and how it would be now with his coming.

It did not always happen, it was true. His dealings took him away for days or weeks at a time. And things went on the same. She was used to his comings and goings, to the many conversations on the telephone, often in Spanish, of which he knew enough to take care of things. *"Tiene usted el dinero?"* she would hear him ask, with an intensity she had come to recognize. And the amount of pesos he mentioned was more than she had ever seen. So much money. She did not know all the numbers even to count it. What would anyone do with so much money?

She could not tell how it would be this time. A month he had been away, in Los Angeles. Making deals. Buying, selling— she did not know what. She never asked him, he never told her. Sometimes he came back, singing at the top of his lungs, smirking like a well-fed tomcat. Then he'd pick her up and swing her around, and say, "Well, my chiquita, we'll do the town up brown. Do some of them nightclubs over in Juarez." But he'd never taken her back over there. She was just as glad.

Other times he complained about the fleabag hotels he'd put up in or the time he had spent waiting for Jose or Gary or Fulgencio or some other stranger to turn up, but these were the only clues she had as to where he'd been or how he'd spent his time. She did not want to know.

Once, not long after he'd brought her across the border, she'd been frightened nearly out of her head. When she was alone, she kept the door locked, as Alex had told her to do. And she seldom went out by herself. But this time somebody kept banging on the door till she had to open it. Maybe it was La Señora who'd rented them the room. But no, a policeman stood in front of her in the doorway, demanding to know where Alex was. She could not tell him, nor could she understand what he was saying, though he tried a few words of Spanish, and she tried to use the English words Alex had taught her.

She was afraid the man had come to take her back to Juarez. But she had been wrong. He ended up writing on a piece of paper, *The feds are wise*, and disappeared. So did Alex for nearly a month—and in that way she came to understand what the words meant. That was the first change, her worrying that he was gone and would never come back. And what would she do then, when her money ran out? The rent was paid, but there was only a little left for food. Then one day he was back. They moved out of the little room in the barrio into another part of the city. After that, she never asked him any questions. There was money, she did not care how she got it. She had a good place to live, with electricity and running water, and food on the table, and clothes to wear. But that had begun the changes. They had moved many times now, from one apartment to another. This was the best—clean, and the toilet worked, and there was a yard for Lucinda to play in. If she needed something, Pilar asked Alex for it. At first, she asked timidly, afraid he would be angry. But he would reach in his pocket and pull out a five-dollar bill, or even a ten and give it to her, as if he didn't care. Sometimes he gave without her asking. But unless it was to buy some present for Lucinda, she had little to ask for.

Now, for the first time, in this place she had a friend, Sarah—Sally, as she liked to be called, and it was good to have a friend. They were all Americans in these apartments, and Pilar was shy about speaking to them—her English was not so good, although she had learned a lot by listening to the television, repeating what it said. But Sally did not seem to mind her having to pause sometimes to reach for a word. She was alone as well, had just gotten a divorce from her husband—"the no-good son-of-a-bitch. He screwed me over plenty, let me tell you." She talked a lot about him. She was teaching Pilar some new words.

That morning Pilar got up early and went into the kitchen to see what she might do to make a surprise for Lucinda. It was a game they had. Sometimes she peeled an orange or a banana and made a little figure out of the peelings. Or she arranged slices of fruit in a design on Lucinda's plate. After she had made her surprise, she would go to wake Lucinda. The child would be lying there, breathing so softly, the flush of sleep on her cheeks, her eyes closed with the long fine fringe of her lashes, her lips slightly parted. Pilar found it hard to believe this was her own child. She would wake her, and watch her yawn and stretch as she came into the morning from wherever she had been. For a moment the sleep would stay with her. Then her eyes grew bright as she remembered. "What is my surprise?" she demanded, and without waiting a moment longer, she ran into the kitchen to see.

"A bird, you made a bird—*que bueno.*"

Today when Pilar went to wake her, she put a finger over her lips. Lucinda caught on immediately:

"*Papá está aquí?*" she asked in a whisper.

"*Sí,*" she said, whispering too. "*Muy cansado.*"

"I will be very quiet," Lucinda said, her eyes lighting up. Whispering was a game, too. She would play the Whisper Game. And the Tiptoe Game, and the Moving-Very-Quietly Game. Pilar watched her elaborate pantomime, and her expression, all very exaggerated. Such a clever little rascal she was—her little parakeet, her mouse, her bee.

"Come into the kitchen, *mija,*" Pilar told her.

"Do you have a surprise for me?" Lucinda wanted to know.

"I have a surprise," she said. "A small surprise. And maybe there will be another," she said. "A special surprise!"

"Something to eat?"

"No, something else."

"When?"

"Later." Sally brought it over to Pilar last night when Lucinda was asleep. Sally had brought other things, candy and books with picture in them, that Pilar and Lucinda had sat and looked at together. "I love that little kid," Sally said, and that made Pilar feel very proud of her. She wanted to give Lucinda her surprise right then, but Alex would be waking soon, and it would not be the right moment. It was different now that he was home. She had been alone with the child for so long, she hardly knew how to act with him there. They had their special ways. She would save her surprise until the right moment. For now, she had an orange on which she had made a face, with raisins for eyes and a smile cut out of the skin. She'd made a little paper cone hat to put on its head and set it up on a glass. Lucinda didn't want to eat the orange man—she named him Pepe.

As soon as Lucinda finished breakfast, Pilar let her go outside to play on the swings and slides at the center of apartment complex. Usually, when she came home from the grocery store, she stayed outside with Lucinda and watched her play in the sandbox or pushed her in one of the swings. But when Alex was there, her whole routine changed. Otherwise, she would have gone first to the store with Lucinda. Lucinda loved to shop in the grocery. They went every day. Lucinda would pick out the vegetables and fruit and put them into a bag. She took boxes of cereal from the shelves and picked out the kind of soap they would use, sniffing different ones till she found a scent she liked. It always took a very long time for them to do their shopping, most of the morning, in fact. And then the swings and slides. Sometimes now, though, Pilar spent time with Sally.

Just as Pilar finished making the coffee, Alex came into the kitchen, dressed in a faded checked shirt that he liked to wear and a clean pair of blue jeans. He still hadn't shaved, but he was feeling good, she could tell, punching his fist into his hand, as though he had new energy he needed to get rid of.

"Did you sleep well?" she asked him.

"Like a goddam brick," he said. "Boy, was I beat. Christ A-mighty. Today I'm just going to re-lax, have me a few beers and lie around. I don't wanna see no inside of a car."

She gave him a cup of coffee—she'd made a big pot, because he would drink many cups of coffee. She poured one for herself, half coffee, half milk, and sat down with him.

"You know," Alex said, "that Los Angeles is quite a place.

Lots going on out there."

She'd heard him say so before. And there was a program she watched on TV that had interested her because it was set in Los Angeles. She liked the palm trees and the ocean. Once she had even felt a desire to go. "All the movie stars live there," she said.

"That ain't the half of it," he said. "Every time I go out there, I think, what am a doing in a rinky-dink place like this? Out there, they've got some style."

She wasn't quire sure what he meant, but she wondered if this was to be a new change. Did he want to move again? After they had come to this apartment with a place for Lucinda to play and even a friend for her to talk to? She could not imagine going to another place.

"I like it here," she said, trying only to sound pleased with the apartment. But she felt a sudden panic. If Alex were to take her somewhere else, she would have to find her way again—learn new streets, find out where the grocery was. Maybe they would not have a playground. It was such a big city—so many cars.

"Yeah," he said, "it's okay. If you got to have a place to come back to when you need it." He seemed almost to be talking to himself. "But one of these days I'd like to live it up a bit. That's what it's all about."

She said nothing. She did not want to go against him. Now she could think only of Lucinda. In the beginning, it did not matter to her where they lived. First the little room with a hot plate and a television and no backyard. Then after moving quite suddenly, half a duplex on a dusty street with weeds and cans in the backyard, and many stray cats in the sheds around—lean and hungry and fierce in the eye. They moved from there, too, because Alex said too many wise guys were trying to nose into his business. They had stayed in another set of rooms for a few months, then moved again to this place.

At first she was alone in the room all day, watching the television. When Alex came home, she sat on his lap on the sofa, and they watched together. And he taught her to heat up food on the hot plate and how to say words in English.

Then an extraordinary thing happened to her. The change

had come upon her more powerfully than any change in the weather. She had not thought about it until it happened. In the beginning, she did not even know what it was, her breasts growing, her waist thickening. Then her ripening belly, her shape enlarging like that of women she had seen on the street. It had been an astonishment to her to find herself like one of them, with a baby inside her, feeling its kicking there in the dark when she was lying alone, awake while Alex lay asleep beside her, or while he was gone. It was like a secret growing in the dark, a surprise that would come when it was ready. And she wanted to laugh because a surprise was coming to her.

How she had wept and sobbed during the labor. It had frightened her very much when the pains began and Alex wasn't there. He said he would be home, and finally he came and took her to the hospital. She had never been in a hospital before, had never felt such pains tearing her apart, not even when she was hungry. But afterward there was the baby. Her child: with golden skin, lighter than hers, but with her own dark lustrous hair. Alex had been the one to name the baby: Lucinda. At first the name sounded a little strange in her ear, as though it were trying to be Spanish. But it was made in America. She liked the sound of it, its music. She made up little pet names to call her—*Lita* and *Lulinda* and *Lucita*. And she carried the baby around everywhere and sang to her and talked to her and watched her while she slept.

She had no thought for anything else while the baby nursed at her breast, filling up with milk till she got drowsy and fell asleep. Or when she fed her with a spoon or held her or shook a rattle until she grabbed it. Alex left her alone with the child. He was gone more and more all the time. And Pilar was glad to be alone with Lucinda. If he was at home, he sometimes looked at Lucinda, as if he were wondering where she came from, as if she had not been made in America but in a strange place and not by him. She did not look like him at all. Sometimes he picked her up and swung her around by her arms or held her upside down. And Pilar was filled with terror that he would hurt her. But Lucinda squealed with delight. Sometimes now she ate with them. But usually it was late when they had their meal, too late for her, with her active body and her young appetite, to wait for them. Pilar used to feed Lucinda in the kitchen and put her in the playpen. Now Lucinda could go out to play with her friends. Lucinda was five.

After he had his breakfast, Alex sat on the couch and watched the game shows on television, then flipped through a magazine. Around noon, he got up, said, "I'm going out to get me some beer and talk to some guys. Then I'll come home and watch the ball game."

After she had done the dishes, she found Lucinda and they went to the grocery store. The car was still gone when they came back, so they went over for a little while to visit Sally.

"See your man's home," Sally said.

"He came in the middle of the night."

"Well, I'm glad to be rid of mine—lying and cheating like the bastard he was. I tell you, I don't know what it is with men— Only now I got to get me a new one. Somebody who'll take care of me and treat me right."

"I hope you find somebody," Pilar told her. "It is hard to be alone."

"You're lucky, you know. You got one that's not underfoot overmuch, that's the main thing—and you got that sweet little kid. That Lucinda," she said. "You want a cookie, honey?"

Pilar smiled, proud of her child.

"Guess she'll be starting school one of thee days," Sally said.

"She is too young," Pilar said. She did not want to think about it—Lucinda going away from her. School seemed as far away as Los Angeles. Lucinda would go to school and learn how to read, and soon she would know more than her mother. Pilar had gone as far as the second grade, but she had forgotten most of what she had learned. She could read Spanish words, some of them. Lucinda already knew more English than she did, for the children she played with did not know Spanish.

"I better go now," she said, seeing Alex drive up.

Sally came out of her apartment with her, and when Alex got out of the car, Pilar said, "This is Sally."

"Glad to meetcha," Alex said, and gave her his hand, a big hand. "Just got back from L.A."

"You have a good time?" Sally said.

"You bet," he said. "Just got me some beer there in the car," he said. "Why don'cha come over later on and have one?"

"Sure," she said, looking at Pilar. "Sure thing."

When she and Alex went back to the apartment, Pilar told him how Sally had moved in while he was gone and how kind she was to Lucinda. It was the first time she had talked to him about someone he did not know. This time he did not seem to mind. Once a boy on the street had come up to her and asked her if she lived in the neighborhood. When she came home, Alex told her not to speak to strangers.

Sally came over with a bowl of popcorn she had made, and Pilar set out some tortillas and chili sauce to eat while they drank the beer. For a while they all watched the ball game, then afterward a comedy. Pilar didn't understand some of the jokes, but it didn't matter. Afterward, Sally and Alex started talking about L.A. Sally had lived there for a year way back when, and they together talked about the places they knew, the best bars to hang out in, and how bad the smog was.

"Used to work in a music store out there on the Sunset Strip," Sally said. "Nice place. That's where I met my ex, damn his hide. He was trying to be a country singer, and used to buy all the albums. Me, I was just trying to get by."

"Ain't we all?" Alex said. "Time you get done working to get from one day to the other, you're about all wore out."

"You can say that again," Sally said.

Alex liked Sally, Pilar could tell. Sally laughed a lot, and it was nice when she laughed. She was not young, and her face had gone hard in a way, especially when she talked about what her man had done. But now she was enjoying herself. And pretty soon, she and Alex were joking with each other as if they'd known each other forever, and Alex was telling her things he'd done in L.A. How he had a friend who had a Harley-Davidson, which was the only kind of motorcycle to have—none of your crummy Jap machines—and how he used to go out and really ride the thing, even on the freeways. He was fixing to buy one. "How'd you like to go out for little spin?" he said to Pilar, pulling a bit of her hair. "Bet that would give you a thrill." Then they drank some more beer and laughed some more.

Pilar laughed with them, for the air was light around them. He and Sally could speak very well to one another, Pilar thought. She admired how they spoke English. Lucinda was lying on the floor watching television, not paying any attention to them.

"By the way," Sally said, "how did Lucinda like the coloring book?"

Flustered, Pilar said, "Oh, I forgot. I haven't given it to her yet."

"Oh, well," Sally said. "It don't make no never-mind." And she took another drink of her beer.

"Well, give it to her now," Alex said. "No law against it, you know."

She went to get it. "Here," she said, giving it to Lucinda. "It is a surprise from Sally."

Lucinda looked at the box of colored crayons and the book.

"You can color any of the pictures, honey," Sally said.

Gravely, Lucinda opened the box and looked at the colors, then at Pilar. "*Me gusta mucho,*" she said excitedly, and for a long time she sat looking at the pictures in the coloring book and putting the crayons in different order in the box, taking them out again, laying them on the floor and putting them back. She asked Sally to tell her how to put them back the way they had come, then she closed the box. Pilar could tell she was sleepy and led her off to bed, putting the crayons and the coloring book on the shelf till morning.

Pilar was happy. She didn't listen anymore to what Alex was saying; she just ate popcorn and drank beer till Sally said she had to get to bed early—next morning she had to go out to look for a job.

"Hey, listen," Alex said, "the night's young. No need to rush off. Hey, why don't we go out on the town and do it up brown? Take in some of those nightclubs over the line."

Sally hesitated. "Well, I really . . ." she said.

"Come on," Alex insisted. "The three of us. Have some fun."

"But Lucinda," Pilar said.

"She's asleep," Alex said. "We'll lock the door. She'll be okay. Nothing's gonna get her."

But Pilar did not want to leave her. Things could happen.

But even if they didn't . . . She might wake up and if no one was there, she'd be frightened.

"You go," she said. "I will stay here and you go—you and Sally."

"Hey, I don't like to do that," Sally said.

"It's okay," Pilar insisted. "You go, and the next time I'll go."

"Suits me," Alex said.

That night Pilar slept badly. In her dreams she was traveling somewhere, but she did not know where she was going. She was alone. When she woke up, she wasn't sure at first where she was. She found Alex heavily asleep on the couch, still in his clothes, his arm flopping over the edge to the floor.

Lucinda was still asleep. Pilar opened the door softly and went outside. A bank of cloud extended over part of the city, but beyond it the sky was a rich blue, so filled with light that everything stood out against it with a sharpness that made it seem caught there forever in utmost clarity. The dark blue mountain closest and the pink mountain farther away, so clear, so bright it was like looking at a picture. For a long time she did not move.

She thought of the colors of Lucinda's crayons, and she remembered her time at school. The teacher had given her a piece of paper and a little box of crayons, but she could not think of anything to draw. She had made a yellow mark on the paper, then a red one. Then a little box out of the red, and a little circle out of the yellow. But some of the children had made flowers and cats and people. That was long ago, long before her mother had sent her out of the house, when the neighbor had told her mother that Pilar was no longer a virgin. For a time she had slept under bridges and in abandoned cars, begging for coins from the tourists and rummaging through the refuse barrels behind the restaurants. Till some other girls told her about the hotel, where she could come and they would give her food and a place to stay, and even pay her money. And there Alex had found her. She was fourteen then.

When she went back inside, Alex was already up and dressed. He didn't want any breakfast—he was going out for awhile, didn't know when he'd be back. She wondered if he had asked Sally to go with him. Once she had seen him put his arm around a woman that he was talking to in the street, and they had gone off together. Perhaps he would go off with Sally—even as far as Los Angeles. She did not know if that was the change he had brought this time.

She went into the kitchen to make breakfast for Lucinda. Soon she would wake her. This morning she had fresh cherries to give her, and after she ate, she would give her the coloring book with the pictures already drawn. And together they would open the box of crayons and make blue dogs and red horses and green houses, with a blue sky and a yellow sun shining over all.

Getting an Education

M ost of the neighbors took in the oddities of Findlay Brightwood the same way they took in everything else: the domestic quarrels of the Ryans; the untidy family life of Dr. Kiely—Eye, Ear, Nose & Throat—whose wife let the kids run wild with neglect; the heavy drinking of the Pattersons, who partied lavishly on weekends, going through her money like water, leaving out a full case of whiskey bottles for the garbage men to cart off the following Monday after their friends had departed in drunken riot.

"Those kids are going to turn into juvenile delinquents," Crystal Munsinger heard her mother say often enough. "They're driving me wild." Or: "Those people are drinking themselves to death. I couldn't sleep last night for the noise."

But though the neighbors gossiped and judged and deplored such behavior, they could not forget the social position of the people involved. It was like discussing the follies of kings. All in all, it made pretty good entertainment

Finney Brightwood was a different case, however. His kind of eccentricity seemed to come of having a head so crammed full of knowledge he was helpless as a baby when it came to the practical side of life and could barely live in the world. He was a college professor newly hired to teach history at the local teachers' college. He'd come all the way from California, bringing his Ph.D. and his mother, a stenographer newly retired from the Los Angeles Police Department with a certificate of merit for thirty years of dedicated service.

Crystal watched him move in across the street, into the modest little house that sat between the money of the Pattersons and the power of the Ryans, who figured heavily in local politics and owned half the town besides, including the great pink stuccoed adobe in which they quarreled. Mrs. Baynes lived on the other side of the Ryans. And though, as Mrs. Munsinger expressed it, she'd been no more than a salesclerk in the local department store and was homely as mud, she'd been married late in life to a man who'd made a fortune in the mines. Now as a rich widow she was therefore entitled to put on the dog and would speak only to the Ryans and the Pattersons.

Crystal's side of the street was a line of neat modest little houses like the one Dr. Brightwood was moving into. So that those who lived in them were able to look across to money and knowledge and power, in an unbroken vision from the Kielys' house on the corner, with the high fence around it to keep the neighbors out but not the children in, down to Mrs. Baynes' two-story mansion with the statue of Cupid in the yard, flanked by a swan. Though Clayton Thurgood, a telephone repairman, commented as the moving van drove off and left Dr. Brightwood in the midst, "All those college professors are either communist or crazy," not everyone agreed.

"He'll be a great asset to the neighborhood," Mrs. Munsinger insisted.

Crystal, her daughter, was the first member of the family to go to college, and the importance of an education had been impressed upon her ever since she could remember. For her mother, the title of doctor, lawyer, congressman called up an immediate awe; anyone who had a profession was a superior being. Education spelled opportunity. Crystal knew that her mother would be overjoyed to see money and social position come her way. But in any case, she wanted her to be a teacher so that she could be somebody in the world and not have people look down on her.

Crystal herself was full of uncertainty. In her sophomore year of high school she'd been transplanted to this remote corner of New Mexico from Lima, Ohio, where her father had sold insurance. The move was to alleviate her mother's asthma, but it had at the same time shattered what little social ease Crystal had managed to develop from her years of growing up in the same town and neighborhood. She had wept to leave behind the two or three friends she had, along with her school and her sense of place. Instead of trees and grass she found cactus and mesquite; miners and cowboys instead of salesmen and company employees—and through it all a nasty suspiciousness between Mexicans and Anglos, as they were called. Her only real friend during high school had been the college librarian, who chatted with her when she went to check out books. "She's always got her head buried in a book," her mother was fond of saying, to Crystal's embarrassment. Now she was starting college.

•

At eight o'clock on the first day of the fall semester, Crystal found herself in Dr. Brightwood's freshman social studies class in a large lecture room on the second floor of the main building. It was a required course, and the room was nearly full. Before the bell rang, Dr. Brightwood appeared. When he walked into the classroom, the girl behind her tittered. He was so short he was all but hidden by the lectern. What was worse, he had the most fantastically skewed eyesight Crystal had ever seen. She learned later that he had but one good eye. As he explained his attendance policy, which was fixed and harsh and fair, the one eye, nearly sightless and planetary, wandered off on its own, now looking up at the ceiling, now at the other side of the room, while the good eye, only slightly off-center, mostly looked ahead. He called roll.

"But you can't tell if he's looking at you or not," Crystal heard one of the girls say after class.

It was true. When he looked at a person, he was looking at two people, and sometimes two students answered from widely separate locations in the classroom.

But he can't help his eyes, Crystal thought, as she sat in the back of the room in an agony of embarrassment for him. To make sure that she was really the one being called upon, she always waited until he actually spoke her name. But several of the students seemed to enjoy the confusion. This trick of his eyesight seemed to leave Dr. Brightwood even more confused than his class, and he would look around wonderingly as though he had suddenly found himself in a strange place.

•

Perhaps Crystal would have thought less about Dr. Brightwood had she seen him only four hours a week in the classroom when she was not fully awake anyway, but he was her neighbor as well. Now of a morning she found herself in his company on the way to school, and he led her at a breathless pace up the hill. Once, as they raced along, Dr. Brightwood explained between breaths that he was a runner, had run the mile at the University when they told him he'd have to take P.E. and had been running ever since. She quickly discovered that he could walk faster than she could run. At the top of the hill, he would take out his pocket watch and check his time. "Not bad," he would say with a certain triumph as she tried to catch her breath. He reminded her of the White Rabbit.

Crystal learned from her friend the librarian that people had been inviting Dr. Brightwood to dinner and that he'd been dropping hints that, being nearly forty, he was ready to get married and would be glad to meet a likely young woman. He had, in fact, spent most of an evening at the librarian's house gazing with his good eye at the picture of a dark-haired señorita romantically portrayed. The librarian had been amused.

It was a surprise to Crystal that Dr. Brightwood would think about women at all, though she could not say why. Nor could she imagine him standing with a dark-haired señorita by his side.

"But I think he'll not be marrying," the librarian said with a smile.

"Why not? Crystal wanted to know.

"I think he's a congenital bachelor," she said.

Congenital. Congenital. Crystal went home and looked up the word to make sure. Were some people born to be bachelors and others not? She was mystified. It was like the pronouncement of one's fate. But the librarian could be wrong.

And everyone had been eagerly inviting him to dinner. But wherever he was invited, he always brought his mother, who monopolized the conversation by talking about the achievements of her Findlay. "I think," the librarian said, "that after a little while, people will stop inviting the new professor."

80

"Well, I'm on my own," Dr. Brightwood announced to Crystal one morning during their race up the hill.

"And how is your mother?" Crystal asked politely, as she had been taught to do, for his mother was in the hospital for a week having her gallbladder removed.

"Coming along nicely, but a little weak yet. It'll be a relief to have her back," he said. "I'm getting tired of cornflakes."

"Cornflakes?" Crystal said, in a burst of surprise.

"That's all I've had to eat."

Nothing else. He didn't know how to cook anything, he told her. "I don't even know how to use a can opener."

Crystal looked at him in wonder: his face was that of a happy child. As he was telling her these things, he seemed somehow delighted with himself.

●

Crystal was trying to be a student and to discover what she ought to be learning. She felt not only ignorant but stupid and wanted to know what would make her smart and sure, but though she studied hard and got straight A' s, it didn't seem to make any difference. She had the sense that she was utterly in the dark. What she was missing or how to find out seemed to escape her.

Dr. Brightwood taught history in a way that made it boring and easy. He didn't lecture or discuss. He spent the class time reading from the text sentences he expected the students to learn by heart and write down word for word on his tests. One always had to remember that certain events happened *about* and not *on* a certain date, *circa* 1500, for instance, and that certain statements required the provision of an *and/or* as part of their testimony. If one left out a *circa* or an *and/or*, the answer was marked wrong with a great red slash. But what dictated the choice of information for the students to memorize was, for Crystal, a mystery without a clue. She had to write down in her notebook that the Straits of Gibraltar were named for Jebal Tariq, the Berber chieftain who had crossed them. Years later she was unable to forget that fact.

A trick of the students was to ask Dr. Brightwood for details of his personal history in order to divert him from giving them more "study suggestions" for his tests. These were far more interesting.

"Dr. Brightwood, tell us about the time when . . ." And he was led on while the class listened with suppressed mirth. He told the class how he came to be a runner and described the various stages of his Ph.D. But just when his history seemed to be exhausted by the only two things he had done in his life, he said one day:

"It's true that now I have to earn my living as a history professor and take care of my mother, but my real career has been as an explorer." His eye wandered around the classroom while a little thrill of interest traveled through it. "On my last expedition to Mexico I nearly lost my life. I went there to explore a cave with a great treasure hidden in it by the Aztecs, but it was under a curse . . . ."

So, Crystal thought, he has had an adventure: so many lives seemed to get on without any. She felt a sudden respect.

At that point he paused, stood for a moment as though waiting for the reaction of the class, then dramatically left the room. A few minutes later the bell rang and the class left in a buzz without him.

As he and Crystal were climbing the hill together the next day, Dr. Brightwood explained his sudden departure.

"Do you know what happened to me?" he asked, with an expression she'd come to recognize. "My false teeth just locked right together and I couldn't say a word."

He told her this with the same sort of directness and amusement that came with his confession about living on cornflakes. It seemed to her that he could appreciate almost any sort of joke on himself. But she'd have died before she told such a thing to anybody. She couldn't bring herself to tell anyone in the class about Dr. Brightwood's false teeth. And it was funny.

•

One evening near midterm, Crystal, seized by a fit of restlessness, spent an hour wandering around the campus avoiding the library. She had walked up the hill from her house in time to see the last stragglers emerging from the dining hall. Most of the time she studied at home, and when she came back in the evening she was reminded that there was a life on the campus that she wasn't part of at all. She was met by a little knot of students, among them Judy Simpson, whom she knew only as a girl all the football players wanted to date—all the mean, rangy boys from West Texas. Each time Crystal saw her, she had a different one in tow. She wasn't even very pretty, Crystal thought, but rather bland, moon-faced. She never said a word in class, never knew any of the answers when she was called on. The girls envied her popularity. Once she'd said that all she wanted to do was get married. It seemed likely she would manage it before the year was out. As for herself, Crystal did not think she would ever marry.

It was a chill evening, not quite dark. The lights were on in the library and the dorms and in one of the classrooms in the main building. Crystal was in time to see the Farnison brothers, Lyle and Rennie, cross the campus carrying a hand organ between them that they were taking to Vespers, held every evening in the classroom now awaiting them. They were not like the fellows who lived in Enloe—a rowdy bunch who spent one Saturday night hurling empty beer cans at the dorm. Polite and clean and nice, they never dated and seemed determined to remain pious Christians despite all the corrupting influences around them. They would never do anything wrong, Crystal thought, not in their whole lives. She could tell even from the way they walked. She wondered what it would be like never to have to make mistakes.

She shouldn't be wasting her time, she knew, glancing at her watch. She had a paper due, a test to study for. Even so, she went over to The Cooler, where she found a group of girls from her class, notes laid out on the long table in back, in the midst of coffee cups and coke glasses. Crystal bought a cherry coke and sat down with them.

"And the Plantagenets," Glorietta Van Duyn mimicked, trying for Dr. Brightwood's wall-eyed look, "took their names from the *Planta genesta* or broom plant." They all laughed.

It was not a very good imitation, really. But Glorietta was an actress and was going into the Theater, and everything she did was a performance. She never sat down, she draped herself into a chair, and all her gestures were larger than life. Crystal envied her, for she had gotten the lead in the fall production of *Camille*, in which she had languished so long and coughed so violently, it looked as though her first play might be her last. But to stand up on stage and do that . . . Crystal thought.

When she left the girls nearly an hour later, she could not claim to knowing more than when she had arrived. She would hardly have time to make a beginning. She walked quickly past the Art Building, where the lights were on and a solitary student was working in one of the rooms. Russell Snelgrove. She knew who he was—he was known all over campus, though he scarcely spoke a word to anyone. He claimed to be a full-blooded Apache Indian.

This conviction had asserted itself one morning at sunrise on a hill over by the edge of the married student housing. At least one couple was aroused in time to see a man in full Indian dress, complete with feathered warbonnet, doing a war dance and yelling in blood-curdling fashion. The rest of the time he walked about the campus in proud silence and took courses only in lapidary and jewelry-making. He spent long hours polishing stones. He was a slender man with lily-white skin, and a distant look. The rumor reached Crystal that he wrote his own pornography and sat and read it at night with great relish. Crystal had never seen any pornography.

By the time she had climbed the hill where the library stood above the rest of the campus, the lights were beginning to go out. She had wasted the whole evening. She lingered a little while on the front steps, looking down at the lights of the dorms and the houses of the town that lay below. She was entirely at loose ends. She thought of the people she knew and didn't know. How was it that people's lives took a certain direction, that they were what they were? Things made a curious sort of twist as they came from the center of another person's meaning into her observation, and seemed to turn wild and fantastic. She didn't know what to think or how to be. There was just all this waiting for something different to happen.

She tried to imagine herself standing in front of a classroom. She saw herself moving her lips with no words coming out. Then laughter.

84

•

Dr. Brightwood kept putting off telling his class the finale of his expedition to Mexico. But finally he was badgered into it. Crystal had been wanting to ask him about it, but everybody had scoffed so much about his tale and made such fun of him she was afraid to take him seriously.

Alone—he told the class—despite the entreaties of his fellow explorers, he had gone into that dark and twisting cavern, lighting matches to find his way. (A snicker at the back of the classroom.) Then suddenly he knew she should not take another step. Lighting his last match, he saw that he stood at the edge of a deep chasm filled with water. There at the bottom lay the skulls of thousands of men. Then the match went out. How Dr. Brightwood found his way back and was happily reunited with his companions was unclear. On that day the class received no study suggestions.

"And how are things going in Dr. Brightwood's class?" the Dean, for whom Crystal worked as a typist, asked her not long afterwards.

"It's so dull," she found herself saying. "He makes us memorize all these facts. And they're not important . . ." She was astonished at herself.

After listening to her, the Dean said simply, "Dr. Brightwood is a gentleman and a scholar." That ended the conversation.

For a moment, Crystal was almost ready to agree and to feel that she had located but one more area of her insufficiency. Yet when she looked at the various labels, *congenital bachelor, gentleman and scholar, oddball,* the figure of Dr. Brightwood became strangely obscured. What did he have to teach her? Perhaps when she reached that ideal toward which her education was to lead her, she would know: there would be instant enlightenment. But for the moment it seemed a questionable promise. Perhaps she might reach the precise point where fact and fancy could be separated, as neatly as Dr. Kiely's fence kept him separate from the neighbors. For the moment she couldn't even be sure which was which. And right now she was ready to throw away Jebal Tariq and keep hold of the adventures in the cave in Mexico, perverse though such a choice might be. The tale, she knew, was pure fiction; Dr. Brightwood, a joke. Yet by a trick of the imagination she had accompanied him some distance on that perilous journey, had wanted to reach out and clutch him by the arm to prevent him from taking that fatal step. In an odd way, the tale, whether fact or fiction, belonged to him, like his watch or his morning race up the hill. It was like a fragment of glass, curious and bright-colored and in itself useless, that she had picked up to save, as she used to do as a child because it appealed to her imagination.

That spring, Johnny Ryan gave Dr. Brightwood twenty-five strawberry plants, which he proceeded to plant upside down.

•

"Dr. Brightwood is such a wonderful son, so devoted to his mother," Mrs. Munsinger said in the tone she kept for reverence. She was sitting by the front room window, where both she and Crystal could observe the familiar sight of Dr. Brightwood giving his mother her daily exercise. The old woman walked in little baby steps, so that it took considerable time for her to reach the corner. It was as though Dr. Brightwood were teaching his mother to walk.

"She can walk perfectly well when he's not around," Jane Edwards had told Crystal. For now he hired college girls to come to clean and cook the meals for himself and his mother. "I take her down to the beauty shop once a week to get her hair done," Jane said. "And she pops out of that car lively as a chicken. But the moment he's around, suddenly she's as helpless as a babe."

That year, Crystal's sophomore year, the newly hired psychology teacher conceived a passion for Dr. Brightwood. Every time he walked past her office on the first floor of Light Hall, she would try to waylay him in conversation or else she would call out to him, "Oh, Dr. Brightwood, hello. Hello, you cute little man."

He would blush like a schoolgirl. It seemed to Crystal that he ran faster down the hall than she'd ever seen him run up the hill. And she thought of what her friend the librarian had said, of what Jane had said, and wondered why some people married and "popped out children like so many peas," as her mother put it, and why someone like Dr. Brightwood was still a son to his mother. It struck Crystal as curious that Dr. Brightwood wore both a belt and suspenders. He was the first person she'd ever known who wore suspenders.

"A wonderful man," Mrs. Munsinger was saying, with that clear and certain judgment she had for applying to the world's particularities and untwisting the skein of right and wrong. "Why, they're talking to Minna Patterson. She's gotten so snooty lately she wouldn't even say hello to me on the street the other day."

Here was, Crystal saw, but one more proof to her mother that it was intelligence that finally meant something in the world, let people say what they would. That was why she was so happy that Crystal was going to end up as a teacher.

But Crystal knew that she was still looking for a knowledge that continued to elude her. Everything lay coiled and indecisive, most of the time afraid to put forth the bud of an opinion. She drifted about in a boredom that was a kind of misery, while judgments flew all around her. But each time she picked one up, she found it only partly workable, endlessly qualified the closer it got to her experience, or else it dissolved like a snowflake.

For her mother, things worked out more simply. She moved things around like the pieces of a dime store puzzle. It all came together neatly as horses in a pasture, flowers in a garden. The pieces formed a picture and no riddle lurked beneath. If you followed the rules, things came out right. But if you drank too much or neglected your kids, they came out wrong. There was a picture but no puzzle. She just couldn't understand why people were so stupid.

Crystal, on the other hand, was always wondering what went on in people's minds. Her own seemed so murky that to find out what was in it was like letting down a hook in dark waters and waiting for one of the creatures that went swimming by.

She took up smoking and shocked everyone by walking into class one morning smoking a cigarette in a long black cigarette holder. She did not smoke at home, only at school. She got a B that spring in Dr. Brightwood's English history course because she cut four times. She still walked up the hill with him in the morning.

That summer Dr. Brightwood and his mother were gone

from the neighborhood for a month. They went off for a vacation for the sake of his mother's health—to a dude ranch in Arizona. Crystal wondered what they were going to do at a dude ranch.

While they were gone, the neighbors noticed unusual activity in Dr. Brightwood's house: there were cars parked along the street in front, coming and going all night long. It appeared that Dr. Brightwood had left the key with the woman who was now coming in to clean for him. While he was gone, she made his home into a one-woman whore house. Johnny Ryan laughed about it, the way he laughed when "Old Finney" had put in the strawberry plants upside down. But Mrs. Munsinger was incensed; it was a disgrace to the neighborhood. It was just that, as she explained to Crystal, the world was full of low types that couldn't be trusted.

•

In her junior year Crystal moved into the dormitory and, since she wasn't in any of his classes, she did not often see Dr. Brightwood. From that point on, she took mostly education courses, which she found more boring than anything she had taken so far. She had to memorize the Seven Cardinal Principles, which had to do with developing character and leadership and demonstrating the proper use of leisure time.

It was with dread that she looked forward to student-teaching during her senior year. Yet she managed to stand in front of her first class and teach the lesson despite the panic that threatened. Though she was sure that none of the students paid any attention, that they waited only for the hour to be over, she managed to keep some semblance of order in the class for a whole semester. She graduated with honors, much to the satisfaction of her parents, and even found a job teaching history and English in a junior high school in northern New Mexico.

But after a year she gave it up. She had no idea what to teach a Mexican kid who lived in a one-room dirt-floored adobe hut in the company of eight or nine brothers and sisters. She went to work for a newspaper but felt equally dissatisfied. Not long after, she married a young reporter she met on the staff.

She continued to receive letters from her mother about people in the neighborhood. Old Mrs. Brightwood was getting more and more feeble. The two of them, mother and son, seemed to be entirely alone—nobody came to visit. Sometimes, her mother wrote, she took over a piece of cake when she baked, and they were always very grateful. Minna Patterson had gone to a sanitarium for a rest cure—"to be dried out," as her mother put it. And Mrs. Baynes, always such a tightwad, was flinging away her money in Las Vegas.

It occurred to Crystal after reading one of her mother's letters that she'd been taking in such details all her life, fact and fancy, bits of craziness and wonder, things large and small, crooked and straight, superficial and devious, excessive and lacking—unable to discard any of it, but having to make space for it all: Jebal Tariq and the Aztec cave, Russell Snelgrove and Mrs. Baynes and her own mother as well. It was like so many fragments of glass that the light shone through, first one way, then another. And each time you took out the collection to add another piece, you found that the light had shifted and nothing was the same.

And yet, Crystal thought, you might add the pieces, but perhaps through it all, curved like a snake or the bed of a river, something was being created, so that after a time you were looking at a strand, a connection, a pattern. For hadn't Minna Patterson been drinking too much ever since Crystal knew her?—though Crystal didn't know why. And wasn't Dr. Brightwood's life but a continuation of what had been?

So that she was not altogether surprised by what happened to Findlay Brightwood after his mother died. Mrs. Munsinger thought he might marry now that he was free of responsibilities and still relatively young, just approaching fifty. And it was with shock and outrage that she discovered that Dr. Brightwood was having a series of affairs—with male lovers.

But then the neighborhood was going downhill, Mrs. Munsinger wrote. Johnny Ryan had shot himself after one of the violent quarrels between him and Bernice: Bernice had driven him to it, she was sure. And Dr. Kiely's youngest son had been hauled in for the second time on a drugs possession charge—she'd always known those kids would come to no good. And Minna Patterson was dying of cirrhosis of the liver. Mrs. Munsinger was ready to move out of the neighborhood and was thinking of selling the house to a Mexican woman who had the down-payment, let the neighbors think what they would.

No, Crystal thought, she was not surprised about Dr. Brightwood.

Then came the final piece of news. Findlay Brightwood was found dead in his living room, apparently the victim of foul play by one of his "boyfriends," as Mrs. Munsinger put it. The place was in frightful disorder, everything torn apart, though there was no reason to suspect robbery as a motive. "To think," Mrs. Munsinger wrote, "that all this time the neighborhood was harboring a degenerate."

Crystal read the newspaper clipping several times. The facts in isolation seemed strangely disembodied: simply a man found dead, his house ransacked, an investigation by the police. To read them meant nothing to her. But then the image came to her of Dr. Brightwood standing in front of his class, looking around in bewilderment as two students answered from different sides of the room. She could hear a buzz of comment and laughter as he told the tale of his fabulous exploration. It seemed to her at that moment that she had followed him down the corridor to his doom, she and all the others—had watched him all unknowing as he came to the edge and stepped over. And to her it had been given to follow his steps to the very last, to be involved without knowing it, watching helplessly while life happened to him. Horrified, she had to sit down. "Oh, poor man," she murmured. And she wondered if, before his wandering eye had been stilled forever, it had lit on anything that had even momentarily illuminated the chaos and allowed it to discover any sense in the world.

Do You Believe in Cabeza de Vaca?

To tell the truth, I've always had trouble with history. When I was young, it was a mighty resistance to facts. My mind balked over dates of kings and lists of battles, refusing to take them in, and for a long time my sense of history was that of little islands of flavor, dimly floating in a sea of time that bobbed up and became the present. I do not remember when I became burdened with a sense of history. Perhaps it came the way age comes, gradually, with the sense of life lived, the augmenting and deed-drenched past. At some point one turns a knob and enters a doorway, as into a great secondhand shop cluttered with objects that have fallen through time to lie dust-covered and neglected for years or centuries, among which, browsing, one picks up this and that, detached from ownership and custom—oh, quaint and curious; oh horror, oh horror—and wonders about their value. There are things that are never got rid of. And there in that debris and chaos are things forgotten that have a curious way of coming alive again, making amazing connections.

But this is a story, not history. So I'll begin with Ed. I met him at a party, and he soon established himself as one of those omnivores who grab books from the shelves because they're struck by a title and read themselves into odd corners, seized by irrepressible fits of enthusiasm, during which they quote long passages to anyone within hearing distance. You know the kind.

"So you're from New Mexico," he said. "Wonderful place. My God, the culture. Indian, Mexican, with an influx of Eastern Europeans in the north—Italians, a few Welsh. I got interested in

91

that part of the country about ten years back. Read everything I could lay my hands on. Oñate, Coronado. The Maxwell land grant. The Lincoln County wars. Kit Carson. Billy the Kid. Have you ever read the journal of Cabeza de Vaca?"

"I didn't know he wrote a journal."

"Fascinating thing. Absolutely fascinating." His eyes, I thought, had the hard, bright glint of the enthusiast of the esoteric. "You have to wonder if any if it's true, his going around healing the Indians, performing miracles. They thought he was—well, no telling what they thought. They treated him like a god."

"I'll have to read it," I said moving toward a second gin and tonic. I didn't admit how little I knew about the region where I'd grown up. For at the time, I'd simply wanted to flee it. But I had head of Cabeza de Vaca, and in the eighth grade I wondered why anybody would have a name that meant *head of a cow*. He was mixed up in my mind with Coronado, who had come north from Mexico looking for the Seven Cities of Cíbola, with their promise of gold and other riches. He stood in line with various other conquistadors. You tend to remember the name of someone known as a conquistador.

In my eighth grade class we were all required to take a course in New Mexico history. I was new to that part of the country, having lived until then in the center of a flat, green little stretch of truck farms on the East Coast. My father had come west to take advantage of a business opportunity that proved to be a disaster— his own version of the search for the Seven Cities. Coronado, in case you don't know it, was killed by the Indians during one of his explorations. It was summer when we arrived, just before the end of World War II. They were having a drought in the area around the squalid little mining town we landed in, and the smell of sun-baked earth hung in the air, laced with the continual dry scraping of the cicadas in the trees. I wandered disconsolately along the stony wash in our neighborhood, waiting for school to start, longing for friends and something to do myself; only to discover that nearly all those in my class had gone to school together since the first grade and stood in the comfortable ambiance of shared mores and family connections and understood jokes. For the first time, my eastern accent sounded alien to my ears.

I sat behind Jane Frances Skillen, who stood out as the exemplar of a blessed and mysterious life. She wore mesh hose and tooled cowboy boots to school, and she had her own bank account. She was a short, plump, soft-spoken girl, with a pasty, lightly freckled face and dark hair, which she had a nice way of shaking back from her face. When she laughed, always very mannerly, her little round face dimpled near the chin. During history class someone usually passed her a note, and I wondered, as I handed it to her, what new and fortunate element was being introduced into her life. Whenever there was a community square dance, the high school boys clustered around her. Once when the box lunches we girls had brought were auctioned off, hers went for at least two dollars higher than anybody else's, and the boy she got to eat with was a tall, rangy, good-looking kid, whose father ran the local newspaper and who ultimately would go off to Harvard. The rest of the time she stood at the center of a huddle of girls, who said things like, "Jane Frances, can you stay in town with me tonight? We can go to the show," or "Jane Frances, let's have a slumber party."

"I'll have to call my mother," she would say without looking different or pleased.

To my mind, she was set apart in some enviable fashion because she rode the school bus home. This was to a ranch somewhere in the Gila valley, which suggested a rough and adventurous life, though she went regularly to the Methodist church and was active in Girl Scouts, and her mother belonged to Eastern Star and the Ladies' Auxiliary and the Sorosis.

I mention these things because, as I stood on the edge of the circle, catching the echoes of a social life I stumblingly tried to enter, the history of New Mexico was simply the occasion where I could sit behind Jane Frances Skillen and dream of being somewhere else.

•

So I read the journal of Cabeza de Vaca. One of the first things I learned from the introduction was how he got his name. It seems that back in thirteenth-century Spain, when the Christians were fighting the Muslims and were about to be slaughtered in a certain battle, a shepherd boy showed the Christians a secret pass through the mountains, by means of which they were able to take the enemy by surprise. The entrance to the pass he marked with a cow's skull, and the grateful King of Navarre rewarded the shepherd with nobility and a change of name: Cabeza de Vaca.

The name, however, had stayed with me from the time I read it in the eighth grade, mainly because of its oddity—a small fact not linked to anything else, and with only the shadow of a human being standing behind it. A curious thing with facts, the way some of them stick, out of a certain perversity that has nothing to do with their importance. And so a nameless shepherd enters History, conquering anonymity and ultimately other people and then . . . but that comes later. For now, let us say simply that it was a bloodthirsty line. Or perhaps given the role of Conquistador, the ideal of the conqueror, you have bestowed upon you an opportunity of killing without self-doubt: a time-honored practice of putting whole populations to the sword in the name of holy purpose and the hope of booty. Cabeza de Vaca's grandfather had subdued the Canary Islands, in at least one instance hanging, drowning, and pulling apart by horses all the males over fifteen, and while slaying the native chief, converted him to Christianity as he died.

Discovery and conquest I accepted quite casually back then—the word *conquistador* suggested an office, an entitlement, something kings hired you out for as routinely as the folks who chopped cabbages. In class I gave my attention to what really mattered: who would be asked to Jane Frances Skillen's birthday party. For I saw her one morning with a little packet of small white envelopes with names neatly printed on the front. These she handed round at the end of the period, before the beginning of study hall, while I watched from behind my book, neglecting for some minutes to read about the Indians being eliminated from history by assorted conquerors of the New World. It never occurred to me then that its inhabitants probably looked upon such names as Balboa, Cortez, Ponce de Leon, and Columbus, indeed the whole kit and caboodle, as a dubious blessing, even if their bearers did introduce the horse.

When Cabeza de Vaca come from Spain to Florida, I learned

later, it was with an expedition bent on doing as well as Cortez had done in Mexico. Cortez had been, in the eyes of some, an upstart, deserving discipline, yet also an enviable model. But the coast of Florida, ripe for plundering, won their attention. The real story of Cabeza de Vaca begins, though, with a lamentable decision by the leader, Narvaez, to separate from the ships and go by horseback to meet them at a sheltered bay somewhere down the coast. They never found the ships. Cabeza de Vaca, being a clearheaded and practical youth, had argued against the plan from the first, much good did it do him. Now they found themselves in a strange, swampy land; plagued by mosquitoes, red bugs, and flies as large as bumblebees, as well as half a dozen other varieties, all bloodthirsty; warred upon by Indians; and attacked by malaria.

All those years I had no idea even of the origin of Cabeza de Vaca's name. It failed to occur to me even that I could ask a question about it. Not that the book or Mrs. Pederson, who taught eighth grade vocabulary and spelling and girl's P.E. as well as New Mexico history, could have enlightened me. Not at a time when the name of Jane Frances Skillen was the one chiefly buzzing in my head. I had yet to discover my lack of curiosity.

One must scrape past cities and culture and manners to imagine Florida, see the Spaniards there in a land stirring with animals and birds, silent but for their cries, inhabited by all but naked men to whom they couldn't speak. At the mercy of this lush, tropical, but alien land. And with less and less hope as they found themselves stranded on a spit of land, swamps all around, dying of malaria, their leader ill, some wanting to desert. And hungry. In this extremity they came up with the idea of building boats and heading for the open sea. How they managed to do this is a matter for wonder, for no one knew how to build a boat; there were no tools or iron or pitch or rigging. There was also nothing to eat.

It is here that my imagination began to take hold, years later as I read. I could see those men, having made it across the ocean, convinced that they could step on shore, conquer the local Indians and rake in the gold, which would be lying in obvious display in villages waiting to be plundered. I could see these men dressed in the costume of the Spanish hidalgo, well-horsed and armed. Men who could wager with one another as to who could behead a man the more skillfully, and selecting a native and setting out on their horses, attempt to do the job with a single sword stroke—using up enough Indians to satisfy themselves as to who had really won the bet. Men who fed human flesh to their dogs to make them more savage in attack. Now as they were lost in a strange land, it was the Indians who assumed the advantage.

I see the Spaniards stripping down. It's a matter of life and death building those boats. Everything must be ripped out of its old context. They melt down their spurs and stirrups and cross-bows for iron to shape saws and nails and axes. And to eat, they kill their horses, though Cabeza de Vaca admits he could never bring himself to eat horse flesh. Even under duress the delicacy of sensibility prevails—for a time. Later he would be glad to eat lizards and rats. They turn the manes and tails of their horses into rope and rigging, cut palmettoes for fiber to use in place of oakum for the boats. And even their shirts they must sacrifice for sails.

Miracle enough that they can put together five boats and launch them, forty-odd men in each, the water reaching practically to the gunwales. By that time they'd eaten all but one of their horses. But that enterprise, too, is doomed to disaster, as the boats are caught in one of those sudden fierce storms that come upon the gulf. Even though Cabeza de Vaca and several of his companions survive the storm, their boat is swamped on the way to shore, and all their possessions, including their remaining clothes, are lost. When Cabeza de Vaca enters New World this time, he is as naked as the day he was born.

Let us pause to watch him struggle to shore. It's November now and cold, and he hasn't had anything to eat except toasted or raw maize since May. Skin hanging onto bones. The poor, bare, forked animal—that's where it begins, isn't it? Unaccommodated man, reduced to skin and bones and the animal instinct to escape death. Survival—that always pricks one's attention: that somehow among all those who perish, someone makes it out, lives to tell the story.

The Indians come to the rescue this round. Took the half-drowned, shivering men to their tepees and gave them warmth

96

and shelter and food. They were afraid, these castaways, that they would be slaughtered, but it was that or huddling together on shore to die of starvation and exposure. And Cabeza de Vaca found the one preferable to the other. For seven more years he would wander the land, cross rivers, make his way through the swamps with their mosquitoes and seven kinds of flies, including the small ones that could leave a horse bleeding all over, live on the fruit of the prickly pear and roots and grubs and oysters, occasionally deer meat, journeying over unknown territory to the borders of New Mexico.

History, so it appears to me now, is born of such events, and then the mind keeps struggling with the experience ever after. The spark of curiosity alone isn't enough. Something must be put aside of the investment in the present, to allow things to live again. Jane Frances's birthday party was too important to be supplanted. Fortunately, I was rescued from my state of disappointment by Mrs. Pederson. She had us write a story using our new vocabulary and spelling words. I wrote one about a man trying to outwit a bronco and getting thrown off each time. It was a humorous story. I had never seen anyone ride a bronco, but I managed to use all the words. Mrs. Pederson chose mine to read to the class.

To go on: We have a man stark naked, stripped of all that Spanish nobility can offer, down to his native wit and strength and will to continue, who will journey in that condition, most of the time hungry, sometimes enslaved or beaten by the Indians, his body in sores, subject to the pricks and stabs of bush or branch, and contending always with the flies and mosquitoes. There is only one large fact—the death that can assume such a variety of forms and still be death. And only one major operation of the will, whether to yield or resist, to continue the suffering; whether in the face of death to resist against the stings and arrows. And only one major recourse—prayer. According to his journal, Cabeza de Vaca prayed a lot, asking for God's mercy and for forgiveness for his sins.

They stumbled on in this fashion, eating or going hungry as chance provided, and as the Indians themselves did—until he and his companions were met with a curious notion: they were capable of healing the sick. The Indians insisted on it. They simply ought to be men who could heal the sick; they must blow upon the afflicted area and cast out the sickness with the laying on of hands. They gave up protesting and did what they were told. Suddenly cast in a strange new role, they added the blessing of an Ava Maria or a Paternoster and made the sign of the cross. And those treated by Cabeza de Vaca claimed they were well, rose up and went their way.

Now comes the strangest part.

They were asked to go to the hut of a man given up for dead, already being mourned by his friends. Cabeza de Vaca's companion hung back, afraid of failure, afraid his sins would get in the way, but Cabeza de Vaca, almost in anger at his companion's want of nerve, went to the sufferer. And though he found him with eyes rolled back and pulse gone, he prayed with fervor that his health would be restored and gave him every blessing. That evening after they left, so Cabeza de Vaca's journal says, others told him the dead man "got up whole and walked, had eaten and spoken with them and that those to whom I ministered were well and much pleased. This caused great wonder and fear, and throughout the land the people talked of nothing else."

The news spread like wildfire. After that, wherever he went, whole villages would turn out, and to cure the sick he was offered bows, arrows, food, hides, the Indians divesting themselves of everything they owned for this man of power.

Perhaps you'll say, "History is bunk" –a historic remark! You can drive through C de V's landscape now, thanks to a man who had no truck with history. What are we to make of all this? I remember an image from a fairy tale I once read, of a princess who had to walk through room after room of an unknown castle. At the entrance of each, giant cobwebs blocked the way, and before she could continue, she had to tear them down. In the dusty gallery we stumble over yesterday's miracles. Who is obliged to believe that Cabeza de Vaca ever existed, much less believe in his story? He could have invented it. Eight years intervened between the experience and his account of it. There is always a story—why not at least make it entertaining for the grandchildren?

Let us suppose that this man, reduced to extremities, light-headed from hunger, slogging on by means of whatever hidden source of strength, all but two of his companions lost, does indeed arrive in Mexico—another Odysseus. But reconstructing that lost time imagines himself a conquistador after all, the role of a god. A fit tribute to his imagination. Or perhaps it was such a fantasy that allowed him to survive in the first place.

About the time a sense of history began to dawn in me, I went to visit my grandmother, then in her eighties. I had seen her only once before, when I was a small child living in the East. I wanted to know about the family, to discover "my roots," as people then were fond of saying. She told me how poor her father's people had been farming in Bohemia, little better than serfs. She married poverty. Then later as a widow with five children, she'd nearly starved. One by one she'd sent the children to the New World to live with relatives; then, thank God, she had been able to come herself.

"I have such a story," she told me one afternoon as she lay on the bed to rest. She was a tiny, wizened woman, with a brace on her leg from a previous stroke and a sharp birdlike face as yellowed as old ivory. And she told me that once in her village there came news of a pogrom, that to escape she had fled to the country with all but the youngest child, my mother, who had clung to her father and refused to leave. My grandfather had thought himself safe enough down in the basement of their cottage, but had kept a single candle burning, which he was sure could not be seen behind the curtains.

But when the shooting came, a soldier's bullet found him out and he died holding the hand of his youngest child.

Whenever I thought of the story over the years, it was enough to bring tears to my eyes. It was inspiring, after all, that somehow amid all the horrors, people struggled on, managed to survive. My grandmother and my mother. And here was I, reaping the benefit. I think of this, a story I have held in my head for years, stringing one sensibility to another. And perhaps it was so for the descendants of Cabeza de Vaca, who could look upon their ancestor with pride and awe, not only for having survived but also for having touched a mysterious power.

For myself, I can imagine it as being the truth. As I follow his story, I see a man forced out of his old life and sent through all the torments of the flesh, till all that's left is a bit of life hanging in the moment, as precarious as a match flame in the wind. Hardly

99

knowing whether he wants to live or die. A man who possesses nothing, can lay claim to nothing but must simply throw himself into the perils of circumstance. Pushed to the point where life cleaves in two, at the wall where one crosses into darkness. With so many dead already, maybe only death lies in the storm of uncertainty surrounding the human will. And so believe, if you can, believe powerfully enough that though death might be easier, you will at least not choose to die. Perhaps if one reaches that state—a state wholly open: beyond riches or fame or conquest or love—one comes in touch with the genius of things, and it pours through, mysteriously igniting certain dormant and hidden powers. A pass through the mountains in a moment of extremity, the power to heal in a crisis of survival: perhaps it is a collection of miracles still gleaming under the cobwebs that joins us to the past. I do not know for certain. There is still the testimony of all those who stood at the wrong end of the sword. Their forgotten voices. A leap into faith on the one hand—or into chaos on the other.

However, though it could have happened, in a important sense, my grandfather was not of those hapless victims. I had never asked my mother about the story, that defining statement of our heritage. I just thought of her as that small child holding her father's hand when he was shot down. But not long ago, it came up on a curious way. We were considering how my grandmother had braved the journey all across Europe and then to New York; and our family from New York to New Mexico. All of us carried so far from the place of our origins. She said she had always wondered what had happened to her father. She was twelve, already working by the time my grandmother made it to the New World. "He was shot down by those murderers," was all she would say whenever the question came up, wiping the tears from her eyes, putting her hand up in a gesture that insisted she could endure no further questions. And when my mother once asked her aunt about it, she got a stony look in a set face, as though she'd trampled on forbidden ground. Naturally, the question nagged at her.

And maybe never would have been satisfied. But years later, a remote cousin who had immigrated some years after World War II, drifted out to New Mexico, and they met. "Bernard," she said to him one day, "you grew up in my father's village—tell me what happened to him."

He shrugged. "Listen," he said, "things like that—water under the bridge."

"But, really, I want to know."

"So why do you want?" he said with a smile. "He's like you never knew him, a stranger. My God, how many years dead?"

"That's not the point," my mother insisted. "It's always bothered me."

"Well," he said, "don't blame me. We never talked, it was the shame of the family. We let our ears burn till it all died down."

I add my grandfather's fate to all the things that I did not know as I sat behind Jane Frances Skillen in the eighth grade. I didn't know either that she belonged to one of the major ranching families in the state and was therefore in a social class well beyond mine or that her forebears had gotten their start by rustling cattle and then, their herds built up, selling short to the Indian reservations. Her great-grandfather and his brother had kept a butcher shop in town, and with his money, Skillen bought land to ranch. His brother, a restless sort, wandered up north to rob stagecoaches. Before he was caught and hanged, he cut a couple of fingers from a young boy's hand in order to carry off the rings he was wearing. But she wouldn't have known any of this, nor I, that my grandfather, who'd been involved in a counterfeiting scheme, had tried to shortchange his partners.

I wonder now if my grandmother believed the story she told about the pogrom, had told it to herself so often it blotted out what happened. Perhaps it was what she needed to survive, assuming that the cousin's story is the truth. Or perhaps she invented it just for me. The angle of the light keeps shifting as it hits the objects in the dust-filled room. And which pose will you take after you've been swung around: sentimentalist or cynic or true believer?

But wait, I confess that I have something of my grandmother's penchant for fabrication. The cattle rustling is all local gossip and heresay—no solid proof, and Skillen's brother is an invention on my part, though I read about such a man—down to the boy's fingers. That's just my way of getting even with Jane Frances for that birthday party. But I want to set the record straight. Okay, so call me a liar: I'm no more unreliable than the next fellow. Yet I do love the truth, if there be truth to the imagination. History is still a problem for me; as soon as I touch a fact, it begins to move and wriggle as though it had a life of its own. I try to hold on as best I can.

The last I heard the great Skillen ranch was being sold because the heirs could no longer afford to run it. Now it takes on a new set of names, joins some other set of destinies. But it's connected to me as well. As I look back and see myself sitting behind Jane Frances Skillen, knowing little of New Mexico and almost nothing of the larger world, I can only marvel at the intricate threads of circumstance that brought us together, one behind the other, as different as the dark from the dawn, mercifully ignorant—for how else could the young bear to live—yet sharing almost everything in common.

Painting The Town

"Give yourself a can of paint and you can cover a multitude of sins. Only take a brush in hand and you got a house of a different color. A red wall, a blue corner, an exterior somewhere between Antique Gold and Up-to-the-Minute Sunlight. Fog Gray, Velvet Purple, Burnt Mushroom—"

"You some kind of poet? That's good—a paint-pot poet!"

"Why I know a town in Oklahoma named Pink. You got it, the whole thing's pink. Not my color, I'll grant you, but you know anybody who'd flat out paint a whole town from top to bottom really wanted that color. Got right inside it and gave the world a new optical opportunity. Fortunately, it's a hamlet."

"Come on. Give the kid a break."

"Possibility, that fleeting thing. Freshness. Cover up the past and you got it: a new surface, blank slate, tabula rasa. You do a public service in this business, kid." That was his Uncle Mort, thin as a match, so tall he'd become round-shouldered stooping in the direction of conversation. His pupils seemed to enlarge as he talked, as if they might take in any amount of light, while he trailed cigar smoke and the smell of himself, cruising the aisles of the paint store.

"Come on, come on. I've seen all the dreadfuls I can stomach." That was his Uncle Oscar. "Like the inside of a migraine headache. Put a brush in some people's hands and what d'you get?—a new eyesore."

Mort threw up his hands. "He thinks eyesore."

"Tell me, kid, you afraid of heights? That scaffolding's pretty narrow and times are it's two, three stories to the ground. Personally, the smell of paint make me sick. I sell the stuff, but I can't stand it."

His Uncle Oscar: short, stocky, whose words came out somewhere between a wheeze and a groan. They were giving him a tour of the store; though he'd been in it dozens of times, it was his first time as an employee.

So much for the killjoys. His Uncle Mort was irrepressible. "The smell of new beginnings—that's what's in a can of paint. You stir it up, see that color come together with the base, pure as cream. Then the first dip of the brush . . ." They paused at a display, freestanding cardboard: a woman, having blazed the first band across a wall, turns to flash a smile of triumphant achievement. Anybody can do it.

"You're in for a long, muscle-aching job," his Uncle Oscar assured him. "Your arms in good shape? You're not careless? God, I hope not. Turn over a can of paint and you got a mess to clean up, not counting the loss of time, to say nothing of the cost of the paint. People are so goddam careless. Makes me furious."

"There he goes; no wonder his nerves are shot."

"The other day some joker comes in here, pulls a can out of the bottom of the pyramid. Always trying it. Stupidity—from the paint store to the White House. You're not a careless type, smokes on the job, drinks?"

"Just trying to get even with me for the cigar. Oscar, you're a pain in the ass. Give the kid some encouragement, will you? Look at him. Tall, good-looking, healthy, full of juice. Reminds me of myself when I was young. Youth . . . Get me greased up a little, I could tell you a few stories."

"Spare him the trouble. Who needs your stories?"

"You're lucky, kid. About to embark on the great adventure. I had a motorcycle then." He leaned toward Matthew confidentially: "I was rather a wild youth."

"Okay. He gets the job done, he gets paid for it. If he don't, no bucks for college, Ellie's son or not. That's the world, kid. You better believe it."

"Don't take it to heart, Mat. Keep your enthusiasm. Color is the alphabet of the emotions. Paint is serious business."

"Goose shit!"

His uncle gave him a wink. They never let up on each other.

"Don't give me any theories. Listen, Matthew, I fell and broke my collarbone in this racket; next I broke my back. Maybe you remember. Weeks staring at the ceiling, months in a brace. Now I get to listen to him bore me to death. It's a living. Ok, so I'm grateful to be in the store selling instead of working my arm, breaking my neck. Let it be a lesson."

"You'd think nothing ever went right in his life," Mort appealed to him. "You're lucky. You get to go back to college the end of summer. You got a life ahead of you."

"If he weren't my brother, I'd punch him out."

"Listen, kid. Man should soar, aspire—invent himself. They teach you that in college? Why he's his own greatest idea. Let me tell you, I think of it often. Leonardo, that great painter, back there inventing wings." While Mort went on, Oscar rocked back on his heels, jingled the change in his pocket, stuck a finger in his ear, and examined the end of it when he pulled it out. Matthew stood by. Nobody was asking him to work his brain; the semester was over. "Looking at the birds and projecting man skyward. Living in the idea. Whenever I think of it, tears come to my eyes."

"So you got gloves, apron, brushes, turpentine, thinner, rags—the works," his Uncle Oscar broke in. "Don't step back to admire your work. And if you get a job you can't handle, let me know."

At this point the door opened, a woman entered the store, and complaint, advice, exhortation dropped to the ground. A swinging curve of the hip that kept lovely company with the movement of the thigh brought her forward as various takes of her face and figure, a variety of subliminal impressions accompanied her approach. A welcome vision, as though she'd come from somewhere else, a foreign country or a different bent. Black hair curling below her shoulders, large eyes fringed with long lashes. But it was not just those. Nor the cheekbones that created two shadows along the cheeks, setting off the wide mouth. Somehow she changed the environment, created her own weather, a changed atmosphere: exciting, unpredictable. Dangerous? She wanted something—she had that look—or had pushed something away from her, like a dish sent back to the kitchen. She was not young.

Bitchy. *Okay, let's hear it. Get what you want and leave me in peace. I've got short breath and falling arches, a nagging wife and bills to pay.* So with Oscar. Mort was ready to doff his cap, bow ceremonially, tap his forehead to the ground. *Welcome, welcome.* Matthew stood between them, flushed at the neck.

"I understand you paint houses," she said, down to business at once.

"At your service, Ma'am," Mort said, with a sweep of his arm. He was going to embarrass them. Make some sort of gesture, gallant and stupid. Oscar jingled change. Matthew shifted from one foot to the other.

"I want mine painted," she said. "Black."

"Well," he said, "we have black paint." An unusual request.

"Good." She smiled slightly, for the first time.

"I don't recall I've seen a black house before," Oscar said, doubtful.

"I've always wanted a black house." The three men weren't going to intimidate her. Matthew was ready to admire her determination. "And now I mean to do it. It'll add a little contrast to the neighborhood."

"Definite contrast," Mort said. "You'll get a lot of old ladies on their porches."

"Lots of grays—painted lots of them." Count on Oscar for irrelevance.

Mort smiled at the woman to undermine him, the killjoy.

"Gray with white trim, white with gray trim, dark gray trim, even red trim." Black was giving him the fidgets.

"I want to be a witch in a black house," she said. A smile, ironic.

"Then you'll have your wish," Mort said. Light on the irony. "I've known some witches in my time, but you don't look like any of them."

Amazing what happened then. She smiled broadly and her whole expression changed. Matthew was fascinated. "How do I look then?" she challenged him.

"Why, you look . . ." Matthew watched. His uncle stood there, a stick fishing for a word. "Wonderful." She laughed, and the sound rippled along Matthew's spine.

She actually touched Mort on the arm, and Matthew allowed himself the thrill of that instant as he caught the scent of her perfume. "I should take you home with me," she said playfully, with almost a growl of pleasure. "You're just what I need." To his Uncle Mort, to that old man!

They arranged for Mort and Matthew to stop by her house, to figure the number of square feet and estimate the amount of paint. He and Matthew would begin the job together, then Mort would go on to another project and help him part of the time.

"Good," she said, emphatically. "It's the best thing I've done in a long time. Next to having a tattoo. Did you know I had a tattoo?" she said right to Oscar. "Maybe I'll show you sometime." His Uncle Mort nearly broke up. She laughed, as she took the pen to write down her name and address. Then they watched her leave. Something hung in the air.

"I tell you," Mort said, "if I were younger that's a woman I'd go for." He made his eyebrows dance.

"She'd carve you into mincemeat," Oscar said. "I'll bet she's had practice. She's no young thing. I wouldn't touch her—"

"You wouldn't get the chance."

Hands in the pockets of his shorts, Matthew wandered around the store. They were done with him. Good thing—he was weary of them both.

"You know who she is, don't you?" Oscar's voice followed him.

"No, can't say I do."

"I thought you were up on all the latest gossip, better than the biddies down at the public library. She's Anna Marconi's sister—some kind of fashion designer. Summers here. And she has a boyfriend, drives a white Bugatti."

"Sure. I know who you mean. Greek god type. Boots, Skin tight jeans. Silver studs down the shirt front. I've seen the teeny-boppers practically on their knees begging for a ride in his buggy."

A series of speculative puffs of the cigar. Smoke over the aisle. Matthew could see the woman, her hair floating on the wind, her hand on the man's arm, as they drove in the white convertible.

So Matthew Brannigan was set up for opportunity by his two uncles. Six feet two in his stocking feet, good build, though he walked as though he had not yet grown into his frame. An open face. Everything to observe; nothing much to hide, few nuances yet. Fond of his uncles, he left room for both, catching a hint of the tragic here, a touch of gentleness there. False heartiness in the one; the groan of resignation in the other. But mostly, he thinks of summer, the sunlit stretch of days.

The house lay at the end of Larch Street, a two-storied rectangle with simple lines, barn red. Black over red—at the end of a row of white houses.

When they arrived, the white Bugatti was parked in front, and he and his uncle looked at one another: they should come back later. They were spared the trouble. A man slammed the door behind him, strode from the porch, climbed in the car and drove off with a roar. They waited a few moments, got out of the truck and knocked. She pulled the door open with a jerk, a vase in hand ready to throw. She gave them a look of incredulity and rage, as though they'd personally robbed her of the chance to let out a large store of sentiments. "Oh, it's you," she said letting her arm fall.

"Sorry to intrude, Miss Cousteau."

"Go ahead, go ahead," she said." Then her face crumpled, and she hastily shut the door. "Goddamit," they heard her yell. "Goddam son-of-a-bitch." Followed by the shattering of glass.

"Rackety times," Mort said. "Think of grabbing her by the wrists and kissing her right on the mouth," he said. He paused to imagine it. "Watch that wildcat turn to sweetness. Ummmm." He shook his head.

Matthew wondered if his uncle got his ideas about women from the movies: he adored Sophia Loren. His aunt Ruth had been a dour woman with a large raised mole just above her left eye. All through his boyhood, he'd stared at that mole, usually during Sunday dinners. She said things like, "Finish your potatoes, Matthew," just as his mother did, and she knitted endless sweaters and afghans. Matthew wondered if only women like Gina Cousteau went only with men who drive white Bugattis. A certain kind of man of which he had a fleeting impression. Whether from the set jaw and angry stride, or from the gray suede jacket and soft gray boots, he caught a glimpse of a sophistication that he'd come closest to in liquor advertisements.

He'd slept with a girl for the first time in high school, an awkward and fumbling affair. And the rare times in college had been, in retrospect, the dishevelments of appetite, in fostering circumstance. He didn't knock them or the chance to prove himself. Actually, he'd been going with a girl since high school, Susan Minton, the daughter of his mother's closest friend. She made endless plans about their marriage, the ceremonial path to where love and sex would meet at the perfect crossroads. Until then he could dream— of what he hadn't the vaguest idea. He thought he wanted to marry her; at least he knew her, and somebody else might be a mistake. None of the other girls he dated promised more than an occasional good lay. But none of that seemed to apply to the driver of the white Bugatti. Here were lovers who threw things at one anther.

"I think I've got it," his uncle said, snapping up the measuring tape." We can start tomorrow."

●

The black paint went well over the barn red. The house would not need a second coat. They worked all that day together, scraping, then painting, but saw nothing of Gina Cousteau. They finished the side wall and Matthew drove by after dark, curious to see the effect. The lights seemed to float on the darkness as though no house were there at all. He sat in the car for a long moment, then cut the engine.

"Why hello."

He gave a start. A dark figure blocked his window.

"What are you doing here?"

"I was looking at your house," he said, embarrassed.

She laughed, a rich throaty laugh. "Admiring your work?"

He laughed too. "I can't even see it. It's weird, you know. The way the lights just float, like something passing through."

"That's nice, she said. "You look at things."

He grinned with pleasure.

109

"Hey, you want to walk to the store with me? I need some company."

"Sure," he said. She oughtn't be out alone at night. If a danger leapt out from behind the trees, he'd go to the ground with it. She could wipe the blood from his forehead, weep a little.

"The evening was so nice," she said, as he got out of the car, "and I got this sudden hunger for something sweet. That ever happen to you?"

"All the time. I'm a chocolate fiend."

"Well, you're a growing boy." She gave him a little poke in the ribs.

It was maddening to walk alongside her. Her perfume, the rippling of her hair, a presence that, like the lights of her house, seemed to float in the dark, ineffable and evocative, made his skin prickle. He wanted to seize her hand.

At the store, they spent half an hour, looking at bags of cookies, reading out the ingredients aloud, getting silly over unpronounceable strings of chemicals ("What is this? Are they trying to poison us?") and speculating about the degree of sweetness. They had to be sweet enough, but not too sweet. In the end she picked out Danish butter cookies and chocolate chip. Not to be outdone, he snagged macaroons, ginger snaps, and something called Growly Bears.

"I think that guy wanted to throw us out," she said, with a giggle. "We weren't helping sell his product. But we bought out the store. You'll have to help me eat some of these," she said, as they walked back. He was fantasizing taking her hand, when she suddenly took him by the arm as they stepped from the curb. He couldn't believe it. He expected her to let go, but she kept her hand on his arm.

Great day, Mort. Peace, Oscar.

"Now we can have our feast," she said, as he stood on the stoop, holding the bag while she unlocked her door. "You like coffee or tea?"

"Sure," he said, though he never drank either if he could help it.

"I'll have it in a minute," she said, taking the bags into the kitchen. "Just make yourself at home."

He walked around her living room as though he'd been admitted to a private showing. He looked at the bookshelves and the masks and paintings on her walls and the plants that grew in profusion on windowsills, in hanging pots. Her things. He saw that the paintings were created not only with paint but strips of cloth, velvet and silk, prints and solid colors, different textures. They looked like large flowers.

"You do these?" he asked when she came back. She set down a tray with a pot of coffee and cups and cookies heaped on a plate. "I heard you designed clothes."

"That too," she said. "But this is my passion."

"How come you want your house black?"

"Oh, I don't know. I wanted to give myself a little excitement, I guess." She gave a shrug. "And I was in a bad mood. Sometimes I do stupid things when I'm like that. Only this time, I'm pleased. I'm going to like my black house."

A simple equation: The man plus her mood equals a black house? Did he drive a white convertible for her? He took a bite of chocolate chip cookie. "Not bad."

She sat opposite him, watching him eat. "You look so good," she said, "I could eat you."

His face grew warm.

"I'm embarrassing you," she said. "It's a terrible habit I have, but you have a wonderful face, you know that?"

He seized at boldness, took her on. Cocked his head and looked at her, first one side, then the other. "So do you."

She laughed. "You're good for me, you know that. Sweet and unspoiled. Hey, you know, your uncle's nice."

He know what she meant. "Yeah."

"There are some decent men around," she said almost to herself. "I have to keep reminding myself."

She stared moodily at the rug, no longer there.

"I guess I'd better be going," he said.

She raised her eyes, came back. But she didn't try to keep him. "Well, I'll see you tomorrow," she said. "Bright and early."

She walked outside with him. "My God, look at those stars,

111

will you. Sometimes I feel like they could draw me right up."

"Well," Matthew said, "you've got something like a black sky right here. You can float along with the lights."

She laughed. "You're something. You got a girlfriend?"

"Sort of."

"I'll bet you do. I'll bet the girls follow you around."

She was embarrassing him again.

"Don't worry, they will. And this car. Where'd you get it?"

"Inherited it," he said. He patted the fender. "If the heater works, the radio doesn't. If you got lights on, you can't use the windshield wipers."

"You ought to paint it," she said.

"You think so?"

"Put designs on it."

He thought about it.

"You just get some little cans of touch-up paint and you can go wild. Tell you what—I'll show you a few tricks," she said. "Come around when you've got a free night."

"You bet," he said.

●

"What's that?" Oscar wanted to know, "A doodle parade?"

The car sat out in front, a fourteen-year-old Mustang, its surface covered.

"Flowers of inspiration," Mort said grandly. "The transcendent landscape. Mountains fixed with fiery stars. An ocean—"

"If you're advertising for us, no thanks."

"Your work?" Mort said. "A mighty hand, a mighty brain."

"I had some help," Matthew said. "I painted the mountains, but—" he coughed, "a friend of mine painted the horses and the Indians."

"What are those over there?"

"Symbols of fertility."

"Hopi?"

"Navajo."

"What's that?"

"Thunderbirds."

"And those?"

"The four winds. Sun, moon and stars."

"Elaborate."

"Nice border."

"Maze design."

"You did the mountains?"

"Is that supposed to be the Last Supper or an Indian pow-wow?"

"Come on, Oscar. Appreciate. Think of the work."

"Paint a whole house in that time."

"What kind of flowers are those?"

"Sunbursts."

"Thought I recognized the glory."

"I didn't know your girl had so much talent."

"More talent in one little finger than . . . Well, I got to go."

"Too bad you got a date," Mort said. "I could tell you a few stories."

"Save the canned goods," Oscar said. "He's invented a whole panorama."

Actually, he was taking Gina Cousteau for a ride in the car. Now that she'd helped him paint it, she wanted to try it out. They'd drive along the ocean and stop and have some fried clams or shrimp. He knew a good place. When she stepped out to meet him, she looked different, younger. She was wearing a loosely knit sweater of blue and white, a scarf and silver earrings. She'd done her hair in pigtails and had put a ribbon at the end of them. "Cute, huh? What d'you think?"

"Terrific," he said, though he wished she had left her hair loose so that he could watch it fly in the wind. He opened the door for her.

They drove out to see the sunset. Clouds floated above the bay, catching the afterglow. The light hung for a long time as they drove, rose melting into gold; then smoke gray across a darkening blue.

"I love being out here," Gina said. "You feel so free, like you could forget everything and start over. And this car. It could just take off over the water, in a flight of sparks."

Not exactly the sleek lines of the white Bugatti, but it was enough. She was in it.

"You like motorcycles? My uncle had a motorcycle when he was young."

"Too noisy," she said. "They terrify me."

At the fish place, they sat on rough plank benches at wooden tables and stuffed themselves with steamers and lobsters. He gave a lecture on the evils of gluttony and greed. "You'd make a great TV preacher." Then a litany in praise of their use of the economy, in the manner of the president. Finishing up with a little commentary in the style of his uncles. She laughed until tears came to her eyes. He was giddy with pleasure, not even guilty about sacrificing his uncles. He'd do worse for her sake. There really were women you sacrificed everything for—fought for, robbed banks for, made a fool of yourself for. All of it. He wanted to sit and stare at her forever, watch her go through all the emotions so he could practice up and get them right. She'd show him the genuine article.

"Hey, do you like to dance?"

"I adore it."

"Just follow me."

It was 3:00 a.m. when they got back, and he had to be up by 6:00. But he didn't care. Wouldn't have cared if his mother vented a storm over him the moment he crossed the kitchen in his stocking feet. He fidgeted while Gina searched in her purse for the key. Was he going to do it or not? "May I kiss you goodnight?" That's what he always said to Susan. The door opened and she turned to smile at him, on the verge of disappearing. His hands trembled. But before he gave way to the impulse, she had her arms around his neck and her mouth to his. Astonished, he hung on till his breath gave out. "My God," he murmured, breathless, then bent down and kissed her again.

"You're wonderful," she said, nuzzling him. "Your skin. That scent, what is it?"

"You really like it?" Expensive, that expression of his vanity. Amazing how her skin and hair had their own perfume; her very presence gave off a scent. Maybe if you loved, breathing was enough. You just drew breath.

He walked back to the car, but didn't get in. For a long time he stood watching the lights float upward in her house, as though they bore her upward too. Lamps ascending into the dark. Then he watched them go out. Where did the light go? Just disappear? He couldn't imagine it.

●

"But I never see you." She had come into the store, interrupting a certain fantasy that had nothing to do with appreciable fact. He suffered a shift in gravity and dimension, a sudden alteration of time and reference. They walked out to the sidewalk, then up the street for a coke. He looked at her in the light of common day—she had claims—trying to figure out where she belonged. Silver bangles shook out the light below her teased hair, now brown at the roots. A band of freckles followed the curves of her cheeks. He tried to remember how he had seen her in the past, in his car, at the movies—how she ate, what she wore. To add her up into a sum of attitudes and qualities. He might have been looking at her from across the street.

"What have you been doing?"

"Working," he said, with a shrug. "Nothing special."

"You haven't even called since we watched the Michael Jackson special."

"Yeah, well, you see, I've had this friend. actually, my best friend at school. He's been worrying a lot about himself. . . . "

"John? Not AIDS," she said, horrified.

"Yeah, I mean, no—not that. Not John."

She gave him a strange look. "What are you trying to tell me?"

"Well, this friend has been in trouble—"

"With the law? Who've you been hanging around with?"

"He thought about it. Almost joined the army, but he's allergic to gun oil and shit on a shingle."

"What are you talking about?"

"Plus he's got a rich aunt." Something lifted his brain like champagne or helium. He couldn't stop. "But then he fell in love."

"So?"

"Love troubles. Hit him hard."

"And you're holding his hand every waking minute?"

"Yeah, I mean, he's been suicidal and—"

"Then he'd better get some help. You can't spend every minute. . ." She paused.

"What does he do while you're working?"

"He's got a job."

"Oh. Just contemplates suicide in his off hours."

"Listen, Susan. It's just that I'm rather involved right now."

"Is it someone else?"

What did he want? "You're free, I'm free." He stopped and looked at her.

"When we're practically engaged? What are you saying? And you haven't had the decency—"

"We're not practically anything," he said. "We never said we couldn't date. We haven't even—"

"Is that all you think about?"

"No, dammit," he said. He'd left off thinking. It was as though only now he'd come upon another language: the way Gina had tossed the hair out of her eyes and smiled over her shoulder at him while they were painting sunbursts on the top of his Mustang; her hair streaming in the wind (he'd asked her to undo her braids on the way home), her eyes gleaming with pleasure as they kept step, invented movement on the dance floor; his name in her voice. When she kissed him, he forgot that name altogether: being called, not back to himself but to another way of being. He wanted to forget the ache of who he was and wake up transformed into a lion with golden teeth or a huge white bear with diamond eyes. None of it quite real; yet he felt he'd just come alive.

"I wish I knew what you were talking about," Susan said. "You're just making fun of me." She was on the verge of tears.

"No, really," he said. "Half the time I don't know what I'm doing." She turned away, and he watched her, her name on his lips. He couldn't say it. Yet something tugged; a little thread still

116

attached to her. "I'll call," he said. "Really I will."

The whole thing was a dream, one that he kept waking from and subsiding into. He was in her bed and she was lying on top of him, tracing his eyebrows, curling his hair around her fingers. He loved the weight of her on his chest, the touch of her breasts, the smoothness of her thighs between his. A woman lying on top of him! There for him to stroke her back, run a hand along her buttocks and thighs. A gift, like a trust. After she'd dozed for a time on his chest, she said she'd been dreaming of red and green grapes, and laughed. He felt relaxed and sleepy, floating in fatness, at ease.

Two hours before, poised outside on the scaffolding just outside her window, he'd been tense with concentration, painting the back wall of the house and finishing up the trim around the window. The window was open and she was just inside, in front of her dressing table. She looked up and saw him, then came over.

"You're here, she said, opening the window the rest of the way. "Come on in." She moved back to give him room.

He set down the paint tray and brush carefully beside him and climbed over the sill. *I wouldn't do that,* his Uncle Oscar remonstrated: *You've got a job to do. So go to it,* Mort said. Immediately, sir.

"Well, here you are," she said gaily.

There in his coveralls, their bagginess surrounding him. He was in her boudoir. She was one for scents all right. His eye jittered over a whole display of vials and bottles, tall and slender, heart-shaped, round; and stoppers, bulb-shaped, pointed, faceted, stemlike. He looked at her. They met in the middle of the room.

"Well," she said.

Question? Invitation? His chest throbbed. *Dangerous business. Don't step back to admire your work.* If he did the wrong thing, she'd probably boot him out. *Just dip in, kid.* He moved toward her, put his arms around her and kissed her.

She smiled back, drew back, took the zipper of his overalls and pulled it all the way down. He reached out and unbuttoned her tunic. She pulled back the sleeves from his arms. He drew her tunic over her head, undid her belt, tugged down her jeans. One suggestion followed another. He wanted to touch every part of her, encircle her waist, feel her warmth, snatch at everything greedily, for himself. But the grace of her nakedness stopped him. He wanted to gaze at her, to keep her in his vision, to stand forever in that fullness, beside himself. The moment he did touch her, he seemed caught up in a momentum that threatened to take him out of control, beyond excitement. Yet he was held back by the gleam of a certain clarity. He learned from her the way he should touch her, allowed himself to be led and then went beyond her response. Knew from the way she moved, the sounds of her pleasure. He followed her, entered her experience and took his place there, found the rhythm, let himself be carried forward by it, to the last breathtaking, frenzied release, when he didn't know where he was going, but only that he had to get there.

"Oh," she breathed afterwards. "Oh."

Now she rolled over beside him, her head on his chest, while he stroked her hair. For a while they lay silent, apart, caught up in their various reflections.

"What are you thinking about?" he asked.

"A man," she said with a smile. "I don't know why. Maybe because I'm happy. Isn't that funny?"

The white car, the black house. A shadow. "Sometimes what you think will be so wonderful . . ." He let her go on, but he didn't want her to. "I adored him, I really did. When he stood there down in the forge, supervising the students as they poured the bronze for one of his sculptures, he was like a god. Everything he touched was strong and beautiful. There was power there."

She was making a picture in his own mind that she must be seeing even more vividly.

"But then," she said, "he never thinks of anything but himself—his pleasure, his time. I tell you, I've sat by that phone for hours waiting for him to call, or just drop me a note. There's always some excuse: his wife is sick, the kids need this and that. He thinks he can have it all."

Susan stood in front of him: *I never see you.* He leaned over and kissed Gina to make her quiet. Pretty soon there'd be a whole confabulation in the room, more real than what was slipping away from them.

"I hate him," she said. "Oh, forgive me," she said. "Why am I thinking of that? You're wonderful, you know. You don't even know it. It's so natural with you, how to be a lover.

"Some men," she said, "it's like feeding roses to a dog."

Then came a sudden banging on the door.

"My God, I forgot. I was supposed to meet my uncle and deliver some paint. It's out in the car."

They threw their clothes on. No point in his going back out on the scaffolding. They went downstairs together.

When Gina opened the door, his uncle looked from one to the other. "What have you been up to?" he asked. "Painting the town?"

"I forgot," Matthew admitted.

"I can see why. No problem. I'll just take the paint."

"I've still got a little work to do."

"Don't leave anything unfinished," his uncle said. "Once you start, do the job right."

•

"Women are to be appreciated," Mort was saying, "but never understood. I've been trying all my life. But then I don't think they know what they're all about either. Or us—they don't understand us any better." He paused to consider that idea fully, saw that his cigar had gone out, tried to relight it, burnt his finger and dropped the match. They had worked till dark, then gone for pizza and beer. Now into their third beer, Matthew felt the alcohol move into his fatigue.

Were you ever in love? He suppressed the question. He couldn't feature being in love with his Aunt Ruth. He remembered her bras and panties in formidable array on the clothesline. Her enemies were dust, dogs, encyclopedia salesmen, and children who picked her flowers.

"I was madly in love twice," his uncle said, as though lifting the question from Matthew's mind. "Or so I thought. Once with a girl named Helen. Beautiful girl. I mean really striking—she could've been in the movies. Jewish. She used to take me home and

119

her mother fed me borscht and potato kugel, just dying for a son-in-law to feed. I put on weight, believe it or not."

"What happened to her?"

"Helen? She ran off with a jazz musician. Mrs. Bernstein cried when it was all over, despite my not being a member of the faith. Helen wasn't really interested in me: a momentary diversion between her last man and the next. I felt devastated—for about a week. By the next Sunday I felt fine. Made me wonder about being 'madly in love.' Later on out in L.A. I found her boyfriend a job, and we all used to go to the movies together."

"You weren't jealous?"

"I think I was relieved. She wanted . . . too much from a man. She went through them like handkerchiefs."

He felt tongue-tied. *Gina*, he wanted to say. All I know is her name. *Pay attention*, she'd said to him. *Pay attention*. To her? To what? It seemed like he couldn't pay attention to anything but her. Fortunately he could paint walls and think of her, let the brush go on its own. Her image swirled in the paint he stirred, and gleamed on the freshly coated wood. It was formed by clouds and cracks in the sidewalk. Her perfume followed him into his sleep. And all of it became the outer reflection of longing. He had not known it could go so deep, whatever this was, like a nail driven through him to that extreme point where life flowed into him and spoke his name, there on the verge of that consciousness that made him separate, himself. That was her language, satisfying a hunger he'd never known existed, and creating one in the process. He ached with a sense of himself.

"I loved your aunt for her finer qualities," he heard his uncle saying. "There wasn't anything really physical between us after the first couple of years."

Matthew looked at him. Giving it up after you went to such pains to get it; he responded with the sympathy of man to man.

"She liked a neat house and her pitcher collection. She'd do anything for me—except very little of that. She'd cry sometimes when I came home from my excursions." His uncle shrugged. "I'm not a saint." He signaled for another beer.

Matthew wanted to ask about his flings, but his uncle changed the subject.

120

"Susan's been around."

"What?"

"Making noises to Oscar."

"Why would she do that?"

"She said you were supposed to call her."

"I never made her any promises."   But he had, he remembered.

"Maybe you didn't have to—you've gone together, what two, three years? Anyway, her mother and your mother . . . She's feeling neglected."

"I've been busy." Too busy for her? After that string of dates one after the other, bringing things up to the not-quite present. A habit. He'd never had to wrack his brains for what to do on weekends.

"I don't doubt it. Well, it's always easier getting in than getting out. Be careful—no, forget it. Things don't happen that way. Anyway, I believe in it, the sunbursts and all the rest."

●

"I've been dying to see you . . . . You never came by and when I tried to call you before, you were never there . . . . I'm so happy you called. . . . Remember all the fun times we had this spring?"

Her voice, reaching toward him, surrounding him, made him somehow dishonest, wearing false colors. *I'm not what you think. I can't go back. Gina, you've ruined me. Susan, the horizons are wider. Haven't you noticed the cliffs? The tracks going all the way to the edge .*

"I'm just not myself. It's hard to say, but I've wanted to be alone." He was going to do it neatly, cleanly. Take her to the movies and break it all off. Actually, he'd gotten a letter that morning that was going to change some things.

"You know, I haven't seen you since you painted your car," she said, when they came out of the theater.

The car, yes. Gina and the car. "You like it?"

She smiled. "It's kind of crazy. But I like it."

"It was a lot of fun."

"You should've called me, I'd have helped. Let's go for a ride," she said.

She'd ridden in it dozens of times before he and Gina went to work on it. Then, it was an ordinary car, somewhat notable for the rust along the bottom. He considered: They could go along the ocean, the same route he and Gina had taken, and could watch the foam break into the darkness in intervals. "The stars are wonderful," he could hear Gina saying. No, they couldn't go along the ocean.

He turned back into the country, along the avenues of dark trees. It didn't help. He drove silently. If Gina had felt bad enough to paint her house black. . . Had she felt that bad?

Susan reached over and put his arm around her shoulder, snuggled up to him. "Come over to the house for a while," she said. "We can put on some tapes and dance."

It was going to be harder than he'd thought. "I really should get back and turn in. I've got a long day tomorrow."

"Just this once. I've got something I want to give you," she said.

He wouldn't stay long, just long enough to get it over with. The house, he noticed, was dark but for a single lamp in the living room. "Where's your mom?" he asked, as they got out of the car.

"She's got a bridge game tonight. Your mother's there too. Come on in." He'd forgotten.

"You hungry?" she asked. "I could put together a couple of sandwiches."

"No, really, Susan. There's something I want to tell you. I just got a letter from my dad and . . ."

"That can wait," she said. "My turn first. Come in here," she said and led him into her room and shut the door. "Sit down," she said. "No, here on the edge of the bed."

"Now close your eyes," she said, sitting down beside him. He could feel her hands on the back of his head, then their pressure as she made him lean toward her. His lips were against her mouth. He kissed her lightly, but she did not let him pull away.

"Susan," he said, opening his eyes.

"You're cheating," she said. "And that wasn't much of a kiss."

She really wanted him to do better than that? Had he ever done much better?

"Come on now."

He did better than that. Before Gina, it would have scared him. He felt a little shudder go through her and then an exhalation of breath. They opened their eyes and looked at one another. Her expression was difficult to read. Breathing rapidly, she moved toward him again, took his hand and put it on her breast.

"What are you doing?"

"I want to, I want you to."

He didn't move, but watched her with a confused mixture of reluctance and excitement as she unbuttoned her blouse.

"Please."

Though he wasn't clear why she wanted it now, he felt drawn and in a way flattered. Perhaps in his new though tentative state, he had something of tremendous importance to offer her. He seized her and kissed her with force, then slipped his hand over her bare nipple. "Oh," she said, "oh." He was suddenly in a pitch of excitement, forgetting everything. He reached toward the zipper of her jeans and began pulling them down, but she wasn't giving him any help, and when he put his hand between her legs he felt her grow rigid.

He pulled away as though he'd been slapped. "You don't want to do this, do you?"

She sat silent, her narrow shoulders and small breasts exposed.

"Put your clothes on."

"She gives it to you, doesn't she?"

"What are you talking about?"

"You think nobody notices? You're not paying any attention. You just walk around doing what you please. It doesn't matter who you hurt."

He stood up, appalled. "You think she's a whore, don't you?"

She burst into tears. "I don't even know her. And she's so old—I don't even see why you like her."

So he'd driven her to this. Without wanting to be, he was sorry for her.

"I love you," she said, tearfully.

"No, you don't," he said. "But it doesn't matter." He grabbed up his jacket. "I think we're even," he said.

"Matthew," she yelled after him. "I do love you."

Back at the house, he was alone, his mother not having returned yet from the bridge game. For a long time he stared at himself in the mirror as though something might be revealed to him if he looked hard enough. "You face is breaking out," he said to his image. "Isn't that swell? You're so big, you're clumsy," he said. "You ought to see yourself. Why don't you get a haircut?"

He slammed around the house, ate the leftovers from dinner—but nothing would satisfy—and went back to his room. At his desk he pulled out a sheet of stationery. He'd ordered it when he was a senior, but had never used it; a gray he supposed was elegant, with an initial M in a darker gray. "Dear Gina," he wrote,

> It's the first time I've tried to write you a letter. It's odd.
> I feel like I've known you a long time, like you're my closest
> friend. Funny, isn't it? How everything can change. For me
> nothing has been the same since the day you walked into the
> store.
> I don't know where I am.
> I look into the mirror and I see a child—timid, scared and
> stupid. But when I look again, I see a man who wants to do
> right and learn and love. Even though I've finished the house,
> can I come to see you again?
>
> Matthew

She called him down at the store. "Of course you can come."

•

He wanted to bring her a present. But he didn't know how to buy a present for someone like her. He thought of flowers, but that seemed corny, and he didn't know how to buy her clothes. It had to be special, part of the language they spoke—of each other. Things he couldn't quite tell her in his letters. Some offering of himself. It took him a long time to decide. One thing he bought, the others he owned. Three things. He wrapped them carefully, went round to the house. He wanted to surprise her.

"Oh, I'm so glad to see you," she said, when she opened the door. "I just got off the telephone." She frowned. "That crumb. Like a bad taste you just want to forget. But you're here. I'm so glad. Come inside."

He brought out the packages from behind his back and displayed them like three cards he was holding.

"For me?" she said, taking one, hugging it to herself. "Oh, I love presents." She unwrapped the first, a shirt of red and gray check like one he'd worn and she'd admired. "I love that shirt." He'd found her size. "Like yours," she said, putting it on. Then she unwrapped the bottle of scent, half a bottle of "Gray Flannel," his big extravagance. He liked the idea of her using the other half. She laughed. "Oh, let me kiss you," she said.

She rumpled up his hair. "What'll I ever do without you?"

"You'll have me," he said, as she unwrapped the third gift, his picture. "I hope you'll never have to do without me," he said. She gave a laugh that sounded almost like a moan. "You'll be here?" he said, worried. "You won't go away, will you? You won't die, will you?"

She looked at him tenderly. "Well, not if I can help it. Oh, you sweet thing. And you've come along now. If only . . ." She looked away. "If I looked at you as I ought, I'd think, 'Here is the son I never had.' Oh, my God."

"But I love you," he said. "I don't want you to be old, I don't want you to die. I just want—you. If you died . . ." He couldn't imagine the world without her. "You'd come back, though. I know you would."

She laughed again. "I'll always be here. For you. But," she said, "it's you who'll go away."

"The summer," he said, "it's going by so fast. And my dad keeps trying to convince me to transfer to school in California. It would be cheaper, and if I go to med school . . ."

"Then you'll go," she said. "You have a future—it's all in front of you, and my future is now my past."

"But you're my future. You're part of it. And I can't go away."

"You're talking like a child," she said, mournfully.

"Okay, then. But I will come back," he insisted.

125

"We'll see."

"I mean that. In two years on this day I'll be back."

"All right," she said, lighting up, as though the game itself were her delight. "We'll make a bet."

"Yes," he said, eagerly. "In two years on this day I bet I'll be here."

"It's a bet," she said.

"And what do I get if I win?"

She laughed. "You can name your prize."

"I want a ride along the ocean. I want you to tell me everything you've never told me. I want—"

"You can have everything. I can only lose."

"What do you mean?" he said, disturbed.

"If I win, I lose. If I lose, I'll still lose."

She stood in the midst of her riddle. Above him with a knowledge that beckoned, but promised to make him no happier once he had it.

"Whatever happens I will lose you."

"No," he protested. "I won't allow it."

She smiled as she approached him. "I love you," she said. "And I like my shirt. I like it on, but you can take it off. You made that choice, you know."

He thought about it. "But you?"

"Oh, I laid a few tracks, but you kept coming. You've done what you wanted to do."

He hadn't even thought about where the tracks were going, not till they'd got here and he was looking over the edge. But I'll go, he thought.

She smiled and put her arms around him. "What you want, you can have."

"Always?"

"How young you are." She gave a little laugh.

•

"A scandal," Oscar said, laying him out. "An absolute scandal. Did you think you were invisible? That nobody would notice?

126

You and that woman!"

"Easy does it." This was his Uncle Mort.

"And if you knew about it," Oscar said, "you ought be strung up. A party to . . . to . . ."

"The delinquency of a minor?" Mort suggested. "Moral turpitude? Let the boy alone," Mort insisted. "He's got enough on his mind."

Oscar scowled.

"He's got a mother, remember. He doesn't need two."

"Was it Susan?" Matthew demanded. "Did she—"

"I'm not going into it," Oscar said, pushing the whole untidy mess down with his hands. "All I know is your mother said for me to tell you you'd better not look her in the eye until . . . well, you know. As long as you're under her roof. She says you'd better go talk to the priest if you know what's good for you."

"What would he know about it?" he said. "What have I done?"

"My God," Oscar said, throwing up his hands. "Though I must say, any woman who'd lead a young boy astray . . ."

The summer may as well have been over, for the huge crack that had struck down the middle of it. A wave of nausea came over him.

"Have you got anything that belongs to her?"

"No."

He had her letters; he wouldn't part with them. The dozens they had written one another, as though under the surface of all they said lay the unspoken that they must wrestle into words. As though he'd never had a thought before. And now he had a way of thinking. And she could see him, more deeply than he could see himself. He loved her for that, for what she allowed him to see. "There're lots of nice girls your own age," Oscar went on. "But then some women are never satisfied. . . .

"Okay, so tell your mother it's over and that's that." Duty done, his uncle patted him on the shoulder. "A fellow's entitled to make a few mistakes," he said.

"Provided they're his own," Mort added.

They left him alone then, went off to argue. He didn't bother to listen.

•

He wasn't going to do it. They could still sneak a little time together before he had to leave. Lunch hours when he'd steal away like a thief, his heart pounding, all his senses poised to see her. To taste a bit of stolen time. And after he drove out to California—he wondered what they'd think of his paint job out there—they would write. He'd rent a mailbox at the post office so that no sacrilegious eye could fall upon even the handwriting on the envelope. In two years he'd be out of school. Free.

It seemed to him that if he threw down everything then and went to Gina, he'd be one kind of person, and that if he gave her up and went on with his life, he'd be another. But maybe it wasn't that simple. And if he did either one, would he look back convinced he'd made a mistake? He could hear his Uncle Oscar saying, "You're just a young guy—you'll get over it." And he could hear his Uncle Mort say, "There are things you never get over—unless you want to be a dead man." At the moment, it seemed easier to die than to live and be whatever he was.

He pulled himself together to begin mixing up the beige paint that had been ordered for his next job, the facade of the newsstand on the corner of main street. ("How about black and white and red all over?" "What are you, some kind of wise guy?")

After he finished, he set the last cans on the floor and leaned his back against the paint mixer. He was contemplating love, betrayal, loss, death, and the white Bugatti parked in front of Gina's house.

"You're really into it. You didn't even hear me. What are you thinking about?" Mort asked him.

He looked up from an inner landscape of confused colors. He shrugged. "Nothing," he said.

Dreaming Crow

White Bird flapping white wings,
—overtaken by darkness.
Come out, sooty one.
Charred by the darkness of the world?

I sat up with a start, head hollow, ringing with dry laughter. Sat up in alarm. Felt the bed under me, the covers in a tangle. I'd landed there in the middle of it, but from what point of departure? Felt my shoulder. Absence. "Crow," I shouted, "Crow, dammit," and in the dark heard the rustle of wings. Hadn't lost him, and if I lost him, I'd never lose him. Haunt me like a demon. But he was here. Had ridden home on my shoulder. And sat with head tucked under a wing while I took off into another crow dream. For of late, I'd been dreaming of nothing but crow.

A sudden light went on, cracking across my skull like a billy club. Hell and goddam! The cops? The landlord? My ex-wife? Bill collector? Insurance salesman?

Just Ernie. Of course, Ernie. And what the hell was he doing in my partial awakening, the switchman turning out the black? When my eyes focused, I saw him standing at the foot of the bed, looking at me out of the silence of long waiting burdened with thought— and Crow with his claws hooked over the chair back. I was trying to reach back beyond the dream, maybe beyond the beginning of my life, that blast of birth, when the sudden, too sharp light dropped me into this year's calendar. Tried to shake the dead days out of my head. A rattling as of abandoned parts. A fog, a buzz, a falling into place: he must have brought me home from Mcintyre's. Maybe, maybe not—he'd done it before.

129

To be on the safe side, I said, "Thanks. Thanks a lot."

"For what?"

"God damned if I know."

"Well, I sure as hell don't."

"Oh." I started to turn over, in an effort to get below the racket in my head. "I must have galloped home on the whiskey. Flown with Old Crow."

"You were roaring loud enough."

"Miracles," I said, to account for the gap between there and here. "There're still miracles in the world."

"Tell me about it," he said, slumping down into the overstuffed chair, into the distortions of springs.

I was not then of a sufficient clarity to take him on. One of his bad nights, I could tell. Had that large sad look in his eye. It would have been a waste of philosophy anyway. "Done any work on the book?" I asked him.

"Tried," he said. "Threw out the whole first section. It's about time. I've been giving myself the lie all year. . . . Now I've got to start over."

"Ernie," I said. "I heard you read it." Could anything still have brought tears to my eyes, that might have had a chance.

He shook his head. "It's not there yet. Not the way it's gotta be."

Crow circled the room and landed on my shoulder. Helpful creature. A burst of distraction. Might've been good for Ernie to have a crow. Take his mind off the damned book he'd been trying to write for fifteen years. An account of his experiences: for those who weren't there in the muck and the horror. Who would never know flaming jungle and wasted life. An experience of consciousness, he called it.

All this time he'd been trying to haul it back, over the distance of years and the gulf of forgetfulness—trying to get it right. Every word. A final monument for those who'd never have the chance to speak.

"How can you stand it?" he said.

"Stand what?"

"That crow flapping around."

"I'm used to him. It feels odd when he's not there. Like a growth you can't get rid of. Gets to be part of you." Performs a service. Lets you carry your darkness on your own shoulder."

"His feet are ugly."

He was in one of his moods all right. Always circled the thing that was on his mind.

"Maddy's coming tomorrow. With Roy."

His wife and kid. Separated. Still loved him. Believed in bridges, in paths around obstacles. Believed that obsessions would melt away and normal daylight return. Believed perhaps in redemption. Their visits left him in the hole for a week.

"Better get some sleep," I told him. He'd probably come up to escape his apartment, or himself. "You're welcome to the chair."

"You mean I can bounce on those springs all night."

"Suit yourself." I'd reached the limits of hospitality. I wanted to turn over. I would sleep again even though Crow would be waiting for me, something growing out of the dark, shapeless at first, then forming his image. Now in one guise, now another, a terrible suspense building, as I lay waiting. God knows what for. For him to speak? So far he hadn't spoken.

•

I think he must be a myna bird, if not a real crow. Your basic black bird. Someone had taken a knife and split its tongue. I have never known anyone who could do that, take a knife and slit a bird's tongue. And I have often wondered where it put you afterward. I have looked into its eye on other occasions and felt all I laid claim to split and shatter like a mirror. Once it spoke. Someone had tried to teach it to say, "All that glitters is not gold." And it had held onto the first part, flying dizzily around the room, spreading a mockery, it seemed, by saying it over and over. Only sound. Not human speech. Split the tongue and take the creature beyond the bird. To what curious sphere?

All that glitters . . . I would not have put it down as the nesting instinct, but every once in a while, I would find a little hoard of things collected: a paper clip, a silver button, a bit of cellophane, a dime.

131

I myself had collected enough bright objects in my time, seizing first on one, then another. All fresh and smart in the gleam of the spanking new. Love and money. Marriage and kids. House and home. All that glitters.

All fallen away. Now the kids were grown and had flown. The house, the life that went with it—collapsed. I'd dropped through the layers and folds of all that had held me up, the structures of the quotidian, and landed here, naked, a creature without a shell, in this derelict gray apartment house, where others had similarly found their level. At least momentarily. For they came and went. Except for the street, the prison, or the grave, I do not know where they could fall farther. Sometimes at night I woke and listened to the wind blowing through me, all my doors and windows banging, and a familiar, yet ghostly stranger wandering through the corridors. Martha, Jess, Lily. Where are you?

Nothing left but Crow. And he had no words now. Not even half a platitude. For a time, I'd tried to teach him his name. Called him Charley. But he wouldn't say it, wouldn't answer to it. Only Crow. The sound of raw bird. I called him as hoarsely as he answered. Out of the mixed flickering of whiskey and dream I would wake to Crow.

●

"Come on, have a drink with us, Jarve," Ernie said, dragging me downstairs.

Down to family. I knew what he was after. Wanted somebody else in the room to deflect the emotional charge. I couldn't stand the voltage myself, but I went down anyway. Owed it to Maddy maybe. I liked her. She was a plain, down-to-earth type, but when she smiled a radiance lived in her briefly, though it didn't happen often. She'd set herself up for a hard life. Had the man she wanted and didn't want any other. They'd been married before Ernie had gone off to play hero, as he put it, and when he came back they had a kid, Roy, sometimes called Mickey, a thin, sallow, hazel-eyed youth, who seemed embarrassed by his father.

I had brought Crow for the sake of the kid, not that he'd likely have an interest. But this time Maddy was alone.

"Lovely to see you," I said, giving her a hug, as though I were back in the social folderol of my old life.

For a moment she clung to me as if to take some comfort from my arms around her. Then she said, "It's useless, isn't it?"

I wasn't sure what she meant specifically: her visit, Ernie's recalcitrance, or the way of things. But it looked like she'd given up on something.

"I can't make him see," she said, standing in the space between Ernie and me. Ernie's back was toward us, his gaze turned toward the back alley, where the garbage cans leaned or lay on their sides from the assault by cats and dogs. From his attitude I could read him. He wasn't looking out but in; if not to the past, to somewhere beyond the present.

"You know, Jarve," she said, as though Ernie had left the room, "I'm not coming down anymore. Finally, I know when I'm licked. And I've been a fool hanging on so long." She pressed her lips together. "It's not fair," she said, angrily for her. "If you can't let go of things and live," she lowered her voice, "then what's the point?"

She grabbed her coat and rushed to the door before either of us could say a word. A shiver started through me, but I turned it off, damning Ernie for getting me involved. It wasn't any of my business. I was just going to walk out myself, but a bottle in the center of the kitchen table caught my eye. By means of the shortest distances between various points, I found a tumbler and poured myself a drink. Then another.

"She's right, of course," Ernie said, following my example.

"Then what're you doing here?"

Ernie shook his head. "Because I'm trapped—in a place I can't get out of. That you can't remember or forget. And there's no other ground. No place to call home. It's like you've lost the world, Jarve." he said looking at me. "And there's nothing else in its place."

Couldn't say anything to that. Figured I'd lost it too. Where was some sweet spot of grass to lie down on, give your body to, and close your eyes and rest?

"I've got to do it, I can't go back on it. There's no peace until *they know*. It would be throwing it away. It was a sickness, Jarve." The muscles in his face tightened. "And how can you cure it if you

133

just bury it?"

Why you? Maddy had wanted to know. Ernie had shrugged: *Why anybody?*

I'd never gone to Maddy's neighborhood or walked past the house that waited for the return of husband and father. To which he had come back—at first. Tried for the normal. Went back to his old job. Thinking maybe he had found his spot of ground. I could imagine him picking up his old life, trying to put it together even as he had the book before his eyes. In a fever to start it. To put his malarial vision on paper. A continuation of the fever that began it, whole scenes replaying vividly before his eyes. But the more he worked, the more it eluded him. Till his whole brain was on fire. He put everything into it. Evenings, weekends, hours in the middle of the night. Ever more consumed.

He lost his job. Tried another, lost that too. Fell farther down the economic scale: short-order cook, night watchman, janitor. A sleepwalker, the book always in his head. Then he chucked it all. How could he play the part when he wasn't there?

"She deserves better," he had told me a number of times. "Why does she bother?" he said, almost angrily. "She followed me here. Couldn't let go. I thought I'd at least clear the path."

He had a disability check coming in. Grocery money. He'd work a day or two periodically, enough to collect unemployment. The rest was the book, when it was going well; the bottle, when it wasn't.

I poured myself another shot, poured one for Ernie. The good guest. Peculiar what people clung to—or abandoned. I'd left too. The newspaper office, the Kiwanis, the First Presbyterian. Just picked up one day and walked out. Let's say I'd been crushed beneath the weight of fact. Lying too long under a refuse heap. Weighty as a tombstone. The heaviness of repetition. The day's disasters, punctuated by the news of a few lottery winners. The weight of the world, yet flimsy as newsprint itself. Wrapping for the day's sink mess. For what? For Crow to pick at.

Once I hadn't gotten the facts straight—so a rival told me and sent me Crow to eat.

●

I see you, Crow, dragging behind you liver and lights, the message of sex, the uneven throb of the heart—all the organs exposed, globules of flesh seeking their function. Oh, it goes beyond the beat of blood, the pulsations of the nerves. These raw things. . . . When love discovers you, it pulls away the skin, fingers all the tingling parts, turns outside inside.

And the eye opens, looking down through the layers. The wound and the eye meet through the hole in the flesh.

●

I woke up to find Ernie banging on the door. It wasn't even light yet. I moved unsteadily to the door, opened it and leaned against the jamb.

"You mean you're just getting up?"

"What's the hurry? Can't even see by the sun."

"Hell, it's about gone down. You've slept through the whole damned day."

"Jeez, what'll l do tonight?" I said, with a sense of loss.

"Come with me down to Mcintyre's. I've got a little cash. I did an article, a protest piece," he said, with great contempt. "But it's money."

When the book came to a standstill, he wrote protests—against pollution and violence and crime, against greed and corruption, against inefficiency and stupidity. It was nearly a full-time job. "Spinning your wheels," he called it. Never touched the real springs. On the contrary, you had to hit people inside, make them see. Otherwise they'd never change.

"Sure," I said. "Why not? Come on, Crow."

"Aren't you afraid he'll just take off when you're walking out in the air like that?" Ernie said, as Crow rode my shoulder.

"His choice," I said. "If he can find a good life elsewhere, I won't stand in his way." Although I wasn't sure why, I'd miss him, sign of my darkness, my faithlessness, all the things I'd given up.

Mcintyre's was beginning to fill when we got there, factory workers in for a quick one on the way home, a couple of guys from

135

the bank, their styled hairdos and shirts and ties offering a contrast to the rest of us. Slumming before they went home to the wives and kiddies. One of the fellows gave me a nod—knew him from my other life. Only now that I had Crow, I'd let go of the amenities. Marks a man. Folks stare, though all the steadies were used to me, God knows. Thought I was a little off. Harmless. Scarcely caused an eyebrow to lift unless somebody was in the mood for a little pleasantry.

Which somebody was. Just as I'd begun to put myself in the mood I'd come to get into. Had sat down and ordered a double scotch. Heading for the fog. To match the smoky atmosphere. When here comes a guy, maybe a foreman; looked like the type: well put together, arms like a wrestler's, tattoo on the left. Clipper ship. Not original. "Baby Doll" below.

"How come you got that crow?" he said, leaning over the end of our table.

"It's his sister," Ernie explained.

"Sister? What is he, some sort of environment nut?"

"Religious. Talks to the birds," Ernie went on. "And other creatures. Rabbits, even moles. All in their own language."

"Let's hear you say something."

I made a half-hearted caw.

"You're full of shit." He turned away and went to the bar.

"Only he doesn't answer," I said.

"Patience," Ernie said. "When he has something to say . . . Actually," he raised his voice in the direction of the guy at the bar, "she really is his sister. Enchanted by a wicked magician because she wouldn't deliver. Been carrying her around for seventeen years. But when she's free," he said emphatically, "she'll tell you the secret—of crowness and black magic."

He was into it. Loved this kind of nonsense when he was in the right mood. Played with the words he had left over: jokes and puns, odd bits of anecdote. He kept it up all evening. I was just as well pleased the guy at the bar ignored us. Might've thought Ernie was making fun of him and caused trouble.

"Her name's Marigold."

All that glitters is Marigold. I ordered another scotch, to have it handy. Ernie, the same. I'd have been glad to sit quiet for a spell. I'd reached that point of silence booze brings me to before I land in the well beyond it. Half listening, I sat contemplating the scene: the colors of the bottles melting in the mirror, words and smoke intertwined. I tried to take a crow's eye view.

"Actually she was a gift from his Aunt Caroline," Ernie said, addressing no one in particular. "Kept birds, filled up every room of her house—parakeets and lovebirds and finches. They all had free run of the place. She liked them better than folks. Less shit."

On the way home he was still making up nonsense, laughing, doubling over. Could hardly walk straight. One of his rare nights. And mine. Somehow I'd forgotten both past and future.

"O Crow!" he said, doing obeisance, "Great Bird, descending to us folks. Giver of light and life."

"Where does he get that?"

"Don't you know?" he said. "In the dark. Always in the dark."

We'd walked up the hill together, our arms around each other's shoulders, the moon tilting over the trees.

•

Certain things I remember vividly. The box on Ernie's kitchen table. "Maddy's stuff," he said offhandedly when I came in for a nightcap. He uncovered a little box and picked up a wedding band. "She shouldn't have hung on so long," he said. "Too many years." He sat silent for a moment, in another space. "Well," he said, back again, contemplating his glass, "here's to her. The good life . . ." He picked up the ring again. "It'll come in handy."

I figured what he'd do. Earlier that week there'd been a big set-to. Brother Crawford, who in the name of his church next door owned the apartments, had surprised two of his tenants in a compromising position. I had seen them coming and going, the girl having caught my attention with her dangling pink earrings and bright pink heels thin as toothpicks. She chewed gum and carried a transistor radio, worked as a cashier at the Dairy Bar. The lad, large, soft, ingenuous-looking type, with a shock of red hair, had been laid off from the parts plant. Brother Crawford told them he'd either marry them or kick them out—thereby offering occasion for the freedom of choice.

They had opted for a life together. Cheaper in the long run to rent only one apartment. The ceremony was the next evening, after work and before bed. The ring would be Ernie's contribution. The present inmates of the Petite crowded inside the little apartment. Patty, who worked at the Roselyn bakery, brought a day-old cake. There were balloons, somebody's notion of the festive. We listened to the ceremony, saw the ring located on the proper finger, and wished them a happy residence at the Petite.

The rest is a jumble. I remember waking up one night, raucous cries in my ears, the lashing of sounds, a terrible quarrel. Then I was looking into a silence so black I woke with an unreasoning terror and lay in the dark waiting to hear some friendly noise. The bedclothes had been fought into the usual chaos. "Crow," I called, turning on the light, trying to push aside the darkness, "say something." I didn't want to go back to sleep. Instead I got dressed and went downstairs, to roust Ernie up.

His light was on. When he was going on the book, he sometimes sat up all night. I didn't want to disturb him, just sit in the room while he was working. I turned the handle and opened the door, saw that he had fallen asleep across the typewriter, head leaning on folded arms. I knew I shouldn't awaken him. But being alone just then was too much for me.

"How's it going?" I asked him, once he'd sat up and shaken off sleep.

"Don't even ask," he said. "It's all junk."

"Maybe you need a breather," I suggested. "Get away from it and let it take you from behind."

He shook his head. "It's me," he said. "It's been in front of me so long I can't see straight anymore. I tried to get inside, to go so far in . . . Now I wonder. Maybe none of it happened like that. Or maybe it doesn't matter."

I noticed the crumpled pages lying on the floor.

I had nothing to offer. His had been the braver route, no doubt. I'd gone down a little narrow alley, found my dead end, and let it go at that.

He shook his head, played with a pen.

Maybe we were looking at two sides of the same wall. I don't know how long we sat in our separate stupors, when suddenly he rounded on me. "What're you doing down here pissing your life away? You going to rot here?"

I was caught up short. So far we'd given each other berth. With forced calm I said, "I'm supporting the Reverend."

"Come on, Jarve."

I'd done my duty by the public. Muggings, shootings, arrests, promotions. The world's a gaping maw—hungry for facts. Or maybe just sensation. A little pinch to know the blood's still in the veins. Thirty years I'd given to it. "Who the hell are you?"

The way he looked at me I knew I shouldn't have said that. He turned away.

"What do you do when you can't get rid of . . ." he said, "when you can't find . . . ?"

I was in no mood for unfinished sentences. I got up and started back to my room.

"You understand me, Jarve," I heard at my back.

But I couldn't say I did. I was too numb. "Sure," I said, and stumbled back upstairs.

●

That was the last I saw him. Two months ago. I think of it as a long silence. I'd climbed the stairs, untwisted the covers and fallen asleep. Then the shot rang out. I don't know whether I heard it or the commotion in the hall. Ernie had a gun, of course. These days you have to have your weapon. I flung myself out of bed and rushed down the stairs, already afraid of what I'd find. Patty was pounding on the door, a couple of others behind her. He'd locked it. I broke in the door, yelled to her not to come inside, but to call the police and an ambulance. By the time the sirens tore up the night, everybody in the house was up and people in the neighborhood had gathered on their porches and along the street, some in their bathrobes.

Brother Crawford appeared, befuddled from sleep, appalled by the noise and confusion that had descended on his property. He

139

demanded to know what had happened. When he knew, his face paled, and he suddenly turned quiet, almost diffident, saying to the police, "Yes, sir," and "No sir," and "Not to my knowledge, sir." Just the week before, they'd come looking for a fry cook who'd been forging checks. But when they'd gone to his room, they discovered he'd decamped, leaving his rent unpaid as well.

I recognized the reporter from the newspaper—had hired him as a kid. When he started to ask me questions, I waved him away and went back upstairs. I had managed to keep my head through the worst of the commotion, but once back in my room I couldn't control a fit of violent trembling. Following that, I sat in a stupor for hours. Somebody would have to tell Maddy, I kept thinking. Who? Images of faces rose to my mind, some of the people I had known in my youth, now long dead. And then my mind became a blank.

•

The time passing was no more than the rustle of crows' wings. Sometimes I slept all day and sat up all night, making a pretense of reading the books I'd checked out from the public library. Not for the sake of knowledge, not from any impulse of curiosity or imagination. Just to take up the time. Thrillers, Westerns, all the junk I could lay my hands on. I read pigheadedly, kept my eyes to the page to avoid looking out or in. My money was nearly gone, and if I didn't do something, I'd be out on the street. But I refused to move. No place to go. Nothing I wanted to do.

My life lay at the bottom of the can, no point in picking through the trash. Ernie at least had tried to capture something real. Tried to find the words. And look where it landed him. Me, I was a facts man, stuck with only a new round of facts, now as dead as Ernie himself.

"Well, Crow," I said, reaching out for him, eager for a little conversation, "you 'spose there's anything to be salvaged from all of this mess?" He cocked his head, gave me a beady stare. I wouldn't find my image mirrored from his eye. What did he see? Probably a large eye, red-rimmed, staring back.

Ernie's father came to see me. He was a large man, both

big-boned and solidly padded, who brought in a smell of aftershave lotion and an unwanted briskness of movement that momentarily and painfully stirred the air. He didn't belong in the Petite, where the odors congregated in the hallway, the stink of disposable diapers mingling with smells of cigarette smoke and yesterday's fried potatoes.

Maddy must've told him about me. I hadn't gone to the funeral. Easier not to go, not to see Maddy or the kid, nor to stand there in the light of not-yet-spring, looking at the bare ground. I wasn't sure why he came, what he thought I could do for him. He took off his overcoat, sat in the one armchair I could offer. Three-piece suit, silk tie—he'd done well in life. A doctor.

"A terrible waste," he lamented. "He could've gone to med school, the whole trip paid for. Wouldn't have had to struggle the way I did. I just can't understand it—all the advantages. The way he treated all of us."

He was indignant all right, the aggrieved parent. And I could understand that. Just didn't want to listen to him. Didn't even offer him a drink.

"I think something must've happened to him over there. Maybe he got off on drugs."

He sat there staring into space, until the silence became crushing. "My God, why did he do it?" he burst out, his eyes brimming.

I reached under the bed for Ernie's manuscript, what was left of it, and handed it to him. I'd rescued it, but couldn't bring myself to read it. Maybe it would only confuse him, but at least he had it. Then I brought out my bottle, and together we finished it off.

●

At first I thought the young couple next door woke me up. Since Brother Crawford had married them, they'd done nothing but quarrel. But I could never tell. The dramas of the day bled into the fantasies of the night till you couldn't separate one piece of nonsense from another. Quarrels and lovemaking, swearing, drunken husbands threatening screaming wives. Crazy laughter and obscenities. No matter who moved in or out, the faces you met on the stairs were always the same.

For some reason I got up and went to the window. Outside the moon was brilliant. A clear blue-purple shadow with a gauzy sheen lay over the trees, plants in a moonlit sea. I opened the window and let the chill air flow in and around me. And I thought of Ernie, of the times we had spent together, drinking and commiserating. I remembered walking home from McIntyre's that night, our arms round one another's shoulders as we came laughing up the hill. And of other nights.

Curious how things look sometimes, the tilt of the moon in the sky, the wash of light. As though everything had arranged itself according to your feeling. As if you were in love and that gave things their hue and color. The sky and each leaf and branch shimmering in the newness of your seeing. When had I looked at the world that way? As a kid? As a youth looking into a woman's eyes and seeing something beyond even myself, something being created there? On my first job in Chicago, when the excitement of running down to the firehouse in the dead of night raised every detail of the streets to vividness? The blood must have beat in my ears then: a woman's touch awakened me, and the world laid me deep in sensation. I must have been a lover.

Now as I stood there, struck with that memory, forgetful in the shimmer of moonlight, I whistled softly. Behind me, from the curtain rod above my head came an answering whistle.

•

Now that I'd had a response from Crow, I was overcome with the need to talk. Poured out my whole history, all my dissatisfactions and regrets. Guilt and frustration. Failures. Talked till my mouth was dry, my throat hoarse. And my hands empty. Got me nowhere at all. Just got thrown back on myself by that beady eye. Nothing from it. So I had to give up. I had to do something though; I had to get out. The room had become a prison.

I'd taken to standing by the window at night, looking out. But the full had passed, and we were back at the dark of the

142

moon. Nothing out there but black branches against the darkened sky. You couldn't whistle the moon back. But I tried it in a mood of experiment, just to see what might happen. I gave a long, slow whistle. And waited.

From Crow came a long, slow whistle.

Again, in the mood of experiment, I did a long note and a short note. I stood tense with waiting. He gave that back too. Then long-short-short. He did it. I kept on, thinking, now he'll quit. But he wore me out first. We'd kept going till I could hardly pucker. But no matter how complicated the pattern, he could give it back to me. I had the feeling he was enjoying himself, that I'd finally hit the spot where his real talents lay.

The next day he landed on my knee as I lay in bed working up the energy to climb out into the day. He looked at me, took me in and gave me a whistle, two long notes followed by two shorts. I said, "Great, Crow," but he just repeated it, flew up and around, landed back on my knee, looked me straight in the eye and repeated it again. It sounded like a challenge. I gave him back note for note. Then he did another, adding a note this time. I gave that one back too. And he went on, calling the tune, you might say. Till finally I could see what was going to happen. His whistles were getting so complicated I couldn't hold the pattern in my head long enough to repeat it. I got all mixed up trying to get it out. He cackled. He was laughing at me. He'd won.

So there I was, not knowing what to make of it. There had been communication. *All that glitters . . .* We could forget about even half a platitude. For the time being, I had run out of words.

•

That evening I went out with Crow for a round at McIntyre's. I hadn't been out of my room for three days or more. I'd eaten everything on the shelves, opened the last can of beans and eaten them cold, right from the container. I had spent my money down to the change in my pocket. Rent due next week. I'd be kicked out on my ear. Had to go somewhere, find something to do with myself. I couldn't put off the next move forever. But the thought of change terrified me.

"What'll you have, Jarve?" McIntyre asked me, after we'd exchanged pleasantries.

"Tell you what. How about a little contest? If this bird here can out-whistle you, you'll stand me a drink."

"What's this?"

"Really. He can do it. No shit."

McIntyre looked dubious, as though he had better things to think about.

"C'mon, McIntyre," one of the regulars said. "This joint could do with a little entertainment."

He shrugged. "What do I do?"

I showed him how Crow would imitate me. Then I said, "Whistle, Crow. Show your stuff." Crow started off easy with three notes. McIntyre had no trouble with that. Then four. Five. McIntyre had to concentrate when it came to seven and eight, Crow mixing up the long and short. He kept it up pretty well too. Got about a dozen. Then he messed up. Crow gave a cackle. I had a drink.

Others wanted to try it. One of the bank guys good with figures. But he didn't last beyond McIntyre. Then a fellow in a tweed cap and a blue denim jacket, feisty looking, pushed himself up to the corner of the bar. He'd memorized the whole of "Paul Revere's Ride" in the fifth grade and could still recite it. Damned if he couldn't out-whistle some goddam bird. He lasted through fifteen notes before Crow got the better of him. His face had grown red, first with effort and concentration, then with defeat, and I was afraid that only a good fight would relieve his feelings. But instead he stepped back and gave Crow an admiring appraisal.

"I'm damned," he said. "He's a smart one."

I had all the drinks I wanted. Every fellow who joined the crowd had to try it. I was carrying on, roaring at the top of my lungs, "Crow, you're a gold mine."

There is always something. Deeper than wisdom, deeper than error, deeper than hope or despair. Always something that escapes your deepest notice: it was still down there, the magma of the heart—the pith, the juice, the old vinegar. Once again I had discovered complexity, only this time it saved me from something worse, from nothingness and the void.

"To Ernie," I yelled. "To the good life!" Tears were streaming down my face, and I was laughing fit to kill. Both at once.

The Turkish March

From the apartment upstairs came the notes of a new piano piece. A relief at first. For Peter had listened to the last exercise repeated so often and with so little improvement he came to hear the wrong notes even before they were struck. Not that it much mattered. The tune, slight and sentimental, jarred him less in the execution than in the sheer repetition. Mercifully, the teacher had sent her pupil on toward a new, if uncertain destination. Peter thought of either a small, possibly humpbacked creature with pale skin and pink scalp showing through thin blonde hair, or else of a graying invalid. For him, the source of error seemed located in physical deformity. Who would be playing at this hour of the afternoon but one cut off from the world of work or school, at the time of day when he himself took a rest and tried to gather strength for his evening round of shopping?

But now he listened. Having established the melody with one hand—a melody immediately familiar, which maddened him for hours afterward without his being able to identify it—the player picked herself up and went on, introducing a new motif. Expectation strained forward as the notes came one after the other, slow, hesitant—wrong. A new start. But no better. She (invariably he thought of the player as she) kept going back to the beginning, determined, it appeared, not to play the whole until she could play it right. Till finally she gave it up, for that afternoon. But the melody assailed Peter from the heights of something perfectly mastered and immediately meaningful to the emotions—quite beyond reach. He sighed and got up, too restless to sleep. For the remainder of the afternoon he took to his newspapers and was lost in the political stupidities from across the Atlantic. Even at this distance, they set his teeth on edge.

•

That evening as he returned with his demi-baguette and strawberries, his cauliflower and lettuce, his breakfast croissant, he had his first exchange with the woman who lived in the apartment overhead. He held the door open for her, a small woman, with a powerful inner determination that seemed to press her beyond the burden of her packages and her terrible bridgework. His sympathy went to her the moment she smiled. Who had done such a botched up job? A front tooth at that, yellow, oversized, mismatched with the good tooth it was anchored to. Metal underneath. He wanted to punch the dentist in the mouth, yank out a few teeth for his pains. The woman was afraid to smile. The bastard hadn't given her a chance.

They climbed the stairs, avoiding cigarette butts and wrappers and other trash on the steps. Earlier in the afternoon they'd have had to work past the motley crowd waiting for their turn at the bell of the second floor apartment: mostly young, dark, nervous, except for a large well-groomed fat man, and a svelte black woman who looked disdainfully upon the scene around her. *Le Clef d'Or,* a sign announced. *Sonnez et entrez.* Buyers of gold. Where daughters could sell off their mothers' necklaces and thieves could fence their loot. A jittery lot, Peter noticed. Keeping one eye out for the gendarmes, chain-smoking, crushing the butts on the steps. The smell of smoke hung in the passage, mingling with the evening's bourguignon.

"A terrible mess," his neighbor said in French. Despite her various parcels, she carried herself with dignity, moving almost as slowly as he did. She frowned, drawing in her nostrils, and looked at him. Her eyes, the soft and luminous irises set in a dark ring, had a complexity of expression that drew him: knowing, skeptical, yet eager, sympathetic. Above the ruined smile.

"As if the hallways weren't dirty enough," she continued. "I've complained to the concierge, but she merely shrugs. Sometimes I kick the butts down from one step to another—right to the bottom.

147

Let her see them there." A flash of defiance from the eyes.

Two dogs inside Le Clef d'Or barked as they passed.

"Tch. And the noise," she said, "it's bad enough on the streets. You can't escape."

He agreed to all of it, still upset by the yellow tooth. What had possessed her to go to such an incompetent? Lack of money? Ignorance? You never knew what you were walking into. Trusting and helpless you went, and somebody took your money and did a number on you. The clown probably soaked her plenty. "Where can you go these days. . . ?" he ventured, breathless from the climb. Who had turned the monster loose in the dental profession? What mentor had passed him on, signed his certificate, inflicted him on the public? He should have gone into politics—there, who noticed?

"They had the cops here last month," she continued, this time, to his surprise, in English, perhaps thinking he had more difficulty with the language then with the stairs. She gave a little smile when she saw his expression—nicer when her teeth didn't show—then took up her indignation. "Someone tried to break in, the burglar alarm went off, the dogs went berserk, the whole building in an uproar. Sirens. Gendarmes. Everybody on the stairs, in the courtyard. A big drama, I tell you. I thought of moving out, but what's the good?"

"The world's gone mad," he said. "Hijackers, terrorists. . ." He could have created a whole list if he'd had the breath, but he still had one more étage to go. At least he'd had the good sense to move in after the commotion. Otherwise his blood would have been up, and this time he might have enjoyed the services of a foreign hospital. But what did it matter? He had come to Paris to die. It was as good a place as any.

"I shudder when I go by," his neighbor complained, nodding in the direction of the Clef d'Or. "The way they look at you. Like they've come from slitting somebody's throat."

"Probably their mothers'," he suggested. They had arrived at his floor. "Do you play the piano?" he asked suddenly. Clearly she hadn't expected such a question. But then she gave a little smile, melancholy and tender, "No, my granddaughter. I hope it's not disturbing you. I could. . ."

"No, no," he protested. "I love music."

Having unlocked the three locks on his door and put the door between himself and the street, he began to wash the lettuce for his salad. He didn't know her name; he'd forgotten to ask. He liked her face, the fine eyes. He was still troubled by the ruined smile.

●

He discovered that on certain days they went to the shops at the same hour. Once they'd passed each other in the market, but his neighbor was so preoccupied she failed to notice him, and he didn't want to startle her. Some evenings he didn't see her at all. She must work then, but not always at the same hours. And her granddaughter must be home alone all day. He was curious about her. His neighbor must prepare her meals ahead of time. He could hear her saying, "Now for lunch, there's a nice bit of sausage, and you can heat up some soup." All he knew was that after lunch the child (young woman?) practiced the piano.

"So you're an American," his neighbor said, when they met again, this time after they had introduced themselves. Sophie Mitkin. Peter Sziv.

"I thought so, though your accent isn't typical. I was in the States for six years. My teenage years," she said, with a rush of pleasure. "I love the States."

"Actually," he said, I was born near Budapest, though I grew up in South Bend." Which she probably never heard of before. In a whole community of honkies, like one big family, eating, drinking, dancing together, marrying one another, going to the funerals of friends and relations. His mother and father working their lives down to the bone marrow. Citizens. The great achievement. They could claim his bloody carcass too.

"My people are Russian," Sophie told him. "My parents came from the same village, though they didn't meet until they were grown and here in Paris."

A young Chinaman, squatting illegally in the empty maid's room on the sixth étage, passed them with a bundle of laundry, greeting them shyly.

"When were you in the States?" he asked.

"During the War," she said significantly.

One of the fortunate refugees. The pure race—it took a dentist's mentality to think that one up. Add it to four thousand years of the might of the stronger, and the displaced person. Humanity by the teeth. They had reached his landing. "By the way," he asked, "do you know the name of the piece your granddaughter's practicing?" He avoided the word *playing*.

"Of course," she said, her eyes brightening. "'The Turkish March.' Mozart. Did you see *Wuthering Heights*? Merle Oberon. Lawrence Olivier. They go to a ball and a woman plays it on the piano. A wonderful film. I saw it six times. I remember every scene, and I could always see myself. . ." She stopped, embarrassed.

Going to the ball like the wild Katherine. He completed the fantasy for her. Charming. He wished his own had been as harmless, even as they had been bootless. Friend, he'd thought, of revolution, assistant to change. Holding cupped hands for the flare of the match, as he played spy for Army Intelligence. Two or three days high on amphetamines, courtesy of his superiors, forty or more hours without sleep while he and Arno, companion in folly, combed the Hungarian countryside, mingled in the towns to gather news of the direction and prospects of that doomed and betrayed revolution. Then back to their base in Austria to drink a bottled of bourbon and plunge into oblivion until they were sent out again. Only youth and a strong constitution could withstand such punishment—for a time. After the tanks came, he was put to the task of resettling refugees, in charge of the whole effort in Yugoslavia. He had written various papers for the U.N. Years later, back in Chicago, he still kept in touch with some of those he'd sent to the States. The grateful owner of a delicatessen, who heaped upon him gifts of his favorite sausage, a musician now battling leukemia, a lawyer for those with claims in Hungary. And Arno was there, grown prosperous in the import business, married to a fashion model, the two of them traveling back and forth to the Europe he could never quite leave behind.

The habits of his old life had made drinking a necessity, a nightly pathway to oblivion. Most nights it was a wonder he got home at all. Once he'd awakened in an alley. Even while Arno was warning him and his own wife nagging at him in the hangdog way that made him want to kick her, he knew it was coming. His liver, his heart—what didn't turn against him? Fortunately he'd kept all his army records. From the government he received compensation for total disability. Money, at least, was no problem. When he was on his feet again, so to speak, he told Arno to find him a place in Paris.

•

She'd never been a beautiful woman, Peter decided, not even when she was young. Though her smile still disturbed him, it was becoming part of how he expected her to look. In the company of the prominent nose, the splendid eyes. Probably she'd never been slender either. Always a little extra in the arms and breasts, extra padding on the hips. The cheekbones, the eyes you couldn't see to the depths of, the full mouth—they had gotten her a husband, maybe a lover or two. Imagining herself at the ball. Imagining passion. The extreme you pushed everything toward. In America, her Russian sensuousness. At her high school they must have looked at her, stood back, wondering whether or not to touch. He tried inventing a past for her, seized on what he took as their common bond: the various dislocations that had brought them to apartments just above one another. To which they both climbed the stairs slowly.

He closed his eyes, tried to disengage his mind from the struggling performance overhead and sleep. He could have shut the window, but he needed air. He had chosen the middle of the afternoon, while the shops were closed, to rest, to rescue his strength so that he could go out to buy the makings of his evening meal. Though the fruit and vegetable stands were mobbed then, as well as the boulangerie where he bought his half loaf of French bread, and standing in line tired him, still he liked the press of people in the streets. It was his social life. His anonymity allowed him the privilege of being merely a spectator upon the scene: housewives--French, oriental, African--all sorts; clerks and businessmen on route home, jostling elbows, winding through the press of people. Finally, all of it was less than nothing to him.

He was alone. No one left except a brother in Toledo he hadn't seen in years and had no desire to see now. No claims on him. His health was shot, his useful life was over. And the uses of that life were now so distasteful to him he woke up at times trembling and sweating, the sheets twisted around him. He could seldom remember the details of those dreams, but they soured his mood for hours afterward.

●

"My daughter brought her to me," Sophie said, "and told me, 'Please keep Marguerite while I go on vacation.' She wanted to go to Los Angeles, where there was something going on. She was divorced then. 'French men are so boring,' she said. 'There are no jobs. I need to find myself.'" He and Sophie were sitting in the café just opposite their street. Sophie was eating liver paté. He was having a salad. Red meat and cheese were bad for him, so he lived on chicken and fruit, bread and salad. He liked the discipline of his diet, though this time he allowed himself a glass of wine.

"What could I say?" She shrugged and offered her open palms. "What is there to say to such discontent? I said to her, 'Go and explore then. There is always such energy in America. You'll find a place for yourself and Marguerite. I kept waiting. One postcard, then nothing. I tried writing her hotel."

"You contacted the embassy?"

"No. I didn't want to cause trouble for her. I didn't know . . . Even now, I say, surely she'll write."

"When was this?"

"Three years ago." Sophie played with the bread crumbs on the tablecloth. "She had no patience with Marguerite. She's an unusual child. She can't stand butter on her bread—it gags her. She used to scream if she saw chicken cut up. She won't eat any meat. Whenever Paulette went to buy clothes, she would hide under the dress rack. And school, impossible. She would soil herself so they'd send her home. Poor thing, and she hates so to be dirty. It's too much for her. She drove the teacher wild. I can't tell you how many days I had to take off from work to go to the school. So I took her out. I have a student from the Sorbonne who comes once a week to tutor her. She likes to read, especially books with pictures."

"She doesn't get lonely?"

Sophie shook her head. "She watches a little television, plays with her cat. Sometimes she likes to go with me to the Tuilleries. She holds my hand in the metro. Occasionally we go to the museums. She likes the cinema. The Indonesian girl who cleans—they're great friends. Then of course her music . . ."

"How old is she?"

"Nearly twelve," Sophie said, "but she looks like eight."

"What will happen to her?" she said, putting down her fork, pressing her napkin to her lips.

He poured more wine into her glass, but she did not touch it. She twisted the corner of her napkin, looked off into space. Then she recovered herself, smiled, lifted the glass and held it to the light, as though proposing a toast. Ruby red, dark, with a gleam at the center. "We're the only ones left," she said.

•

What would happen to her? he asked as he listened to her play—this violation in the logic of generation. For the world, she was an idiot, not of intelligence but sensibility. And Sophie and he were two of a kind. Time was nearly finished with them, ready to throw their carcasses aside. Time for him meant waiting. The color of time had changed, now that illusion, expectation had dropped out of it. Slowness on the stairs; pill bottles on the shelf. The neighborhood with a restless surge of blacks, East Indians, orientals, coming from who-knows-where, living who-knows-how. Bombs on the Champs Élysées, in Le Magasin. Time was a dark rush that soon enough would drop him too.

Now she could play the "Turkish March" all the way through, and there were passages that kept the proper notes and rhythm. It was clear that she liked the piece, for certain phrases leapt past the notes toward a suggestion of triumph. But she had no control. The piece came patched with repetitions, new starts, uncertain passages. For him, it became those errors and repetitions. He lay in bed every afternoon listening for something that might be called progress but error dogged her. Hopeless. He could never sleep. It wasn't her playing that kept him awake, but his own disquieted mind, going round and round with the latest absurdity in the Middle East or Latin America, the most recent piece of corruption he'd read about. For every day he read the newspapers, French and American, with the avidity of an addict, the fascination of a man watching an anthill.

Like folds in a sheet of paper, the lines of history crossed and intersected his, Sophie's lives, turning things awry, creating the inescapable before and after. He often thought of this when they were together.

The two of them met now on Fridays for their dinner together, the night she worked late. By then Marguerite would have eaten, watched television a little, and gone to bed. She did not practice in the evenings for the sake of the neighbors who might want quiet then. The fat man on the other side felt no such constraint, but practiced his trumpet with impunity, even sometimes early on Sunday morning.

"Before we left for the States," Sophie was telling him, "there was a wonderful year. My father was rich then; we lived in a beautiful house and I had lovely dresses. But even then I knew. One day a fine house; the next day, broke and on the streets. My father was like that."

She had accepted casual elegance like the weather. Expensive restaurants, good wine at the table. A governess.

"He had a radio station then in North Africa. The Germans wanted it, but he wouldn't sell. Of course they wanted to kill him. We had to leave everything with only a few hours' warning. I remember he spent the night burning papers." Other things she would not speak of.

In one of his recurring dreams, people kept moving, running, falling into shadows in unknown territory. His life had been given to this ambiguity, this struggle.

"I loved it aboard ship. The captain was very kind to me. Always showing me things in his cabin. It was a wonder my father permitted it. He let me blow the boat whistle. Each time he did, two Indians would say, 'It was just like that the last time—they blew

154

the whistle just before we were torpedoed.' The passengers asked me, please would I not blow the whistle." She grew animated as she spoke of her youth.

She had been happy then. When she came back to Europe— but before she could tell him, a police car whipped past, followed by an ambulance.

"My God, it's right here in the neighborhood," she said, standing up. "Look, there's a crowd."

"Our building," Peter said.

She went white. "Marguerite! She's alone. Oh, dear God, I hope nothing's happened."

He leapt up to pay for their dinner.

She was trembling. "I just want to satisfy myself she's all right."

When they arrived at the apartment, bystanders filled the sidewalk. The ambulance was in the driveway that led to the courtyard, and someone was being carried down on a stretcher. The concierge was talking to the gendarmes. "Who is it?" Sophie asked around her.

"Robbery. The Clef d'Or."

"They shot the woman. In the head."

"Is she dead?"

"Imagine—with all the dogs barking."

"They knew the place. They did something to the dogs."

"Her husband was away."

"Is she dead?"

"No one seemed to know. The ambulance shrieked off down the street, and they were allowed to enter the building. Sophie hurried up the stairs.

•

Marguerite is ill, he read on a note that Sophie left under his door. I am staying home to take care of her.

For a number of days no sound came from the piano. He telephoned once to ask how she was. Sophie had come up the stairs to find Marguerite hysterical. The shots ringing out, the sirens. The

155

first robbery had left her terrified. This time she developed a fever. She didn't know where she was.

Where could you step, he thought, but into the fevers of the mind? From the flower seller he bought daisies (marguerites), and some bonbons and asked the concierge to take them up. He'd seen the child only once, from the back. Hair dark like Sophie's. Small for her age. He wondered if she had Sophie's eyes. She must be a pale child, from being deprived so much of the sunlight. Would Sophie take her to the park down the avenue when she was better?

He'd come across a crippled veteran there at the entrance on his way back from the post office the other day. He was wearing a ragged overcoat and held out a can for coins, at the same time ranting and waving his cane. Whether denouncing the government or swearing at those who passed by indifferently, Peter was unable to tell. He was unshaven, possibly drunk. They have saved a place for you on all the metro cars, he thought; one has to stand and give you a seat. On the other side of the park, a Vietnamese woman with a baby held out her hand. "For the baby," she said.

When he saw Sophie on the stairs, the flesh of her jaws looked heavy and her eyes were tired.

"How is Marguerite?"

"Better, thank you. Tomorrow I'll go back to work. The concierge will look in. I'm going out for strawberries," she explained. "They're her favorites. She smiled. "I used to pick them when I was young—in the country they grow wild."

He was relieved. The mother would never return. Sophie must know that as well. What sort of life included Marguerite? Better to unzip the past and step out. Poof—it's gone. She'd gotten a face-lift maybe and gone on the most recent crash diet and exercise program, bought a new wardrobe and had a lover who thought her accent adorable.

He was entertaining these possibilities when he heard again the first notes of "The Turkish March." Shaky. She was badly out of practice. And she'd never play it well. Not like the woman in *Wuthering Heights*. Not anything close to what Mozart had in mind. But she was back at it.

He would see Sophie again. He would sit across from her

and listen to her story of how she'd come back to Europe after the war and found every aspect changed, how she'd wept over leaving her friends behind, her other life. She didn't know a soul in Paris. The flat was so cold she spent hours in bed reading, far into the night after the rest of the household was asleep. It was her only real pleasure.

"The Turkish March." And who remembers the Armenians? The jumble of history knocked in his head. Marguerite had gone back to the beginning. And he was again prepared to hear another version of that much-patched piece. Gradually she took hold of the melody. He wondered if she'd like to go for a picnic in some quiet place, the Bois du Boulogne or somewhere farther out in the country. Perhaps Sophie could take a day off during the week when there would be fewer people. He would buy strawberries and search for a bakery that made the good tough French bread now so difficult to find.

He drifted deeper, the melody enticing him like a conjuration, her playing of it fused now with that intimation of form that danced beyond the notes, calling up somehow the taste of strawberries, the image of Sophie's eyes, luminous and dark, her yellow tooth and jagged smile. Separate, yet blending as a single sensation; for a moment, all contained. His chest rose and fell in rhythmic breathing. He let go and fell asleep.

The Old Hotel

If you found your way out to the old hotel in the years following the Korean War, leaving the blacktop north of Deming and churning up dust for miles on the narrow dirt road that crossed the range, you'd have wondered that anybody still inhabited the place. It looked abandoned, like the shell of an older, more extravagant life. By then one side of the porch that swept the whole front end had broken off, and the columns were split as though they'd been struck by lightning. An effort had been made to give the exterior a new face, but the boards had soaked up the paint, eating up money and will and enthusiasm, till finally you could see the line along the side where the effort had been abandoned halfway down. It was an attempt to catch things before they hit the downside forever, but it was all patchwork, and no amount of it could turn things around. The whole place was sagging under the burden of weather and time, so that if you went inside, you'd have expected every door to hang crooked in its frame.

If you came looking for Jack Whedon, the owner, chances are he was off somewhere "looking after his interests," as he put it, leaving the management to his wife, Penny, who kept things going in her own fashion, and to their daughter, Jewel, who had to grow up there. Jack had made a deal with old Jesse Harris, who'd have run things into the ground with his drinking alone if two wars and a change of style hadn't sent away his clientele.

"Put some arm and back into the place and you've got yourself a gold mine." The old man had brought him back to Deming and was treating him to a few drinks after showing him around the place. "Why you could make it into the showplace of the county. That hotel made a fortune in its heyday. On account of the springs.

Folks all crippled up with arthritis and rheumatism walking away sprightly as a roadrunner." And now that the latest conflict was over and that great general was in the White House and the Communists were cleaned out of the government, the days of glory were coming back. Maybe Jack could turn the place into a fancy dude ranch. "What I wouldn't give to be young again," the old man said, "and watch the good times roll."

Jack took it all in, whiskey breath in his ear, as the old man leaned toward him and tapped the counter for emphasis. Jack had come from managing a restaurant and then a so-called nightclub, where the ranch hands came to drink and dance, but he didn't have much of a head for details and had allowed himself to be overcharged by the wholesalers and cheated by the help. At the moment he was standing at the lag end of opportunity, looking for an opening for his talents. He was intrigued with what he could do with a hotel in the middle of the desert: the great dining room and parlor across the front, the two extensive wings with balconied rooms that faced one another across the mesquite. A windmill to generate electricity and a well for water. An old stables—they'd even kept a milk cow—and sheds for the chickens. All of it watered into existence by the springs that bubbled up from deep in the rocky ground and fed the bathing pool. There was something grandiose in the isolation of the spot, the cactus-studded landscape stretching away to the blue imprint of mountains in one direction and twenty-five miles to the nearest town in the other.

"I'm thinking of taking over the Hot Springs Hotel," he told his wife that night. "Old Jesse is going to let me buy in."

"*Let you!* Why he's been trying to unload that white elephant for as long as I can remember."

"It looks pretty run-down," he admitted. "But it's all solid underneath." It would be a challenge to scrape away the old paint, replace the rotten boards, tackle the hotel as if she were a ship that would take dominion of the desert once more. Think of what it would do for the county. Bring people out there to drink and dance, not only the townspeople but the folks down in the valley. Give them something to do on weekends. Then when he and Penny got a little cash, they could really put the place in shape. They'd go after summer people and guide hunters in the fall.

"And work ourselves into old age and bankruptcy, whichever comes first. It would take a fortune."

"You've got to see the place to appreciate it. I know—at first I wouldn't have believed it myself." Besides they didn't have to do everything at once. The place had a history in those old boards. There was local color; there was charm.

For a moment Penny Whedon was taken aback by this excess of imagination, for in the past Jack had never entertained more than the notion of stepping into a good spot and making a killing the next instant. But now that she'd nursed him through a couple of failures in which circumstances and other people seemed less to blame than his own stupidity and flaccid amiability, she wasn't about to give him any margin. Finally, after he'd painted the prospects in colors that came gleaming from the liquor bottles in the mirror at the back of the bar through a haze of whiskey and self-deception, she laced into him with such scorn he felt the hollowness of a man who hasn't eaten for three days. The next morning he went to the lawyer's office, where the old man, hardly able to believe his luck, sat in a quiver till Jack signed the contract.

"What the hell," Jack said. "Opportunity, that old bitch, don't come but once."

Although she'd been dead set against the idea, when the time came Penny packed up their things and acted as if she were moving up in the world. Whether or not she believed it, she worked like a demon along with Jack, running back and forth to town for paint and wallpaper and a hundred other items, arranging for loans and credit, hiring the help and getting a good write-up in the local paper, with pictures on the front page.

They turned the old dining room into a restaurant; that is, they added a few tables and printed up a menu. Then they cleared most of the furniture out of the parlor and put a bar at one end under a large gilt-edged mirror and called the rest a dance floor. On weekends they brought in a three-piece band—saxophone, violin, and piano—which played with more energy than talent. But the place was lively. Folks came from town, from the valley, even a few from fifty miles away. It was a novelty, the old hotel. People

160

had known about it long enough to have forgotten about it. Teddy Roosevelt had lodged there, and one of the deer heads hanging in the dining room was attributed to his prowess. Even a few tourists came to spend a night in one of the four rooms Jack had managed to refurbish.

But when the summer ended, they were deeper in debt than ever. The circle of reputation was still too narrow, too limited, to appeal to more than casual curiosity. The hotel was too far off the beaten track to draw much of anybody during the week. And weekends were unpredictable. There were bars enough for the young bucks who wanted to get drunk and pick a fight, lodgings enough for tourists, resorts enough for a chosen clientele. No one came any longer for the healing powers of the springs.

By the time Jack let the regular help go and faced a winter of struggle as they tried to gather their resources for spring, he was ready to give up the place as a bad job. He was a man of brief enthusiasms and quick discouragement, and he'd known even as he signed the papers that he had taken on more than he could handle. He took a part-time job in the valley as a bartender, and rumor had it he was fooling around with a woman in town. But curiously, Penny worked harder than ever. She made the hotel her domain, hanging on, scraping by, clinging to the place for cold comfort. Perhaps now that she was in it, she couldn't let go or wouldn't because she'd always had a stubborn streak. At times she wanted to laugh: Jack was such small potatoes, thinking he could fool the future with his halfway measures. She could see through him all the way to his backbone, a man who could only think small, but enough for him to outsweep his talents. No wonder he was a disaster. It would have taken a certain magnitude, a flourish to bring it off—the talent for risk, for adventure. And money. She could recognize the means even if she couldn't imagine the measures. Meanwhile she entertained her own schemes. Bad as things were, she couldn't wholly cut herself off from the sense of possibility. Suppose something should come their way; say a land developer passing through, a wealthy investor. Till then she honed the practical side of her nature to a fine edge. She put aside every cent she could, paying the creditors just enough to keep them at bay, scrimping on meals, piecing and patching. She stopped

161

going to town unless it was necessary, for otherwise she'd have to take Jewel to the movies and buy her ice cream. From now on they'd do without.

At first Jewel had been delighted by the old hotel. She went through all the rooms, opening the doors with a wonderful thrill of imagined adventure, watching motes of dust float in the light that entered through the tattered curtains. She was certain to find a fortune in gold under one of the old beds, and lifted mattresses that had been raided by field mice for their nests and yanked open reluctant drawers. She looked for clues to an unsolved mystery such as she read about in the Nancy Drew books. But she turned up only a few stray hairpins and some fragments of yellowed newspaper. For a time she played over and over the records she found in the shelf of the Victrola in the parlor, listening to voices that sang hollowly of obsolete longings and dead loves. She tried the old piano, which had taken new felts and a tuning to bring its dead notes to life. During the summer there was the interest of seeing who'd come up the road and park in front. She could lie in bed and listen to the high sweet notes of the violin, rising above those of the sax and the old piano, and listen to the last words before the car doors slammed. But after a few weeks of that she lived only for the school bus that took her to the one-room school in the Mimbres Valley. During the winter blizzards she stared out the window at the snow and dreamed of running off to New Orleans and living on a riverboat, or to San Francisco and crossing the Golden Gate Bridge.

II.

Sometimes at night Jewel was awakened by the howl of coyotes cutting through the indigo stillness across great distances. It was as though she'd heard their voices before, howling through her sleep, though she couldn't remember, and she wondered what they wanted, hurling their voices to the moon. Sometimes she imagined them coming in close, putting their noses to where people had walked and their ears to walls, listening to the breath of sleepers. And a shiver would go through her at the approach of their wildness. Sometimes, from the room next to hers, she heard human voices, but it was even harder to tell what they wanted. Jewel would try to remember how it was where she lived before, in town—the schoolyard where she played. But even when she came back to the town, she knew it had forgotten her, as though she'd been carried along by a river to another part of time and space. She wasn't sure where she lived; she floated somewhere between the voices of coyotes outside and the voices on the other side of the wall.

"When I married you, you said we'd be rich. And where is all that money? And all those good times? I had a better life during the war, all those boys wanting to buy a girl a drink and have some fun. And what have we got on our hands? A dead loss. I don't know why I don't pick up and go back to town, or away to somewhere with real human beings. I know about you—just leave me here to drudge while you cat around and have yourself a time."

"So that's what you were doing while I was overseas."

"What did you expect?"

Suppose her mother did leave. Then she'd be there alone. And when the coyotes howled again, Jewel heard a new note, one that went beyond any words she knew.

"All right," she heard her father protest, "let's just leave and go on back to town."

"What the hell would you do there?"

"Get a job."

"Who'd hire you after this? And how would I show my face in the street? How could I look anybody in the eye?"

Such nights succeeded those days that Penny found fault with everything, tongue-lashed anyone who crossed her path, so that even the cat did well to hide. And the outcome was always the same.

"Christ!" Jack would mutter, when he again reached the point where nothing he could say would make any difference, as he already knew. And Jewel would hear the springs complain as he turned over and took refuge in silence. She'd have been glad to go back to town herself, for she was the oldest child in school and had nobody to talk to except her teacher. Miss Blackburn gave her chores to do that made her feel important and brought her books from the public library and told her she could do the best lettering of anybody she knew. Jewel painted signs for over the doors that said "Exit," and "Walk, Do Not Run," and wrote the day's spelling words in colored chalks on the blackboard, inside a border of flowers. In one of the library books, she found poems she could memorize and learned to recite "The Wreck of the Hesperus" and "The Song of the Shirt." After school, if she could escape from helping in the kitchen, she scouted the land beyond the hotel for arrowheads or drew pictures of the mountains or played some of her old pieces on the piano.

Without telling Penny, Jack put the hotel up for sale, but no buyer stepped forward. That done, he seemed absolved of responsibility. He spent less and less time there, going off to prospect for manganese and feldspar, or sitting with his cronies at the bar where he worked weekends. So that he wasn't around when Henry Betts, a lawyer from Deming, came out one afternoon. He had a mission of some delicacy and was just as well pleased to find the wife instead of the husband.

When he had telephoned, she couldn't figure out why he should come unless it was on the wings of some disaster Jack had perpetrated. He could have traded the hotel for some worthless mining claim or delivered them to a scheme that was bound to leave them worse off than before. More likely a secret debt was about to strangle them—back taxes or Jack's liquor bill. Or even worse: by this time he could have made some woman pregnant. Her fears raced over the groundwork created by suspicion while she prepared her face for sociability. Meanwhile the lawyer was taking his time, looking around with interest.

"I've heard about this place," he said affably, "but I never made it out here before this. My Daddy used to talk about it."

She invited him to sit down on the brocaded rosewood sofa she'd had Jack restore to the parlor—her special pride.

"Lots of nice antiques you got here."

To keep herself from fidgeting, she offered him coffee, for she had some on the stove in the kitchen. When she'd done that, and they'd arranged themselves and were clearly waiting for whatever had brought them to this moment, the lawyer said, "I've come to tell you about a woman who needs a home, a special kind of home."

If he'd come looking for charity, they had none to spare, but she knew enough to keep quiet till he'd finished. Miss Viny Trilling, he went on to explain, came from a good family, had grown up like you and me, but when she came to be an adult, she'd taken her childhood with her and couldn't tell the difference between what was in her head and what was happening in the world. Or didn't want to, for at times she was as sensible as you and me and other times she was crazier than a coyote. Lately, she'd seen from the porch a man she claimed had visited her in a dream and promised to carry her away to the mountains and make her his wife and give her a child of her own. Nothing would dissuade her from this illusion. And sometimes she'd slip out of her room and go roaming the streets, even in her nightgown, looking for him. Her brothers were at a loss—there was nobody at home to take care of her. They wanted her to be in a place where she wouldn't cause embarrassment but would be well treated. And he named a sum for this purpose that Penny could scarcely believe.

She had a hard time hearing the rest: that Miss Trilling would have to have fresh strawberries with cream when they were in season and oranges in winter, the big, sweet navel oranges from California. And there must be a feather quilt on her bed, and nobody must open her trunk but herself. Penny could only think how much she could put away and what it would take to hide it from Jack, who just then appeared, back from his latest foray into the hills, face grimed and his jeans and boots gray with dust.

"Got caught in a sandstorm," he said by way of greeting. He came forward, a slender man with a scraggly red mustache and an apologetic stoop to his shoulder, and shook the lawyer's hand.

"Go wash," Penny said. "You aren't civilized. And I won't have you on this sofa."

He gave a good-natured shrug and retreated. He went down to the springs, threw off his clothes and stepped into the pool. He let the heat close around him and the water lave his tired muscles. Like a caress it was as he floated. He closed his eyes and almost fell into a doze. For a moment all his troubles fell away, and he let himself drift into the pleasure of his fatigue, his body loosened from the pull of gravity. He allowed himself a certain luxury of sentiment, enlivened by the whiskey that had eased his homeward journey: things would work out. They'd go forward into the future. His girl would grow up and find her way in the world. Daddy's girl. He thought how she was growing toward the woman she was going to be, how the child and the woman were blending together. Sensation and feeling became a single glow he was melting into. Then the water became too hot for him to stay in any longer, and he emerged looking as though he'd just been boiled and peeled.

III.

Actually the Whedons were visited by what at the time was a double stroke of fortune. Not long after they agreed to take in Viny Trilling, they received a letter from a certain Everett Ferril, who used to come to the hotel as a boy with his parents and had fond memories of the place. He had recently retired from his teaching position in a private school in Switzerland and wanted to spend some months at the hotel writing his memoirs. He hoped the piano was in tune because he wished to devote time to his music. And he would like to hire a horse for long morning rides into the mountains.

They spent the next weeks preparing for the boarders. Mr. Ferril appeared first, a much younger man than they expected. Though he was impeccably dressed in suit and tie when he arrived, they didn't know what to think of him. He looked un-American, if they let themselves dwell on it, an unknown quantity, shaped by a life in a foreign place. A life that had left its marks and channels in his face as though he'd brooded over it but never resigned himself to it, and that gave him a look both worldly and unsatisfied. Something intense and barely subdued played under the surface like an electrical field that made his hair go awry and gave a spark like anger to his eyes. Which were everywhere, taking all in—the hotel and Jack and Penny herself. But Penny was not to be rattled. She didn't care what he was like or what he saw as long as he paid his bill and gave her a future. Then he stepped forward, kissed her hand, and gave her smile so full of charm that she was struck by the novelty and entirely won over.

"You're right welcome," she said.

By the time he was settled in, Viny arrived. Penny and Jack

went with Henry Betts to meet her at the train station in Deming, where she arrived with her brother Frank. "Take good care of our Vinita," he said, as though he couldn't bear to part with her. "She's our most special girl."

When they arrived back at the hotel, Jewel had just come home from her last day at school and was waiting to meet yet another stranger. She was not yet used to the first and ducked around corners to avoid speaking to Mr. Ferril. He was quite a tall man and seemed to look down at her from a great distance. A very gallant man, her mother said, who cast a spell with his foreign culture and manners. He spoke both French and German, so that his speech held a different flavor from what she knew, spiced with foreign words and the names of cities Jewel recognized from the outdated globe in her classroom. She was so awed by him she'd laughed when he kissed her hand, and was so embarrassed by that rudeness, she was perfectly tongue-tied in his presence. By contrast, her parents, whose speech and manners seemed suited only for a land of barren rocks where cattle foraged, didn't seem to care about the difference.

Viny Trilling was another matter. She was a child, newly born every second. When she looked at Jewel with unclouded eyes that seemed more violet than blue, a moment's terror overtook her, for her eyes seemed to draw Jewel into a territory that was both familiar and tantalizing, but one she dared not enter for long. She could hardly take her eyes from Viny's face: the pure brow, the unspoiled complexion without freckle or blemish, just the faintest touch of pink along the cheeks. She was like a china cup, but with a stubborn tilt to her head and a stubborn set to her jaw. She was twenty-eight years old.

"You can show her where her room is," Penny said, after Viny had offered a surprisingly strong, frank hand all around.

"I'll want to see the kitchen first," Viny said.

"Whatever you like," Penny said. "Jewel will show you everything."

She's used to having her way, Jewel thought enviously.

"I'll put away her things," Jack said.

"You be careful with that trunk," Viny said. "And mind you don't open it. It's got my things."

Jack required the help of Mr. Ferril to carry the large brassbound trunk to her room.

"I traveled to Europe with one like that years ago," Mr. Ferril offered. "I didn't know anybody still used them."

"Break your back, don't they?" Jack said, glad to set it down. Meanwhile Jewel took Viny toward the kitchen.

"Where do you keep the dishes?" Viny wanted to know.

"In the dining room."

"That's what I want to see."

Jewel opened the china cabinet so that Viny could survey the stacks of plates and bowls and saucers. "I'll need a special bowl for my strawberries."

"I know one," Jewel said, and brought out a little china bowl with lavender flowers around the edges that she had often used herself, it was so light and elegant.

"'Amaranths," Viny exclaimed. "The perfect thing."

"It's yours then."

And she smiled with such radiance Jewel had to look away.

During that spring she and Viny and Mr. Ferril were treated to strawberries and cream every morning for breakfast. Viny always took the longest to eat hers, saving one until the very last. They teased her about it—she only did it so that they could envy her and she could lord it over them. She'd laugh with pleasure, hold up the strawberry on her spoon for all to admire, put it in her mouth and close her eyes, shutting them out of her exquisite pleasure. Jewel envied her; yet she always ate hers right up. Viny the Hoarder, Jewel the Greedy, they called one another. And Mr. Ferril, what was he? What did they want to call him?

They hadn't thought, he went on so quietly while they teased each other and laughed. They never considered him part of the game, he was too . . . grown up. And they both had to look at him, as though they needed to discover more than how he ate his strawberries. Though he chatted and told anecdotes that made them double over with laughter, he seemed quite beyond them, as though he could, if he wanted, refer to some private store of superiority. He treated them all—Penny, Viny, and even Jewel—as if they were ladies, but quite impersonally, as if he adored them all and would have extended this courtesy to any woman, even if she stood before him in rags. He praised Penny's cooking, though it was of the meat-and-potatoes variety, mediocre and overdone. He went round the old hotel with a memory attached to every object and corner, piano and Victrola and porch and dining table. How extraordinary he could remember so much about all the mere objects of their daily existence. He told about former guests, whom he remembered in vivid detail and, it became clear how, even as a boy, he could recognize human frailty and turn it to ridicule. Jewel liked his way of making fun of people, because he made fun of himself as well. With his presence, together with Viny's, the place grew lively, glowed with a life borrowed from somewhere beyond it.

But he never said much about his present circumstances. There was no mention of a wife or family, or a home he came from. He'd grown up in Michigan, but had lived all his adult life abroad. He had a low opinion of the students he had taught; "rich men's brats," he called them, "like pieces of spoiled fruit." He didn't explain why he had left Switzerland or where, as a man in his forties, he might be going. "He must have money," Penny was fond of saying, implying that he also had everything else—good looks, nice clothes. And what was he doing here?

"Mr. Flight," Viny called him.

It was a peculiar summer. Just at the point where Jewel was about to close the door on her childhood, she was asked to live it all again. Penny had taken her aside. "You'll have a job this summer," she said. "And you'll be paid for it. Ten dollars a month in your bank account." She could buy clothes for the fall when she'd be going into town for school. Meanwhile she was to be a companion for Viny. Jewel readily agreed; she'd never had so much money before.

The summer was an invention, created from whatever fell to hand. When they discovered a litter of kittens in the shed, apparently abandoned, they fed them with eye droppers until they could eat on their own. They sewed little dresses and caps for them and made elaborate visits to one another and invented conversations for their babies. They explored the attic as well and took down tables and chairs to make a special house in one of the unused rooms. Sometimes at night Jewel slept with Viny and they lay awake late like girls at a slumber party. Though once Viny woke her up in the middle of the night moaning and crying out.

"What's the matter?" Jewel asked her. "Did you have a bad dream?"

"I'm the matter," Viny said, sitting up. "Why was I born?" she moaned, rocking back and forth. "Oh don't turn on the light, don't let me wake up." She sat blinking when Jewel did so, and rubbing her eyes. "Where will I go to find my love? He was here and then he was gone."

It was peculiar, her living in a dream that way, and Jewel wondered that she should have miseries like that when she hadn't a trouble in the world and didn't have to do anything she didn't want to. She could let each day go wherever she wanted and do as she liked. She didn't have to cut up vegetables or help with the dishes, though mostly she shared whatever chores Jewel had to do.

What particularly took Jewel's fancy was the trunk of clothes Viny had brought with her, all old: cloche hats of velvet and stiff ones with broad brims; hats with plumes and bunches of feathers and rings of pearls and artificial flowers and veils. Dresses of crêpe de chine and taffeta and velvet, and scarves and shawls embroidered with peacocks and roses. Gowns that trailed the floor and silver shoes and beaded slippers. Her dress-up clothes.

Since Viny's arrival, Jewel looked forward with quickening interest to what the day would bring, as though each day were to be lived without the burden of the previous one. And time flowed without being time. It made her feel guilty somehow, like living off the fat of the land. If, now and then, she was seized by a moment of misgiving, she would go to the mirror to remind herself that she was growing up. The first thing she would buy was a bra. The summer would come to an end and she'd be ready.

"How do you like Viny?" Jack asked her one day, out of idle curiosity.

"She's okay," Jewel said with a shrug and immediately felt she'd betrayed her.

While they went their way, Mr. Ferril sat at the piano in the parlor, limbering up with scales, then filling the hotel with music. Jewel envied him. Though she'd taken lessons up till the time they'd moved into the hotel, nothing she played was ever perfect. And now she was a year away from her music. The teacher had let her work on songs in the songbook to play while the younger children sang, but what she knew kept slipping away. Mr. Ferril could play pieces like "Clair de Lune"— which Jewel thought was the most beautiful music she'd ever heard—and works by composers. Sometimes he struck chords that filled the whole place with sound. "Rachmaninoff," he would tell her, one more of his foreign words. When she looked at the music he left open, it appeared so complicated and difficult she could only wonder how anyone played it.

One morning after she and Viny had admired themselves in the full-length mirror Jack had helped them move from the hallway into their special room, Viny wanted to attend a ball in the parlor and dance to music on the Victrola.

"But Mr. Ferril is practicing," Jewel said.

"We'll wait till he's finished," Viny said reasonably.

Jewel didn't want him to see them, and when it was quiet, she took off her gown to go and see first that he was gone. But as Viny was dancing to the music with an unseen partner, he appeared. Jewel felt a sudden rush of shame. She was too old to be caught like this. But curiously, he went up to put the next record on the Victrola and said to Viny, "My name is first on your dance card, madamoiselle. I hope I may claim the honor."

"Of course, Mr. Flight," she said, and gave him a gloved hand and allowed him to lead her to the center of the floor. They sailed around the room as though an admiring crowd were witnessing. Viny's dress swirled out around her, in a sheen of pink silk. Movement filled the tune of the waltz and made it less plaintive, and for a moment it was possible to imagine other dancers, other voices. Jewel envied her and the way the pink dress curved across her breasts and fitted her waist and flowed to the floor. She'd yet to have her first formal, and she wanted one, and to go to a prom like they had in high school. When they finished the waltz, breathless, laughing, they grasped each other around the waist. Mr. Ferril's forehead glowed.

Then he started the record over again and asked Jewel to dance.

"I can't," she said. For though she counted steps and concentrated, she always tripped over her partner's feet.

"Just follow me," he said, taking her hand, looking at her in a way that intimidated her.

"Just put yourself inside the music," Viny said.

Jewel clutched her dress up into a knot so that it wouldn't trail, and tried to follow, blindly, stumbling, till her face was hot and her hands were moist.

"A little practice is all that's needed," Mr. Ferril said kindly. "It's all anything needs," and he squeezed her hand.

She couldn't bear it. She stood there in the silver shoes that slipped against her heels and felt the summer collapse beneath her.

Viny plucked her sleeve. "We're late," she said. "The carriage is waiting."

She was glad to flee from Mr. Ferril's gaze, but she couldn't put from her mind the picture of Viny dancing.

"We'll teach you to dance," Viny said when they were together.

"I can't," Jewel said, without understanding why. She knew she would adore dancing with Mr. Ferril if she could dance like Viny. She'd seen films of Ginger Rogers and Fred Astaire, and she could imagine being whirled around a ballroom. But it was possible to imagine herself doing it only if she didn't attempt it.

It was more than she could bear to see Mr. Ferril almost every time she turned around. Though he practiced the piano in the mornings after breakfast and sometimes worked in his room, he seemed to have a great deal of time on his hands. He had bought a new car, a Hudson with silver fenders and a wide body, not long after his arrival, but after he'd taken them for a brief excursion and they'd reveled in the newness of it, he apparently had nowhere to go. It sat in front of the hotel.

"So what'll we do today?" he asked them one morning after breakfast, as though he had so far advanced into their company they were a threesome. Jewel looked at him uncertainly, but he appeared to be waiting for his answer from Viny.

"Let's go on a picnic," Viny said, clapping her hands eagerly. "We can pack sandwiches and go on an excursion and eat outdoors."

"The car," Jewel said, hoping she wasn't being forward. "We can go in the car."

"Absolutely," said Mr. Ferril. "A wonderful idea."

Penny packed sandwiches for them and made a thermos of iced tea, and they drove off for the City of Rocks, a few miles from the hotel. It was not so much a city as a chaos of rocks, as though the earth in a mad moment had flung out boulders in every direction. They made a great heap on a small rise where they'd been pushed above the ground, and the soil having settled among them, grasses and mesquite and a few small cedars grew out of their midst. They gleamed white in the sun as they approached. The sky was brilliant and cloudless, with a solitary hawk cruising above.

"I'll bet anything could live here," Jewel said, as they surveyed the boulders. "Snakes and mice and rabbits and scorpions and—"

Viny was momentarily startled by a lizard.

"It's weird," Jewel said, "I wouldn't want to be here at night."

"I didn't think you'd scare that easily," Mr. Ferril teased her.

She ignored him. "Let's climb on the rocks," Jewel said to Viny. "I can go highest, I'll bet." She scrambled up among the boulders to the point where she could look out over the desert and down at Viny and Mr. Ferril standing together. "Come on," she yelled. "It's not hard. You can see everything."

They reached her finally, took in the view of the mountains, and sat down on the rocks to catch their breath.

"The world's out there somewhere," Jewel said.

"And luckily we're here," Mr. Ferril said, "and it can all go hang."

That was the way with adults, it seemed: they were ready to condemn something before you had a chance to try it out, like a secret they wanted to keep for themselves and never let you in on it.

"I'm going down," he said. "My stomach is about to digest itself."

Jewel didn't care.

"Do you think it's a grand place?" Viny asked, gesturing toward the expanse.

"Yes," Jewel said. "I want to see Paris."

"I saw a picture once," Viny said, "of a tall tower. They said it

173

was Paris." They climbed down to the base of the rocks, where Mr. Ferril had spread a cloth under the shadows of some cedars.

"What could be better?" Mr. Ferril said, taking a bite from a ham sandwich. "Sky like this and sun and rocks. You never know how good food can taste till you eat it out in the air."

They ate and drank hungrily, then Jewel jumped up again, ready to explore.

"What energy," Mr. Ferril said. "All I want to do is sit here forever and watch the clouds." He leaned back against a boulder.

"That would be boring," Jewel said, "with nothing ever happening."

"What do you want to happen?"

She shrugged. "I don't know. Something. There's all this waiting—and nothing happens."

"The same wherever you are," said Mr. Ferril. "All this waiting for something that never happens. And if it does, it's too late."

He reached down and broke off a blade of grass, put it between his thumbs and tried to blow on it. "I used to do this when I was a kid." She hated him just then, throwing out something mean and then playing with a blade of grass. Speaking from that superiority of his she had no defense against. She looked at him as though he'd spoken a curse. She made a face, so he couldn't get away with it. She was sure it wasn't true.

"I want to go to school," she said, emphatically.

"Yes," he said in a dull voice, "I suppose you do."

Jewel was mortified that she had revealed herself so openly.

"Itching to run out into the world, are you? Well, it's not all it's cracked up to be, and there are things I've done in it I wish I hadn't." He cracked his knuckles, then picked another blade of the grass. "Grass is wonderful stuff," he said. "Trample it down and up it comes."

"You've seen lots of things," Viny said. "There and there," she said, reaching over and running her finger over the lines of his forehead. "Those are all the things."

He smiled and took her hand. "I'd rather be here with you than to have seen any of them."

Jewel had heard men say things like this in films, only you knew it was false even when you wanted it to mean something, even though everything came out with happy endings. Mr. Ferril was lowered another notch in her opinion.

"You don't know anything," she said, going off. He'd put her in a bad mood, and she wanted to take a swipe at him. She went around a boulder to chew on a long grass stem and dream about school starting and the clothes she wanted. She was impatient now for the summer to be over; it always got so boring. She wanted to forget about Viny and Mr. Ferril and take her thirty dollars and go shopping. If he wanted to sit there with her and Viny when he could be off speaking French and walking along the Seine and seeing the insides of cathedrals, he must be like the donkey that wanted horns instead of ears. Or like a monk or a man shipwrecked on an island. Only he'd come to this place out of his own free will. So he must be crazy. Or maybe wicked. It occurred to her he might indeed be wicked, but she didn't think he'd killed anybody.

She'd been watching the way he acted in the hotel, as if he'd come to stay and wanted everybody to like him. Easy and familiar with the women, as though he had crossed some invisible boundary and gained their territory. She'd never seen a man act like that before. With her mother, for instance. Touching her arm, or putting his arm around her shoulder when he asked for something, making a little joke and laughing when she laughed. It was shocking, though her mother seemed not to mind at all, but even to welcome it. A change came over her then, like the sun moving out of a cloud, and she joked and laughed till the color rose to her cheeks and she looked warm and pretty and pleased. Between her parents there was no such intimacy. They either moved behind a cloud of indifference or acted as though they had the goods on one another and would give no quarter.

Mr. Ferril was gentler with Viny, more tender, occasionally taking her by the hand and saying, "Look here, isn't this lovely?" and showing her the sunset or a rock with veins in it. And she would smile at him, her eyes glowing with pleasure. But it was the same pleasure she had for the sunset or the other things that gave her delight. Sometimes, though, she would scuffle with him the way the

175

kittens tumbled with each other.

With Jewel, it was different. He'd never touched her except when they had danced, but she found herself wanting him to look at her, wanting him to laugh with her the way he did with her mother. And when he said to Viny, "Isn't it lovely?" his voice touched a nerve that made her shiver. Sometimes she wanted to kick her legs and bang her head on the floor just like a child to make him look at her. She was awkward in her desire to please him without knowing how, angry that it should matter, because he was such an old man and she disliked him besides. When he did look at her, she pretended not to notice.

Toward the end of the summer, Viny's brother Frank, and the lawyer, Henry Betts, came out to the hotel for an afternoon's visit. They all ate in the dining room, a small group in a room of empty tables. Then Viny insisted that Jewel come to sit in the parlor with them. When it was nearly time to leave, Viny and her brother hugged one another as though they never wanted to separate; then Frank held her at arms length to look at her again. "My darling," he said. "My rose of Jericho."

"The name of this place is solitude, Brother," Viny said, "and its song is sung by the coyotes."

"She's a genius," Frank said to Penny and Jack afterwards. "Only she's never had a place to be it before. She lives differently from you and me."

That night Jack had a brainstorm and lay in bed under the rush of his enthusiasm. Think of it, he told Penny, they had a real start this time. With Viny there year-round and Ferril staying on indefinitely, they could attract other boarders. Build up the summer clientele. With a little luck, they could make a real go of it.

Penny could see him lying there, an ill-defined lump under the covers, eyes wide open to receive the gleam of the future. All caught up. He was such a fool she could almost pity him. She tried to be patient. Surely, she argued, they ought to let well enough alone and see if, for once in their lives, they could get a little ahead. What was the point of taking on risks they couldn't cover?

"But we've got a chance, don't you see?"

"Birdbrain," she said, and turned over and went to sleep.

176

Jack lay awake a little longer, staring into the dark. Then turned over as well and folded his arms across his chest. He wasn't about to fight her. He'd go back to his cronies and his mining claims and his woman in Deming. Penny could do as she liked.

IV.

Penny had it in mind that the dawn of one of these days would find her far from the hotel. She saw a woman sitting alone on a train, in hat and dark dress and pumps—stylish without being conspicuous—while the vortices of travel whirled away behind her. She could almost watch herself looking through the window at towns speeding by while the wheels thundered out distances. She kept putting money away into the secret hoard she'd started even before that image of herself possessed her fantasy. But now that it was there, she let it carry her forward to different cities and other men. She wanted to go somewhere in the world where nothing would hang onto her. She wanted to shed her present life the way a dog sheds water, leave the hotel and all the things that had gone awry to fade beyond memory, sealed up in a room she'd never open. Even Jewel didn't belong in this picture of herself, because Jewel could only remind her of where she'd been. And Jewel would be old enough to fend for herself one of these days. Jack wouldn't let her starve, he and his whore. They could all do as they liked—it wasn't any skin off her hide.

In some ways, they were two of a kind, she and Jack, and at times she looked at him as though he were part of a conspiracy. He'd done all right, wandering among his cronies and whores, going off on his fruitless hunts for manganese and feldspar. Anything that would take him away from the hotel and to the price of the next drink he'd do. Short of stealing—and maybe that too. He'd never need a cent more than he had. But her little hoard was growing. She even gave Jack a crumb now and then for the sake of good will and a clear path to the future. And because he couldn't let her get the better of him, he'd put a little cash her way when he had it. He'd got himself a partner, a worthless sort of blowhard, who knew everything about the country and had only till now avoided being rich for the sake of some obscure principle.

But fall was coming and the moment she'd have to look Jewel in the eye and deny her what she'd been counting on. For if Viny was their bread, Jewel was their butter.

Indeed it was coming on September, but nobody'd taken her to town for school clothes, though Jewel kept nagging about when they were going. The plan had been that she would stay in town with the Folsoms and go to high school. Though she was only thirteen, Miss Blackburn had said she was ready. But every time Jewel mentioned it, Penny put her off.

Finally, knowing she couldn't dodge the question any longer, Penny made her come back to the bedroom and closed the door and told her. "I know you've been counting on going to town and boarding out this year, but you've got to understand that we're hanging by a thread and can't afford it."

Jewel couldn't believe it. "But I could work, I could babysit and wash dishes and—"

Penny shook her head. "Maybe next year, when you're high school age anyway. Besides," she continued, "those schools don't teach you anything you can't put off for a year. Besides," she added, as though this time she had the real clincher, "You'll get a better education right here. I've talked to the principal and to Mr. Ferril, and he's agreed to be your tutor. You can go on with your piano and he'll teach you French—said it was a good way for him to keep in practice. Why, you'll have a real European education."

But Jewel was not mollified. All she could think about was being in town, where she could go to the movies with girls her age and giggle over boys and have skirts to wear instead of jeans.

She went off in a fury that was new to her, and made Viny cry because she told her to go away and leave her alone. She sat in her room in a stupor of disappointment, then went out back to where Jack was killing chickens, a job he hated. She stood by while a headless chicken jerked and flung itself around the floor of the shed, the other chickens nearby clucking their distress.

"Daddy," she said, following him to the pump, waiting till the water washed over his hands. "Daddy," she said, trying to keep her voice calm, "how come I can't go to school like we said?"

The fumes of the day's whiskey fuddled his brain, and the

178

hand that held the axe belonged to someone else. Then anger burned him: he felt unhinged by circumstance, and the look in her eye made his own eyes moisten. He'd have enjoyed the luxury of giving way, of sitting right down with a good drink and huddling his woe with an endless compassion.

"I could work. Mrs. Folsom said she'd be glad to have me, and Jonie's there."

"Young girls need their folks," Jack said, suddenly convinced of this. Young girls wanted to wander off by themselves, and all heedless they went down dark streets without knowing what was waiting for them.

He concentrated his small red-rimmed eyes on his hands, lathering them up, rinsing them off, examining the stubborn dirt under the nails. "Why, you got the chance of a lifetime right in your own backyard. That Ferril will teach you things that'll take your breath away."

"I just want to go to high school," Jewel wailed.

"Actually, the principal was against it," Jack said. "Didn't want to set a precedent. He said, 'That young gal should wait a year.' He was thinking of you doing your best. And meanwhile you won't have to leave Viny. Because it would break her heart, you know." He gave her a direct look, "You wouldn't want to do that, would you? She'd take it mighty hard." He walked back to the shed to pick up the headless chicken.

Jewel had been momentarily silenced. Of course, she'd have missed Viny. More than her parents, though she didn't like to admit it. Viny took up a space that no one else could fill. But that didn't change anything. "I'll have to go sometime," she said. "Viny has her own life."

"Well, and you got yours, puss," Jack said kindly. "You don't have to rush it all at once." Time enough to know what a hard place the world was. He felt he was doing the right thing by her, protecting her for her own good. There were usually good reasons for doing almost anything. And he tested that theory on the basis that he felt better than he expected to, found himself on solid ground for a change.

Jewel ran off to her room, her head full to bursting. Suppose

179

she just ran off to town, took the money in her bank account and hitchhiked across the country. Suppose she killed herself. But though she tried, she couldn't live in her disappointment. Her consolation, such as it was, came a few days later when they went into town and she bought a new skirt and sweater with her savings. Then she and Viny went to an adventure film while Penny went to the stores and shopped. Viny put her head down whenever the hero was in danger.

From that time on, Jewel nursed a sense of blame toward Viny. It was her fault she wasn't going to school. She knew it was wrong, but she couldn't help herself. Viny had created her circumstances without knowing it, had helped create the net that bound them all, tied up the knots of possibility. The hotel bound Jack and Penny; they held on as though it were their invention out there in the desert. And now she had been pulled into the trap. Viny was free—she could travel in any space and come back and be what she was. She would never be hustled out of her domain to be locked in the narrow, closed space that Jewel resisted and that everyone she knew had entered. Had it been possible to hate Viny, Jewel would have been glad to do it. But Viny was without malice; her only harm lay in being what she was.

She tried to put herself at a distance, as though Viny presented a treacherous quicksand that would keep her from moving where she needed to go. But it was impossible to get away.

"I've got something to show you," Viny told her one afternoon in her usual way, recognizing no change between them.

"What is it?" Jewel said, without interest.

"Come and I'll show you."

They went to her room, where she opened a drawer and pulled out a small leather pouch. From it she took out a rabbit's foot. "I thought I'd lost it," she said joyfully, as she held it up.

"Is that all?" Jewel said cruelly.

But Viny paid no attention. "It's a coyote charm," she said.

"To keep them off?"

"No, to bring them," she said.

"Why would you want to go and do that?" Jewel said, her interest quickened. But she went on, "It's just an old rabbit's foot."

Viny didn't answer for a moment. Then she said, "They're

part dog gone to the devil, and you can't tame them. They howl for the part that used to lie in front of the fire, only they can't have it. They'd be too comfortable, and the desert's the only place for them. So they howl for the sake of what they are."

"What's the point of that?" Jewel said. "And who'd want them close anyway?"

"They make you remember being out there with them."

Jewel gave a shrug, tired of the game.

"It works by moonlight, by the full moon," Viny said, picking up the charm. "We can go out then."

"It sounds dumb," Jewel said.

"You see this hotel," Viny said, as though she hadn't heard. "It's under a curse."

More nonsense, but she could almost believe it. "Why?"

"Because it's here and it has no soul,"

"You think it ever had one?" Jewel said in a mocking tone.

"Of course it did, every place has one. You have it for a while, then you have to let it go wandering on. You can't hold onto it. But if you try without it, everything goes out of whack."

In some ways Viny was uncanny. "I don't know what to do," Jewel said, in a rush of misery.

"Here," Viny said, holding out her hand, "I'll give it to you."

"That's all right," Jewel said, putting her arm around her. "You don't have to give me anything." There was nothing Viny or anyone else could offer her.

"It'll be a secret between us," Viny said, putting it away.

V.

Jewel did take refuge in her piano lessons, though not at first. When she took out the yellow-covered John Thompson music books and tried her old pieces at the keyboard, she made so many mistakes she wanted to tear up the music. Afterwards she ran off to weep in her room. Mr. Ferril kept telling her she had real piano hands because she could reach a whole octave, and he told her she was very talented. He bought for her the notebooks of Anna Magdelena Bach, and she practiced when she could, Viny sitting in a chair beside the piano, quiet, not disturbing her, as though it were nothing for her to hear the same piece played a dozen times. They created a schoolroom as well, moving the bed out of their special room and moving in a secretary. Jewel was learning French and reading *Ivanhoe* and *Julius Caesar* and *Romeo and Juliet*. Sometimes they read passages aloud so that Jewel could get practice in public speaking, with Viny for the audience. And so that Jewel would learn how to use words, Mr. Ferril made her write poetry. He kept pushing her; the more he pushed, the harder she tried. He was inviting her to go somewhere beyond anything she knew, but she had no idea where he was leading her. She had come to idolize him and was afraid that she wouldn't live up to his expectations. At the same time a kind of quarrel lived in her, ready to flare up into rage.

"There's a girl in France just eight years old who writes poetry that puts philosophers to shame," he said once. "Don't you want to do something like that?"

"I'm not eight years old," Jewel said.

"That's not what I'm saying."

She didn't want to write poems; they sounded stupid. But she learned to play "Für Elise" and "Malagueñia" with such aplomb that Mr. Ferril kissed her on the top of the head and called in Jack and Penny to listen. "Mighty fine," Jack said. "Nice touch, don't you think?" And Penny said the other kids would be jealous if they knew.

She could have spent hours at the piano. She had caught on finally, and it came easily, the notes in her mind moving her hands. She skipped through the pieces one after the other. When she played particularly well, Mr. Ferril put his arm around her and said, "That's my girl."

He went to town to buy her a book of Mozart's sonatinas, and that evening they went to the piano to try the first. She was very excited.

"Here, now," he said, "come with me. I'll get you some music paper, and you copy it out. That way you'll know it. You sleep with that music in your head and let it take hold of you. That way you'll play it. Do you understand what I'm saying?"

She didn't think she did, but she wouldn't admit it. She was filled with uncertainty. She wasn't sure what he wanted of her, something more than playing the piano.

"The passion is there—all that remains is for you to let it out." She remained silent.

"Look at me," he demanded.

She was beginning to feel suffocated by his presence there in the room. But then he smiled, and gently pushed the hair away from her face. "A lovely girl," he said gently. "Young and lovely and full of promise. Kiss me," he said.

She leaned over and kissed him on the cheek.

"Now on the lips," he said, and this time bent forward and kissed her lightly on the lips. "You see," he said. "That's a kiss between friends. It's a little doorway to be entered. Whole realms and countries to be imagined."

"Kiss me again," he said. But she turned away.

"I'm trying to help you," he said. "I'm trying to make something of you. You're young but not stupid. Try not to be stupid." She turned to leave. "You want the world, don't you? You may as well get it on your own terms. At least before they beat it out of you."

She had no idea what he was talking about.

He gave a little laugh. "I suppose I'm frightening you. Maybe that's a good thing. Think of me sometimes," he said, before she closed the door. "Tomorrow Mozart. Both purity and passion—you can't get better than that."

That night she lay in bed, reliving the kiss like a tune that played itself over and over in her mind. She felt it on her cheek and against her lips. She could call up the sensations in those spots that linked with others and collected in a place she wasn't sure about. Because when she touched it, she was sure she shouldn't, yet it seemed all sensation flowed there and made her feel more herself. She didn't want him to kiss her; she wanted him to kiss her until she didn't want any more. She'd do anything not to be drawn to the next kiss. And she touched the place that seemed itself a doorway, herself a doorway that things might enter. She didn't know what to do. It was the first time she'd been kissed on the lips. Now it was something she didn't know how to live with, for it led beyond itself. To honey and anguish. She wanted something desperately, but had no idea what. Not Mr. Ferril and not music and yet those too. He

183

had an idea about her that she resisted, but she had none about herself.

"Do you want babies?" Viny asked her a few nights later, when they slept together.

"I don't think so," Jewel said. "I think they'd be horrible, crying all the time and having to be changed and fed."

"A child is real," Viny said.

"Of course it is, but you and I are real,"

"It jumps and plays, and that's different from what's in your head."

"Of course it is. Lots of things are real."

"Yes," Viny said, touching her forehead. "When I do this, I know it's all in my head and outside it's real. Only it's different with a child, because it lives in its head, but it's outside. And you can talk to it—and say what's in your head. And it knows. It's different from other people. And if you had a child, it would be yours."

"I don't want one," Jewel said.

"What do you wish when you break a wishbone?"

"To go away from here," Jewel said.

"I want to marry Mr. Ferril," Viny said.

Jewel lay in silence. "You can't do that," she said.

"Why not?"

"Just because. Suppose he doesn't want to marry you. Suppose he has a lady somewhere else. It's a stupid thing to say."

She wanted to pinch Viny and make her cry and push her out of the bed. She wasn't supposed to want Mr. Ferril. He belonged to her, only she didn't want him.

"Besides," she said, "he's a wicked person."

"He's a wicked person," Viny said, "but he's a good person. He takes me down to the river to look at the birds. We're going to catch a bird; he said he would."

"That's stupid," Jewel said. "What would you want with it?"

"To have it," Viny said. "Like the kittens. Only a baby would be better."

The lessons went on, but though she thought everything would be changed by that kiss, Mr. Ferril acted as if nothing had happened. He seemed to have lost interest in her, to have lost

184

the focus of his idea. He never said, "Don't you want to be a great musician? Wouldn't you like to play all over Europe?" or any of the notions he'd teased her with. Her playing went badly; the harder she tried, the worse it got. And after the lesson ended with his putting a record on the Victrola and dancing with Viny, she sat there glumly, full of disgust. If he'd asked her, she'd have refused, though she wanted him to ask. If she could only play the piano better than anyone in the world, then Mr. Ferril would give her all his attention. She watched Viny laughing and clinging to his arm, their hugging afterwards and it was more than she could bear. If only she could lie on the floor and kick and scream, but she couldn't do that either.

Suddenly it occurred to her: what if they went off together and took off all their clothes down by the river? Viny wouldn't have cared. She hadn't thought where Viny and Mr. Ferril went on their walks together while she practiced. Maybe Mr. Ferril had kissed Viny a long time ago, because Viny was beautiful and they could dance together like Fred Astaire and Ginger Rogers. When they went out that afternoon, she left the piano and watched them disappear up the road. She wanted badly to follow them and spy on them. The next day when they were going to take the silver Hudson into town, she deserted the piano and ran out to the car because she couldn't bear to be left behind. Mr. Ferril accidentally closed the door on her finger, and she cried. She knew she was being allowed to go because of her finger. Though they ate dinner at a Mexican restaurant, she didn't enjoy it. Her finger wasn't broken, but it would be a few days before she could go back to the piano. That meant she could go with them on their walks. She saw that Viny and Mr. Ferril held hands and let their arms swing as they walked.

But even after her finger healed, the lessons went badly. Mr. Ferril's mind seemed to be elsewhere. He was virtually silent over breakfast, and when he went into town, it was by himself. For the first time since he arrived at the hotel, he'd received several letters all in one week. He started to use the telephone once but thought better of it, jumped into the Hudson, and went into town.

"If you have a baby," Viny said one night as they lay together, "you can tell it words, and it will say them back, and then it will make up things to say. Isn't that fun?"

"Are you going to have a baby, Viny?" Jewel asked, pushing herself up on her elbow. "Tell me, are you?"

"Mr. Ferril says I can have one if I want."

"But you can't do that, Viny," Jewel said. "It would be wrong."

"No, it wouldn't."

"You're not even married."

"I don't care," Viny said, stubbornly. "He has to go away first. But if I have a baby, it will be real."

"Who does? Mr. Ferril? Where's he going?"

"I don't know," Viny said, "but he'll come back."

"Does he love you, Viny?" she asked shyly. Perhaps that too was something that entered a doorway.

"He says so."

"But if he doesn't come back, what'll you do then? It will be terrible," she said, as though it had happened already. She knew she'd gone too far.

Viny whimpered softly beside her. "A baby would be real," she said. "Don't tell," she pleaded. "It's a secret between us. Promise— you have to."

No matter what she did, it would be wrong somehow. If she told, Viny would cry and tell her she was mean and maybe never forgive her, and Mr. Ferril would hate her. And Penny would blame her for not saying something before. If she kept the secret, she'd be miserable and never have a moment's peace. But suppose Viny only imagined a baby without ever having one, or suppose Mr. Ferril came back and married her. That way she could go to school and everybody would be happy. She was willing now to let Viny have him.

VI.

Mr. Ferril left them soon after, saying he'd been called away on business, but that he'd return as soon as everything was settled. He took only a small valise and left the rest of his things and paid his room and board for the next month. He kissed the women on both cheeks, as the French do, he told them, and drove away up the road. Viny waved to him until the car disappeared.

After he left, the hotel settled into dullness. Jewel let her music go and only played when she was seized by the fear she would forget. Her French and math books lay entirely unopened. Penny didn't say a word to her about studying. Lethargy took hold of everything. Even if something needed desperately to be fixed, it was left. The sink got plugged up and the dishes went unwashed for days before they called the plumber. Jack slipped in and out without anyone noticing. Penny could tell Jack a dozen times to nail a loose board, but when it got fixed was another matter. Sometimes things ran out, like bread or eggs, but Penny didn't seem to care. Jewel and Viny spent a lot of time playing checkers and listening to soap operas on the radio, or if it was Sunday, to Jack Benny and Edgar Bergen and Charlie McCarthy.

She ignored Viny much of the time, but Viny didn't seem to notice. Viny moped around the hotel, played with the cats, and sang to herself. She had a hard time getting up in the morning and looked pale and irritable over breakfast. Not even the advent of the large, sweet navel oranges from California revived her. She looked at the brilliant fruit and pushed the plate aside. For long periods she sat in her room and stared out the window.

Then the lethargy was pierced by voices. Penny and Jack seemed to spend half their time quarreling.

"If anything's going to get done around this place . . ."

"Sand down a rathole."

"It's what I hate about you," Penny said. "Like you've forgot Viny's here and keeping food on the table."

"I know all about it, but I got things to do. And Viny's being taken care of."

Their exchanges were as brief and fruitless as they were necessary to their existence. Jewel stayed clear of them, because it was like entering a cross fire to come between them. But then something created a tension in the air that was almost like a purpose. Jewel wasn't quite clear what was going on. Whatever she overhead was fragmentary and inconclusive, but clearly it had to do with Mr. Ferril.

"I never liked that man," she heard Penny say, "not from the first moment I laid eyes on him. I figure it was in him to do something like that."

"You'd never know it the way you two carried on."

"Listen, he was our bread and butter, and all I did was be nice to him."

"Yeah, I'll bet. I had him figured for a ladies' man from the very first go."

"Just what do you have in mind, Jack Whedon? When I want to go roving in the clover you can be sure I'll make the most of it."

"I 'spose you would."

"And isn't it just like the pot calling the kettle black?" Always, just before Jewel could figure something out, they went on to their own private grievances and let her hang with a suspense that finally drove her to Mr. Ferril's room. She opened the wardrobe and fingered the cloth of his finely tailored suits, the tweed jacket he wore on walks. The smell of him still lingered in the room. She looked at the pile of books he left, the Shakespeare she had read from, a novel by Stendahl, and the plays of Molière. A crystal ashtray still held ashes and cigarette butts. She found a little notebook with his handwriting, listing his expenses. He had a peculiar way of making a seven. As she leafed through it, a photograph that had been taped lightly to the back cover fell out.

When she picked it up, she saw a family. The woman, petite and slender, with her hair swept up elegantly, stood next to a young boy, almost her height. She held his arm as though she depended on him, and although he faced the camera, he seemed to glance off to one side, but whether at her or something outside the frame of the picture, it was impossible to tell.

The two of them seemed linked together by the same eye that looked outward and somewhat askance and took in everything with the same humor and touch of superiority. And the same energy played in their expressions. Behind them stood a man taller than the boy. Jewel looked at them closely. These were his parents, where his origins lay, the ones who called him Everett and told him he mustn't spoil his supper and to watch out for the cactus thorns, who sent him to school and expected him to study diligently and mind the teachers. Behind the trio were the columns of the hotel, white and smooth in the sunlight. The hotel was young then, the paint still fresh, and all, it appeared, was whole and sound. Others were gathered on the porch. Jewel could make out the edge of a rocker and a man's leg extended. On the back of the photo was a date: June, 1919. She wondered why he had left it behind.

The rest was negligible. A crumpled handkerchief. A fringed bookmark. A paperweight. A mixture of French and Swiss coins on the windowsill. These Jewel examined one by one; they'd been in his pockets as he'd walked the streets of foreign cities. Then she put them back where she'd found them, left the room, closing the door quietly behind her, and never said a word about having been there.

At that point, with a sort of grudging truce between them, Penny and Jack kept things mostly to themselves. When Jewel asked questions, they told her Ferril had gone away and wouldn't be back. He had business matters to settle. And quietly Jack and Penny gave themselves to speculation.

"No wonder he wanted to come here. Seems strange now we didn't know anything about him!"

"We never asked, you idiot."

"When I think of it—him being around our girl and all."

"Now you think about it."

"And what did you think with all the money coming in? Well, it's all catching up with him, poor guy. I don't know though. I think he was planning to come back, even wanted to. He left all his things—there's some expensive stuff there."

"Maybe that was just his way of clearing out."

"I don't believe it," Jack said. "Maybe he just wanted to start over."

The way Jack wanted to do. His partner had just told him about the assayer's results on some rocks they'd brought down from the Black Range. If they could find an outfit willing to go to the expense of taking out the ore, they might have a good thing. And if the hotel did go under, as he thought about it now, he could put his time where it would do the most good. Penny could get a job in town as a receptionist or a telephone operator. That would carry them along until he hit pay dirt. He'd have to find the right moment to put it to her. For now he'd bide his time.

It didn't take too much evidence before Penny got wind

of Viny's secret. She cornered Jewel one afternoon and said to her, "Maybe you know something I don't know. But the way Viny's been sick these mornings means only one thing, far as I'm concerned. What can you tell me about it?"

Jewel shrugged. "I can't help it if she's sick."

"Nobody said you could."

It was curious, though, the train of Penny's logic. If Viny was pregnant, it could be one man as well as another, and Jewel was party to yet another quarrel.

"What do you take me for? As if I'd lay a hand on her."

"Well," Penny said, "you never know."

For once Jack rose to ire. "You think a man's got no honor?" he said. "Taking advantage of a poor woman who doesn't have her stock of wits."

"Well, someone did, unless it's a virgin birth."

"And you still can't believe what's right in front of your eyes. All that high-toned culture he slickered you with." Jack gave a little laugh. "And you didn't even keep an eye on her."

"How was I to know? And say what you want, that Viny has plenty of wit." She knew how to flirt anyway. She could play with a man like any woman, for all she was a child. Penny could see that. Even so, the bastard should have left her alone; he didn't have to stoop that low.

They blamed each other for not being more careful and blamed Jewel for not looking out for her and in the end decided there was no help for it. They couldn't take her anywhere to bring it off, because it wasn't legal, and if they tried to do it illegally, Viny could die or they could get themselves in trouble and even land in prison. Nor could they just sit by and take the money and let her have the baby, though Penny'd have been glad to do that if she could get away with it. But she had enough saved up to take her to California and keep her going till she got a job. She was philosophic about it: all good things came to an end eventually, and if you could make anything out of them first, you were ahead of the game. All they could do now was call Viny's brother and let him take her. The moment she was gone, Penny would buy her train ticket.

When Penny told Jewel that Viny would have to leave, she

burst into tears.

"What's the matter with you anyway?" Penny said. "You were all broken up because you couldn't go off to school. Now maybe you can go."

But it didn't seem to make any difference. Viny begged not to go and wouldn't be comforted.

"Don't let them send me away," Viny pleaded as they lay in bed together for their last night before she went away.

"I tried," Jewel said. "Only nobody will listen."

"I can't go away," Viny said, "because of the baby, and because he'll want to see it."

"But when he comes, he'll come to where you are."

"But that's not the right place," Viny said. "Let's run away."

"Where would we go?"

Viny lay silent. Then she said, "Listen, I've got the coyote charm under the pillow. I want you to take it."

"I thought you gave it to Mr. Ferril," Jewel said.

"No, I only showed it to him. I'll give it to you. Here," she said.

Jewel took it and leaned over and kissed her on the cheek. She thought about it and kissed her on the lips.

"Only you have to use it while I'm still here."

"I don't know how."

"Be quiet in there," Penny said at the door. "You can't lie there talking till all hours."

"Take it," Viny whispered, "and go outside after everybody's asleep. Just hold it in your hand and they'll come round."

Jewel was afraid of the dark. She didn't like the idea of going outside in the cold or meeting creatures in the dark. She didn't think anything would bother her, though she couldn't be sure. But she couldn't refuse Viny on her last night.

"They won't harm you," Viny assured her.

"What am I supposed to do?"

"Nothing. Just wait."

Jewel put on her bathrobe and slippers and listened for sounds from the next room. Then she moved to the door, opened and closed it quietly, and slipped down the hall to the front door.

Off in the parlor sat the piano she had neglected for so long, a black rectangle in the shadows, and the Victrola under the gilt-rimmed mirror that caught a gleam of light from somewhere. The floorboards creaked beneath her movements, and she had to pause between steps so as not to wake anybody.

The front door complained when she opened it, and she went out quickly. It was bright outdoors, though the moon wasn't yet quite at the full. She descended the steps, watching for the loose board, and walked out back past the springs. It was a clear night filled with stars. On the ground a light powdering of snow had left a few traces. Carefully, she walked out through the mesquite and yucca trees far enough that the hotel was a large irregular shadow behind her. She let the silence gather around her till she heard only the rustle of night things. And how do you know they are there? she wondered.

But as soon as she thought it, she knew they were gathering in the bushes, circling her. They moved on paws that were quick past stealth, their tails poised and their noses in the air. She felt the wildness behind their eyes and the hunger that went straight to the moon. The hair stood up on the back of her neck. Even though she couldn't see them, she felt the pulse of their blood. She caught her breath and pushed away fear, and let her breath out slowly. They had made a circle around her, and she stood at the center. It was as though she could feel herself entering the space, taking possession of it. She thought of all the people she knew, Jack and Penny, Viny and Mr. Ferril, and she didn't want to be any of them. I want my own experience, she thought. She didn't know how she could get it. But the circle seemed to hold all the shapes of possibility, the ones that entered dreams and those that the daylight brought to form. Dimly, if only she could catch hold of them, were projections of the future. There were hidden things, and things she could almost see, that appeared closer, moving and shaping. She had never known anything like this before, nor had a sense of the future growing out of herself. In a moment it was gone. Even while she tried to capture it, the coyotes had moved away and the night took up its usual sounds.

She walked back toward the dark shadow of the hotel, past the low wall that surrounded the hot springs. A mist rose from the pool and evaporated in the air. The moon glistened on the surface of the water, but if something dark collided with the reflection, she didn't notice. She was intent on a vision of the future. She could see a time when the hotel would be gone without a trace and she'd be out somewhere in the world. She wanted to rejoice because she was certain she would be free. And she wanted to weep as though she were mourning the deaths of all she had known, something of her own death as well. But there was this she had lived. And what would remain of it for her to remember?

The Afternoon of the Pterodactyl

Home from school. He let himself in with his key and slammed the door behind him, then stood listening as the silence put itself together around him. He liked to announce his presence to the house just in case it had been hatching something to surprise him with while he was away.

"Robert, is that you?"

He wasn't expecting his mother to be home that early in the afternoon. He moved through the hallway to the kitchen in search of enlightenment. She had been shopping, and he found her in the midst of emptying the grocery bags that stood atop the kitchen table and in the chair seats. Very likely she had arrived only minutes before him. Onions, tomatoes, a head of lettuce, and a package that looked to be meat lay along the sink. A bottle of wine stood on the table gleaming darkly. He waited for her to emerge from the refrigerator, where she was putting produce into the vegetable bins.

"It was a slow afternoon," she said, coming over to him and giving him a hug. The presence she leaned over him with, something beyond the scent she wore, lingered after she moved away. "So I took off early."

Something else was afoot. He could feel the nervous edge of preparation. "I have to give a report," he said. His news.

"Oh, what about?" Though she was surveying what was left to be put away, she turned in his direction. She could divide her mind like that; he took the available half.

"Something prehistoric."

"Ah," she said. She unwrapped the meat and left it exposed on its bloody paper.

"I have chosen," he said, as though it were a significant matter for her attention, "the pterodactyl."

"I don't know that one," she said.

"It was a reptile," he said, "that became a bird. They've just found a small one—a real link."

"Imagine," she said, selecting a knife and moving to the stool in front of the sink. He'd had her for a small quickened moment, but knew he couldn't hold her for long.

"Their wings are like leather," he said, trying for it. "It's not one of the feathery kind like the apteryx."

"Interesting," she said, subsiding.

"Wings like a bat, but still it's a bird."

Then she said, "Paul's coming for supper."

He might have guessed. Expectancy, like a rush of wings, filled the air, and it seemed, as it so often did, that he had nothing to meet it with. Paul had been there a lot lately. He took a little sharp breath.

"Is it important?"

She looked at him. "One doesn't know those things beforehand," she said in a low voice.

He could never quite read her mood on these occasions: tentative, even apprehensive at times, wanting to put the best light on things: it would be good to have a man in the house. There had been others. They came past him, tousling his hair on their way to her. When he was little, he hung onto their arms, their hands, trying to waylay them in that one spot on some impulse that wouldn't come out in words. Desmond, three back before Paul, used to wrestle him to the floor and pin his chest with his hand and laugh while he kicked and flailed. Once when Robert had gotten free, he ran at Desmond and tried to kick him.

He remembered them all, their faces bobbing foolishly above the horizon like balloons after they had vanished from his life, and sometimes even in his dreams he heard their voices. *Alice*, they called to his mother. *Alice*. For the many voices that spoke her name, it all added up the same thing: *Come Come Come Come*. He heard in that syllable. *I want you, I want* . . . And then there was a voice that didn't want. *Don't ask, don't ever ask me that.* The *Want* voice was stronger, more powerful. Sometimes he was afraid his mother would disappear into it, but that had never happened. The *Didn't Want* voice was sometimes angry, sometimes shrill, sometimes even pleading. And sometimes it came out stronger than the other. But in his dreams he heard them both, and he couldn't tell where they were coming from.

Meanwhile he had stood by, fending off the strangers with an imaginary sword, while his mother hovered at his back. *Only wait, please wait,* he called to her inwardly, not expecting her to listen. Finally they'd all gone through the doorway and into the past, and with a little secret gloat he couldn't help feeling he'd managed it all himself. Only they'd left him a bit ragged; they took something with them, even as they left something behind. A flavor of themselves that both drew and repelled him. The shape of their bodies was different, and their voices went deeper. They could move furniture and repair broken toys. They could throw a ball and hoist him up on their shoulders. They bore another kind of smell that made the living room different. And now Paul had come, and he didn't know what to think.

"I'll call you when it's time," his mother said. "And make sure your room's picked up."

He went off to his room, hung up his jacket in the closet, and emptied his book bag. She was always insisting about his room even though it was his. He arranged his books on the desk, sharpened two pencils in the pencil sharpener Paul had given him, and set them next to his composition book. Paul had given him things: a poster of horses galloping across a field; books about the stars and animals in Africa; various cars for his collection, including a small dump truck that actually dumped. Sometimes it worried him that Paul was in his room this way, but he liked the presents. When his mother worked late, Paul came to take him for hamburgers and a movie afterward. Before that, he'd had to come home to Mrs. Matthews, a tall, raw-boned woman, who lured him to watch the soaps by sharing her peanuts with him. He preferred the outings with Paul. Paul never wrestled with him or made up to him, and he always let him choose the movie they went to.

But even so, he had to remain on guard. Once when it was still dark, a noise had awakened him, and he went to the window in time to see Paul leave the house, pausing to give his mother a kiss that must have used up all her breath. He'd never spoken to his mother about this. She never kissed him on the mouth that way. His mother's other boyfriends had become extinct, but Paul had moved into their lives. He wondered if Paul had any interest in the pterodactyl.

He studied the picture his teacher had copied for him. So this clumsy effort at a bird stood with its leathery wings. Leather. It had come up from running along the ground, carved out a new career for itself. And now stood with the encumbrances of its lizard past. He puzzled over it for a while. Suppose Paul not only stayed but came down the years with them. Suppose that happened. He could barely remember his father, only the empty place he'd left behind. And when someone else stood in it, it seemed even emptier. Robert couldn't stand in that place, though he wanted to, but when someone else stood in it, he had no place at all. Then he felt something at his back that threatened to swallow him up. His mother didn't seem to notice, even when he stood guard, sword bristling.

He wondered if Paul could fill up that place. It would make everything different. Sometimes he hoped that would happen. He liked it when Paul clapped him on the back and said, "Come on, pal, we're going for a night on the town, just the two of us." And when they were together, he liked the way Paul walked up to pay for their food and took out his wallet. He liked Paul's thick hands and the hair on the backs. But he liked to be alone with his mother too. He liked to watch her get ready, when he was the only one there and she sat in front of the mirror and put on her face. He watched her rub the color into her cheeks, then apply eyeliner with a little brush, and her lipstick with another kind of brush. Then she would turn toward him and say, "How do I look?"

Once she'd asked Paul that, and he'd said, "You look good enough to—" He paused, as though he didn't have the right word. Then he said, "No, you look even better than that." And went over and seized her by the waist and whirled her around. Both of them laughed, and Robert laughed too and said, "Do it to me." And Paul had whirled him around.

He sat dully over his notebook. He could describe the pterodactyl, but the picture said more. It gave you strangeness and then held back. The longer he looked, the more the creature drew away from him, clacking its teeth once more over its shoulder before the aeons swallowed it up. He stared blankly at the paper.

At least it got off the ground.

"The pterodactyl," he began, "was a lizard that decided to be something else." He wondered how the idea had struck its brain. He tried to picture it, but it was hard to see how the creature had lived, how it had risen up from being belly down, crawling or perhaps scurrying across the savanna. And why some things remained what they were and never became anything else. The room ticked around him, so that he had to look to see what it was up to. Everything was where it belonged, so it was probably making little noises of satisfaction. It ticked the way he did when he was little and his mother dressed him up to go somewhere: proud of itself. The room made him nervous. If he was to find out anything at all, he'd first have to create a world where the pterodactyl could exist. Impossible to do in his room. He got up from his desk and went down the steps to the basement.

Upstairs he kept his clothes and slept and worked at his desk and watched television, but everything he liked most to do was down below: games and puzzles, his electric train, and his collection of cars. He could lie on the floor and send them wherever he wanted them to go, sometimes shooting off in all directions. He could leave things out until he came back to them—against the rules upstairs. He kept his own country down there with its kings and soldiers: King Boris, whom his countrymen had dubbed "The Avenger." But now Robert cleared everything away: the king, the citizens, the dead soldiers from the battles of the past few months.

First the climate. Tropical—moist and warm. He saw a landscape full of lush grasses and ferns and thick with trees a hundred, even a hundred and fifty feet tall. Conifers. He'd had to look it up. He'd found a good book in the school library that described the world of dinosaurs. A lizardy world. Full of reptiles, all sizes. Huge ones and little ones—some as small as frogs. Warm-blooded and cold-blooded. A reptile world for millions of years, as though nature had just the one idea but lots of ways of bringing it off. And there they were, big and little, eating all the time. He could see the brontosaurus, all seventy feet of it, feeding endlessly on leaves, on ferns and leafy plants, then reaching up into the palmlike cynars, the ginkgo trees, and swallowing down a ton of food a day without even having to chew. He imagined eating all day long, just stoking it in. And doing it slowly, browsing and eating through the hours. He saw their mild eyes as they cropped and breathed and swallowed. Eating the world.

And he saw the meat eaters too, moving fast and striking hard. All around he could hear the tearing of flesh. They were teeth and spikes: sharp cutting teeth as long as ice picks, teeth like meat cleavers with serrated edges, rows and rows of teeth in a head of two thousand grinding teeth. And spikes—spikes for thumbs and spikes for toes, to stab and kick their prey to death. It was different, he supposed, to be this kind of animal that went toward meat instead of vegetable, and made a kill and then slept it off while the stomach took over. He looked up into the maw of the great tyrannosaur: it could swallow a man whole; it could have swallowed him like a piece of candy. Looming over the landscape on the lookout for something to devour, to fuel itself up with its own weight every week.

That was eating all right, in a world full of eating. Chomping and chewing. Little eaters and bigger eaters, with their open jaws and teeth, their clamoring palates.

They had a brain for food. Maybe that's what they were all about. A little brain that took them through aeons and aeons. Plants, animals trying themselves out, trying to be bigger and take up more room than anything else, gobbling everything along the way. Maybe plants were scaly like the reptiles themselves, filled with bumps and prickles, none of them knowing anything about seeds or flowers. And all around this landscape clumped the big reptiles, some sluggish and lazy and slow. Others quick despite their size, running on four legs; or running on two, balancing with a tail. Giants. They rose like mounds from sets of stumps and soared upward into rows of teeth. He could see their big heads swaying like stalks among the trees.

It must have been a noisy place: the ground shaking as they clumped along. Even with the mild ones that fed on plants instead of each other. But the carnivores—watch out! He could see them knocking up the turf, clashing with their tails, tearing with their teeth, rising up on their huge hind legs, and grappling one another with their arms, twisting round their long necks. When they fell, it was an earthquake, shock waves all the way to the edge. Poom! Poom!

From upstairs he heard the doorbell, and his mother's footsteps. If he went up now, he could be there. Paul and his mother wouldn't be able to say anything he didn't know about, though sometimes he caught them talking with their eyes. Their glances leapt over him to some higher meaning. But at least he could talk to Paul before dinner. It used to be he could never think of anything to say when Paul came to dinner, and he made up a bunch of nonsense: "What if a goldfish flew in the air. What if a turtle ate ketchup." Then he would double over with laughter. This was little-kid stuff, and he could tell it drove people crazy after ten minutes or so of excruciating patience. He didn't do it anymore. "How are things at school?" Paul was certain to ask him. He wasn't ready yet to say anything about the pterodactyl.

Perhaps he should have chosen tyrannosaur. He already knew about that. Only the tyrannosaur didn't make it. All the great monsters had had it easy—so the book said. Lolling around in their tropical paradise. But the world changed, and there they were—stopped cold. They'd put on all the armor plate and spikes enough to kill an army, carried around all that meat. Tons of it. Dinosaurs and brontosauruses and triceratops—back then too it was an age of specialization; they couldn't get rid of their heavy equipment. And whatever had hit them, like a comet that shut out the sun, they started dropping to the ground.

Meanwhile—now he was ready to come down to it—there was one smallish sort of lizard who'd spent his career dodging the feet of all the bigger ones. He'd gotten good at it, keeping one step ahead of the stompers and the claws. Lean and quick— just trying to keep from making a long flying curve up to those rows of teeth. Dodging into bushes, scurrying along the ground. If something

200

loomed above and reached down into the shadow that had fallen on you, you couldn't fight back, just kick and wriggle on the way up to the maw and down the hatch. It must have been quite a sight, if you got your head up at all, to stare up at all those rows of teeth. Or maybe there was some guy not even very much bigger who got his hooks into you.

Okay, Robert figured, so you spent all your time running from something after you, trying to find some insect to snap up on the way. And things were getting worse. Especially when the climate started to change and the seas began to rise up onto the continents. Quick, out of the way of everybody looking for a meal. Escape, only escape.

Robert sat back to think. The lizard-not-yet-pterodactyl had him pretty well stumped. He could see into its quick little eye, feel its trembling body. *Caught*, it whispered. *Let me out of here*.

Something must have happened. Only whatever it was didn't just come down out of the sky. That happened only in the movies, and though you clapped, you really didn't believe it. Oh, he did when he was little. But the lizard was desperate. What's the good of being a tiny dinosaur when everybody else is so big? *All those teeth*.

But it hadn't stayed entirely on the ground scurrying around on all fours. Some did; it didn't.

"Let's say," Robert said, sitting up. "Let's say it was an ordinary afternoon. Creatures chewing or snoozing or looking for food. The swamp diver had just come up. A creature who didn't know if it wanted to be on land or in the water. Sitting there on a rock. Sometimes she likes to come up out of the swamp and dry off once in a while. And there's a lizard running, a bigger dinosaur slashing at his heels.

"Closer it comes, and closer. And just when it's about to reach down and scoop up its dinner, the little lizard reaches up with its arms and grabs onto branches and pulls itself up until you can't see it in the foliage.

"The swamp diver saw it all," Robert went on. "Afterward, when the lizard appeared, still shaking from its narrow escape, it told him, 'You've got something there—that's a trick to keep in your bag.'

201

"The Lizard didn't know exactly what it had done—it had to think about it." Robert paused to do the same. "But it could feel in its arms the way it went swinging up. And it remembered, and kept on doing that and kept on." After a while, Robert thought, even that would get old. "Then it got another idea when something came after it fast. It started leaping from one branch to another."

"That's it," Robert said, and held his nose and let himself fall backward. It did it until it was written across its brain: Escape. That way it could escape. Like the first time you ride a bicycle. When you know something you didn't know before, only you don't know what it is. If you did something often enough, then maybe it became a part of you. A whole new idea. The little creature stood before him. He was looking into its eye, but the eye was focusing on something beyond. It wasn't food it wanted. It wanted something else, wanted it terribly—beyond anything.

"What do you want?" Robert asked it. "You get to escape, don't you?"

But it only shook its head.

It wasn't enough, not for this lizard. Things were getting worse and worse. The climate getting colder, seas still rising over the land. Hunger everywhere, till the skies were a single roar. Punctuated only by the crash of a great body to the ground. Poom! Poom! Like a mountain falling over. Robert had never seen such carnage. Death, death, death. A death-glutted landscape.

The lizard didn't know where to turn. It spent most of its time leaping from one branch to another, afraid to be on the ground. It would have been glad to leave the ground altogether, if only it knew how. Then somehow a little gleam entered its head, moving around in the dark. All dark but for the little gleam. And while the aeons passed and the dinosaurs crashed to the ground or sank into the swamps . . .

"Dinner," Robert heard his mother call down into the basement.

Wait, he wanted to say. Wait, I haven't done yet. But he knew they wouldn't let him delay dinner. And he was getting hungry. He roused himself and went upstairs to wash his hands. The smell of roast hung in the air, and when he came into the dining room he saw everything was ready. Paul was sitting at the table carving the meat. The bottle of wine had been opened and their two glasses had been filled, two bulbs of ruby red. He noticed that a third had been set at his place with a small amount in it. "Hello, Robert," Paul said. "Come and join us."

Robert stood for a moment watching as his mother brought the salad to the table and set it down. Then she sat down, and both she and Paul looked at him expectantly.

Behind him the pterodactyl looked down at the new growths on its arms and beat its leather wings. It was such a struggle, and it wasn't even a bird yet, not really—just one more creature that tried itself out along the way. And even the birds still had to escape from one another. Only sometimes you could escape.

Paul had put a piece of meat on his plate, and his mother was helping him to vegetables. He pulled out the chair to sit down. He couldn't disappoint them.

"You must be hungry," his mother said. "Did you finish your report?"

"No, not quite," he said, and he looked from one to the other as though, like the little lizard, he was trying to reach for a new idea.

The Blind Musician

When he appeared at the Placido Recreation Center, from outside in that open, sun-swept, if dusty, afternoon came a chorus of voices, "It's Frank," "Hey, Frankie." "Hola, Frankie." And the kids on the steps made way for him, holding open the screen door, as though for a celebrity, while Carlos, the sneaky boy who made trouble and blamed it all on others, whom she'd banished outside once and for all, at least for that day, guided him to a bench at one of the long tables. The helper now, who'd earned or slid his way past reprimand, he gave her a smirk, while she took in the stranger. A formidable man, with his large torso and big hands, his black western shirt with its trim of pearl buttons—movie star or gangster?—giving him rather a formal presence as he took possession of a table scattered with games and coloring books. Though his dark glasses made his expression opaque, she caught under the fringe of mustache lips full and soft, almost feminine, that made his face seem exposed, what with its scattering of dark pockmarks, likely from some childhood disease.

She found herself staring at him, not wanting to speak. She'd never been confronted by a blind man before, certainly not in such a compelling shape, and the ordinary formulas of sociability fell away as so many small pieces of shattered glass.

"I was down in my old haunts," he said, in a voice soft but with an inflection that could have been taken as casual insolence. "Thought I'd drop by and see who was around."

Carlos lolled against the wall, one leg bent behind him, waiting perhaps to see if she would tell him to leave, making a game of it, while the other kids pressed against the screen that had already begun to push in lumpily with their hands. "Why don't you come inside?" she said, turning toward them. They laughed and whispered in Spanish but kept where they were. If they came in, it would be in their own good time, the way a cat enters a doorway. She knew this and also that they would not protect her from having to make response to the newcomer.

The blind man reached into his pocket for cigarettes, strictly against the rules, and, tongue-tied, she watched him negotiate the flame of his cigarette lighter toward the end of the cigarette. "Cipriano still work here?"

"He takes the kids to the ballpark," she said, relieved that so ready an explanation fell to tongue. There were only herself and her supervisor, Mrs. Santiago, just now off purchasing supplies, whose confident authority could deal with any such threats and infractions of rules. She should have been there.

"But pardon my bad manners," he said. "I'm Frankie Lucero," and he extended his hand for her to shake. She put forward a hesitating hand of her own, as though it might be lost in his. Even his name seemed too familiar or slight to contain him.

"Caroline Nolan," she told him, though it was Carrie at home, and the kids there alternately called her La Carita, the dear little one, though she had to wonder if it was an ironic commentary on their conspiracies against her. Or else they called her by names that meant *flame, the fiery one*, because of her red hair and flashes of temper when they teased her too much.

"Ah, so you're the Nolan girl," he said.

"You know me?" she said. His name she dredged up now, from some piece of violence and outrage whose echoes circled briefly through the town and the high school corridors before being displaced by another, more current piece of notoriety. But there was no such reason for him to know her. She felt a small rush of alarm, as though she'd been caught at some secret guilt.

"Hear your father's managing the Longhorn, trying to make it into a fancy place." He gave a little laugh that could have been a commentary on the futility of the undertaking. Was that how he knew her? With something of the mockery intended. for her father?

It had been an old bar and dance hall where only Mexicans came to dance, but now it had been bought out by those who were bent on making a killing off vacationing Texans. A piece of local color. As manager, her father had gone on to what promised to be another of his doomed employments. His stock in the family never held very high, and it was only through a series of large threats and small brutalities, especially when he had a few drinks under his belt, that he could maintain it. It was her mother who kept up the slender bridge to respectability by working part-time as a physician's receptionist.

The ash on Frankie's cigarette had dropped to the floor, and Carrie got one of the cans they used to hold water for paints and gave it to him. If Mrs. Santiago turned up, the door would hardly have closed behind her before she said, "You know smoking isn't allowed," and put him in his place. It was a lapse of certainty, unprovided by youth, and inexperience that gave him an opening—she knew this, knew also she was being held responsible for all that occurred there. It unnerved her as she struggled to find a ground from which she could speak something out and make it stick. But she was in a place she didn't belong, her summer job owing to the intercession of her father's boss. The kids knew they could ignore her, and she felt deprived of moral force.

Carlos had moved to one of the chairs at the table, as though each word that passed between these two people was too important to let slip away. One of the kids outside ventured in, then another, till, except for the ball team, more kids surrounded Frankie than had ever come inside for the games and projects. Only two of the girls ventured in, and they stood grinning at each other, as though from their own daring.

"When did you come back, Frankie?" one of the kids asked. "I've forgotten," Frankie said, shaking his head. "Time," he said, "who thinks of that? Sand down a rat hole, water down the creek," he said, with a small turn of his hand, letting it all go. "Every day with its own color, some burnt at the edges. I don't look at the calendars anymore. I don't think of dates." He subsided into silence. "It takes a while to get used to being a blind man."

"You did some driving, Frankie," another of the boys said admiringly.

"Screw it," he said. "I've done lots of things that never did me any good." A wraith of smoke circled him.

"Hey, Frankie, give me a cigarette."

"Get lost," he said. "You think I'm such a big man?" he said, turning in the direction of the voice. "Only one thing makes me big," he murmured, turning away, "and it made all the difference." They still hung there, as though he might yet utter the saving word that would let them past his disdain to claim their kinship.

"Where's your guitar, Frankie?"

"Getting a little rest. Now quit pestering."

Finally the kids trooped out: he'd let them down, somehow. They thought perhaps they had something to show off. Only Carlos remained behind, whether out of some obscure loyalty or simply to annoy.

"You play the guitar?" Carrie said, with a quickening of interest.

"Yeah," he said. "I had lots of time on my hands."

"What do you play?" she said, emboldened by the fact. Even the minor key of his answers didn't put her off. She'd have liked to play something. She, too, had time, a crushing weight of it that delivered one day after another to the same leaden inertia. She didn't know what to do with time. There were odd moments when snatches of music came into her head that spoke so deeply to something unspoken she seemed almost on the edge of some vital recognition. They merely teased her and evaporated. She didn't know where they came from, nor could she identify them. They were nothing of what she heard on TV or what the kids at school listened to.

"Just about anything," he said. "Let me hear a tune twice and I can play it. Whatever's in the air I can catch ahold of it. Buddy Holly, Aretha Franklin—Doc Watson, who's blind like me. All the ones that come and go. Old stuff, new stuff. Folk songs, what the cowboys sang to keep the cattle quiet. I like those—" He paused. "But mostly I make my own music."

"Oh,"she said. And what sort of music would it be? Something ominous and dark as the man himself? Black and blue. Like the rumble from dark underground craters. A tumble of rocks. Exploding into smoke and noise. Only that? An unbearable shriek and scraping that would make her put her hands over her ears? Nothing soft? Soft as his own lips, or the insolence in his voice. In that instant she knew she had to hear it.

"Would you bring your guitar?" she said. "And come and play here?" She was caught up short by her own suggestion. Clearly, she had no business to do it. But why not? she defended herself, as she bumped around for justification. The kids would love it, she told him. And even thought it might lure them to coming there, even as his presence seemed to draw them suddenly out of the secret kid places into which they disappeared.

"You think so?" he said.

"Oh yes," she assured him. Her mind spun ahead with the thought of an event that promised to lift a day off its stultifying plane, like waking to find your hovel turned into a palace. More often than not the kids came, looked with a dull eye over the array of games and puzzles, gave a little shrug, and left with a clatter of the screen door. The games lay about like things discarded. Checkers and Chinese checkers, Parcheesi and Monopoly, decks of cards. Downtown the video games offered a moment's distraction. Or if they were old enough, the entertainment at the bars. They had to wait for that, content meanwhile with the TV.

"I'm not sure you'd want to hear me play," he said.

"Why not?"

"Once I played," he said, "and the coyotes set up such a howl, they nearly wakened the dead."

She didn't laugh.

"Then the neighborhood dogs tore each other to pieces. After they'd got the cats and the possums. I figured I'd better quit playing," he said, "or I'd have the whole town after me."

She was beginning to catch his style. It led her on—all she could think to say was, "I'd really like to hear!' And she shouldn't have done it.

Frankie seemed to consider. "Well, I might just do that," he said. "I don't mind a little excitement now and then."

She felt a little line of sweat break out just beneath her hairline.

She had to keep this job, had to have the money. "Well,"

208

Frankie said again, pushing back the chair, taking up his cane, "it's time for me to hump along." Carlos moved in at once to guide him out. "Good to know you, Carrie," he said. "Be seeing you."

He left then, and she watched from the doorway as he felt his way along like an animal in a tunnel, until he disappeared past the broken tree on the other side of the street.

She took Frankie Lucero home that day as a perplexity that worried at her, but that, at least, occupied her mind. She had gotten on to another of her obsessions. They came to her and spiraled in her mind, and she was unable to get rid of them. The way certain people ate. How they chewed and swallowed, what they did when they got grease on their hands or got a spot on their shirts. Or the way people walked. She found herself in a constant stare, at the movements of thighs, the insinuations of hips and buttocks, the angle toes turned in or out. Joggers and runners bounding along or trimming their steps into allotments, springing up light and quick, or thunking along. She looked for a key that unlocked their character or fate. The puzzle nagged at her. The cripple, twisted up into himself, rocking along. Or the long-striding, loose-limbed man she crossed the street with, who seemed to walk into the future without looking both ways. He left her afraid for him. And for the little hobbling old woman whose head jerked on a thin stalk, who didn't have the eyesight to make any movement that didn't terrify her. And had they all agreed on what the world was as they walked into the moment? Did they move on something other than the stretch of an unvarying boredom? Or was it only she stranded there without a clue?

It was always the same. It didn't matter, when she came home, whether there was chicken or spaghetti for supper; it all came with the same insipid flavor, like ancient leftovers. But Frankie gave her preoccupations a different cast.

"I couldn't get the sewing machine to work," her mother said, by way of greeting. Carrie shrugged it aside. "I wanted to get that hem fixed. Now it'll have to wait. They can't fix the machine this week. They make these things to break down." Her mother seethed over such frustrations.

She came home to find some part of life had always broken down, in need of repair, or turned to disappointment. A tooth hurt, the carburetor had gone bad, something her mother had ordered hadn't come or came in the wrong size, the wrong color. These complaints formed a counterpoint with her father's—about the cook and the waitresses, and how the help you got these days didn't want to put out. And that brought in the school system and the government. Everybody had his hand in the till, trying to get something for nothing. The high school kids wanted big bucks but didn't want to work—no wonder they sold drugs or stole and went after each other with knives and guns. And none of them knew how to spell. When he was in school he was the champion speller in the class.

None of it was of the least importance. She could see her father was a failure, trying to hold onto his shaky status with Clark, who owned this new venture, as well as a hotel and a bar, who had both the largesse and the narrow shrewdness that came with the smell of profit, and who would toss her father aside like old rags and put someone else in his place at the flick of an eyelash. The other businessmen knew it as well, but they condescended to drink with her father, listen to his dirty stories—you ought to hear that Nolan, he's got a slew of 'em—argue town politics, all the time speculating among themselves about when old Nolan would get the ax. She could see the rage that burned beneath her mother's stolid resignation and the banality that ruled the household as the only means of keeping the world at bay. These things she'd always known, for they reached down into the well of her childhood. She hadn't forgotten them. It was as though she looked at the world from underneath its skirts, or from the roots of trees. Out of the curse of some fatal lucidity, she couldn't forget what she knew—

—although she was supposed to. She'd have preferred to forget everything, herself into the bargain, do what everybody else did, but she couldn't. What was there to live for? Sometimes she amused herself by looking in glamour magazines at advertisements for clothes, trying to imagine herself into the life that went with them, but she couldn't make them fit. At times she wondered if she were really human. The most she could imagine was climbing a mountain, standing on a peak above the world, and looking at cliffs and peaks rolling away beyond her, standing there in complete silence. But what she would do then except jump off she had no idea.

She was waiting for Frankie to come back, no doubt like the kids herself, trapped in some unwarranted expectation. Something to break up the monotony of beads and shells and pieces of leather; picture books of plants and animals and birds of the Southwest, all lying there like so much inert matter. She tried to invest these things with interest, convince the girls to make bracelets out of shells or necklaces of beads. But, smiling, they shook their heads—it wasn't what they wanted to do. But what did they want? She put out jars of paints, red orange blue violet, and hoped they would pick up the brushes and take her to some fresh excitement. Instead she experienced a certain dismay that they wanted to color in the coloring books meant for the younger children. "You can draw your own pictures," she invited them, showing them paper and crayons, but the blank paper seemed to intimidate them.

Then one afternoon Frankie appeared again.

"I'd hoped you'd bring your guitar," she said, when she saw he'd come without it.

"Broke a string," he said. "My last one. I ordered some more—they'll be coming any moment." She wondered if that was an excuse, whether he'd really bring his guitar.

"Yeah," he said, "I was playing so hard, I like to broke myself in two." He laughed soundlessly.

She could almost see and hear the voice hurled into song. The soft lips opening and making a cave to enter that was a darkness without a bottom. That's what she saw now. For finally she had asked Mrs. Santiago, "Do you know anything about Frankie Lucero?"

The wonderfully smooth skin of Mrs. Santiago's face, that almost translucent softness ripening toward some final sweetness, darkened with her thought. "Don't remind me," she said. "He was such a mischievous boy—always in trouble." And she poured out a litany of his excesses. How he'd taken to drugs, gotten in with dealers in El Paso. Suspected of robbery, though it hadn't been proved. A homicide, though it had to do with others. Mrs. Santiago knew his mother, whose life had turned to dust and ashes. She'd begged him to join the army. "He shouldn't be here," Mrs. Santiago concluded. "It's not good for the kids to see we let him come. The next time he bothers you, you tell me."

But there he was again, in the same shirt with the pearl buttons, presenting a challenge, perhaps defying explanation, pushing aside the warnings she should have relied on. And if he'd come because of her, she had unwittingly invited him. Now she was being asked to betray him and to take the consequences if she didn't. Since his first visit she had been brooding over a question, and now she put it in front of him. "How do you make up your own music?" she wanted to know.

"No particular way," he said, with a little shrug. "You just make it up as you go along, with whatever you've got." He paused. "Even if it's garbage, even if it's old tires and pieces of dead meat, and somebody's cancer—even if it's the worst things you can think of."

"Who would listen?" she said. She meant no insult.

"You think I like being what I am," he said. "You think I'm bragging. You don't know anything. I'll bet you're still a virgin."

She felt her chest tighten. "What would that prove?"

"I'll tell you," he said. "I'll tell you there are things that just sweep you up before you know what to do with them. They drop you over the cliff—that's how it happens." He was tapping the table erratically. "But now at least I can play."

A certain dark pride seemed to flicker in him. He wouldn't play just for anybody, she could tell that. She didn't think he'd play for her, but she was desperate to hear him.

"People get the wrong idea," he said. "They think you can get it by boozing it up and screwing and throwing rocks and getting high. Drugs and screwing. I'll bet you do that, too."

He confused her, the way he could say one thing one moment and contradict himself the next. Actually, she kept pretty much to herself—the boys seemed afraid of her, and the girls talked boy stuff. Sometimes she went to dances, got out on the floor and threw her arms and legs around. It didn't matter who you danced with, or if you danced with anybody. She didn't try to defend herself. "I just want to hear you play," she said.

He gave a chuckle. "In that case . . ." he said. "Only I can't do it here. I'll give you a call sometime, when I get the urge."

She told him that if she wasn't home not to leave a message but to call her back. She knew she'd have to pretend it was somebody else and find some reason to be gone, say she was going off to see a film. Mrs. Santiago fortunately had been out for lunch, so she didn't have to say anything to her when she came back. And for a week or so, his promise was the secret thing she carried around, what she took home from work and mooned over when she did the dishes.

It didn't occur to her that her mother would have any idea Frankie would be calling her. Not till she sprang it on her. "That Lucero fellow called," she said. "What nerve! Mrs. Santiago told me he'd been pestering you. She wanted to warn me." She looked at Carrie, as though she was a creature bereft of sense. "One of the kids told Mrs. Santiago he'd been hanging around. She feels responsible. And why didn't you say something? I told him if he called again I'd call the police."

She was caught short, with nothing to say.

"That's all they need, those Mexicans, they're bad enough as it is without some ex-con to give them ideas. I want you to tell me if it ever happens again."

So it was finished. She wouldn't hear Frankie play, but he would continue in her life as an absence, there to haunt her. Would she ever know what it was she hoped to find, in that dark thing, so endlessly dark that kept pulsing inside? She knew it only as some formless shape with a little flickering incandescence at the center that kept at her. Frankie might have reached it, come to know it, at least for himself—enough that he could look back at her with whatever he could manage of pity or scorn. As her mother cast her eye in her direction, that *it* grew white and fiery, but whether, as she stood among the accused, what crossed her vision was the glare of a spotlight or the flashing up of that incandescence, she couldn't say. No words would take her there, but she was suddenly clear about what it meant to stumble into blindness and then take up the guitar.

Venus Rising

The presence of his wife lingered at the edge of Jacoby's consciousness as potently as the surroundings announced her absence. When he came home in the evenings now, the house was not only dark from the outside, but filled with darkness when he entered. He let himself in like a man who might be taken by surprise and prowled through the rooms as though he were trying catch a thief in the act of robbing him. When he was alone in the house, the least noise startled him, and he would leave off what he was doing and listen with strained concentration. At times his mind began to wander, and he would begin to hear bits of nonsense, until he shook his head and brought himself back to the task at hand. Even so, a persistent hum followed at his ear, like a voice speaking below the level of intelligibility. Sometimes, though, he heard words spoken as if she were there speaking directly to him. At these moments, he would turn sharply as if to catch sight of her and then, in the pose of utmost stillness, listen again, straining to catch the sound of her voice.

This attitude was new to him. He was a man who heard what he wanted to hear and did as he pleased, who was galled by any suggestion to the contrary, saw it as an accusation of some lapse on his part, some mistake or failure. When his wife was alive, he frequently left her words hanging in the air as though she'd spoken them to herself or the cat or the chair he sat in. Very likely she was used to this, for she seldom said, "Did you hear me?" or gave any sign that she expected an answer. Now it seemed as though her utterances had left their vibrations still hanging in the air, a sort of ghost speech that, given just the right atmosphere, was stirred into sound again. For the most part, these were trivial things: "I don't have any place for my cookbooks," or "There's hardly any room in the garage any more," or "We've run out of bird seed."

Were she there he would have shrugged them off with the same annoyance he had always felt. Now he waited to hear even such trivialities and went about slamming cupboard doors and clattering dishes and silverware when several days went by and nothing came. Although he had been alone for some months now, he had no desire to break his solitude. From his work as manager of his father's metal shop, he came directly home despite the insistence of his partner and the other fellows he used to stop with for a drink on the way home. After hunting through the rooms, he showered away the grime of work, ate hastily standing up, then read the paper, drank a couple of beers and went to bed. He slept as blankly as an empty sky. Weekends he watched football on television and sometimes a late-night movie.

The summer had come and gone. As he worked into the fall, a busy time of year, he was aware one day that the leaves had fallen and the meadows were covered with tow-colored grass that looked as fine as hair. The bare trees webbed the neutral sky, and it occurred to him that it was all over for another year. "The color must be glorious in the hills just now," her voice spoke up and reminded him. He was standing at the window looking into the yard. A few brown leaves still clung to the oak, and the ground was covered with maple leaves. The scarred stump of the plum tree he'd cut down stood in the middle of a bare space. "You know that's not true," he said irritably. "You know better than that. The leaves are over." He looked back into the living room, blinking into the silence. He had to hold himself in: there was a kind of stupidity even in the workings of memory, and what did come back to him was completely out of kilter. Every year she'd said the same old thing. And he was assaulted by a sudden anger that her presence should linger in the dullness of repetition, in the things that had worn grooves in his hearing during the twenty-odd years of their marriage. He moved restlessly from one room to another, finally pausing again at the window.

He had cut down the plum tree one autumn in a fit of resentment over the stench of rotten fruit on the ground and the hordes of wasps hanging over it. His wife had been aghast when she'd come home and found what he'd done.

"I did all the jam from that tree," she protested. "Those plums made the best jam."

"You can just as well buy plums in the store, for all the trouble that tree gives us. Stinks up the whole neighborhood." He'd made a concession this time to nuisance, for ordinarily he liked the feeling that nature was giving him something for nothing, even though, as with the jam, you had to put your time and sugar into it.

"It wouldn't be the same," she said grimly.

The curse of woman was not, he thought, in the sweat she brought to a man's brow, but in her logic.

"All the jars I used to give at Christmas."

"It wouldn't hurt you to buy the damned fruit."

She didn't though. Since the tree was gone, she gave up any of its suggestions. He remembered how one morning she'd been surprised by the blossoms. The tree had come out during the night and when she'd come downstairs, it was in full bloom. "I didn't even know it was there," she exclaimed. "It was like a vision."

Now the sky was dark with the approach of coming rain. "If you look," her voice said to him, "you can see Venus rising." In a passion of irritation, he went into the kitchen and pulled out another beer, set it aside and went into the bedroom.

He knew that he should go through the closets and get rid of her things. But each time he made an effort to begin, the intention flagged, and he left everything as it was. He opened the door, looked at her clothes hanging limp and motionless. He'd found it difficult to touch her things, to put his hands on stockings or lingerie, to gather up her dresses. The softness, the flimsiness of the materials almost repelled him, and the bottles of her toilet water had always aroused in him something both insidious and questionable. For some reason, he ran his hand down a pink satiny lounging robe, then a shirt of some velvety material. He thought of her wearing the different textures next to her skin, of the feeling of them moving against her breasts and thighs.

He went into the bathroom and for some reason ran the water for a tub, stripped off his clothes and got in. He never took baths, preferring his two daily showers, but it felt good to lean back and soak. He closed his eyes. Often when they were younger, she used to step naked from the bath, her skin fresh and glowing, and come forward to where he was, moving in a slow, teasing way, lifting a shoulder, giving a turn to her hip, looking at him with half-lidded eyes. Perhaps she was inviting him to view her, to see what suggestions she aroused and let her know what she was in his eyes. Then she would exaggerate her movements, and finally, turn to the mirror and stare critically at her body and her face, then dress, taking up one piece of clothing at a time.

Usually he kissed her and ran his hand over her back, then went on to whatever he was doing. He didn't care to make love to her just then, to break in upon the afternoon or the evening with something that would powerfully distract him. For she seemed to be imposing herself on him in a way he wasn't clear about, and though he never said as much to himself, just below the surface lived the doubt that this display of her physical nature entitled her to respect. He preferred to discover the female form next to him in bed in the early morning, where it had arrived under the cover of darkness. Then, his own energy awake and primed, he would summon his wife from sleep, nudging and caressing her until she responded, not quite fully awake. He shaped her response until she seemed ready and yielding, then entered her. Afterwards she got up and made coffee, fried eggs and bacon. Washed, dressed, satisfied, he attacked his breakfast hungrily while she sat over a cup of coffee—she never ate the first thing in the morning—watching him as though he were satisfying her hunger as well.

He was thinking of her now as he lay against the porcelain of the tub, seeing her in her younger years before she allowed herself to get fat and he'd awakened her mornings only if felt hard-pressed. It seemed that he could feel her presence more strongly than usual, that if he opened his eyes he would find her image wavering before him. He could see her clearly, her small well-shaped breasts, her slender hips, her full thighs. He didn't dare open his eyes for fear her image would leave him. He felt an almost overpowering desire to reach out and touch her, followed by the hope that she might extend her hand. But as he waited, her outline began to fade, and when he opened his eyes, he sat looking into the steam from the water. He sat without moving, allowing himself to drift back slowly.

Then he emerged from the bathtub, toweled himself down and went into the bedroom for clean undershirt and shorts. He caught a reflection of himself in the mirror, looking as though he'd surprised himself. He stood for a long moment in front of her closet, took out the pink lounging robe and put it on. A strange sensation overtook him, one he couldn't identify. He took it off and put it back on the hanger.

That morning he measured the space where a shelf could go in the kitchen, went down to the lumber yard and bought a length of cherry board that would show a nice grain when it was varnished. Home again, he cut it into lengths, carefully dadoed the sides, fit it together and applied a coat of varnish. It had been a long time since he'd worked with wood. In his youth he'd made furniture, and for a time he worked as a carpenter, finishing interiors for tract homes. But when his father's partner left, he went into the business—it would ultimately be his. He stamped out parts to order, did some body work on farm vehicles. When they'd bought the house, he had no interest in doing any carpentry, though his wife at first had asked for a broom closet, some shelves. They'd never got around to those things—he'd always been too busy. Now though, when he picked up his tools, they felt familiar in his hands. After the varnish had dried, he sanded down the shelves and gave them another coat. He wanted the varnish to have a soft glow, so after the second coat was hard, he spent a number of hours during the evenings after work sanding the wood and giving it a final rubbing of pumice.

On the weekend he fastened the shelves to the wall just under a narrow cabinet at the side of the stove, and gathering together the stack of cookbooks she'd kept on a chair on the back porch, he arranged them alphabetically by author along the top shelf. On the other, he placed a small copper kettle that had belonged to her grandmother and an old coffee grinder. He felt a sensation at the back of his neck, as though someone had been staring at him, and when he turned his head, he was certain that she was standing just inside the doorway.

He stood still for a moment to lure her back by his silence, his receptiveness. He felt dizzy and had to lean against the counter.

If she were indeed watching him, looking at him, she'd come back for her bookshelf. He wondered what she would think of a broom closet. He sketched out a simple drawing for it, measured the space, considered the proportions, and on the weekend went down and bought lumber, also cherry wood, and brass hinges. The project took longer, what with cutting the boards, gluing the widths, shaping the inside of the door so it would fit the opening nicely, finishing the edges. He worked evenings varnishing and sanding, the hours passing until, exhausted, he fell into bed. But he couldn't sleep. He lay awake, his mind busy with the project. In the shop his work grew mechanical. He waited for the end of the day to go home and finish the broom closet. He did not dare ask whether she would come, whether it would make a difference.

But when he put it in, he didn't have the sense of her standing there as he'd had before, and when he turned he had no particular sense of her image. He stood there for some moments admiring the wood, then surveyed the kitchen. It was a dark kitchen, made darker now by the fine wood of the shelves and broom closet. She'd once given the walls a coat of paint, but even that had grown dingy from the layers of grease and dust built up over the years. And the cabinets were nicked and scarred with wear. A dingy place. It would take him the whole winter to replace the cabinets, put in a new sink and paint all the open surfaces. As he stood there thinking of the task, he felt a sensation in his shoulders as though someone had touched him. He didn't turn around, he simply stood trying to keep hold of the sensation. Then he put his fingers up to test it.

He didn't hear her voice any longer, but it was as though they kept up a continual conversation. He kept her informed of his progress. "After I get the measuring done, I'll order the wood. All cherry," he promised her. "It'll have a glow, I tell you." He would start in with the cabinet that would hold the sink, do the ones above and beside it, then work to those over the stove. At first it was hard for him to work, the garage was so cluttered with junk he'd collected and stored over the years. She'd complained about that. There was hardly room for the car; it was one of the first things he'd heard her say when he was there alone. Piled on the floor, crowded against the wall was all manner of scrap iron, along with outdated farm machines he had bought at auctions and things he'd saved out of habit—jars of bent nails and used spikes, old spark plugs, rags and other odds and ends. He'd never known exactly what he would do with these. At one point, after an argument with his father, he thought of opening his own shop, doing something with wrought iron, painting the old separators and cider-making machines and selling them for planters and other decorative ends. He never launched into any of these schemes, but neither could he be persuaded to get rid of the stuff. You never knew when something might come in handy. He associated himself with this part of the house. The bathroom he used as a necessity; the bedroom he occupied as an uneasy interloper, put off by the scalloped curtains, the flowered bedspread; in the dining room he was rewarded for having provided. The garage was his.

His wife, at one point, had suggested that they make the garage into a sewing room that they could also use as a guest room, since they never had any room when her brother's family came to visit. But he wouldn't hear of it. As long as the stuff was there, it held the promise that he might do something with it. But if he cleared it out, he lost dominion forever to curtains and carpets and something that had always made him uncomfortable in his own estate.

Now he moved some of the old machines outside. If he wanted any real space, he'd have to clear it away in several truckloads, but he'd find time for that later. He made what space he could for the lumber, moved his saw to a better location, parked the car out front. He worked, measuring and sawing and gluing and assembling. He took some days off work to buy materials and to plan the work. He became so absorbed in what he was doing that he would discover half the night had passed, and if he were to function at all he'd better get a few hours' sleep.

One night, as he ended his labors by sitting at the table drinking a beer, he got up and took one of his wife's cookbooks from the shelf. He leafed idly through it, considering roasts and stews, cakes and pies. The elaboration of food had never been of interest to him, though there were certain things he loved: corn on the cob, a good beefsteak tomato, and chicken noodles. He hadn't asked much of his wife in that respect; in fact, he had a suspicion of unfamiliar dishes, what might be lurking under the surface. Now it occurred to him to wonder over the many ways a dish could be prepared. Had she, even on occasion, made herself little delicacies? He saw her sitting over a dish of mushrooms stuffed with crab meat. He wondered if she'd looked forward to his absence on certain evenings as a time she might indulge in a bit of culinary infidelity. As a matter of curiosity, he took down some of the other books, read about curries and stir fries. It must have been difficult cooking such things only for herself. Had she had company? One of the neighbor women? If it had been a man, he could imagine his coming, the smell of cooking in the air, of his being called to the table, tasting, looking at her appreciatively. And then—but it occurred to him that there had never been any unusual odor of spice in the air, nothing different when he entered the house. Yet, there they were, a whole shelf of cookbooks that he had rescued from a precarious stack on the back porch. Perhaps she'd sat here as he was doing now, turning pages, dreaming over recipes, imagining whole feasts.

And what would he do in the kitchen once he'd finished it? All this labor after she was no longer there to benefit. He thought of those ceremonies performed for the dead, where the relatives put out plates of food. In some way he felt he had done all of this work for her, but to what end and purpose? He was a practical man and usually he'd asked such questions before he undertook any project. Or if the answers didn't satisfy him, the project didn't go. This time he had been carried along, planning, figuring, building and replacing without the slightest consideration of cost, impelled by some intuition that moved in the direction of a sensation he occasionally caught. Brought here to the glowing wood and gleaming tile and fresh paint that now seemed an ironic comment on his efforts. Suppose he stood in front of the stove and filled the kitchen with the smell of exotic dishes, would it make any difference? He felt stunned by the wall separating the living from the dead. Yet he felt compelled to woo back his wife by leaning into all the unrealized possibilities that had lived in her words, her gestures, all that had been spoken or left unspoken over the years.

It was winter when the kitchen was finished. The cherry

wood glowed over the sink; new tile gleamed on the floor. He'd replaced stove and refrigerator. Curiously, he felt no expectation of her presence, as though all his labor had been preparation for something more. He stood looking out over the sink into the backyard where the ground was covered with snow. It was quiet and the bare trees stood against the pale sky, tinged with rose above the setting sun.

"Feed the birds," he heard her say. She'd always fed the birds. She'd spent half a fortune on bird seed during the months snow was on the ground.

"Lots of birds die because of the snow," she used to say. "They can't find food."

"Hell, they've been doing it since before the bird feeder was invented," he countered, wondering why it was always women who took on the things that nature did just as well by herself.

She had no answer for that, but she continued to feed the birds, watching their activities as she stood over the sink washing dishes. Sometimes she would pause and go for the binoculars and her bird book. Cardinals and blue jays were all over the place, and various kinds of sparrows. She had a great fondness for woodpeckers.

She'd had a bird feeder attached to one of the trees, but he didn't see it out there now. She'd put it up herself. Perhaps it had fallen and if he looked he was likely to find it buried under leaves and snow. He left the kitchen and went down to the garage and surveyed the piles of rusted parts and old iron, the salvage of years, the things he'd hung onto in a fierce, saving way. The effort it would take to clear the place out depressed him, though there was no reason why he should bother. *It's piled up to the ceiling*, a voice said, perhaps his own thought. A load or a piece at a time he'd added it to it, and now it sat in a random collection giving out its peculiar smell of old metal and rust.

You've never made anything out of it came the voice in his head. It was quite true. He wondered what he'd had in mind all these years. He had an overwhelming desire to be rid of it. He backed up the truck as far as it would go and spent the next few hours heaving it full of junk. The first thing next morning, a Sunday, he drove it to the dump. The work got to his back, and he had to leave off for several days. He chafed with impatience. He wanted space, wanted the evidence of space under all the clutter.

At one point he came to a pile of iron rods and poles lying on the floor. He picked up several, started to throw them into the truck, and put them down again. He surveyed them thoughtfully, struck by a sudden inspiration. That afternoon he took one of the poles, cut various rods, welded them together until he had a tree with a number of branches, a spike welded at the top. Then, heating the rods he attached large nails all over the metal branches. He want outside and with a snow shovel cleared away the snow from the stump of the old plum tree. Then he attached an extension cord to his drill, took it outside, and bored a hole in the center of the stump.

His new creation was too heavy to stand alone, so after clearing away the snow, he used a strip of metal to encircle the stump, pounding it into the hard ground, and in this mold he poured cement and set in the iron pole. Against the bare trees it looked quite barbarous, the iron spike sticking up, the nails bristling around it. He surveyed it with wonder that he had made it, that he'd such a thought. For the time being, he left the rest of the garage undone as though he'd now accomplished whatever had been important.

For several days he looked at the iron tree from the kitchen window. It took possession of the space around it, a tree of thorns, assured that nothing would come near it. He thought of his wife going out to put seed in the bird feeder that had once been in the tree. He had forgotten the bird feeder. He thought of going out and looking for it, but he hadn't thought to buy bird seed. He went to the bread box, took out a loaf of sandwich bread and started forming it into little balls, which he put into a plastic bowl. Then he put on his coat and hat, went outside and stuck them all over the nails on the tree. Once he was back in the house, a few sparrows flew up and took away the pieces. Just before sunset a flock of starlings flew over and settled all over the iron branches. The dark birds made a strange impression on him. Then the neighbor's dog started barking and all the birds flew up. But for a flash of an instant, before the birds had risen in flight, they had given him the impression of leaves on the iron branches.

223

He stood looking out the window, but no more birds came. The house, the yard were filled with a profound stillness. He didn't want to move. The trees, the snow, the birds, everything was like a set of syllables that one might read if only he knew the language. He stood until the sun became a red gash on the horizon, until the colors faded with just a faint tinge, until that too was gone and he saw Venus rising and then the moon.

The Demon of Forgetfulness

Surrounding him were the brutalities—the knocking of pipes; the voices of domestic warfare: masculine bombardments, feminine air raid sirens, kamikaze kids; the batter and clang of garbage cans and dumpster lids; the bloated enthusiasm of t.v. announcers and the bombadoom of rock stations. E. V. Gaines was trying to invent a metaphor for these assaults, one that would render justice. He'd left his mind open for it, bidden it to enter—*the ravening wolf leaps to gobble up the sun*—but it was eluding him. He wanted the perfection of the word, the apt expression. He owed to Melissa Harmon the strain he was putting upon his mental resources. He was writing her a letter—an occasion.

He was always writing letters; it was the chosen occupation of his days, that and taking his poodle, Cicero, for his afternoon walk. He wrote letters of protest to editors and letters to the consumer complaint departments of corporations and letters to city magistrates and state officials and congressional leaders. These were his official correspondence, for which he received canned responses from those trained to put off the irate, the disenchanted or disenfranchised—the crackpot and the crank. Occasionally he found himself on the other side of an argument with another news subscriber, a flurry of letters passing back and forth until they gave up, unconvinced, totally winded by argument.

But this was a personal letter, a labor of love. He'd found a book in the library and picked it up to read because he liked the name of the author: Melissa Harmon. It was a novel in the cause of earthly justice, with characters who kicked against the pricks determinedly and had their hearts in the right place. Every afternoon he absorbed himself with a young widow done out of her inheritance by a brother-in-law she'd had every reason to trust—though he'd tried through numerous veiled innuendos to seduce her while his brother was still alive—and her efforts to get it back. Each afternoon he brought his concentration to the book, but he had not finished it. He'd rather let it go, letting his mind wander off the page. Everything still hung in the balance, and he was afraid he'd feel cheated even if the heroine got her money back and the brother-in-law received his comeuppance. He wanted more. He wanted someone to stand beside him in the face of the irrevocable and make a few trenchant, believable strokes. He read cautiously ahead, desultorily—afraid Melissa Harmon would betray him into hurling the book across the room. Then, fortunately, someone checked it out. But that was after a pleasant hour of studying her picture, during which he found himself in an imaginary argument about whether the book could offer any consolation for betrayal. Melissa had held up her side of the argument with eyes that at least hadn't settled for anything mindless. Yes, it was a good face, though hard to make out from some photographer's aesthetically induced shadow: middle-aged, holding a certain toughness. Experience, he thought; she's had a dose. He'd sent off a letter to her publisher, written with the sun sliding along the varnish of an oak library table, on paper aging into ivory he'd found at a garage sale. A month later, she had responded.

Now he was writing her about the harassments of the manager of his building, the trumped up complaints against him and his dog. Carmody, the super, drank—it was well known—had been drinking since his wife died, and complaints from the tenants about the heat, the trash in the halls, and other matters went begging, sometimes for weeks.

On the previous Friday, Carmody appeared in a dirty T-shirt, breathing fumes, ready for a fight—a thick man, with a heavy jaw, a downward pull of flesh at the pectorals. He stood in his doorway like a side of beef. Gaines repeated the conversation for Melissa Harmon's benefit:

"*Look*," he said, "*we've had one too many complaints about that dog of yours and now you're out of here.*"

"*Who complained,*" I asked him—at first politely, "*and what about?*"

"*Your dog keeping the neighborhood awake half the night.*"

"*What night? He's always inside here with me, curled up—asleep.*"

"*They say you had him out.*"

"*Once for a moonlight walk. I don't permit barking. Complaint dismissed for lack of evidence.*" I am a foot shorter, he wrote, but I had defiance in my eye. He could not forego a little pride—he hoped she would not take it ill.

"*He was howling in the apartment.*"

"*Complaint dismissed for extenuating circumstances. He howls when Dominick turns up the juice on his stereo. Hurts his ears.*"

"*Don't give me any of your smart-ass lip. You see this paper?*" He waved it in front of me. "*It's an eviction notice, get it?*"

I fear, he wrote, *that my upstairs neighbor turned on me in a surge of vengeance. He is a young man*, he went on, *Dominick by name, with a certain bent toward the Dionysian*. Almost every weekend he'd turned up his music as loud as it would go so that he and a friend could dance around the apartment naked. Gaines knew this, though he did not mention it to Melissa Harmon, by virtue of the time Dominick had come to the door holding in front of him only a large fan of peacock feathers. *You can imagine*, he wrote, *the difficulty of acquiring*—he crossed out *acquiring* and wrote *benefiting from*—*a good night's sleep*. Trapped below, Gaines had spent those nights wide-eyed in the thrum of electric guitars, the vibrations of the drums and the thumping of dancing youth. He did not want to interfere with their revels, to add further persecution to what was no doubt a difficult life. But sleep was impossible. And the heaving of the building in what seemed a visceral surge made Cicero's ears hurt. He sent up long siren-like howls, and Gaines had difficulty quieting him. The thumping kept up for hours. An incredible energy—he could envy it. Various requests, at first mild, then more insistent, had brought no response. *I appealed to Mr. Carmody, the manager*, he wrote, who put him off with three or four obscenities and a wave of the hand—*Finally, raw-eyed, desperate*, he continued, *I accosted the*

227

youth in the hall and told him I would summon the police.

It was therefore with a certain surprise that I found Carmody at my door with an eviction notice. Indeed he had trembled all over. His son had found him the apartment, assuring his father that it was the least he could do for him, and weren't they fortunate at the rental, considering the way things had skyrocketed. But this would present no financial burden after all. *I saw myself out on the street*, he wrote. *It would not do well for Cicero. He's an old dog, and stiff in the joints.* In his terror, he grabbed the eviction notice out of Carmody's hand and started humming the Dead March. (It occurred to him now to wonder if it had been an eviction notice or just any notice Carmody had picked up to threaten him with. He hadn't looked at it.) *I took a turn around the room humming The Dead March and then strode out into the hall, went up the stairs and knocked on Dominick's door. Dominick happened to be in just then and when he appeared, I hummed it for him as well and started down the hall, knocking on all the doors. I hummed rather loud, you see. The super was right there at my back, but all he could do was yell. You have to take the enemy by surprise, by an ironic turn*, he advised Melissa Harmon. He hoped that she had a taste for irony.

"Look, you go crazy on me. . . ," Carmody had yelled. He couldn't let Carmody yell him down, so he started barking like a dog. Old Mrs. Waterson, he recalled with a certain delight, started banging pots and pans. Dominick danced around him in the hallway. Carmody retreated—it was too much for him, and the whole melee turned into something of a social occasion. Usually the inhabitants passed one another in the halls like shadows they didn't want recognized. Afterwards, Gaines had written a letter to the owner of the building. He wrote down the dates and times he'd noticed whiskey on Carmody's breath. Then, thinking of the man's wife, he'd crossed it all out and started again. He simply complained of being unfairly evicted.

The owner came around and arbitrated a grumbling peace. And now in the flush of that triumph he described it all to Melissa Harmon. The manager standing there dumb-founded while he hummed the Dead March; the other tenants entering the excitement as he marched up and down the halls, waving the eviction notice. . . . The rapier touch of satire, he told Melissa Harmon, sometimes

228

counted for more than the blast of a blunderbuss. The woman who'd banged the pots and pans, nearly eighty-five, had lifted herself off a sick-bed so as not to miss the excitement. And afterwards she'd shaken him gratefully by the hand.

He hoped that Melissa Harmon would try her hand at satire, naturally in the cause of justice.

"I am happy to know that you triumphed," she wrote back two weeks later. *"I believe in fighting the good fight—and I am very pleased that my book inspired you."*

He didn't tell her that this was not exactly the case. For the moment, he put aside the question of inspiration. Rather he had the need to explain the persistence of the fallen world. *The world is an unweeded garden,"* he quoted, and proposed to her his theory of humanity, much brooded upon over the years. A number of the people walking around were pure meat—just material goods issuing from the heart of nature ever busy restocking the shelves. Carmody, for one—though he was good for fixing pipes, if only he'd tend to them. He'd wept when his wife died, Gaines remembered, though he'd done nothing but yell at her when she was alive. That was as far as he could go. But some few had been taken over as they came into the world, accosted by wandering spirits returning to put on life again. These he called "interlopers," not angels or guardian spirits, because they were, in his view, a mixed blessing. They got in the way of things falling to their lowest level and allowing human beings to be just one more animal—which might, in fact, improve matters. But because they'd come from somewhere else and knew the ropes, they were trying to bring things up to their level. Only it was like trying to build the Tower of Babel out of lego blocks. The creature part was stuck to the earth, just trying to crawl away to a hammock and lie there with the cat on its stomach and a mint julep in its hand, or going off to hang around a bar trying to sweet-time some large-breasted pushover. *The interloper,* he wrote, *is like a nagging mate, always beckoning you towards a realm of fiery thought, trying to convince you that's where the action is.* But only the interlopers remembered such a place, he told her, and their view of it kept dimming the longer they had to struggle with the recalcitrance of things. Sometimes they forgot it altogether, and they couldn't apply for a new dose. He thought he could have been one of those dimming spirits himself; only a certain spark of protest kept him aroused.

Even before he received an answer, he was writing her again. Things had come round to another pretty pass. In between letters, the super had left him alone, perhaps because he was having prostate troubles, and Dominick had made a compromise that worked well enough. He and his friend danced till midnight and then turned off the music. Gaines was grateful, had even sent a note of appreciation. Then the music started up again, louder than before—until all hours. The building, on its way to wrack and ruin, was now only half-occupied. Dominick was the only inhabitant on his floor. The state of things very likely gave Dominick his occasion. And it could be Gaines was the only one disturbed, but lately he'd learned a Chinese couple had moved out, after pouring a can of red paint down from the third floor onto Dominick's windows.

My life dins in my ears, he wrote. *I am ringed by demons.* These, too, were part of his theory, but he didn't bother to explain. He'd been so caught up in the disturbance, he hadn't been able to think about anything else. He walked about absently, unable to find things he'd been holding in his hand a moment before. He'd grown savage hunting for his keys, his glasses, Cicero's leash. Unable to concentrate, always drawn back to the sore spot. That evening he was going to confront Carmody, and obsessively he rehearsed the conversation. As he imagined all the possible alternatives the dialogue repeated itself in his head for hours instead of the five minutes it would take up of real life. It was unbearable. Writing the letter gave him a moment's release.

As he wrenched himself out of the mire of his thoughts, something struck him, and he wrote, *The greatest is the Demon of Forgetfulness.* This was true failure, he thought, among the larger failures of his life. When that demon held him in its power—forget about inspiration or any higher mystery—everything else fell away, and when he went to look again, he couldn't tell what had eluded him or where it had disappeared. Sometimes he rummaged in the dark as he walked about abstractedly, the same way he went looking for his misplaced keys or the electric bill or the stamps he'd bought. Had he somehow misplaced his life? His pen trailed off in a dim, inconclusive line. The sun glared in his eyes from the library window, and he couldn't get the blind to shut. He was going to abandon the letter. Then suddenly—and he was struck by the effrontery—he wrote, *I wonder if you'd do me the favor of sending me your picture. Yours is a face I would like to keep in mind.*

His son came to visit him that evening. When he stepped into the little efficiency apartment, he made the place seem too small to contain him. Gaines could not keep from a certain amazement whenever his son appeared. Who was this man and where had he come from? Impossible that he'd issued from his loins: Elliot. He stood there, the top layer of a palimpsest of discarded images that belonged to boyhood and beardless youth. Now a face softening pinkly towards middle age, a beard bristling with gray while the balding head—as though there'd not been enough hair to go around—picked up highlights from the ceiling fixtures. The athlete's body had signaled its departure: Elliot did work out at odd moments, but the years had shaped a comfortable paunch under his neat dark suit. Age and the business lunch, his father thought. The evening cocktail. He tried to peer past the evidence to the quick-footed youngster.

"Well, E.V."—it was hearty man-to-man these days— "you doing okay here?" His son glanced his eye over the formica and plastic while the voice trailed into a kind of uncertainty.

"Not bad for a young guy," Gaines said—it was expected of him.

"Amazing the way they plan these units," his son said. "A place for everything."

The achievable goal. Except for the person living in one, Gaines was tempted to say, but his son would take it personally— too hard to watch in all that grim sincerity. Efficiency covered a multitude of sins, for every day he did battle with the opposite. Horses' asses were everywhere, some bigger than others. Always a new one entering on the scene.

Gaines contented himself with one small prick of reality. "If they'd only keep the place up . . ."

"Yeah, that trash in the halls is disgusting. Those horses' asses never keep up with their jobs." Gaines had hit the right nerve.

Perhaps his son would also notice that the molding was shot all around the shower, or register the ugly stains in the lavatory, the warping of the tiles under the sink. The construction was cheap—self-proclaiming as it went up, tacky on the way down. If his son did notice, it might get registered as one more violation of the larger plan, done in by another set of horses' asses. Next would come the philosophic shrug: life had to move on, in any event. Kids to educate. A house to keep up. Car payments; furniture installments. All the demands. And the old man. Couldn't live on his Social Security, so he had to chip in. The old man needed it after all. He'd been sick—lost everything—they were just lucky he didn't have to languish in a nursing home, adding to the deficit.

"You could always come back . . . We'd be happy . . . "

"I'm well off here," Gaines insisted. He'd had his moment in their midst, sitting there like a rock in their path. An impediment. They had their lives, and his was into the leftover stage. He had only his dog to walk. His singular duty. Being alive was enough to call for a certain guilt. But being in the way was unendurable. If his grandson swept past him to his friends, his activities at school, it was only natural. He'd loved him as a tot.

"You still haven't unpacked that box," Elliot noticed.

"No, I'll get around to it sometime," Gaines said, not sure he ever would. Meanwhile it sat next to the wall under the kitchen table. He wasn't even sure what it contained: remains of his former life haphazardly collected when he took sick. Residue. Detritus. He saw that one of the seams was split, one side caved in, though the cord still held. His son was still standing, his easiest transition to being somewhere else. He invited him to sit down.

"For a little bit, I'm on my way to a parents' meeting." He laughed. "As if I needed something else to do, but they're trying to raise funds for a drug abuse education program. He subsided into a chair.

"How about something to drink? I've got some apple juice."

"No, really, I just left the supper table. Barbara feeds me too well."

"And how's my grandson?"

"Terrific. Made the swim team. He was thrilled, let me tell

232

you. He's even got college on his mind, forget high school. Every minute in the pool doing the butterfly, and hungry as a tiger when he comes home. I bet the food bill's gone up twenty per cent."

It was good to be proud of one's son. When he had a phone, Gaines used to call to pick up the news, but decided finally he'd rather live without one. There was a pay phone at the grocery if he needed it. "And Barbara?"

"You know her—they're always asking her to run some drive, head up some new charity, but she's had it up to here. She's taken up quilting."

He couldn't keep up with them. They pursued their lives as though they had to trap them before they got away. While his was a few scraps lying in a box. And brawls in the hallway. "And you?" he said. "Still burning up the track?"

His son laughed. And the laugh seemed to go back to something he might have wanted to remember, if he could just hold it a minute. "You know me—I can't sit still. I got to be doing something." And apparently the moment was calling for just exactly that, for he stood up. "Well, E.V."—he could have been chairman of the board—"tell me—do you need anything?" He looked around again as though the missing item would announce itself. Then he pulled out his wallet, and Gaines' first thought as it fell open was that a man shouldn't carry around that much cash, at least not in this neighborhood. His son took out a hundred dollars, paused, then pulled out another. Gaines couldn't help staring at the wallet, like a schoolboy waiting for his allowance. A little whistle shaped itself inside him as though he'd found a nickel in the street.

"Buy yourself a little goodie," his son said. "A little treat on me." He shook hands with his father. "Well, E.V., I gotta go. I'm already late for the meeting."

"Good to see you."

For some moments the room seemed to bear his son's imprint, then subsided into the hum of the small refrigerator combining with the flavor of his and Cicero's occupancy. Alone again, the idea he'd stumbled on returned to harry him: the demon stealing things into forgetfulness. And what was it? And when? And would he ever yield it up?

Only a week later came a letter from Melissa Harmon:
Dear Mr. Gaines, she wrote. *I have sent you this picture to remind you of things you don't want to forget. I hope that it will help you to fight away the Demon.*

The picture elevated him. She had actually sent it; he could look directly into her eyes. Though he couldn't tell from a black and white photo, he had the distinct impression they were gray eyes with flecks of violet. He set the picture on the kitchen table until he could think where he might put it to advantage. He wanted to do her justice.

It was a fine day out, after a stretch of cold weather that was enough to convince one that winter would never end. He put a scarf around his neck and pulled a cap over his ears, then took Cicero's leash out of the drawer. The dog always recognized the sign of the day's adventure and did an eager dance. On the path through the park, Cicero kept pulling ahead to be let off his leash to ramble on his own. It was against the rules, but since no one else was in the park just then, he let Cicero go. "Now don't stray," he admonished him.

He stood absently at the edge of a little pond where Canada geese sometimes landed, honking insistently, then joining into an idly moving flotilla. He'd once seen a heron there, first standing, then with his approach, poising itself for flight and taking its long shape over into the trees. Here he was. Staring into the watery sheen. As he looked into its mirrored surface it seemed like the polished surface of time under which everything now lay, all the things that had fallen to the bottom, no longer themselves but a rotting goo. No matter how much you'd packed in.

When he got sick, the last things that had given him his moorings had been stripped away. Emma had died the year before. And it had been half a dozen years since he'd been a copy editor in the newsroom of the local paper. He'd gone round a time or two to visit some of his cronies, but mostly they'd retired or left and those who were there, still in the momentum of the daily round with its gossip and complaint, didn't know what to do with him.

This time, when he got sick, it was the house he'd had to let go of, his furniture and possessions—even the geography of his old

234

life. They hadn't expected him to live. They'd put papers into his hands he'd signed casting all away. Why should he hang on? —there were bills to pay. And then miraculously he was up and around, everything gone. They'd brought him back to the Midwest to take care of him. What money was left over, he'd put into their house.

He didn't like the Midwest, flat, mindlessly green. And even though Deming was the town his son was glad to escape from, it was the place that had held his life. He missed the mountains, the desert, even the dust storms. All his life had been lived in their midst. When he tried to bring to mind the configurations of Cook's Peak or the Three Sisters, or the way the clouds rolled above them, their outlines were dim, half rubbed out. And the color of the sky. The space as it rolled toward the horizon—

Suddenly he remembered the dog. He started calling, looked around frantically. For a moment, silence. Then Cicero came panting up. "Oh, Cicero," he said gratefully.

When he arrived home, he found all hell broken loose. The ancient, rusted plumbing had burst at some important juncture, letting out a rush of water. The bottom floor was flooded, and some of the apartments on the floors above had gotten their share of water. His own door stood open, a large puddle in the center of the room. The hall was tracked with mud and footprints. Cries of dismay from above. Gaines saw that the box he'd never opened was now standing in water. He lifted it up and set it in the sink to drain, quickly pulled out the contents and left them in sodden piles.

Then he went upstairs. Dominick was berating Carmody, while old Mrs. Waterson was trying to tell her side of things. She'd been in bed resting when she saw the water creeping along the floor. She'd thumped her broom on the floor, then tried to call. The phone rang and rang but nobody came. "Imagine," she said. "Somebody could have died in there."

"You see that, you see that!" Dominick kept repeating. His stereo equipment and various tapes and discs lay in loose disorder in the hallway. Absolutely ruined, he insisted. He was going to sue. Gaines surveyed the mess. There in the debris were Dominick's nights of abandon, the gestures he had flung into the air. In spite of himself, Gaines found himself trying to comfort him: he was good for a moment's commiseration. It was loss after all. Then he went into his own place. He'd have a little peace and quiet at least—one couldn't push sentiment too far.

He took a mop to the water on the floor. Then after he'd put Melissa Harmon's picture in a safe place, he spread a towel over the kitchen table and spread out the sodden contents of the box, whatever Elliot and Barbara and had thought fit to save when they went through the house. His first temptation was to throw it all away. But carefully he went through the mess, separating the papers that stuck to one another. Things that had sat in the bottoms of drawers, old receipts and papers, buttons and photographs, old Christmas cards. He found pictures of Emma, some of the photographs with Elliot as a boy. *Gene*. That was what her voice had called him all across those years. And in the office he was *Vic*. The pictures in the little album weren't at all damaged, except for a few that had slipped out. He found himself among these. He was sitting somewhere, most likely on the patio with a shape beside him he found difficult to make out. Water had damaged one side of the snapshot. His demon, he wondered. And with a little laugh, he recognized a pot of cactus. There he was. The patio, the house. Where they all had been.

He knew what he wanted to do. He wanted to go downtown and buy a small gift for Melissa Harmon, something that it would take him hours to shop for and which, when he found it, he would recognize as being exactly right. And he wanted to buy a frame for her picture. He'd put it inside with his own just below it. He would have her to look at, to look past, in fact, to try to recall that flavor, that stream in which everything still flowed and in which lost things lie.

News from the Volcano

Rising up from land flat as sheet metal, the rock, sheer and huge, unprecedented, is a ship moving across the desert, its dark shape bearing straightaway, wherever it is headed, not to be put off course. Aeons ago it rose towering above the land, lava overflowing from the molten core. Now the core is all that remains, the rest worn away by all that time can do. Only the core—a relic of ancient catastrophes, before any were present to know what they might mean. Hardened now and silent.

But now and then the moon rises blue in the dust of ancient memory. A haze of particles hanging suspended in the air, as though from that time when the volcano erupted. Who knows how they've gathered or where they came from? They gather above the rock, above the desert, above the occasions of earth below, as though reminded by the original disturbances of the air. So I see it now, as the moon rises three-quarters full. And with a light that comes from somehow beyond it.

It sends its bluish haze over a huddle of adobe houses, from which the small lights float in the surrounding indigo, and the smells of chili and beans and fry meat mingle with the evening chill. The light touches on the headlights of the trucks parked alongside, as though they were closed lids, gives a sheen to their metal casings and leaves the land beyond a dark sea. Prickly pear and yucca, ocotillo and scrub cedar raise dark silhouettes from darker pools. Along the road cars are moving, and among them is a stranger moving this way. He moves the way a shark moves toward a school of fish, a dark rush in the direction of the unwary.

Up the road a neon sign sets its glare against the landscape: a gas station-grocery-cafe, still open. Many times I have gone past, watched the customers enter and leave. Sometimes I've taken my loaf of bread and left change on the counter. Lupe I know from hearsay, for she does not speak much, at least to me. Perhaps she feels my gaze upon her and draws away, not wanting anyone to know too much. But I cannot get enough of certain faces, wanting to know what has shaped them. I only know I must not look too long. There is something frightening in too close a scrutiny. I keep close to myself and see things as they come.

Tonight Lupe sits inside as she usually does, on a stool behind the counter, waiting for Lorenzo to return to help her close up. He'd left her alone all that afternoon, away on some errand. He may have driven all the way to Gallup—he does that sometimes. She had already cleaned the grill and wiped the counter, totalled up the day's receipts. Whatever came in now belonged to tomorrow—it is good to begin the day with something.

A truck pulled in, three boys in front, two more sprawled out in the bed. Lupe knew the truck—Manuel's. They were headed to the dance in Farmington. She could hear them outside. "No, man, you're drunk already." "Look with your eyes, man." "It's the Russians—they've set something off." "Why them?—maybe it's us." "You're crazy, man. We'd have heard it." "It's from outer space. A spaceship—a huge one." "Not that big—don't you know any science?" "I know the moon when I see it—only that's different." "I want another beer."

It was a game, of course. But there was a difference in the cast of things. They could tell as they stood in front of the truck, looking at the sky. They broke their pose just as Lupe reached them. "See, look how strange it is," they showed her. And she stood with them, her arms hugging her shoulders over her thin blouse. She'd never seen the moon like that. Just now a plume of cloud fanned its surface, trailing across like a scarf. Splotches of light and shadow lay over the dark vegetation.

A different moon. Where had it come from and what did it mark? Perhaps it was a sign, if she only knew what it meant. That is always the way—it could be this or that. Her grandmother had been one to know. She could read the world like a map of secret journeys—there are some who can do that, who seem to be born knowing. She could enter certain moments like a doorway and see what pulsed beneath, even if she could not tell the exact shape of what was coming. She could tell people where sickness came from, the violence in the flesh, and if an ill wind was blowing. It was something. Though perhaps not enough—perhaps it is never enough. One keeps looking for news; perhaps that's why I stare so at the things around me, waiting for them to speak.

Lupe's grandmother was dead now. Lupe had seen her lying at the threshold of her hut, left behind by the soldiers who carried off her chickens. They laughed as they caught the squawking birds. And the one who struck her down, who can tell? Or the others they left, scattered in the postures in which they had closed with death, set upon with the marks of whatever impulse or intention had overtaken them. Rumor caught these things and breathed them on the wind. But the soldiers had disappeared as they had come.

Lupe turned to go inside, and Manuel followed her in to pay for gas. It was his truck, he'd bought it used and took jobs hauling. He had a sister and a mother to support. Though he wanted to go off on his own, down to Albuquerque to look for work and perhaps for a certain freedom, he didn't stray, not even for better wages. Lupe liked him—he was older than his friends, held something in his face she could trust. "You going to the dance?" he asked her.

She gave a shrug. She didn't know, Lorenzo was so late in coming.

"We could wait till you lock up," he said. "You could ride with us—in front."

She'd have liked to go with them. But she didn't like to leave when Lorenzo wasn't there. "I'd better stay," she said.

"I could come back," he said. He wanted her to go. "Unless," he said. "you have someone else."

"No, there's no one else."

Very likely it was Willie he meant. Willie was always asking her to go with him. He had a motorcycle and liked to roar down the highway with a girl at his back holding on with her arms around his waist. I've seen him many times, getting in his brags, you might say. There'd been a number of girls eager for the thrill, but Lupe was the one he wanted. It was easy to tell by the way he looked at her, as though he were trying to take her with his eyes. But she'd never sent a glance in his direction, was never lured by his roaring down the road.

He was trying to make a special link between them: they knew more than the others. They were above doing what the spoilers had done. He had found Indian somewhere in his blood, past the blue eyes and white skin that had corrupted the original purity, and he'd come West to find it. He brought his camera with him, and his power lay in that. He took pictures of road kill—that's what the hunter's skill had come to. Having left the buffalo to die by thousands, this was what civilization had brought—dead creatures in the road, and the effete beef steak. He took pictures of junked cars and litter and dumps and faces from which every dream had fled. Warnings and reminders.

There is always laughter in his eyes, when he turns his glance on Lupe, though when I've passed him I've caught something cold and sharp that goes right through and doesn't disappear. And he turns away as though he's already revealed too much. I too draw back. I have no wish to meddle. There is always something back of his expression when he's flirting with the girls, taking their measure, taking the square root, storing things away for the next time— something quite beyond them that perhaps he doesn't see himself. But his attraction works like a scent drawing to him all that might speak to his contempt.

Perhaps Manuel was relieved to know he didn't have a rival, for Willie was always asking her to go. "Maybe you'll come later," he said, taking up his beer and the change. "Save a dance for me." And he gave her a smile that she held onto after he had gone.

The truck started up, moved out onto the highway and was gone. It was quiet now but for the refrigerator making cold, and the buzzing of the fluorescent lights inside taking the beer cans into their glare. She doubted she would go to the dance: Lorenzo would be too tired.

Once or twice a month he took her: she knew it was for her sake. He'd come through the door around closing time and say, "Let's go have some fun," and they'd climb into his pickup and go to join the crowd. Lorenzo didn't dance himself, but stood on the edge among the spectators, drinking a beer and talking intently to whoever might be standing next to him, man or woman—he knew everybody. But he always kept an eye out for what was happening on the dance floor. If things started to get rowdy, Lupe had only to look for his nod, and they would leave. There were always those who hung around the edge, usually outside passing around a bottle, sometimes hooting and laughing, hoping for a fight. It was a question of whether they'd get bored and go off to further adventure or start something there. More than once the sirens came shrieking down the road, and someone got carted off to the hospital. Lorenzo kept a sharp eye in his head.

Lorenzo had had a wife once, but she'd run off to Denver with another man. Her lover had disappeared long since, and others had followed. But somehow she'd remained in Lorenzo's life, even though she never came back. If he went to see her, he never said. She called him at least once a month and told him her latest round of troubles and asked for his advice, and sometimes money. For a time he'd given her both, but the money blew away like scraps the wind had brought and would, as far as she was concerned, bring again. Now he gave neither, but listened to her stories. From time to time, he was with a woman. Now he had no one, though there were women who'd have been glad to have him. He was a generous man who liked people around him, but who kept back a certain melancholy he never imposed on anyone. People liked him.

A restless mood came over Lupe. The night was growing too long, and the lights were not strong enough to keep certain shapes from invading from the darkness outside, nor the cans of beer and the packages of snacks and loaves of bread solid enough to keep her solidly among them. She got these moods. And you could watch her struggle against them. I can remember when her look spoke only of this.

When they had first arrived, she and her mother, it felt strange to her to stop moving. She felt the moving still in her body, and a danger of falling over if she stopped. It was strange not to see one landscape shifting into another, whether they were on foot or in the waddling buses. She could not believe that if she closed her eyes the same objects would be standing in front of her when she opened them again or that she would wake in the same bed in the same room, the mountains beyond the window still solidly standing, and Lorenzo's place down the road.

She refused to go to school—they had to bring her home. She wouldn't be separated from her mother, though in many ways she was no longer a child. When the two of them came into the store, Lorenzo gave her sweets. When her mother sank into the drunken stupor that lay at the end of her pursuit of safety and could no longer take care of her, Lorenzo gave her credit. And when her mother went off with the man who took her by the hand and led her to his car, Lorenzo took her in and taught her to make change and add figures and how to brew the coffee and cook hamburgers. She had finished growing up there.

The other girls envied her. Like one chosen, she had been given a place where she could earn her own money and put it in the bank. She had a future. She could go where she pleased, though she seldom left her place behind the grill or the cash register. She could lead her own life and didn't need a man if she didn't want one. She sensed their eye on her, their gaze as sharp as desire. But what was there to envy? The dark rush of her dreams? Sometimes she dreamed of animals devouring one another that lived like a menace just under the surface. She'd crossed boundaries where she'd had no wish to go and who would care to follow? For she'd had experience, and no one could wipe it away. And what was there to be done with it?

She heard a car door slam and hoped it wasn't Willie come to lean over the counter to try to lure her in his direction. She had no idea why he continued to pursue her. Lorenzo never spoke to him. She was always pressed back by the tightness of a face that seemed to close behind some secret scorn, while his eye let nothing escape his notice. Then, unexpectedly, his face would break into a grin and he would tell her a joke, a bit of gossip he'd been saving up: who Manuel was sleeping with and which of the boys liked Lupe. He had something to tease everyone with, those he wanted to get the better of. He tried to tease her about Manuel, but she never blinked an eye.

He never had enough to do, it seemed. He was always

242

around. Sometimes he showed off the photographs he took of mountains and desert plants to sell to tourists. Compliments made him smirk. There were times she saw Willie every day. He'd come in and pull down a loaf of bread, a can of soup, a jar of peanut butter, as if eating were a matter of indifference to him, slap some bills down on the counter and leave without a word, sometimes without his change. Or he might come in for beer and disappear for days on end. He'd be off in his room, chain-smoking, his music turned up loud so he wouldn't have to listen to the noise of cars. Sometimes he slept all day and went prowling out at night. Sometimes he stayed drunk until he felt like being sober.

But it wasn't Willie come to pass the time. It was a stranger. He stood with his back to her as he filled his gas tank, then replaced the hose and came inside: a tall man with a pony tail pulled back from a narrow, bearded, hawk-nosed face. He closed the door and surveyed his surroundings as though to take a reckoning. She caught the restless glitter of his eyes, a film of weariness over something leaden and driven.

He did not offer to pay but placed himself on a stool at the counter. The lights were off in the kitchen; it was too late for food, but Lupe did not tell him so.

"What do you have to eat?" he wanted to know.

"Omelet," she said, "or a sandwich. Ham or cheese."

He considered the choices as though they were the only things he'd ever be tempted to eat.

"Till tomorrow morning," she explained.

"I could be lying half-starved on the slope of Pike's Peak by then."

She didn't deny it. One could be anywhere, without so much as a piece of bread. He wanted an omelet with ham and cheese and coffee—lots of coffee. She put on a pot on the Silex in front and went back into the kitchen to beat up the eggs, take out the cartons with the ham and cheese. She watched him while she worked. He drummed impatiently on the counter, glanced in her direction when any noise came from the kitchen. He took out a cigarette, lit it, took a long, deep drag and let the smoke out slowly. He set it in the ashtray and left it. She saw him reach towards his belt, draw a

243

hunting knife from its sheath and lay it on the counter. She hadn't seen it under his jacket. It had what looked to be a bone handle with dark streaks, perhaps a design carved into it.

He gazed at it for a moment, then took it up, ran his thumb across the blade in a way that suggested that he wanted her to take notice. He glanced up in her direction, but she'd felt his attention coming and had ducked away in time. This was something she had no business with, she knew it under her skin, but it would be hard to keep away from it. He turned the knife over in his hand, familiarly, as though he'd gotten it as a bargain and he could take pride in whatever the knife might bring him. A certain energy pulsed out of his weariness as he turned the knife back and forth cutting the light into metallic slices.

She didn't want to look at it, the way it cut the light, the restlessness of it in his hand, as though straining in the direction of what it had been shaped to do. It knew killing. Lupe saw at once. The knife had killed someone. It had leapt into the place where killing was and caught the secret scent. Who knew how it had happened? But it was glutted now with what it knew, even if it had blundered into that space, been caught blindly or risen up and driven forward in a flash. The man was hectic with the consequences, but he could not get rid of the knife. It was joined to him now like his flesh.

He set the knife down, then pushed it to one side when she brought him his food. This gesture was for her benefit, she was no fool— to show her it was subject to him. She asked him if he wanted catsup, then came with his coffee. She wondered why he hadn't threatened her before, hadn't robbed the store of what he wanted and gone on his way. There was food enough to cram into his maw. The threat itself was enough to get him whatever he wanted.

But maybe he wanted to be reminded of something, the smell of cooking in the air, the aroma of coffee. She filled his cup. His hand trembled as he took the mug, raised it to his lips. A bit spilled over the edge. It was the knife—it had him in its power and wouldn't leave him alone. The knife had no interest but itself.

Every now and then he paused, his fork poised as though he were listening, perhaps for something that pursued him or something that had momentarily stopped, as though a buzz had been set ringing in his ears that wouldn't shut off. Till he was weary of it, sick to death of it. She could see how he was trying to push it away, rid himself of it as he tried to eat, as he tried to chew his food back into savor and to warm himself with coffee. He craved the ordinary and was working to get food to his stomach before it gagged him and turned to sawdust.

She breathed sharply. The knife was greedy too, as it strained against its moorings. It would spare nothing. In the fullness of its impulse it was trying to get her to form the image of her death, make it coalesce before her eyes. It wanted her to reach toward a source of terror, where its power lay. If she tried to run away, it threatened to pursue her. Not because of anything she would do, but because she was there and had seen it. It wanted her powerlessness. If Lorenzo wandered in, heedlessly, it could rise up against him. He could walk right into it. She saw that and stepped into uncertainty.

She put herself back into what she knew, those nights when the countryside had turned into the shadows of fleeing forms. They were all joined together in the shadows, pursued and pursuer, having shed everything but the one impulse that bound them. It lay at the bottom of the world. Out of it she could imagine her death. The absence of herself standing there—that was her death. It formed a space of stillness. The part of herself she was most familiar with would die. And whatever it was that lay behind it—that would leave her too. But she let go of that. She would not give it to him. It did not belong to him. Though she was looking at him, she seemed not to see him at all.

When he'd stopped eating and made a swipe with his napkin across the last of his food, he stood up and took his knife. "I'm finished now," he announced. "You can open up that drawer and give me what's in it."

"I'll give you nothing," she said. "You'll have to pay."

He looked at her like a snake risen in his path.

She did not let go. Neither did she pretend to innocence. She had passed beyond that long ago. She looked directly into his eyes with the knowledge of what he had done. "You have to pay," she insisted. "You've eaten, you've filled your car with gas. Now you have to pay."

She had no pity and asked for none. The knife had no pity. It was looking to make an excuse of her weakness, to bury itself in that. But she had let go of her life—it did not matter.

"I have no money," he said, as though it were a joke. "When you have this, you don't need money."

She stood there like a wall: he could kill her if he wanted.

He didn't move. Perhaps he caught a sense of what she knew and how the space between them joined them now. She was no accomplice. Or perhaps it was her voice that struck him, twisted inside him. It had found him out, gone to the bone. That can happen—I have seen it. It made him want to let go of all he knew, as if there were a moment in which both of them might rise above their images to something else. Everything wavered in that effort, that possibility. Then in a sudden movement he flung down the knife, reeled as though it had taken all his effort, and threw himself out the door. He stumbled and nearly fell before he reached the car.

Lupe did not move. For a long moment she seemed to stand outside her body. The knife had put her there, and now it was lying on the floor. She would not look at it. Dizzily she sat down, trying to regain herself. She tried to call to mind whom she'd seen that day, who had come for gas, for food.

She did not notice when the door opened again. And when Willie came up behind her, he startled her.

"You falling asleep?" he said with a teasing laugh. "Who's the guy who left—friend of yours?"

"I never saw him before."

Nothing to make a difference. "I thought you'd be closed up now. Why hang around. Let's go to the dance."

"No," she said. "Not tonight." She wanted to pull the grin off his face like a mask.

"You always dance with me. Just to tease, I bet."

"I dance with everybody."

"You don't trust me."

She shrugged. "Lorenzo would take me, but he's not back. I won't go till he comes."

"He's not your father—he doesn't own you," he said meanly.

"What's he saving you for—himself? The big man." His foot struck against the knife. He bent down for it.

"Don't pick it up," she warned him.

"Why not?" He stood up with it.

"It isn't yours," she said. He turned it in his hand, watching her as he fingered the blade. "It's a good knife," he said. "You don't find one lying around like that every day. Finders, keepers."

"Fool," she said, turning away, as he toyed with it.

"I've always wanted a knife like this."

She tried to ignore him.

"Look. Go with me," he insisted.

And if she went with him . . .

"Or you'll be sorry." Willie turned away, as though the threat would hold force without him, and strode out the door.

Now he had the knife. He would go where it took him. She would be sorry, he'd promised her that, when he turned again in her direction. He was asking her again to reach into the fear that filled the space the knife was ready to make. To live in that darkness. If she looked into the space, would she see only the blank tearing of flesh, the deep wounding that asks for revenge, the endless chain? What was to be saved, and what would save her? She stood for a moment as though waiting for news, for something else beyond her to come to speech, if it were there to speak. That was the question, the one that takes us to the depths, nailed by the moment, to listen for our lives. She could hear, she could almost see a great struggle roaring in the dark on the verge of some upheaval. She expected it to appear in front of her, but when she ran outside, into a brisk wind that was raising up the dust, the road was empty. The moon was still rising.

Uncle Lazarus

The fog had come in on something other than little cat feet, damp and impenetrable, and Mason Chalmers insisted that Kitty Bean let him off at the other side of the bridge that led down into Prospect Landing. He could get up the hill to his house on his own. Save her a trip over the winding dirt road and having to back out of his narrow driveway. As it was, she'd be some little time making her way back to the camp she had rented. Who knew when the fog would lift? He wished he could offer her a place to spend the night, but his house was emphatically occupied.

"Afraid to be seen in my company," she teased him.

If anything, he was afraid to be seen in his own, things having broken free from their moorings, it not yet being clear where they might settle. Everything seemed tentative, up for grabs. But he was in better spirits than he had been for months, thanks to her.

He leaned over, placed his hands on her shoulders, drew her toward him, and allowed the kiss to become an occasion in itself. "I'll be up next weekend," he said.

She put a finger up to his lips. "Best to make no plans."

"No," he agreed, "it's a poor idea. But . . ."

"You'll see me when you need to," she said. "And who knows, I may go off on one of my wanderings."

The years had not taken away her liveliness, her pride or determination. Her green eyes held their depth and sparkle above the lines in her face—she was still a beauty, her red hair a halo of fire around her face. And she was as maddeningly unpredictable as ever. "But you'll come back?"

"Of course I will. Haven't I always?"

"There have been some mighty long gaps in your appearances." The thought of her going off once again left him hollow.

"We came together long ago and maybe there's something yet to be plucked from the future. It's still ripening, you know. Meanwhile you've got work to do."

Was she putting him to some sort of test?—it was quite like her.

"Do be careful, Mason—let me give you warning. That situation of yours has an ugly turn to it. Family or no, those folks are not on your side. I never did catch the scent of benevolence in Emma. Nor her kids, except for Nancy—poor thing. At least she had the sense to clear out."

"I think you've guessed it," he said. "Leaves you with a hell of a lonely feeling."

This time she leaned forward, put her arms around him and as they kissed, he was taken up more forcefully than ever into what he'd always felt for Kitty Bean. "It's been a great moment, Kitty," he said, when he'd caught his breath. "One for the annals of time. There aren't all that many..."

"Your time and my time anyway." Her lilting laugh tripped down his spine like an arpeggio. She started up the motor, and he left her, reluctantly. He turned to watch her go, with no thought of moving until the last suggestion of her truck lights had dimmed into the fog.

It wasn't all that late, only a little past sunset, but it was dark already. Light trapped by fog. *Brouillard*—he liked the word that had lingered out of his college French, perhaps for the just right occasion. He had seen fogs a-plenty, but this one made him seem afloat as well, to put in a special call for clarity. The harbor was pretty well socked in, but for one thin veil trailing towards the hill, nothing to suggest, though, that the fog would lift anytime soon. He stood in its midst, trying to get his bearings.

He walked over the bridge toward the store where his sister, Emma, sold gas and night crawlers and boating supplies, soft drinks and groceries. His first thought was to walk on past—seeing her would only put a damper on his spirits. The years had settled them into a series of enforced pleasantries, a cover for a distrust he acknowledged but didn't like to dwell on. He would never have told her about Kitty or anything that mattered to him. But he was in need of a few things to tide him over—a loaf of bread, a jar of peanut butter, a can of coffee, and a little cream to put in it. He'd have a cup of coffee with her, just to delay going home. No doubt his niece and nephew had cleaned out the pantry and refrigerator by now, as they'd been in the habit of doing all that long summer. Whatever else had occurred during his absence he didn't care to speculate about.

He had no one to blame but himself. He'd been hit during a vulnerable moment, not long after Hannah died—left there in an empty house with only his cat, Samson, and Charlie to come in to help him keep the place fixed up. Charlie did his shopping and was creditable with a hammer and nails, but not much good with housekeeping. There was cat hair over all the furniture and a century of dust—or so it seemed. The house smelled of neglect. "You can't go on living like that," Emma scolded him. "The place'll go to wrack and ruin. And there's your health to think about. That Charlie is about helpful as a crutch."

Then there was the problem with the well. First he got sick from what doctor decided was food poisoning. Nothing he had eaten, he was convinced of that. Luckily it occurred to him to have his well water tested. Full of e-coli bacteria, it turned out, after having been good pure water for thirty years. The only conceivable source was Herb Watkins' goats on the land just above him. But Herb stoutly denied his goats had anything to do with it. They'd been neighbors for a dozen years, the goats having come into the picture some months before. Mason's alternatives were a law suit or a new well. He chose the well, as a matter of economy. It might cost him four thousand dollars, but a lawyer's fees, the pressure on his nerves, and bad blood on his borders were not worth the price.

His sister took issue with him, though it was none of her affair. But she had raised him, and had returned to her old habit of correcting his life and issuing dire warnings. "You let him get away with that? You'll put yourself out of house and home if you don't watch out. You need someone to handle your affairs."

It was clear what she had in mind. Her daughter, Marlene, and Vernon, her son-in-law, had presented Mason with an offer to buy his house—with the proviso that he would continue to live there. Thereby keeping it in the family. Keeping alive all the memories of Marlene's visits there when she was young. They'd be on hand to help take care of the place. He wasn't entirely convinced. He could smell something of motive, and very likely Emma was behind it—trying to do something for the younger generation, getting her ducks in a row. Her older daughter had come to grief, though of exactly what kind Emma refused to reveal. Marlene and Vernon were the objects of her anxious care. If he agreed, they'd have something after he was gone: his land was getting more and more valuable all the time. Their offer, he thought, was on the skimpy side.

He knew he was going to have to make some decision about his house; sheer inertia had kept him from making a final will. He resisted any idea of selling the property and moving to an apartment; he'd lived in the house for over thirty years and was fully determined to die there. It was the outer casing of his personality, of the life he'd lived within its walls. The old farmhouse he'd bought and redone had space and character. The kitchen with its pine cabinets and tongue-in-groove pine floors, full of light. The sun porch where they'd taken their meals and watched the light dim behind the old barn. And the garden. Outside he'd planted sweet peas of varied colors, and Hannah had her roses. He thought of all the auctions he and Hannah had gone to, looking for furniture with good wood, now pieces they'd prized over anything they could have bought new. And his study with its shelves of books, mostly history and biography, along with Shakespeare and a set of the Great Books—he'd always been a reader—his computer, and on the walls a couple of landscapes his mother had painted with a delicate touch; a certificate from the community commending him for his volunteer work.

If he sold the house to his niece, he'd have a little extra cash. He could pay off the debts that had come with Hannah's illness and his own time in the hospital and have something left over to leave to Charlie, who'd been with him for the past fifteen years. He said he'd consider it.

Apparently that was enough to convince Marlene and

Vernon to come up from Augusta that summer, ostensibly to visit and to help him get back on his feet, but it became clear they had no intention of leaving. They moved in on him and took charge, as though they owned the place already.

They were hardly in the doorway when they told Charlie he was no longer needed. No use keeping him on, simple-minded as he was, unable to follow instructions unless you repeated them three or four times and supervised his every move.

"But it's his job," Mason insisted. "He's been with me ever since he hurt his back up at the mill." He'd put his foot down, but behind his back, they made Charlie's life so miserable, Charlie had left on his own. "You'll save twelve thousand dollars a year," Emma told him sagely. He was furious, not simply that they'd taken advantage of his weakness, but that he'd slipped into a certain lack of nerve.

As he drew closer, he saw a car sitting in front of the store, with Emma outside filling up the gas tank; she stood talking to the driver as he was counting out the bills. She knew everyone for miles around and pumped her regulars for gossip as they bought groceries and parts and fishing tackle and bait. Mason's brother-in-law, Homer, a taciturn man and exacting mechanic, serviced their boats and trucks. The two of them had put by a tidy sum at one point, but had lost considerably in the stock market.

"Well, Norman, you drive careful here in this fog," Emma said. There was a little conversation between them.

"No," Emma said. "After Marlene reported him missing, they had half the state out looking for him. Well, you heard the commotion. Helicopters flying over. Dogs tracking through the woods. Homer was gone for three days dragging the bay, along with the others—left me with all the work. He's dead tired. And I'm dead tired, let me tell you. All that labor for nothing."

The driver must have sympathized. Mason drew closer.

"I'd hate to say it, but . . . I'm sure he took his own life." There was a catch in her voice. "Nothing to live for after Hannah passed . . . Didn't leave a note or anything. . .That's right—the memorial's coming up the end of the week."

He felt as though someone had landed a punch in the gut.

He'd gone off without telling anybody where he was headed. Marlene and Vernon didn't have to know his every move—they weren't his keepers. It was a piece of resentment on his part. He hadn't figured they'd put him in his grave while he was gone.

He waited till she had a chance to put the bills in the cash drawer, glanced in to see that she was alone and stepped inside. She had sat down on a stool behind the counter and opened the newspaper, perhaps to see what they were saying about him.

When she looked up and saw him, her normally impassive face—eyes that didn't miss a trick—was fixed in something more powerful than dismay. She stood up jerkily, pressed her hand to her mouth and gave a half-suppressed cry.

"I know why you've come haunting," she said in a tight voice. "They couldn't find your body and you don't have the peace of the grave. Oh, Mason," she said, "that it should come to this." She held out a hand as though to stop his further advance. "We all understand . . . how sometimes you can't go on. Just tell us where the body is," she said, "and we'll bury you right and proper. And where you've put the will."

He was himself astonished, even beyond hearing the news of his own death. It was his ghost she was seeing, even as he stood there in his Red Socks cap, his blue chambray LL. Bean shirt and tan slacks and Rockport walkers, vigorous and substantial, though his beard could have done with a little trimming. She was of too practical a mind—his will, eh?—he'd have thought, to let in the supernatural with the first whiff of the untoward, but she used to scare him with tales of ghosts and hauntings when he was a boy, maybe believed in them. Or else had wanted to induce the right sort of behavior on his part—he never knew. Perhaps she had planted him so securely in the other world, had so much now invested in his demise she couldn't draw back.

He could have held up his arm with its good solid flesh and type-O blood and invited her to give it a pinch, but for some reason he wasn't ready to undeceive her. The fog perhaps—must have put him in the mood.

He opted for a profound silence. He could hear the hum of the fluorescent lights on the ceiling and in the refrigerators. "Death

253

is a hard thing, Emma," he said finally in a husky whisper—when you *haven't* run out of things to live for."

She was silent as well, having to reconstruct his fate. "What happened to you, Mason?" she said, with a hint of desperation. "We've searched everywhere."

"I went fishing, Emma."

"Fishing? Why, you haven't been fishing for over a year, not since . . ."

"Fortunately, I got out of the slough of despond. Ray Thompson came along.

"You don't know Ray—a regular cut-up when he was young. Sold me a boat once that I swear had the inclination of a horse forever pulling toward the stable. And we've drunk many a beer together. Great fisherman. I can remember a time . . ." Though the power of invention could have taken him by a longer route, he let it go. "He'd rented a camp up on Matawamkeag and came down after me. Hadn't seen one another in I don't how long. Just came and collected me and took me off in his truck. 'Mason,' he said, 'let's see what we can do. This is just the lake for white perch— And you know as well as I do they're the best eating of all. . .'"

"You went that far?" She was putting things together. "So that's why your truck's right here—parked in front of the house. And no note or anything, about where you'd gone. We thought . . ."

Yes, I know what you thought. He watched her as she made an effort to work out the perplexity of things. He tried to make a space for contrition—he hadn't meant to give anyone trouble over him, but things had gone beyond him, and he was being carried forward in the momentum. It was no longer possible to continue what he'd been experiencing lately—an odd detachment from his own life.

The only help he managed to give her was to extend the plausibility of his fiction.

"Only once I got fishing, the old appetite just came back. Ray had some business up in Houlton, so I got up early that last morning and went out on my own. I was out there in the middle of the lake when a line squall came up—a real doozey. Tried to get back before it struck, but it hit that boat and turned it around like a leaf, and the waves kicked up and suddenly I was swept out into the lake."

"Didn't you have a life jacket?"

"It got so hot before that squall came up, I took it off. Never figured anything like that would happen. Had it lying there right in front of me."

She stared at him, unblinking, but whether she'd swallowed the tale was unclear. The phone rang, and they both gave a start. When she turned away to answer it, he took the opportunity to slip away. He'd floated in the front door, so to speak, and caught her unaware, and it seemed a good moment to drift out again, disappear.

He counted on her to work things out afterward, figure he'd been playing her like a fish. Right now she was too rattled to think straight. Moments later he could hear her calling after him, but the fog was against her. For good measure, he ducked into the trees and stood there, fueling another emphatic silence. *I am a figment of my own imagination*, he thought.

•

"So tell me about your life," Kitty Bean said to him. They'd taken the motorboat out on the lake over to a spot near the far shore that Kitty said was promising for white perch. It was warm and sunny, a fine day in August, moving toward September. You could tell that things were winding down, the leaves of the trees having grown rusty, as though they'd done their duty for the year. A few branches of the maples were going red in the swamps. But the goldenrod, all different species with their various heads and shapes, and the other late summer flowers—asters and sunflowers— were still offering their vigor. And he had cause for celebration because Kitty Bean had come back once more, come for him, and they were sitting together there on the water, with a picnic basket of food she'd put together, thick meat sandwiches, and potato salad, dill pickles, chocolate chip cookies, and a thermos of lemonade.

He was back in another place and time—past his domestic troubles, past all thought of politics and war and the drift of the country, past the need to sort through the fictions that daily confronted him in the newspapers and on television and brought him to anger and cynicism. Small comfort that Hamlet had had a similar problem. But now there were just the two of them sitting there with most of their lives behind them, but still holding the vital thread of what had brought them together after all their separations. She had come for him, just come out of the morning in her truck and said, "Mason, here I am—I've come to spirit you away." And what could be better, out there on the lake with a fishing pole in his hand and Kitty sitting across from him.

He could reach all the way back to origins: Kitty Bean, Kitty Bean. His cousin's name had reverberated in his head with the rhythm of promise and delight, like a sky full of colored balloons. In kindergarten, he'd spun himself around with the rhythm of her name, and she, too, had spun around and around, the two of them breathless and giddy out there on the playground. Until, at the center of the whirling, a flame shot up and engulfed him, heart and senses, liver and lights. He'd turned about in that flame through all his childhood and youth, even when her face had grown beyond his remembrance of her. Through the years that turned it was the flame of his longing.

His first experience of loss came when he was six and his aunt and uncle moved off to New Mexico, taking Kitty with them. "Kitty's your cousin," his mother said. "You'll have to find another girl friend." But then there was the tentative rediscovery of one another the summer his aunt and uncle came back East for an extended visit. The two of them were inseparable, hunting frogs together and fishing off the end of the dock. He'd given her his pocketknife, he reminded her. "Still have it," she told him.

"Then when I came out to New Mexico that summer to help your folks with the orchard, they treated like a member of the family." A feeling he'd never had with his father, or Emma, seven years older than he, who took over the household when his mother died. His aunt made his bed and washed his clothes and plied him with food, and his uncle taught him to ride a horse and let him drive his truck.

"Well, you were."

"The thing I chiefly remember," he said, "when I had the words to tell myself was that suddenly I knew what love was. It was a discovery. My head was all full of you, but it was in the air, and I'd got hold of some of it—people treating one another not just like they mattered, but as though they could *see* you, see who you were and actually loved *that*. Maybe I'd never have known how it could be done . . ."

She smiled. "My mother said she thought you were love-starved and undernourished as well. 'That tight-fisted brother of mine—I never could find much sugar in the bucket.'—that's what she said."

He laughed. "Maybe that's why she kept trying to feed me,"

When they sat down to breakfast, the food was spread before him like a feast. Eggs and pancakes, bacon and sweet rolls. Though it was Kitty he wanted to look at, his Aunt Mary also took his notice as he watched the way she prepared a meal, the way she handled every vegetable and piece of fruit—as though a single lettuce leaf was something to be prized. And the way they were all gathered around the table, his uncle Clyde and the three girls and his aunt. The smells that lingered in the air, a distillation.

"It wasn't just food," he said, taking up one of Kitty's sandwiches. It was what you put into it, the feeling when you sat down to eat it. More than what you put in the stomach. . ." It was moments such as these—ports of entry, he liked to think of them— where you entered a certain space that belonged forever to your imagination. Among all the seething possibilities of things coming together and falling apart, you had a sudden hope of clarity about what mattered. And whatever happiness he'd had in his life, it was owing to those moments he carried with him that served as a kind of paradigm for what he tried to create for himself.

"Too bad we didn't get married," he said to her.

"With two families beating on us about the idiot children we'd produce," she said. "There'd have been hell to pay."

He'd written Kitty love letters all the time he was in the army, but he'd never gotten any response. Kitty told him later that she'd never received the letters.

"We didn't have to have children," he said.

He had a bite on his line and tried to set the hook. "Got away," he said. He baited the hook again.

She shrugged. "I didn't think about that at the time. As it was, all I could do was go my own way, beat my head against stone walls. Not that I got all that far— Probably we'd have ruined one another. You had a good long marriage, a place in the community," she offered. "Nothing to sneer at. I've been a rolling stone."

Indeed he'd loved his wife, though he'd have said now there was something left over that he'd never found a place for except in his imagination. Ironically, they'd been childless. Meanwhile Kitty had had five husbands, owing to, he thought, no one being able to meet her match. Very likely she'd have been too much woman for him as well. Most likely she'd come into the world with a certain elevation of spirit, and hadn't settled for anything less.

"When you married that first time, I was wild with jealousy." What was jealousy but the flame turned green?

"Gus?" she said. "I gave him a hard time. He probably had reason to be jealous of you."

•

And what would he find now when he came back home, hardly his own anymore? Not simply occupied—usurped. Very likely Marlene would be working on the afghan she was copying out of some women's magazine. And Vernon would be planted in front of the TV, where he spent most of his time when he wasn't writing the Westerns that were going to make him rich, if not famous. He'd never been West, though he read Westerns by the dozen and took his landscapes from the pictures he saw in the *Arizona Highways* he thumbed through in the library. Nor did he know anything of the habits of horses or cattle, or, Mason concluded, of men and women.

Meanwhile he palmed off his badly typed efforts to anyone who'd read them—maintaining they was at least as good as anything on the shelf in the Rite-Aide. Mason had been a captive audience. These were narratives filled with lawlessness and violence—hold-ups, cattle-rustling, train robberies, shootings, hangings and general mayhem. "You might throw in a little sex," Mason suggested at one point, "just for the sake of variety. It's what people like to read about." Vernon worried over the subject for a while, then whipped a sheet out of the typewriter to show him. Mason was struck that he'd managed to do the job in a single sentence: *And then Nat Darby entered the saloon, took one of the girls upstairs and had his way with her.* "I needed that," he said.

During these labors, there were nearly three hundred pounds of him to keep stoked up. Mason did the cooking. That summer with Kitty had permanently influenced his ideas about food. During those years she was in charge, Emma had been able to put food on the table, mostly things she got out of a can. She could fry an egg and do up potatoes and macaroni and cheese, and she passed that knowledge onto him when she ran off to marry Homer. His father was gone most of the time, as captain of a ferry boat that went over to Saint John, and Mason fended for himself. Sometimes when he was home, they went out to eat. His father would go into the restaurant, leaving him to wait outside in the car. When he'd finished his meal, he'd bring Mason a hamburger. Once, bored with waiting, he got out of the car and went up to the window to look inside. His father was sitting practically next to the window, a plate in front of him with a steak and potatoes and all the trimmings. He ducked down quickly.

Once he learned what food could be, he decided to learn how to cook and had his Aunt Mary show him all her recipes. He carried home this new knowledge, and during the time he was in college on a scholarship, he earned his spending money weekends as the cook in a small café. After his marriage, he did his share of the cooking.

Usually he started the day with baking biscuits for breakfast, and at least twice a week, he baked bread. Much better than the store stuff. He made pound cake and oatmeal cookies and yeast rolls. He gave much of it up for church bazaars or sent it round to the neighbors. Friends he invited over for roast chicken and dressing and mashed potatoes and gravy and vegetables that weren't cooked to death. And his homemade strawberry ice cream was cause for celebration. His niece and nephew tucked in three square meals without the blink of an eye; at least Marlene helped him afterwards with the dishes. But the way the two of them packed it away, going through his meatloaves and mashed potatoes, loaves of bread and plates of cookies, all the groceries and ingredients out of his own pocket—the way they sponged off him, had turned him cranky and sullen.

When he suggested to Vernon that they chip something in for all they'd consumed that summer, his niece was not pleased. Finally, after waiting a week, they handed him fifty dollars.

He walked along trying to imagine how he would arrange his appearance. If the TV was on, he could enter without their hearing him, just appear out of nowhere. Would they, too, take him for a ghost come back to his old haunts? Full of portent, and not exactly friendly. By now Emma had very likely phoned them up. Would she have raised the question of how he'd managed to keep hold of that baseball cap in the middle of a squall? "I was sure it was his ghost— like to scared me half to death. Only now I'm wondering. But if he's not dead . . . but can he really be alive?"

More than likely, Samson would settle the argument. Mason was sure he'd jump down from where he'd been curled up in his favorite chair, or else come out from under it to rub up against his leg—a dead giveaway. The cat had missed him terribly when he'd been in the hospital, had been all over him when he came home. Since Vernon and Marlene's arrival he'd spent a good deal of time hiding under Mason's favorite armchair. They didn't like the cat. "Now what's going on here?" he could hear Vernon saying. "Folks all stirred up thinking you're dead. Maybe you can fool my mother. . . "

He would spare them further ambiguity. He was now ready to emerge—solid, reanimated—out of the fog. "It's your Uncle Lazarus," he'd announce to them, "—come back from the dead." And when they'd taken that in— "I have a message for you—you can pack up your stuff and clear out. Tonight you can spend with your mama. And come for the rest of your things tomorrow. Charlie'll be here to help you." The idea had just struck him.

Charlie—of course, Charlie. Back as before, as he deserved to be—rescued from betrayal. If he would come back . . .

That meant that he had one more place to visit before he set foot in the house. It would take him an hour—more with the fog—to get to Charlie's trailer, where he lived with his wife, Jenny. Whereas Charlie was slow, Jenny was quick, and together they'd made a decent life. Their two grown daughters, both married, worked part-time waitressing in a restaurant up the coast.

Mason could take a little credit for him. He'd come upon Charlie when he was a juvenile officer for the county. Charlie had run away from the foster home where he'd been placed, having been shunted from one relative to another, mostly neglected and very likely abused, and was living on the streets. What to do with him. The kid was sixteen and on the verge of getting into real trouble. Mason did what he frequently did with the kids he worked with—he took him fishing, taught him to fish. He'd found that out about some of those who came his way—if they took to fishing and enjoyed the companionship, they could get a glimpse of something beyond what they knew. He saw to it the boy got through high school—he wasn't the brightest, but he could get that far. And he was willing to work. He earned some real money working for the paper mill in Brewer, till he hurt his back. Then Mason took him on—Charlie needed work, and Mason needed somebody to help him keep the place up.

As Mason approached, Charlie's dog, a combination golden retriever and Newfoundland, made such a racket that through the window he could see Charlie get up from his armchair, slowly because of his arthritis, and move toward the door to see about the ruckus. Mason waited for him to open it. "What's got into you, dog?" Charlie yelled out into the fog.

"Hello there, Charlie," Mason said, stepping in close, while Charlie quieted the dog. "We haven't seen each other for a while."

Stunned, Charlie stared at him for a moment, as he stood there in the fog, then came hurtling down the steps and threw his arms around him. "I knew you weren't dead, Mr. Chalmers. I told it to Jenny. I said, 'I don't care what anybody says. He'll be back.'"

A big man, Charlie, and for a moment it seemed to Mason he'd be swept off the ground, what with him and the dog leaping up.

"Well, it's a good thing I'm here—" Mason said, when they'd got their footing and he'd caught his breath. "—seeing the state I left things in. I don't need to draw you a map."

Charlie gave a little self-conscious laugh.

"Come over to the house tomorrow," Mason said, "that is, if you're willing—after all this nonsense."

261

Jenny, who was standing in the doorway looking over the scene, didn't wait for his response. "Of course he'll come," she said. "He's been moping around here all summer. I'll be glad to get rid of him."

"Make it about nine," Mason said. "We'll have a cup of coffee—you and me with no interference—and I'll make you a list of what needs doing."

"You want me to pick up some doughnuts on the way?" Charlie asked. "I mean, if you don't have anything on hand."

"I'd count it lucky if there was a sack with crumbs in it. Chocolate icing on mine." He couldn't remember when he'd last made doughnuts; maybe he'd get out the recipe one of these days.

He'd be busy for a while. He'd have to send Charley for groceries before he could do any cooking. Meanwhile he'd throw open every window, air out the whole place. Change the sheets. Remove all trace of recent occupancy. He'd see if Mrs. Gresham would come in to do some cleaning, or one of the other church ladies. He had an accumulation in the closets and basement, stuff that had piled up over the years. No point in saving it. Some of Hannah's clothes he could give to the church for their rummage sale. And now that he was free to live, he'd make an appointment with Collins, the lawyer, to make out his will. His house would be his own, and when the time came, he'd be leaving it in good hands.

Exiles

"He's been through hell, Suz," Peter said. "Nothing original—just one more extension of the current hell we've been creating for ourselves. The Albanian version—" Peter had stopped by on the way to his house just up the road, ostensibly to see how she was doing, but five minutes into the gin and tonic she'd offered him Suzannah knew what was really on his mind. He brought out a letter with foreign postage for her inspection, and Suzannah considered a handwriting of broad clear strokes and a row of foreign stamps, black on gray. "I don't know what's coming off—I never know who's mucking around with power these days. Things are so volatile there, one disruption after another. They're mostly crooks and spies, for all I can figure out."

The Spanish afternoon denied any trace of skulduggery, but insisted vividly on pomegranate trees and ripening melons in the extending fields. Geraniums and roses cast their reds and pinks about the edges of the patio. "All the way up here I just kept thinking about him. I'm afraid for him and Anna. Maybe we could get them out of the country for a while—at least till things cool off. I've been trying to convince them to go to Paris."

He looked at her as one with ready sympathies, a fellow conspirator. "They can travel out of the country now, only none of them have any money." He shrugged, acknowledging the irony. "They have that freedom anyway." Peter, of course, would be footing the bill. He'd made it his life, taking up the cause of people on the run—persecuted writers and artists, people in every sort of political danger, even musicians down on their luck, actors out of work—sponsoring and befriending them. Indeed he'd been Suzannah's mainstay and support through all her own trouble—the merely personal. He gave her a kind of reassurance, his faith that certain things mattered, held firm in a world torn apart by ethnic conflicts and struggles for power, by bombs and money.

So here was the latest victim. From Eastern Europe or Latin America, parts of Africa they came, seeking his help and protection. A friend had told them of him or the friend of a friend. Peter provided an oasis, whatever money and connections could do. They were devoted to him—men and women, whatever their various races and tribes, religions and sects. She'd met a few—mostly Eastern Europeans, uprooted intellectuals, torn from their cultures, hoping for a way back after years of exile. And though there'd been some few along the way who'd borrowed what they never intended to return, or taken advantage of him in other ways, in one case turning on him viciously, none of it fazed him. He'd spent most of his inheritance on such humanitarian efforts, traveling behind the Iron Curtain before it fell, smuggling out manuscripts, letters and news, gathering up personal accounts, translating poems and stories, which he published in an obscure magazine in Geneva. Except for his sometimes neglected career as a sculptor, this was his life.

She guessed what was coming—he was trying to involve her in the drama, perhaps to take her mind off her own situation. Appealing to her own sense of exile and tentativeness. The question was still in her mind, whether to give up her house now that she had nothing to keep her in Andalusia and go back to the States or just to sit there, a permanent visitor, and let life happen to her. As opposed to Peter, who was a citizen of the world.

"Has he been in prison?" she asked. An obligatory question. Being in prison, escaping from prison were constant threads of Peter's narratives.

He gave a wry smile. "No, by some miracle. He didn't do anything overtly antagonistic to the regime. The threat was always there—his wife and children were harassed as well. He never took up political issues in his novels, but there everything is political. Under the old regime, you couldn't say, 'There are no goods on the shelves,' without being considered subversive—I suppose that is a political statement. But now it sounds like he has a new set of spies to contend with. "

It always dismayed her to learn that one set of evils had been exchanged for another, that the hope of progress you tried to live with suffered so many detours.

"All those unreconstructed hardliners," he went on. "Those in power never let go without a struggle. They're still entrenched—"

Now there was a new danger. His friend had published a piece demanding that the files collected by former spies and informers be opened to the public. He'd roused a storm in political circles, even among other writers and artists. "But I think they're largely creatures of the new power structure," Peter said. "Not Karlo. He's a feisty sort, very intense—he never lets down. They couldn't intimidate him. The police called him in I don't know how many times. He didn't scare."

How dreadful it all was. Just when you thought the bastions had been stormed and some new light was being let into the cellars, you discovered the old rot was still there, giving off its fatal corruption. She didn't want any of it, didn't want to think about it. There were too many items in the news as it was: Ruanda, Kosovo, East Timor. Iraq, and always the various rumblings in the Middle East or India.

"He can stay with me as soon as I can get the repairs done, but you've seen how things are." A poplar tree had keeled over during a wind and damaged the roof and one of the bedrooms of the abandoned farmhouse Peter was rebuilding. The workmen would come when they could get to it. "It's just that—"

Yes, the situation was pressing. She couldn't refuse him, even ignoring that she was in his debt. After all, she was in the house alone—she had room to take in a whole family, if need be. Her sisters from the States had been to visit, but just now she was without company. "Let them come by all means," she said, before a certain dismay set in. She would have to deal with these people, what they represented—their very presence would demand it. Deal with injustices she had no way of addressing, suffering she could hardly assuage. In some ways it might be a cruelty—offering them merely a respite from things she considered unimaginable and then throwing them back into them. Unless they simply fled. But even then— She would have to summon up suitable words as she took in

265

her visitors, instead of sinking into her own inner space, as she did now, sometimes staring out over the garden until Elvira came to her in the fading light to tell her supper was on the table. Or else if she sat reading, she would suddenly rouse herself to discover the book had fallen open in her lap at some odd page, while her mind had wandered.

"Good—you'll like them," Peter said, getting up to leave, mission accomplished. "Like I say, Karlo's intense—almost too much so at times—I could tell you some stories. But there's such a warmth, such passion . . . And his wife is lovely, very brave. She speaks English well."

Various phone calls during the next few days, and it was arranged, though not as they'd planned. Karlo was eager to come; his wife, who had an office job, would remain to look after things. Better not to have it look as though they were beating a retreat. Later perhaps— Suzannah's own concern with appearances was less dramatic. Wouldn't it seem awkward—that was her first response—to have an unattached male in the house? And cause comment? She was sensitive to conventions—she was, after all, a foreigner. As though sensing her hesitation, Peter offered assurance. "The workmen should be finishing up not long after we get back. I'll have my new studio then and invite everybody over."

First Peter would drive to Barcelona to pick Karlo up at the airport, and they would spend several days in the city before they appeared in the village. Meanwhile she had Elvira prepare the guest room and primed herself to meet her visitor with a combination of sympathy and admiration: he'd done what she could never conceive of doing, lived at the edge where everything was at risk. She tried imagining life as a single breath, a single space of hazard. What sort of man was this—what had his experience done to him? She was unprepared to answer such a question for herself. By comparison, she seemed to have so little at stake. If it came to it, she wondered, what would she stand for? Could she claim any sort of courage? She doubted it. Nor did she have Peter's selflessness and dedication.

Her husband's business had created a world—she'd served it, had raised two children, now settled in their own careers in the States, had given her spare time as a volunteer to help teach

266

English. That phase of her life over, she felt a certain relief—no more entertaining, no more tasteless jokes—but she had nothing to replace it. She knew herself only from the mirror, an uncertain image: a woman aging, without a clear future.

•

On the day of arrival, she was nervous, as though she were being put on trial. Elvira answered the door, and Peter brought him in. They were quite a pair—Peter, tall, big-boned, with a large head, broad freckled face and thick dark red hair, who completely dwarfed his companion: small, slender, almost a head shorter than she herself. Yet he was an immediate presence. Proud nose, square jaw—sharply cut features. She was reminded of a hawk chick she'd once found in the road, which she'd approached tentatively to see if it was injured. It gave out a shriek that seemed to involve every cell of its body. All hawk—don't touch. Something to be reckoned with. And this, she thought, was Karlo. But when he smiled, she saw no bird of prey.

Indeed his face lit up when he saw her, and she read interest, eagerness. His smile was almost boyish, forget the shoddy dental work. "Very please I make your acquaintance." He took her palm in his. "To your house, which you so kindly offer, I offer the world's smallest writer." He added a grandiose gesture, inviting her to laugh at him. "My books, you pile them up, and they are higher than my head."

"You're boasting," Peter said. To Suzannah, he said, "Don't confuse this with humility—you'd be making a mistake."

"The world's smallest writer is welcome," she said.

His eyes sparkled. "I saw you before," he said. "When you didn't know."

"Me? Where?" she said, surprised, looking to Peter in her puzzlement.

"Peter and I walk on the beach this morning—he told me there is the lovely lady you stay with. Suzannah— If she had been Helen, she would launch a thousand ships. And now I see you."

"You see what a difference you made in the day," Peter said. "We waved, but you didn't notice. I didn't want to break into your

267

reverie."

"Ah." She had indeed gone out that morning, walked along the beach as she often did, as if she could walk out her inner confusion, lose herself in the vistas of sand and sea—so self-absorbed in that state she didn't trouble to notice anything else. But she'd been seen—it made her feel strange, almost as if she'd been exposed, spied upon. She gave a little laugh to conceal her discomfort.

If he was enjoying a certain triumph at having caught her in a private moment, the softness of his look suggested that he found it precious. A romantic, she decided. Not at all shy. She'd come across them before. Gallantry above everything. A male thing—or maybe a European thing. To be lavished on any woman whatever her age. She grew skeptical before it. Entering foreign cultures had always intimidated her. All the things you could trip over, misinterpret. Americans blundered in like golden retriever pups, their innocence making a shambles.

Then it occurred to her a tone had been established that might offer both of them a cover. They could banter with each other, concealing more than they revealed, taking nothing seriously. Perhaps she had been given the key for getting through the next couple of days. She tried for some image of the spot in the Balkans he'd come from and what it might mean to be an Albanian. She knew something of Romania and Yugoslavia, but, for him, things had been pushed over another notch. What did it mean to come from the poorest, most isolated country in Europe? She couldn't quite take him in, though he and Peter seemed to have the ease of an established friendship, two men not too far apart in age—Karlo looked to be in his mid-fifties; Peter, somewhat older. Peter brought in his bags, and they got him settled in his room. She explained how the shower in the adjoining bath operated.

Afterwards in the living room, a glass of sangría in hand, Karlo looked edified, almost glowing. "Let me know if there is anything you need," she said. She'd invited Peter to stay for dinner—Elvira had prepared paella, and for the first time since Warren's death, the meal was served in the dining room with its handsome carved furniture. Karlo looked around appreciatively. "Very beautiful," he said, his gesture taking in wood and tile and brightly decorated plates along the walls. "I can tell you love things that are beautiful."

The tone was genuine, the words carrying a kind of recognition that gave her a little burst of pleasure. After their initial argument, Warren had left the decoration of the house entirely to her. Whereas he'd have torn out everything, modernized the old farmhouse with the most expensive fixtures money could buy, she'd found craftsmen to restore old walls and tile-work, to redo the floors. She'd searched in the city for furniture and tiles and found a gardener to put in plants and flowers. There was something more than pleasure in all of it, as though she were reentering a former life, bringing it to consciousness. In the end Warren had been won to something like enthusiasm, especially when his associates looked around and said, "Nice place you've got here."

She tried to ask Karlo about his work. "Later, I will explain," he said, "I will give you my life."

Oh dear, she thought. When she went to bed that night, she was exhausted, yet all keyed up. She slept restlessly.

When they met in the morning for breakfast, Karlo was full of energy. Already he'd gone for a walk, and seemed more at home almost than she. Elvira served them café con leche, brought them hard boiled eggs, a plate of cheese and ham and toast with butter and jam. "How good you are to have me here," he said, palms extended. "I wake in palace like the Arabian nights."

"It's a pretty modest palace," she said, smiling. "I'm sorry your wife couldn't come."

"Yes. Better for us both. She can speak the English. I can only . . . " His hands moved into the space where vocabulary failed him.

But he could look at her. Whenever they came together, his expression made a place only for her, his gaze intent but receptive, as though to see her in pristine clarity. It made her feel as she had when he told her he'd seen her without her knowing. Perhaps the absence of language brought into play something more basic or primitive, more observant and receptive. More passionate. Was that the word? She hesitated before it, there was such immediacy in the notion. As though his eyes were open, informed by some vision that he alone had access to. She had no idea what he saw—would have been glad to stand back from herself and see it too. Maybe it wasn't there at all. For herself, she found it difficult to form a clear picture of him, grasp a sense of his experience beyond what Peter had told her. A film, a scrim seemed to lie between his image and her eyes. She sensed a deficiency. She could only add up the daily facts of his presence.

The work at Peter's was going more slowly than expected. A lot of his roof had to be reconstructed. Materials hadn't come. Various delays. She was relieved that in the days that followed Karlo actually made few demands on her. The routine of the household went undisturbed. Most mornings he was up early and after a walk on the beach and their meeting for breakfast, he went to his room or set up a card table in the garden to work. He was intent on finishing the draft of a novella he had brought to Spain to work on. Whenever she glanced out at him, she found him frowning with concentration. Sometimes he worked all day. Sometimes he stayed up till all hours like some night animal tracking its prey. How intense the impulse that carried him—she envied him.

But if he came to a momentary block, Peter was there on his motorcycle to whisk him off. Quite a picture, the two of them. Karlo would mount on the back, clasping Peter around the waist, and off they roared to the beach, to the surrounding towns. She loved to watch them take off. A motorcycle—somehow it was fitting.

She tried to negotiate a state of affairs where her visitor could do as he pleased without feeling ignored. As the days passed, she felt she should rouse herself from her torpor—do something for him. "He must be bored . ." she started to say to Peter.

"On the contrary, for him, boredom would be self-indulgence. He has all he needs."

She felt rebuffed. "I just thought he'd like to meet some other people," she countered. "A dinner party—."

"Of course," Peter said. "I was just trying to reassure you. . . . "

They went ahead with the plan, bringing together those who formed what might be called their society, a combination of Spaniards and expatriates. The Porters and the Welds, British couples who'd retired there to escape the climate at home, were on hand; an American couple on a Fulbright, as well as a French painter

Peter knew, who had come for the summer; a couple of Spanish journalists down from Madrid for the weekend; the owner of a local bookshop; a German winegrower Warren had cultivated; and a Bosnian translator who had left the country during the civil wars.

It was more than she'd bargained for. After the usual introductory chit-chat and the first glass of sangría, the hubbub began to drown out the single voices, but over at the edge the conversation grew increasingly declamatory. The Americans were embittered over the way politics was creating a witch hunt at home. But what had Spain been through?, the journalists reminded them. The rest of Europe? The Bosnian was eager to blame the Europeans and the Americans for the state of things in the Balkans. The shelling of Dubrovnik—that's when they should have stepped in. "You think only of yourselves," the Bosnian said. "You are drunk with your ideal of goodness. You play with triviality while world falls into ruins. Democracy!" He could have spat.

Karlo leapt in. "You think the Iron Curtain is gone, everything is clean as rain. Only look—corruption, corruption everywhere. You have heard the pyramid scheme—everybody loses their money." He explained in detail. "You cannot imagine—. It is like a hell. Underground—people tearing each other—like sharks."

She'd been standing with the Porters, who'd been trying to hold onto the notion of a friendly gathering. "You've got to start out with solid institutions," Bryan Porter said, leaning over to Suzannah, as though revealing a secret. As in India, she thought. She caught the cigar smoke on his breath. "Otherwise, you're just done for, aren't you?" He sent his hand in a downward plunge.

"I don't want to think about politics anymore," his wife, Gwyneth, said on the other side of her. "It gives me a headache." She was a small woman with watery blue eyes and blonde hair turning toward gray. "I just want my *Guardian*, my good English marmalade, and a little dancing now and then. That's not much to ask, is it?"

"No, dovey," her husband said, "though I could do without the dancing."

She gave him a little punch, and looked at Suzannah, to draw her into being amused. She was trying to help.

"Now a group of informers, out of the old ones," Karlo

went on, gathering momentum, gesticulating wildly. "They can't stop being what they are. Like scorpions—they cannot help being scorpions. There is a secret file on me, others—"

People looking at you with hostile intent—and how, Suzannah wondered, could you maintain your innocence in that? No one was invisible. No, there were always eyes on you.

"Oh dear," Gwyneth murmured as she sipped her drink. "Having to be like one of those little feisty dogs, all so worked up."

"And with very sharp teeth," Suzannah said. Something like acid scalded her mouth, and she had to excuse herself. If only one could take refuge— In what? Not innocence certainly. She refilled her wine glass. An old ploy. Wine made her rosy and voluble, excited her into being charming.

"How can we live—if we don't purge away these evil things?" It was becoming a drama— He was forcing people to listen to him in spite of themselves. "Why the files should be open? Otherwise, I tell you, the future is poisoned. What are we, the writers, the intellectuals?—not cunning like spies. No, we forgive the wound and do not ask revenge. Otherwise how can we live?"

His plaint ran like a litany in her head, as she went off to the kitchen to tell Elvira to serve the food. Perhaps it would bring a little calm.

If there was something to live for . . . The smell of food assured her that there was. It was beginning to make inroads into the consciousness of the guests. Or perhaps the discussion had reached one of those peaks at which, for the moment, there was a necessary pause. At any rate, there was a movement toward the table as soon as Elvira and her daughter, Beatrice, set out the platters of paella with its rich combination of seafood, chicken, sausage and rice. They brought platters of fresh tomatoes and avocados, baskets of bread. Politics dissipated into the homey and personal. Gwyneth asked Suzannah how her sister was, and Peter wanted to know if the Porters were organizing a trip this year to Lorca for the bullfights. "Lorca?" Karlo pricked up his ears. "Look, I carry him in my pocket. He is the prince—my poet. Just like Alexander with *The Iliad*."

Gwyneth smiled, puzzled, then moved past distraction, "Of course—it's the great event. We're dying to see 'El Cordobes.'"

"You enjoy the slaughter?" Karlo said. "You don't have enough?"

"It's a great art," the Porters insisted.

"And my Lorca, yes, he loved them."

"You must see a bullfight while you're in Spain."

"For the cruelty?"

"For brilliance and daring."

Afterwards, little conversations sprang up in various parts of the living room at the edge of a central bonfire that roared on until, finally, after the others had departed, Karlo was left with Peter and the two Spanish journalists, who raked over the state of things in the Balkans, speculated about the future of Kosovo and what Karlo would be going home to, if he did go back. This group finally broke up around two in the morning. Peter apologized to Suzannah for keeping her up so late. After Peter left, Karlo poured himself another drink and paced up and down, apparently replaying what had gone on before. "Goodnight," she said.

He looked up, came to himself. "Oh, I am sorry. Please forgive me—always I am carried away. You will not get your sleep." He came to her and took her hand. "Thank you," he said. "You did this for me—I am grateful for all you do."

When you were poor, you became rich in gratitude. She had learned that much in her various travels in the world.

Had Warren ever been that poor? Suzannah wondered. She was keyed up herself, as if she had just witnessed a gun battle.

●

When her husband was killed in an air crash leaving Singapore, her sisters, as well as her children, tried to persuade Suzannah to come back home to the States as soon as possible. Why would she, a woman alone, want to stay in Spain? Her older sister, Margot, came over for almost two weeks to help Suzannah through this period of loss and confusion, though Suzannah suspected that Margot very likely thought her better off. It had been a difficult marriage. For all his success in the overseas management of a consulting firm, he seemed perpetually angry that his singlemindedness had landed him only the number two spot in the firm. His rage shaped a family life in which he bullied Suzannah and sons into some version of perfection that kept changing—or else he ignored them. Away for months at a time trying to win contracts for his company's services, he took an annual holiday reluctantly so that Suzannah and the kids could reconnect with their relatives in Connecticut. His own parents were dead, and he avoided his sister, who was habitually short of cash. Earlier in his career, his job had taken him to Indonesia, Yugoslavia, and Romania.

Margot had tried Bali and Belgrade, but Bucharest had been too much for her. Spain, she decided, was far more civilized. She couldn't fault the beaches of Andalusia and the chance to sunbathe. But after two weeks she was glad enough to get back to the familiar environment of New Britain. "Now you must put yourself together and go on with your life," she insisted. "You're still an attractive woman. And you know Gordon Mason—he still asks me about you. He's doing well in that pharmacy— He runs it now."

"Aren't you getting a little ahead of the game?" Suzannah protested. "As if my first thought was another man. How can you? I know you didn't like Warren . . ." She burst into tears.

"Oh, Suzy," Margot said, putting her arms around her. "I just want you to be happy for once . . ."

"And what makes you think," Suzannah said, drawing back, "that I wasn't happy?" Her face was hot.

Margot looked at her in dismay. "Oh dear," she murmured. "But at least consider the house," she said. "I know it's a hard time for you to be practical-minded. "It's so *big*," she said, holding out her hands, looking around her. You'll rattle around in it like a pebble. And who are you going to keep company with—yes, I know, you've introduced me to the Porters and that woman with the wart on her lip. But you know how it is with a single woman. All the married women think she's after their mates and . . ."

"Please, Margot," she said, "This is the life we built here, Warren and I. You wouldn't have chosen it, but . . ."

"So I ought to mind my own business—indeed I should," she said. "You were always the one who wanted to go your own way, and if that's what you want. . ."

"I don't know what I want," Suzannah cried. "How can I

know—here, now?"

"I just thought you might need a refuge. We're there." She offered herself, the rest of the family, with open palms.

A sudden image of them all with open arms amused her. And beyond the prickly surface of Margot's affection was something she could count on. "I know—"

Though she was glad her sister had come, bringing the feel of the air she had breathed in the past, a sense of continuity, her own unresolved state made another presence a distraction, if not an irritant. She was hardly reluctant to see her go. Just as she was relieved to get past the visits of condolence from people she scarcely knew, the messages she had to answer. *"Your husband was a man of utmost integrity and large ideas. He pushed himself to the limit."* Indeed. His titanic energy had exhausted her. At times she wondered if he'd enjoyed his life.

When she'd done what was required, signed the necessary papers for the lawyer and accountant, worked past the bureaucratic snarls, and was now waiting for the accountant to settle matters of taxes and inheritance, the house loomed large and empty and quiet. She had wanted to be alone. She was reminded, though, hearing Elvira, their cook, and Beatrice, who kept the house spotless, laughing and gossiping in the kitchen, that she was a stranger here. Even though Suzannah spoke Spanish fluently now, there lay that zone where sound subsided into silence, and she was teased by a music half heard, by a space around and beyond words, shimmering with implications. Some inchoate possibility or nuance that beckoned, only to elude her.

Into that mood now Karlo had stepped. And though, like her sisters, he had always lived in the same place, where his writing made him truly a part of the culture, it struck her as they talked that he was as much an exile as she. A kind of spokesman for those who suffered and yearned in silence, still he was caught in the net of lies and intrigues that shaped the common anguish.

"You look around," —his eyes darting furtively— " you don't know who are your friends. Some artists, writers now they are mad at me for what I write."

At least he was led by some deep unswerving impulse. In the

light of his, her own loneliness seemed a pallid affair. Simply a series of moves from one place to another occasioned by her husband's work. Just when she'd got settled in a place, found connections, a common bond among those similarly situated, she'd had to pick up and move somewhere else, saying goodbye to friends from Australia or Britain or Germany or Japan, with whom she'd exchange Christmas letters, but seldom, if ever, see again.

She'd felt oddly shaped by Warren's business, his motive for being there his only real focus—that left the real life of the place untouched. Meanwhile she'd had to carve out some sort of life for them—find schools for James and Edward, do volunteer work with agencies that worked among the poor, socialize mostly with Warren's associates. Her role. For his part, he kept them in comfortable quarters, found servants to look after the cooking, clean the apartment, tend the garden. There was a car and driver to take them to markets and schools and clinics, to restaurants and gatherings. She'd hired tutors, tried to learn the language she heard in the street, now, it seemed, a garbled language of many tongues. That sense of ever keeping an ear cocked without fully understanding had given her a sense of how dependent she was on the good will of even the least of those who washed her clothes or prepared her food, as she pretended all the while she was fully in charge. An odd play of mutual preservation they enacted, she and her servants, who wanted only to cling to their good positions and not be sent away. Their mingled insecurities bred a curious sort of loyalty in those who loved her, a barely concealed contempt in those who could only see her game. She'd survived, however, with her life a bricolage taken from the various cultures she'd been exposed to.

The oasis was those few weeks in Connecticut with her sisters and nieces and nephews. Family. A life that seemed more solid, more meaningful than her own, with her children in international schools, finally going off to college in the States. There lay continuity, stability—a certain desirable boredom. The family had been in the town since the post-Civil War era, rooted there.

So that what happened now surprised her, her resistance to go back to all that she'd missed over the years. "Really, Suzy," Margot wrote as the weeks lengthened into months, "I don't understand you at all. All those years you've never had a home and couldn't wait until you were back on native soil. . . . And Jim has married such a delightful girl."

Poor thing, they thought of her—having to keep uprooting herself and the kids, starting all over again. Yet despite all the years of looking at herself through their eyes, what surfaced again after those coveted visits was that she was no longer of the common mind. She'd stepped beyond the mold that shaped her earlier life and would feel almost as much an outsider if she moved back.

Foreign speech with its varying accents, the richness of skin colors, the differences of atmosphere and orientation, the smells of different food cooking—these were the stimuli she responded to now and she found a curious reassurance in them. She missed a certain innocence and energy she found back home, but its trivializing influence, its bumbling self-assertion put her off. To whom could she speak? Those friendships that had formed out of the sense of the temporary were particularly intense. Given their common condition, their ethos of the temporary, her friends opened their lives to her, and, in effect, became her family. She felt she'd left some part of herself in each of the places she'd lived. Perhaps if she could retrieve all these fragments and put them together, she sometimes thought, with more hope than conviction, they would yield a whole greater than the sum of its parts.

•

She had been making herself sort through the boxes of stuff that had moved with them over the years and had sat gathering time in the closets. Things she'd forgotten. Correspondence and papers she burned in the fireplace; clothes she would distribute among various charities, wondering now why she'd kept them. Old treasures the kids had given her—these she put aside. She found an odd assortment of things—some shadow puppets she'd never unpacked and a tiger carved from teak.

Then a box with her old paints and drawing things and a sheaf of her various attempts. She'd carried them with her over the years, always knowing they were there, but leaving them aside. She brought out a little painting of Warren she'd done not long after they were married. What a struggle to get him to sit still for her. She smiled as she contemplated the youthful features. Not bad, she thought. She'd caught a certain expression, a kind of constant that had traveled down the years of aging features—both proud, with a touch of arrogance, and defensive. Next a drawing of their old cat, Tobey. A striped yellow cat they'd had to leave behind with her mother when Warren took his first job abroad. She couldn't tell whether he remembered her on their visits home. There were a few landscapes, unfinished drawings mostly—a couple of her better efforts from high school. She'd never thought of herself as painting seriously; yet she'd held onto these early efforts. She'd even taken an art class during one of their sabbaticals in the States and for a while she'd been stirred by an intention. She discovered a little sketchbook she'd carried for a while, recording rice fields in Bali and some willows along a river in Romania. She'd meant to do something with them. But there had been too many distractions—she'd found it hard to carve out a solitary space, to make room for herself. She lifted out a box of pastels she'd bought in Hartford, barely used, and a box of water colors, a pad of paper.

She sorted through the brushes, found an old favorite and smoothed out the hair. She looked over the tin of paints, red and yellow, orange and blue, and felt an old excitement. She went for a glass of water, then looked around for subject matter—something simple. Fruit. From the bowl on the dining room table she selected two pomegranates and three green figs and arranged them on a white plate bordered with a blue and yellow design. She studied the arrangement for a moment, moved one here, adjusted another there. The red and green cast their juxtaposed reflections on the plate. Yet to try to capture the effect seemed quite beyond her. Tentatively she put down a wash, laid in another, then found herself growing intent upon what she was doing, forgetting everything. After she'd laid in the washes, she took up a pencil for some line, deepened the colors. Gradually the painting emerged.

"Ah, you paint," Karlo said, coming up behind her. She hadn't heard him approach.

"Oh hardly," she said, flustered, caught again. "I just . . ." But she had no desire to explain.

"Of course, I knew it," he said, as though he'd made an important discovery. "Art is truth and beauty—"

"Oh," she said, "I'm just doing a little water color." It was too much to stand before truth and beauty, even if they came only with small letters. Hastily she closed up her paints.

•

Since Karlo's arrival, she had the sense that time and motion had shifted from a gray stillness into a rapid current, set in motion by Karlo's intense preoccupations. Disoriented, she wanted to stay where she was, keep the future at bay. Yet when she turned away, it was to a fading past. She tried to extract something hard and firm to take to the present moment, but her recollections seemed part of another landscape. With Warren she had shared a life. But even the remnants of grief couldn't sustain it, offer proof of her experience. She lacked further imagination.

But Karlo seemed a free agent—a presence, whether he was working on his novella or roaring off with Peter. Perhaps he was simply enjoying himself, unaware of the challenge he offered her. (Damn the unpredictability of workmen, who had conspired to set him so emphatically in her midst. Peter was all apology, but what could he do?) Karlo was grounded in purpose, she was adrift. She yearned to reclaim her space, not have to answer to anybody. Yet who did she have to answer to? But the prospect of being alone, rattling around in the house, as Margot put it, daunted her as well.

She tried to stand back, decently attentive as a hostess, but at the same time a woman who had her own concerns. The phone still rang constantly—something from lawyer, accountant, Warren's firm, various businesses, family, friends and acquaintances. She made herself go out for lunch or coffee with this one and that. These occasions left her with a sense of dissipated energy. On the other hand, Peter seemed determined to have her join their adventures. More and more they were a threesome.

Indeed the day at Agua Amargo was a gift. Peter knew the

place from his various wanderings around Andalusia, but it had been a while since he'd been there. Though he was certain they'd prostrate themselves at his feet in gratitude for his taking them there, he was, he told them, killing two birds with one stone. First there was the wonderful sandy beach. They could swim and lie out in the sun. And there was a taverna where they could have lunch. But for him, it was the stuff he could scavenge on the beach. The treasures— what he could turn up for his sculptures. It was a particularly good beach for that. Suzannah marveled at what he could do with bits of driftwood and bone, with feathers and shards of glass, even pieces of old tire, plastic cups, bits of metal and rusted wire, dented beer cans. The stuff you kicked aside in disgust—unless, of course, you were Peter—or a child. If only you could go back to a six-year-old's intensity . . . . His studio was a little museum of odds and ends that he'd reclaimed, waiting for their translation into forms that Suzannah found sometimes whimsical, sometimes formidable, like forgotten icons.

They arrived at a little cove framed by hills falling away to shelves of rock and stony outcroppings. To one side was a sandy beach, quire perfect for swimming. And how inviting it was, the water pale green and gold with the sun on it, sliding over colored stones. The rest of the beach was scattered with such stones, and rocks and shells and bunches of seaweed. "Perfect," Peter said. "We've got the place to ourselves. Just look at the colors." As if they'd all been hit by the same impulse, the three of them were one, each moving along, bending, picking up stones or shells, examining them, showing them off. "If you find a pure round one, white . . .but translucent," Karlo said, "I will trade for this beautiful . . . Look, it has a landscape on it." "What can this be—I've never seen a green like it. It can't be natural—and the shape." "It's a piece of tile," Peter said. "I can use it, if you don't want it." "By all means."

Suzannah looked back at their prints in the sand. Kids, she thought. Or maybe just idiots, the sun beating on their heads, turning their brains into mercury and salt. It was hot, she was sweating. She bounded over the hot sand, dumped her treasures next to her towel and ran down the beach into the water. "Oh," she cried, it was so wonderfully cold. She waved to the others. "You're crazy not to be in here," she yelled and plunged in. She swam out until she was breathless—out and farther out. Then she turned onto her back and floated with the waves, her eyes closed, giving herself to the lulling movement. How lovely. A wave dashed her.

She swam back in until she could put her feet down on a tussocky spot. She couldn't see Peter, but Karlo was swimming toward her. He tried to stand near her but he was beyond his depth. "So you tempt me," he said. "You think you're special because you have your rock." He tried to push her off. A struggle—he was much stronger than she expected. But just at the point of conquering, he dove down into the water, came up a little farther out, shaking water from his head and laughing. "This is Karlo's rock," he boasted. "The rock he rules. His kingdom."

They got out of the water together. "Where's Peter?" She didn't see him anywhere. He must have gone somewhere beyond the point.

"He will wander for miles," Karlo said. "until sundown—past hunger and thirst. He will forget us entirely, forget everything except popsicle sticks and pieces of plastic. Meanwhile we will starve."

"Yes," she agreed. The two men, she thought, understood one another.

Peter returned, full of enthusiasm, as they were drying off. Not only had he found inspiring bits of flotsam, but a pair of earrings someone must have laid on the sand when she went in to swim. It would be a sacrifice but he would give them to Suzannah. "How lovely," she said, admiring the earrings, silver with little figures set with red stones.

"Now I must find you a treasure," Karlo said. "Maybe not now, here in this moment. But I will find one."

As though they were in some sort of competition. "What tribute," she said. A male thing, she supposed. Never outgrown. How laced with ironies. Peter hadn't the slightest interest in her. Somewhere in the past there'd been a rocky marriage, and afterwards, from the oblique references he sometimes made, some short-lived affairs. Women loved him, but she suspected darker regions of temperament. Now he seemed interested mainly in what

281

he found on the beach or what was thrown up on the tide of political absurdity. Only Karlo was caught up in some momentary fantasy. She wondered what his wife was like.

"Look at this." Peter called their attention to the skull and vertebrae from some small animal he'd found. "I might have done something with the earrings," he said, but bones are more useful. And just look at this piece of root. Wonderful shape."

Karlo rubbed his belly. "I appreciate you have a great talent and you're now exploding with ideas. . ."

"We're starved," Suzannah said.

"In that case . . ." Peter said, and led them in the direction of the taverna.

There a young Italian woman remembered Peter, welcomed his friends, and at his request, showed them the kinds of fish that had been brought in that day that she could prepare. They chose a large fish with firm white meat that would feed the three of them, then sat down at a table under vine leaves in a little space of shade in the dazzling afternoon. They ordered a bottle of wine, exchanged toasts, attacked the bread and then the salad brought to them, and waited, teased by the odors of the cooking fish. Suzannah had never been so hungry.

The fish, the wine, the afternoon—the time went in a single rush of pleasure the three of them were reluctant to let go of. They drank a second bottle of wine and ordered a third. "I could stay here forever," Karlo said.

"I hope you will," Peter responded. "What's the news from home?"

Karlo shook his head. "Yet when I think of Tirane—it is such a beautiful place." They reminisced about Peter's visits to Albania. Karlo dramatized how he'd once outwitted some petty official by mimicking a superior and ordering him to give Karlo a permit and funds to attend a writers' meeting in Belgrade. Through Karlo's imitation, the official came across as particularly dense. The afternoon ended in great hilarity, and Suzannah yielded to their entreaties to go with them to Granada the next day to visit the Alhambra. She had planned to go to Madrid—she had business there. But it didn't seem pressing.

It turned out to be a peculiar day. They were late getting started, waiting for Karlo, who appeared in suit and tie and smelled of aftershave. "You've been all that time primping?" Peter said. "You expecting an audience with the last of the Moorish kings?"

"I always hear about the Alhambra," Karlo said, as if he could not fail to live up to the occasion. "The name of God written 9,000 times in one room alone."

All during the drive, he was pointing things out, as though to preserve each thing in its special quality. The stray dog on the road, the flock of sheep moving into the hills, certain trunks of the olive trees, as they rayed into vastness over the hills. He was exhausting.

A long drive to Granada and there it was, the walls of the great palace overlooking the old section of the city below. They bought their tickets, signed up to enter at one o'clock and were on their way to a spot where they could eat the sandwiches they had bought when Peter let out a yell and turned sharply, "Ladrón!" Thief," and took out after a man shouldering his way through the crowd. Other people started shouting. Karlo and Suzannah tried to follow, but their path was blocked, and it was impossible to see. A struggle apparently. Then the police. An increasing crowd pressed around. They'd grabbed the man, and Peter emerged with his wallet. He had to go the police station, however. No, they shouldn't wait for him. He could see the Alhambra again anytime.

So she and Karlo gave themselves to the porticoes that looked like lace in stone, admired the efflorescent color and design, the pools and fountains, the pavilion of lions, the gardens. A marvel, all of it. And how splendid to walk there, two ordinary people in a place that had been stripped of its history. A seat of power once, lost by a man more taken up with a woman than with the threat of extinction. "A dangerous illusion—power," Karlo said. "You think it belongs to you. Somewhere in the universe you listen and there is laughter."

She and Karlo spent a good deal of time in the gardens, with their exquisite roses, all colors and scents. Suzannah leaned over to smell them. Karlo did his own scouting, calling her to this one and that. After they'd made their way to the Generalife and then to the exit, Karlo pulled out from the inside of his coat the rose, a mixture of pink and yellow, they had found the most alluring and presented it to her. "For you." The promised offering. She had worn Peter's earrings.

"You can get into trouble for things like that," she said.

"What is there but trouble? It depends on the kind you want."

The next morning when she sat down to breakfast, she found a piece of paper on her plate with a verse printed out:

Why was I born between mirrors?
Day reflects me
and night copies me
in all its stars.

"Lorca," Karlo said, as he reached for a piece of melon.

What splendid egotism! That was him all over—to be part of the atmosphere, part of the air she breathed.

The following day the sheet printed with large generous strokes was on the table on the terrace, where she usually sat in the afternoon.

Free me from the martyrdom
of seeing myself without fruitage.

A knife went through her. Had he chosen words for her? And then another slipped under the door of her bedroom:

With a cape of wind
my love flung itself to the waves.

He wasn't at breakfast the next morning. He had business with Peter in town, Elvira told her. But he had left the book of poems beside her plate. "Read some Lorca today," he had written across a scrap of paper. Perhaps, she thought, she could find a verse that would protect her like a sword stroke.

•

But she wasn't called upon to marshal her defenses. The game, the contest, whatever it was—was shunted aside. For some days a sense of distraction caught at them, something immanent in the air, like static. The situation at home did not bode well. One of the factions had succeeded in creating havoc in the congress, and the political situation was close to anarchy. "The lies and callousness," Karlo raged. "More arrests and human rights violations. And what will that solve?"

He and Peter had long debates about which faction would win out, whether or not he should stay in Spain and send for Anna, what would happen if he went back. They could take temporary refuge there, Peter argued, with an eye to Paris, that refuge of expatriates, or even the States. Then after several days of brooding, of moods that ran from outrage to despair, Karlo appeared, looking as haggard as if he'd spent a month on a binge. "Pardon me for my very bad temper these past days," he apologized to Suzannah as he sat down with her for breakfast. "I have been terrible company—a great impose—how do you say? on my hostess."

She tried to reassure him—but he waved her off. "No, inexcusable to make you a party of my part." He took a sip of coffee, sat silent for a moment. "Everything strikes here," he said, as he struck his chest. "But no more of it." He pushed it all aside. "I made up my mind. Yes, finally Karlo has to do that—stop making an ass of himself. It's about time. These past days—like a nightmare. Anyway," he announced, looking at her with haunted eyes, "I am going back. I will call Peter to arrange for the ticket."

He spoke as if it were his only choice. She felt a sudden chill, could almost have wept.

"You're surprised? Maybe I am too. But who would speak for them? These times—maybe they will be worse before they get better." He shrugged. "If I don't go back, I betray something— It is where I live, what my life has been. My experience, their experience—it's the same. That's where my books came from. Without them, what they have given me, what would I write? There are those who trust me."

She envied him. She no longer trusted even herself. At times her sense of reality seemed like foam disappearing into sand. Karlo belonged somewhere, at least on his own terms. And when he left, she'd be back where she was before. The thought left her reeling.

The rest of their breakfast was taken up with small details, questions of what could be arranged. After breakfast he called Peter. Though Peter was surprised, concerned for him, he understood immediately and set about arranging things. Karlo would be able to leave the end of the week. Though he went back to work on his novella, a tension hung in the air. The day reflected him all right—all his moods, all his unpredictability.

"What I am in this kind of world is all right—nothing to lose. It comes down to myself—what I am."

"But aren't you afraid sometimes?" she asked him.

He looked at her. "And you're not?"

"And you've just told Gwyneth you'd go to the bullfights. Right after—"

"Even when I speak of the slaughter, the cruelty? But I must understand—I must see what Lorca saw, the deep emotion he discovered, that lives in his poetry. I must know that. I have come to this land of Spain and I will see what is here and if it is the same as what I know already. Perhaps I will discover. And you will come with me?"

It was more than a request. "I don't know," she demurred. "The blood—I'm afraid it will make me sick."

"Yes," he sympathized. "In the newspapers you don't have to look at it."

•

It was difficult to imagine the Porters as bullfight enthusiasts, but they made their trip to Lorca an annual pilgrimage. "It's the whole drama," Gwyneth said. "Putting their lives on the line just for those few moments in the ring. Absolutely thrilling, the courage of it."

"And the art," Bryan said. "It's such an art. Right now the bulls are at their prime—we'll see the real fighters."

Peter was less than enthusiastic. "Cruelty raised to an art," he said.

"Look, old fellow, that's all those bulls are good for. Most of them end up as beef anyway—except for the really fierce ones—the *toros bravos*. Very selective. For them it's a pampered life for four or five years. And then the final moment of glory. What more can you ask?"

"How about a willing cow and a little spot of flowery

meadow," Suzannah suggested, as she adjusted her straw hat.

"A slaughter for public entertainment," Peter said. "What's the moment of truth these days?"

"Come now," Gwyneth said, as she directed them to the cars. "It's the heart of Spain— Flamenco and bull fights—you can't have one without the other."

"Ritual," Bryan contended. "Probably goes back to the bull sacrifices in Crete."

"Once they sacrificed human beings," Peter said. "Young girls, children. Now it's murder."

"Maybe that's why they call it war," Karlo said. "So they can do it anyway—without ceremony."

"Come on, you killjoys," Gwyneth said. They distributed themselves among the various cars. Suzannah tried to avoid the Porters' vehicle because Bryan was such an erratic driver, with sudden starts and lurches that made you grateful for seat belts, but they insisted she go with them. Peter drove off with Karlo while Bryan loaded the trunk with a chest of cold drinks and the food they'd packed for the occasion. They'd also brought pillows to sit on.

Tickets in hand, they entered into the babble of voices inside the arena and found their seats in the sun. Foolish to buy seats in the shade, the Porters commented—before it was over all the seats would be in shade anyway. They watched the Spanish women make their entrances in their brilliant dresses, red, pink, yellow, with white ruffled sleeves and ruffled skirts. In the stands beside their men they were like exotic birds. The atmosphere was festive, expectant, the sun blazing. Then music to stir the blood. The grand entrance. First the officials, then the players in the drama—the picadors on horseback, the bandilleros, the matadors, all in their costumes.

Actors in place, the chute opened and the first bull came pounding into the arena, entering a strange space and a new experience. A force meeting an uncertainty. Suzannah stole a glance at Karlo next to her, his eyes riveted on the bull. Her breath caught. Peter had told her the bulls now were smaller, bred down for the bullfighters. Even so, it was more than enough. The sheer dark force of it, the horns that could gore and kill, the great head, the dewlap. It could still force its way into the mind with a single dizzying impression— You could still imagine a god rising out of it, out of nature and taking its form. A tension flowed through the crowd as one of the bandilleros ran the cape across the ground and the bull charged after it. Did it favor the left horn or the right? How would it charge? That was what you had to watch for.

Behind her Bryan was handing round bottles of beer and soft drinks and, gratefully, Suzannah took a lemonade. It was hot now—Karlo had shaped a hat out of a newspaper to shield himself from the sun. Gwyneth handed round the chicken sandwiches she had prepared. Suzannah held one in her hand, not sure if she could eat it. They were watching the picadors on their blindfolded horses stab the bull with their pointed spears. The bull lunged at one of the horses, throwing the picador to the ground. A gasp from the crowd as the others tried to lure the bull away and get the man to safety. Her stomach was a knot.

Now the two central figures of the drama emerged, matador and bull. All thought suspended, she entered into the dance between them, the series of veronicas made of charging bull and shifting cape. The excitement of the crowd was a palpable thing, the shouts of olé, with each skilful pass, the closeness of the horns. She almost forgot to breathe. And how expertly the bandilleros cast the sharp decorated sticks into the vulnerable spots to fire things up for the final encounter. Now with the muleta, the sword concealed underneath.

The moment seemed to break apart and she was spiraling inside it. The man had known from the outset what he faced, but the bull had to awaken to its fate and saw now the instrument of it, saw and would throw himself at it, trample it to the ground, if he could. As if in that moment of pure ferocity, in the recognition of the force that shaped its death, it too attempted to shape a death for what threatened, the process moving beyond the bull itself to something almost human. In the same moment, the eye and consciousness of the man were connected to the two eyes of the bull, both looking at the death that hovered over them. The passes very close to the horns now caught them in the deepest intimacy, as if only they existed, the spectators in the stands melting into illusion. Intimate as lovers, seeing nothing but each other, the flash of the cape, the maddened rush toward it, each knowing the other beyond all knowledge.

"Truly, this is art," Bryan Porter breathed behind her.

But she was dizzyingly caught up in what she had always known but never knew before. If anyone had so much as touched her the atoms of her being would have shot out in all directions.

Then the thrust of the sword, the gush of blood, the staggering animal. The bull came crashing to the ground, as the crowd went wild with applause; flowers rained from the stands. But for Suzannah came an overwhelming rush of disgust as the victorious torero received the ears and tail. She sat staring at the half ton of carcass being dragged from the arena and couldn't breathe. She wanted to get up and go outside and see no more, but there were five more bulls to watch.

Afterwards she could scarcely remember any but the first contest. She didn't know what she felt about it, couldn't find any suitable words. She barely listened to what the others were saying on the way home, the various distinctions between bulls, what marked a bull as having particular mettle. The fierceness of the Miura bulls. She was glad the Porters were so knowledgeable. Karlo, who had come in her car this time, scarcely spoke, seemed oddly subdued.

It was late when they returned to the house. She was too tired to think of eating, though she badly wanted a glass of wine. She offered one to Karlo. "I am very grateful for all that has been," he said. "Now the ending," he acknowledged, for he and Peter would be leaving the next day for Barcelona, where he would catch his flight.

"You have given me new life," he said, as he took the glass from her hand. "Let me drink to you."

"To your safe return," she said, as they clinked glasses.

He stood looking at her as though he were memorizing her features. "We'll miss you here," she said.

He set down the glass, came and put his arms around her, dived in for a kiss. "I love you," he said.

She did not resist.

"There are many marriages," he said. "I have a wife I love

289

very much. But I love you too—we are together in my soul. Sleep with me."

"I can't," she said, drawing back. "I just can't."

"Oh," he said. "How terrible for me."

The next day he was gone. Just as he was leaving, she discovered his book of Lorca's poems on the table and ran after him with it. "No, no," he said—"for you." She stood with it as the car pulled away. He waved and blew her a kiss.

•

The day's mail brought a letter from Karlo. She recognized it immediately. An envelope with slanted blue striped edges and stamps of gray on black, the large printed letters of her name and address. She had to prepare herself to open it, for what always engulfed her in a curious set of emotions. "You entered my space," the first letter said, "and I knew immediately I loved you." What she had done she couldn't imagine. "If you don't love me," she read in the second, "don't answer."

Did she love him? Love. To be so caught up, consumed. Had there been anything that could do some damage? Everything seemed so divided, fragmented. Yet she had written him.

She tore open the envelope: "My darling," she read, and entered the letter like an obstacle course. Not just for the tortuous English that pushed sometimes beyond the syntax into ambiguity, sometimes into sheer nonsense while its intended meaning plummeted toward the outrageous, but the repeated insistence on whatever emotion happened to rule, the underlinings in red ink for emphasis when all was emphasis.

"I think of you always. Your last letter gave me a high pleasure, like always. Your soul is beauty. When I say the name Suzannah, I think it must be the name for love."

Oh, come on, she thought. She should take up painting again, he insisted, be an artist: "I see you as a very particular woman. Creating everlasting fire—that is your task."

If nothing else, his letters connected to what she remembered of his time there, the way the days had reflected him, the way he'd made her see and value her surroundings. Even if she was his fantasy, his invention, perhaps she was drawn toward being seen in a way she hadn't seen herself. She read his letters as though they might lead her to whatever she was searching for.

Maybe he needed his fantasies to get by—his own situation was real enough: "I am writing you from a café—bullets are whizzing in the air around us. Who knows what will happen next? The ministry of culture is finally destroyed financially. My job too. You remember how people's savings were stolen—three billion dollars. How cruel! I could have gone to America, my wife and I—but I didn't take the money. It was stolen from others. How could I?"

She began to worry about him.

The artist, especially, works without thinking of death, though it is all around. Maybe he works because there is always death. I think of that moment in the bull ring. I see the bull. I stand looking into the eye of that death rushing toward me. Always I have struggled against the forces that would take from me my life—even more, my light.

Love also pushes the artist to create. He tries to live with love. You haven't lost the sense of beauty. You know how to laugh—to weep. You are so human. I will carry always the image of your face.

It was a letter she read many times. Meanwhile the letters from home were becoming more insistent. When was she going to put the house up for sale? Indeed she had been approached by a friend of Warren's in Madrid, who had made an offer, a generous one. She told him she would consider it, but she was no closer to a decision than when he had first approached her. What was she waiting for?—she couldn't say. Was she all right, her sisters wanted to know. Margot could come and help her with the packing and moving.

In every direction she temporized, putting people off, resisting any decision. She chided herself for her inaction.

Then suddenly the letters stopped coming. A month went by, then another. She asked Peter if he'd heard from Karlo, but he, too, hadn't received any news. He'd tried to call Karlo at home several times, but the telephone was out of service. "I'm really worried about him this time," Peter said. "You never know what can happen. Anybody with a grudge and pistol. I've tried to contact someone I know in the embassy to see if he can find out anything. I may have to go myself."

She resumed her long walks, not just on the beach but into the countryside as well. Sometimes she drove out to the villages and walked through the streets, observing old women sitting in doorways, the men in the taverns, the children playing ball in the streets. Although she wasn't doing anything, it seemed that what she was doing was profoundly real. She seemed to live in a solitude in which she wasn't alone. It was more than enough to be struggling with her own shadow.

She was afraid for him. She had an image of him falling between two mirrors, never to be reflected again in her day or night. She'd begun to read the poetry he left behind, tried to imagine how he'd responded to it. She read it in Spanish; then she bought books of other Spanish poets.

She took out his last letter, pushed away her fear for him and wrote a long response she couldn't have written before. What happened in the bull ring now struck her as the outward expression of something hidden that she had caught at last. She wrote out a verse from one of the poems she had read:

You are what I am
neither more nor less than nothing.
dream of a body that bleeds,
a soul that dreams blood.

A strange poem that sent shivers up her spine—haunted her. She found the words compelling even as she resisted them. Even as she finished writing the letter, she knew she would never see Karlo again. She'd send the letter anyway.

When she went to post it, she found a letter from Margot waiting for her. "We so look forward to the time when you'll be part of the family again," she read. "Do let us know when you're coming. We'll gather everybody together for a royal welcome."

She stared at the sentences, reread them several times before they connected with her understanding. A royal welcome. But somehow she knew she couldn't go back. And if she stayed in

Spain . . . She didn't know what her experience would be, but it no longer mattered, her not knowing. She would simply let it come to her—come the way the light came. There were moments when she let herself be surprised by light: when she stepped into the patio and let her eye move over the reds and oranges of the bougainvillea as the sun caught it and the red amaryllis, the roses and the geraniums. At that moment they reminded her of blood.

The Death of the Cat

I.

Is it the back room where it begins, through the little passage that once held the table with the perpetual dolls' tea party, cups and saucers Lauren had since come to identify as willow ware, from Japan—connecting to the shed-like part that held two great piles, one of kindling, one of coal for the various stoves and fireplaces in the house? For the winter took its toll, and endless fires in fireplace and woodstove had to be kept stoked to keep life warm enough to get through it. Snow. *Falling in great flakes. Sticking to your coat sleeve. Wet wool smell. Snow falling and still falling, piling up to the porch, up to the very eaves, with only the chimneys poking through—Snows of all the years.* She couldn't see over the banks after her father had shoveled the walk: they made a tunnel for her to walk through.

Is the beginning there, in that dark place where the coal came tumbling in through a chute, roaring a black stream into a pile she wasn't allowed to climb on, for most certainly it would dirty her clothes—though she sneaked back sometimes and took odd shaped pieces from the kindling heap to pound nails into? *Oh, the cat's been in the coal pile again.* There, where if you went in, you quick came out and shut the door against the cold and the coal smell and a lingering sense of the unfamiliar; where the snow shovels leaned against the walls in the posture of waiting and the feed stood in bags for the ducks and chickens in the side yard; and where the cat had her kittens? *"I'll put a cardboard box for her in the back room. It's too cold outside. She can have her kittens there."*

Or does she enter the past by the front door, or even the kitchen door off the side porch, by way of the trellis hanging with wisteria, humming with bees and wasps visiting between the wisteria and the climbing rose at the side of the walk leading back to the garden bordered with zinnias? It is a question Lauren has been puzzling over. Her childhood has been locked away for so many years like a sealed room she never wanted to enter. Somehow forbidden, as in the fairy tales. *You may have all the keys to all the rooms, save this one. This door you must not open.* The key trembles in her hand, different from the others. Glowing now. Light from the fire has fallen on it like blood. *Fire roaring through the house like time, charring walls and ceilings, leaving black boards and cinders.* Now that there is nothing left, she circles round her childhood house. She holds up the key.

To enter by the front door would be easiest, past the porch with its swing and all the places it would go. *Philadelphia, Philadelphia and O-hi-o.* A white house with square white pillars. She stands there before the porch. An elegant house, for all it was drafty and cold. *Antebellum.* So, then, almost a hundred years old. *Antebellum, antebellum*—the words sang through her childhood and down through the years—remembered elegance. But how could it have been? Now the town she left fifty years ago sits in the backwaters of no-time, in less than elegant decay—with a modern part trying to pull away like an obstreperous offspring towards the highway sprawl that got her there. Her old neighborhood, a slum, no hint of elegance in the houses that remain. Hers is gone—not a trace, razed by a fire, in which a child died. She read this, a little news item in a newspaper all the way up in Maine, where the family had fled after the fire. Her house where they lost their child. *Go on now, you have the key. For curiosity is the key. Curiosity killed the cat. But the cat died giving birth.*

So what is there to reclaim? She could try the various ways she'd entered the house—it was a house abounding in doors. But did it matter where you entered or what was there, or even that the cat had died? So much has gone by—in fact, a whole parade of cats. She can't remember now what the cat looked like, or even its name. Her father once spoke of a tortoise-shell cat—was that the one? Odd that even then when she stood sobbing for hours, in a grief she had never known, fathomless, as though a chasm had opened under her feet, she had no real image of the cat. Was that why she wept—because she could not see her?

It was Christmas, and the house quickened with the season. Not only were the doors and windows all along the street decked with holly wreaths, ending in the downtown strung with lights—so that everywhere you turned it was Christmas—but the tree was up in the living room. Excitement growing about what Santa might bring. And there was to be a party. People coming, breaking into the daily round, the familiar smell of mother-and-father presence. A different rhythm: her mother in the throes of preparation all week, she somehow always underfoot, trying to sneak a candy, or a nut, a bit of icing, a silver ball. Presents to be wrapped; hors d'oeuvres to be created; cakes to be baked: her mother trying to be everywhere at once. Eggnog—where was the recipe Mamie had given her? And hot punch—to the telephone to call Viola Foley to see if she would lend her punch bowl and cups. Could she get enough meat for the meatballs? For it was wartime, and meat was in short supply.

Bessie, the cleaning woman, came in all that week to help in the kitchen and to clean the house from top to bottom, from the arctic bedrooms upstairs with the only bathroom in the house—that guests would have to climb the stairs to use—to the living room, dining room and kitchen down below. The living room had been refurbished with a whole new set of slip-covers her mother had sewed on for months, all in a flower pattern to brighten up the sofa and chairs—it got so dark in the winter. Lights covered the tree, angel hair making green and blue and red and yellow halos around them, and glinted from colored balls and tinsel. Flames danced up from the logs set on the andirons of the fireplace. The room was set aglow—from the mahogany of her father's bookcase, where the Harvard Classics stood like soldiers pitted against the dark, to the crook of the stairs where the secretary reached up its glass-fronted shelves, on top of which the cat sometimes surveyed the whole of the living room.

Her father had come home a little early the night of the party, so that they would have time to eat and he could bathe and dress and build the fire and see to it there was enough wood to last the evening. He was in one of his rare good moods, making puns that her mother thought deplorable.

Her father was a disappointed man, Lauren now knows. Perhaps it explains why he had to ridicule people, pick flaws, bully to have his way. He was supposed to have become someone important—a doctor or a lawyer. But his own father had died when he was young and he'd had to sacrifice all his ambitions, and had never done anything more important than become president of the local Kiwanis Club and help with the annual food drive for the underprivileged. Baskets for the poor. He ran a small container factory with his brother, her uncle Melbourne, whom she'd seen only once. He was a casual fellow, "trying to be a hale fellow well met," her father said with contempt—for whom nothing was ever pressing, and who left her father all the real work, while he ran the sales end in Manhattan.

Most of the time there were quarrels in the house, as when her mother bought an extra pair of shoes or didn't cook something to his taste or when he wasn't satisfied with what she did with the household money. Tonight, too, there was a little tiff. "You've got too much lipstick on," her father said.

"Good heavens, Jerome, it's no more than I usually wear."

"And rouge, for God's sake. You look like a French whore."

Her mother reddened under the comparison, so that the rouge melted in with the color of her cheeks and little sparkles came to her eyelashes. In a low voice she said, "It's our party . . . Why are you trying to spoil things?"

"All right, all right—do as you damned please."

Her mother hastily wiped her eyes and went off to the dining room to get out the good dishes and the sterling silver. "They'll be here any minute."

The warmth of expectation closed round the momentary lapse, and in the kitchen Lauren had the giggles and kept dancing on her toes. She had on her patent leather shoes and a dress of tartan plaid, and imagined she was a pony. *Pony, pony, run with the wind.* Then she was a dancer, dancing with the wind. She could stay up only long enough to greet the guests; then it was upstairs to bed with her. A promise had been exacted, but she would see. There were solemnly sealed promises and negotiable promises; she had an instinct for the difference.

Then the grown-ups started coming, those great towering figures guarding the portal to the mysterious region they inhabited. First, Miss Gwen in her fur coat, and Dr. Mack, as she knew them, he, entering red-faced from more than the cold—oh that nose of his!—and cheery, shaking her father's hand, "Well hello, hello, Jerome. How's with the old boy? And this lovely girl—growing like a hollyhock, I tell you, and prettier than Shirley Temple." "I'm taking dancing lessons," she told him. "You'll be a marvel," he said and tweaked her nose as Miss Gwen took off her fur coat for Bessie to carry upstairs to the bedroom, and stood splendid in a dark-blue dress dotted with rhinestones, like a night sky—with one of her famous plunging necklines. "I don't see how she gets away with it," her father would say. "Décolletage to and beyond the pale—and I don't just mean skin. How can they learn anything in front of all that cleavage?" For Miss Gwen was a high school teacher and taught math. "It's V for Victory," he would add with a laugh. She had her hair dyed as well—in Salisbury, twenty miles away, so that it wouldn't be known, but who can keep such a secret?

"The way Mack dotes on her," her mother would say, marveling.

"Like a slave," her father said. "She's tamed him and maimed him. No wonder he drinks."

"Oh, Jerome," her mother protested. "He's like a cavalier. And he knows how to hold his liquor."

"You like his style, eh? Well, don't get any ideas. He's probably too drunk to see what she looks like under all that makeup."

They never went to Dr. Mack for their dental work. "I want a man with a steady hand," her father said, "when it comes to working the drill. He could pierce a hole in your eyeball."

But she could only look at Miss Gwen in her stunning dress and take in her dark hair and her rouged cheeks and bright lipstick, all the flavor of her presence deepened by the scent of her perfume. Her heart leapt when Miss Gwen handed her the packages she'd brought, one of them a small package wrapped in a silvery paper with a splendid bow, the most beautiful package she had ever seen. It had to be hers—she wanted to tear off the wrapping right then, only it wasn't Christmas yet, so it had to go under the tree to keep company with the packages from her aunts. Dull packages with dull things inside. Useful things. Socks and panties and slips. When her aunts visited, they gave her a dime or two to buy a savings stamp to help the war effort and gave her mother advice about how to cook for her father. "Jerome can't stand a tough piece of meat," her aunt Felicia warned her. "And a sponge cake should never be heavy—you want it to melt in your mouth. It's the extra little effort in beating the eggs."

They opened the door to Mr. Ed, the bachelor, bald as an egg, with a little rotund belly tucked under a gray wool vest. She admired the chain of his pocket watch when he took off his coat. It had a seal on it with a mermaid. His laugh tickled her. "Fussy as a woman" was her father's opinion. "Walks like he has a dime up his ass."

"How can you say things like that?" her mother would protest. "He's the nicest person in the world."

"Pfff. *Nice.*"

Lauren thought so, too, for he collected stamps and gave her his duplicates for her collection. The optometrist arrived on his crippled leg, in the company of his beautiful wife, Elizabeth, who came from money, her mother used to say in a low voice, and helped her Milman to a good thing or two. And then Miss Letty, who walked with a cane and kept a parrot.

Bessie took their coats, and her mother led her guests into the dining room and invited them to try the eggnog or take a cup of punch from Viola Foley's punch bowl. Viola herself wasn't coming—she'd called in the middle of the afternoon but had sent over her maid with the bowl. Jonathan would be there, unless he had a house call.

"I do so hope Jonathan can make it—at least for a little while. Things are so hard for him just now," her mother said.

"You're sweet on him, aren't you?" her father said. "Wish you could have married him, don't you?"

Her mother reddened. "What makes you say things like

299

that, Jerome? Heaven knows I admire him, the way he treated Lauren when she had the grippe. No one could have been more attentive."

"You didn't pay the bill."

She kept running up to the window to be sure to see him first and greet him before her mother did. It had begun to snow again, and she could see a deeper coating on the porch. Icicles hung from the eaves. *How cold it was to put your mouth around one. But so delicious. A slice of cold that sang through your teeth.* Dr. Jonathan still wasn't in sight, but here came Jimmy Calhoun, the tallest man she'd ever seen, who'd once given her father an exploding cigar. He sold insurance. He stomped the snow off his boots.

"Well look who's here," her father said. "Didn't know you'd been invited. Well, come on in, you inverted exclamation point."

"Are you deliberately insulting me," Jimmy said, holding onto his coat, "or is that your idea of a joke?"

"Better than your idea of one," her father said, with a little laugh.

Her mother gave him a look that was both angry and pleading.

"Let me tell you one about an insurance man," Jimmy said glumly.

"Why, Jimmy, honey, we're overjoyed to see you. Now you give me that coat and come right here," her mother said. She had her hand on his arm, and he was somewhat mollified. "I want you to try some of this eggnog. If it's not the best you've ever tasted. . ." And she steered him into the midst of safety.

Her mother hated it when her father insulted people. "You do it all the time," she would say after the party was over. "What is it that gets into you?"

"I can't help it if they're so goddam sensitive. So what if he is a stick—can I help it? I'd just like to have a nickel for every buck he's lost on the ponies."

The party was in full swing and still Dr. Foley hadn't arrived. Sometimes her mother cast a look at the door, frowning slightly. She didn't want to set out the buffet supper until everyone had arrived and had had at least one cup of punch. The eggnog, too, had been suitably spiked. *Spiked is when you pour in the rum.* It seemed smart to know grown-ups did this. People filled the living room and the dining room, and even overflowed into the kitchen where a serious conversation was going on between the dentist and the optometrist. "But Hitler has to be stopped or all of Europe will be destroyed," the dentist said. The optometrist shifted his weight to ease his leg. "It's a bad business, though, our getting into it. All our boys getting killed and wounded." "That's war," said the dentist. "Think of what they say about the Jews, how they've been rounded up. No saying how many dead." "They're nothing to me," said the optometrist. "They've got all the money anyway. Seems like we could do with a few less of them, considering our boys are getting killed."

Dr. Foley finally arrived, stomping his galoshes on the mat and brushing the snow from his hat. "Oh, Jonathan," her mother said, as he came in bringing the cold, "I was afraid you wouldn't be able to come. I'm so sorry about Viola." Her mother put her hand on his arm. "She gets these attacks so often. I haven't seen Viola for such a while."

"Yes," Dr. Foley said. "She's been getting these migraines frequently lately. Rest seems to do the best for her. And a compress on her forehead."

"I'm sorry she has to miss all the fun."

"It's a shame," he said. "I'd hoped a party might do her good." They seemed to contemplate the fact that not only she was deprived. "I won't stay long. I just wanted to say 'Merry Christmas,' Ginny. I have some news, but it can wait a bit."

They stood smiling at one another as her father came up. "Glad to see you, Doc." The men shook hands. "Good thing you decided to take a little time off from increasing the population. Or maybe decreasing it."

The doctor laughed. "I have only a medical degree—nothing in divinity."

She stood sashaying back and forth, no one paying any attention to her. Suddenly she ran up and tagged the doctor on the arm.

"Hello, kitten," he said, and whisked her up and held her over his head and swung her down between his legs. She gave a little shriek of pleasure and begged him to do it again.

"You're still up—it's way past your bedtime," her mother said. "Up to bed immediately."

"Just a little longer," she pleaded. She knew she had an advantage, for it was a party, and nobody wanted a fuss. She loved it when Dr. Foley came to the house. Once it had been just for her, when she'd had the grippe, but more often it was for her mother, who had spells of shortness of breath.

"Now to bed," her mother said.

She pushed her advantage and made her bargain. "If I go right up to bed, can I take one present and open it up in my bedroom?"

Her mother vacillated. "Just one."

She didn't even go around and say goodnight to everyone. Forgetting to give her father a kiss, she snatched up the silvery present with the glorious bow Miss Gwen had brought and went upstairs with Bessie to help her undress. "What are you getting for Christmas, Bessie?" she wanted to know.

"Lord knows, honey—a chance to rest my feet."

"I hope you can rest your back too."

"I might try that," Bessie said, with deep laughter. "Good night, honey bun," she said. "You sleep well now. Me, I'm going home and get me some supper. I'll be back tomorrow to help with the cleaning up."

From her bed she could hear the noise from the party below, but she wasn't thinking about it. She sat with the present in her lap, turning it over and over in her hands. There in its silvery paper, it held its secret. How badly she wanted to open it. But then once she opened it, the surprise would be gone. Finally, she worked the paper loose at one end, slipped her hand along the edge and broke the two halves apart. The silvery paper slipped aside, and there was a little box. How lovely there was something else to open. Inside, on a lavender satin bed lay slender flask of blue glass filled with perfume. She unscrewed the gold cap: Miss Gwen's perfume. She inhaled deeply—how fragrant it was. She dabbed a little behind her ears and sniffed it again. She put the cap back on. She wished everything had such wonderful scent. How lovely it would be filling the house. She imagined a whole world filled with scent.

An idea struck her. She slipped out of bed and into the hall. She could see perfectly well. A small lamp burned on the table next to her bed—the base, a dog sitting in the opening of a doghouse. The hall light was on, too, and the light in her parents' bedroom, where the coats were piled up on the bed.

She took the cap off the perfume bottle and went from coat to coat, dabbing a bit of perfume on each collar till they all smelled lovely. Then she put the cap back on. She heard someone coming upstairs and slipped under the bed, her heart pounding.

"I wish you didn't have to leave so early," her mother said.

"You know how Viola gets." It was the doctor's voice.

In front of her, two pairs of legs came down to the ankles and made feet in shoes. She could have reached out and touched her mother's high-heeled pump or run her fingers across the toe of Dr. Jonathan's heavy man shoes—but she didn't.

"Such a shame," her mother broke in. "I know you suffer."

"Ginny, dearest—there is something I must tell you."

There was a pained moment of waiting.

"There's a terrible shortage of doctors and. . ."

"Oh, Jonathan, you're not going?"

"I must," he said. "It would be on my conscience if I didn't."

"But we need you here. We—"

"Seltz will take over while I'm gone."

"I will miss you terribly."

"You know I love you."

Love you. Love you.

"You *will* write?" her mother said. "I couldn't bear it if I didn't hear from you—just to know you're all right."

"You know I will. And will you answer?" She heard the doctor slip on his coat. There was another pause, a low sound, almost a moan from her mother. Then she heard the creak of floorboards as they left the room and descended the stairs. She slipped out from under the bed and crept back to her own room. She lay in bed awake, the noise of the party louder than before. For a while she made caves in the covers and pretended they were inhabited by finger people. Then she rubbed her eyes and watched the little fizzles of color sail across the dark sky of her vision. Then she fell asleep.

III.

The cat, she read years later, was worshipped by the Egyptians as a goddess of pleasure. On their visits to the shrines they bought little cat mummies the way tourists buy postcards.

"When a cat rubs up against you," her father said once, "it's not showing affection for you, but taking its own pleasure. They care for no one, those creatures. Just keep them fed. Independent as hell."

"I don't see it that way," her mother said. "I think they feel affection if they're treated well."

"Pure sentimentality," her father said. "That what I love about women—they can't think beyond their feelings. That's why they have no moral history. Can't imagine giving affection to a creature without getting something back."

She looked at him for a long moment. "That would mean frequent disappointment," she said in a low voice.

"Are you contradicting me?"

"Not at all. Or maybe you do get something back in spite of everything."

"Whatever are you talking about?"

She was lying on the floor letting the cat rub up against her head and nuzzle her face. "Don't get too close to that cat," her mother said. "They have fleas."

"She likes me," Lauren said. She loved the cat. She put her head down to hear it purr.

That Christmas she got a small phonograph you wound up and put a record on and set the needle on the edge. Each record played a song. She played the songs over and over.

There was a jolly miller who lived on the River Dee.
He worked and slaved from morn till night,
No lark so blithe as he.
And this the burden of his song
Forever used to be:

I care for nobody, no not I
And nobody cares for me.

She liked the way it sounded when the phonograph was winding down, and the sound was like a gurgle deep in the throat. Years later she still remembered the song. Sometimes she wondered if you could take the miller's statement at face value, or was he simply some loveless workaholic so stuck on the dollar he didn't have any friends, and was shunned by everyone. So that he had to pretend to a good thing. It was a question.

"Lauren, take that phonograph up to your room and play it there."

"Why? Don't you want to hear the music?"

"I can't hear myself think. I need to talk to your mother."

"I want some pretzels."

"In the kitchen then."

She got her pretzels and hung about the doorway without showing herself. There was trouble in the house, and she had been the cause. The day after the party her mother received a telephone call from Viola Foley. Had her husband been at the party? she wanted to know. And if he was there, what was he doing? Her mother had been taken aback. Why yes, Jonathan had been at the party, though he didn't stay long. What was the matter? The matter was the scent of perfume on his coat collar. All this with people listening in on the party line. Her mother was mystified. Perfume. It was only after she'd spoken with Miss Gwen that things came to light.

"Lauren, do you know anything about Miss Gwen's perfume?"

The bottle was empty but for a tiny drop in the bottom. She'd put it on when she was playing dress-ups with Janet Elsley and Suzannah Robertson, and they, too, had dabbed it behind their ears. She'd put some on her dolls. She brought the bottle to her mother. "Why that was the present for me," her mother said. "Why didn't you ask, honey? Did you put some on Dr. Jonathan's coat?"

"On all the coats. I wanted them to smell nice."

"Oh," her mother said. "Getting into mischief, I see." Yet she didn't seem angry. "Well, you did make them smell. It's a perfume that lingers. I'll have to call Viola and hope everybody that listened in the first time is listening now."

"She watches his every move," her mother said to her father the next day. "You see how innocent it all was."

"Where there's smoke, there's fire," her father said.

"What do you mean by that?" her mother said. "There wasn't even any smoke."

"Not here maybe. In any case, fires can burn without it," her father said.

"Really, Jerome, you get on my nerves."

He was determined to pick on her mother. Sometimes he did that. She could tell when he walked in the door if he carried a pick in his hand. Sometimes she hid behind his chair and popped out to surprise him. If he was in a good mood, he said, "Hello, little monkey." But tonight he was peeved, and said. "Come out of there. You're getting a little old for that."

"And what do you do in this house while I'm away all day working my ass off?"

"You know perfectly well what I'm doing—I'm cooking and cleaning, and sewing and mending. I'm keeping house and cooking your meals."

"You'd rather be off working in some factory, I suppose—being part of the war effort."

"Maybe I would."

He raised his eyebrows. "Rosie the Riveter," he said, "I can just see it. You there with all the factory girls."

"Some people believe in patriotic duty," she said. He'd put his foot down over her leaving the house and taking a job. It was a sore point both ways. Her father had tried to enlist in the Navy, but they wouldn't take him. But the doctor had gone.

IV.

It was bitter cold the night the cat died. The wind whistled around the house and through the cracks. But she didn't know about the cat. Not till she'd kept asking and asking if the cat had had her kittens. She'd been waiting for the kittens. Waiting to see them born. Waiting to see them open their eyes and lap up milk.

She could dress them up in doll clothes.

But did it all happen before she and her mother went on the train? One morning her mother had packed a valise and put in some of her clothes as well. She found herself dressed in her woolen skirt and white pullover and dark blue jacket, with the blue beret she hadn't worn before. They were going somewhere, on the train. Leaving the house. A cab pulled up outside to take them to the train station. Her mother sat in silence as they drove down the main street past the Sussex hotel and the A & P and the drug store. To the place where the stores ended and the houses began—and there was the station with its water tower set below the street just before the bridge the train went through. You had to take the stairs down. She'd held onto the iron railing. Her mother bought their tickets— to Philadelphia, and they stood waiting on the platform until the train came chuffing in. Those arriving descended. The porter took their valise, and they followed him aboard.

"Why are we going to Philadelphia?"

"To stay with your grandmother."

"When are we coming back?"

"Honey, we're not coming back."

"But what about Daddy? Isn't he coming?"

"No, he's not coming. Daddy will get along just fine."

It was strange. The train was shaking her, taking her away from her Daddy and first grade. Trees, houses, people swept past. *No Daddy, no Daddy, no Daddy.* Mama and Daddy, like two pillars that held up the front porch. "How come Daddy isn't coming? Questions. Her mother was looking pale, her eyes watery, and every once in a while she dabbed at them with a handkerchief. Then she took out her compact, applied rouge and lipstick and powdered her nose. The train kept rushing forward. *No Daddy.*

On the day after the cat died, she was standing in her mother's bedroom watching her put on her face in front of the mirror. She loved to watch her mother dress and her father shave. She liked the little brush he used to put lather all over his face, and the way the razor made a clean path through it. She adored the smell of witch hazel. She loved the way her mother brushed her hair and then wound it up into a coil and put in combs to hold it up. Her mother was going to her Saturday-afternoon bridge club, and Mrs. Langford was coming to stay with her. She didn't like Mrs. Langford because her hands were cold and limp and covered with brown spots. And she never let her do anything.

That morning she wanted to go out to the back porch to see if the cat had had her kittens, but her mother wouldn't let her. She'd whined about it during the day. Why couldn't she see? Where was the cat—why hadn't she come in? She always came inside in the morning.

"Honey," her mother said, turning to her briefly before she began to put on her makeup, "I'm sorry, but there isn't any cat any more. She died when she was having her kittens."

Died. She didn't know *died.* What was it? She strained towards explanation.

"What happened to her?"

"We don't know—she just died. That means she's gone," her mother said.

"And her kittens?"

"They died too."

She couldn't believe it. There was no way to take it in, no place prepared. "But where did she go?" The tears were coming then.

"To heaven maybe—somewhere. But now she's gone."

The tears became sobs that took over her whole body—wrenching sobs. "Why is she gone? What happened?" She was sobbing so hard she couldn't breathe. Great wails she didn't know were in her came out. She couldn't stop crying, though her eyes were raw and her nose kept running.

Ordinarily her mother would have put her arms around her and soothed her and stroked her hair and wiped her nose with a handkerchief. Only this time she stood with strained patience staring into the mirror. Finally, she turned to her and said with a sternness she didn't recognize: "The cat is gone—that's all there is to it. I want you to stop crying—right now."

V.

How long before it happened? She was a year or two older, but the war still raged on. Something was in the air, but she didn't know what it was. First it was manifest in the strained silence when her father came home from work, in the sudden outbursts from her mother, sometimes of shouting and screaming. And what had brought them about was puzzling. Once because she'd forgotten her umbrella at school. Once when she'd broken a glass. Once because she'd lost a dollar on the way to the store. The laughter was worse. Only it wasn't laughter. Just thin scrapings from where the spring had gone dry. It made her put her hands up to her ears. The quarrels had gotten worse: why had she come back and why had he taken her back? What he'd promised and what she'd promised. And what she spent the money on. He wouldn't give her money to run the house—she'd just drink it up. Bessie would do the shopping and the cooking. Shouting and pleading. Or just shouting.

Suddenly there were other voices in the house, other presences. Her aunts, whom she'd seen once when they went to her other grandmother's funeral and twice when they came to visit. Now they were installed in the house: the ones to give her breakfast in the morning, to object if she wanted corn flakes instead of soft boiled eggs. And when she came home from school, they were sitting over their cups of Constant Comment. Her aunt Felicia, who looked like a spoon, with skinny arms straight as rulers; and her aunt Flo, lumpy as a feed sack. They both looked like her father, with his nose and chin, but with pale blonde-white hair instead of black. His nose made for a strong face, but on the women it left little space for beauty.

They were women who knew the value of a dollar and whose sense of utility was like the starch they gave to their dresses. Bessie was sent away, and the two of them shopped and mopped and cooked and mended and ironed her dresses and plaited her hair. It was as though the day came mounted on a little wheel they had to keep from jumping off the track and crashing in a heap. She learned never to ask about her mother; she continually caught hints of her existence though seldom of her reality.

309

I always thought Jerome could have done better. She had a wandering eye, that one.

She didn't know her mother had an eye problem. Her aunt Flo was always telling her to stop squinting and to move over into better light to read.

Jerome said her hand was on the arm of every man she knew. More than friendly. And then, of course, the letters. I hope Jerome burned them.

She didn't know when or how she knew that Dr. Jonathan had been killed in the war: he'd been trying to get to a wounded G.I. during one of the battles in North Africa. Or whether his death had begun or hastened her mother's dissipation. Or where she was left on account of it. She saw less and less of her father, who was now down in Washington, for things were getting worse on the production end of the business. There were shortages of materials, and he was hoping for a government contract.

"What do you want to be when you grow up?" her aunt Flo once asked her.

"A dancer," she said, even though her lessons had been stopped.

"You'd do better to learn some secretarial skills," her aunt said. "Dancers starve to death."

It was her first real experience of hatred. But she never saw things the way her aunts saw them. Certain images she clung to all down the years, stubbornly, as though claimed from the last vestiges of fading sight, where things blur into confusion. She saw her mother sitting in front of the mirror brushing her hair, twisting it into a roll and pinning it up on her head. The rich chestnut color—the way her hair caught the light when she entered a room, as though something inside her had turned it on. Her features she couldn't be certain of. She had only a single photograph, of her mother as a young girl before she was married.

There was another image, perhaps more crucial. She was left with that puzzling moment on the platform after they'd descended from the train. For they never got to Philadelphia, no more than the porch swing had taken her there. They were to change trains at Wilmington. She had hold of her mother's hand and was still asking questions as her mother picked up the valise and they began walking toward the station. They were caught up in a crowd of people, porters bustling around them. It was fearfully noisy. Then the pace of her mother's walk changed, as though intention had gone out of it. She sensed bewilderment or loss of nerve. Her mother paused, opened her purse, and pulled out a train schedule. "Where are we going now?" she asked.

"It's all right," her mother said. "There's another train. We'll get home in time for supper."

A sense of some terrible wrong seized her. More than disappointment. "Why? Why are we going back?"

"Who would be there in that empty house?" her mother said distractedly. "Who would feed the cat?"

The Orange Bird

The crate from Spain, long awaited, arrived at the gallery that morning. Mildred was all agog, a kid getting a birthday present, hovering over Mark as he cut the wires and pried up the planks. Carl and Antonia stood by, witnesses of the grand opening. She'd been on pins and needles for months—would the shipment arrive, would Diego come through? This was her baby. She winced as the nails came out, as though Mark might damage something, and it would be hell to pay if he did. He worked loose the lid, took out the packing. A blast of color struck him in the eye. Careful of the baby, he lifted the top canvas and set it up on a chair. The four of them stood back appraising. There it was: a vase of red and yellow flowers like fried eggs, a drape to one side; in the background an amorphous mauve shape next to what could have been a corner of the Alhambra. In front, a lobster, cooked and coral. On the other side, a basket with clusters of grapes spilling out, two apples in the neighborhood, an orange bird behind. As a finishing touch, the surface offered a crackled effect. Breathtakingly awful.

"It's beyond imagination," Mildred enthused. "Just look at the color."

Mark caught Antonia's eye, but her expression was neutral. "You can certainly see the Spanish touch," she said. He covered his mouth to avoid some expression of horror, to still the laughter that threatened to double him over. Mildred shot him a glance, dismissed him. If she'd caught his disloyalty, it didn't matter.

"Well, Diego's really done me proud," Mildred said, turning the paintings over to Carl, who did most of the framing. Eleven more lay in the crate, looking as though they'd been cranked out by a machine. "A black frame," Carl said, "to lock in the color. Or maybe silver." Carl, expert at measuring and cutting, never had an opinion about anything he was asked to frame. Just so there were no complaints from the customer. Antonia was a different kettle of fish.

"I'm just thrilled," Mildred said. "It's so hard to get a still life that'll go over. People get bored with the same old stuff. I've seen too many pumpkins in my time. I've got to call the Steens." She went off to do so at once.

Thrilled. To have hit upon Spanish kitsch instead of the mere domestic species. No doubt offering employment to how many struggling, or maybe not so struggling, Spanish artists.

"Thrilled? She can't believe that's art," Mark said to Antonia after Mildred had left for the bank. "It belongs in Wal-mart."

"Does it matter?" She was a small energetic woman in her fifties, a photographer, who supplemented her income by working part-time in the gallery and by doing weddings. She liked the connection. She and Mildred had been on friendly terms for years. A few prints of her photographs, studies in light and shadow, offering haunting contrasts, hung on the walls, attracting an occasional buyer. To Mark, these were the best work in the gallery. "Believe me, Mildred knows what she's doing. She's had to learn the hard way."

He tried for a title. "'The Afternoon of the Lobster Quadrille'—how does that grab you?"

"It's a pretty inert lobster."

"A more Daliesque approach? 'The Cornucopia's Lament'? 'Sancho Panza Strikes Again' or 'The Persistence of Indigestion'?"

"You haven't quite caught the essence. It has a certain genius," Antonia said, cocking her head, as though to capture it more fully. "A genius of badness—that's hard to come by."

"I think Mildred's outdone herself."

Transcending the typical, the banal, the decorative, this was their bread and butter. Landscapes of houses and trees decked in summer green; seascapes with foam, and sometimes dramatic clouds; the snows of a New England winter—the "yesteryear stuff," he called it—what would go well in a dining room or over the mantel of a fireplace. Technical skill to the grommet. ("Don't knock it,"

Antonia said. "Considering the way they come out of some of the art schools these days. Can't draw for shit."—"I don't." he insisted.) Still anybody could have painted them. No character, no signature. Early Motel. Late Professional Building. For the suburban nests of the up and grasping, fine for bank or doctor's office. It didn't offend—maybe even convinced people there was a place for art. For artists. For himself—or so he hoped.

He figured he'd hit it lucky when Mildred took him on his first year out of art school. Except for the one or two who'd landed on their feet, who'd somehow gotten connections and were consistently selling their work, most of his buddies had either gone into advertising or some form of computer graphics. A wonderfully talented water colorist was taken on by a greeting-card company. Left to his own devices, he'd managed to cobble together various part-time jobs. For a time, he worked nights in a bakery, after which he threw himself exhausted into bed. Then the gallery job opened up, offering him a glimpse into the art scene and actually allowing him time to paint on his own. For the moment, at least, he felt he was struggling in the right direction. If most of the stuff Mildred sold was nothing he'd ever paint himself, at least he didn't have to think about it. His work there was varied enough to be interesting: talking to potential buyers, trying to connect them with what they were looking for, whatever it was, or else setting up the shows. These were often the work of artists who combined fabric and flower arrangements, did playful treatments of animals, or water colors of river, lake, and rocky abutment. Occasionally Mildred took in a painter who moved in the direction of abstraction or did something unusual with color. He'd hung a couple of shows that moved toward the pretty good.

So far the only work that genuinely interested him was Antonia's photographs. When he tried to tell her how good they were, her face reddened, as though he'd discovered a secret that couldn't bring her any benefit. "I'm very grateful to Mildred," she'd say, as though her talent was owing to her as well. "She actually has one hanging in her living room."

Her first years Mildred had taken up young and promising artists and given them shows, even though their work mostly didn't sell, and more than once she'd been left in the lurch. She hadn't done that for quite a while, but had subsided into success. She had, in fact, hit the jackpot several years back when she'd been the one to handle the contract for the paintings and assorted art objects for a cluster of condominiums going up. A number of artists both in the area and outside had been commissioned to do paintings, even a few sculptures, suitable not only for living and dining rooms, but for bedrooms and hallways. Mildred had made it into a real competition, had worked up a lot of publicity in the papers. Artists had submitted slides for the project, and Mildred had made the selections. They'd filled up the place with beach scenes at sunrise and sunset, flower arrangements, birds in flight. Pinks and peaches, vibrant greens and blues and lavenders going from sultry to misty. The impression apparently, was to make the Midwestern city dweller believe he'd been transported to Florida. "Mildred made a bundle," Antonia had told him. "Really expanded her collection. You should see that place of hers."

By all descriptions a real showplace. Expensive woods, stone fireplace. One of the best private art collections she'd seen in the city. Not just prints and ceramics by Matisse and Picasso—the Names—but lithographs by Romare Beardon, paintings by Wayne Thiebault, Alice Neel, Chuck Close, and other notables. Work that took not just money—apparently she had plenty to throw around—but an eye too.

Mildred was a puzzle to him. Her little-kid excitement over the hopelessly bad seesawing with her aim to live with the good stuff. For investment purposes? To show she had class? She knew how to make a buck—you had to give her that. But beyond that? He wanted a way past equivocation, to where their sympathies might join—especially when she said just before the shipment arrived, "Hey, what are you painting these days? I'd like to see your work."

He was flattered, yet reluctant, at the same time curious to see what her response might be. Actually, he felt pretty good about what he was doing. He hadn't found an approach that satisfied him; he was still trying to break loose from the school stuff he'd done, mostly abstract expressionist displays with heavy impasto and a lot of surging shapes, work that now struck him as turgid and derivative, whatever praise he might have received. Now he was working into a more figurative mode, trying to use color with more finesse. After a long love affair with the German expressionists, Bonnard had become his idol.

Then she mentioned it again. "When are you going to bring something in?" When he did, taking in half a dozen of his recent canvases, Mildred set them up along the wall, regarded them with a critical eye. "You're working out of the dead stuff," she told him. "That's good." Hardly the enthusiasm that met the Spanish still life, but better than nothing. "Keep moving. Bring some more when you get them done."

He couldn't help an occasional fantasy—her giving him a show, inviting him to her house to see her art work . . . . All very unlikely, he told himself.

"Twelve of them," he said to Antonia. "How in the hell can she sell twelve of *those*? Impossible."

"You want to bet on it," Antonia said, giving a little ironic smile.

"Okay," he said. "You win, I'll buy you a beer at Stefanelli's."

"If I lose."

"I'll buy you a beer anyway." If he could manage it. Right now he was pressed from all sides—student loans, a car going bad, a nagging weakness in the chest he hadn't yet taken to a doctor.

She laughed. "You're on. Only if you win . . . "

"Trade me one of your photographs for one of my paintings."

"A deal. You look like you could use some coffee. I'll make some." She moved toward the back.

"Thought it was my turn."

"You can do it next time."

He was bone tired. He'd stayed up most of the night working on a painting that refused to jell. Tonight he'd take a break, head off to Stefanelli's and sit around with the old Italian men still in the neighborhood who frequented the place. For some reason he felt more at home with them than with the young guys that hung around. They were no longer trying to prove anything—a relief. Especially if you had everything to prove yourself. It was his only social life, as much as he could afford. As it was, he made barely enough to pay

316

the rent on an apartment in a rundown, blue-collar neighborhood, the living room serving as his studio. He'd rigged up a set of lights so he could work nights after he got home. Usually Mark managed a couple or three hours of painting, but sometimes stayed up till all hours when he really got going. He dared not do it often—he couldn't risk falling asleep on the job. He lived for his two days off, Sunday and Monday, when he could work uninterruptedly, sleeping late and working all day. He'd lost touch with most of his college friends. When one of them called, he was eager enough to talk on the phone but was vague about future meetings—at least for the time being. To all intents and purposes, he'd gone into hibernation. He had work to do, had to see what was in him.

The first of the Spanish still-lifes sold the next week. It was just what the Steens wanted. He drew a quick sketch of them in the little book he carried in his pocket: a large, hearty woman with graying hair, who wore huge earrings with smiley faces, and her balding mate, who spoke in quick explosive bursts: "Terrific color—light up that north wall come winter, won't it, hon? Terrific color."

"I was sure you'd like it," Mildred said.

Antonia gave him a significant look. Okay, one down. Mildred hung up a second and sold it the same week, this time to a woman who came in with a handsome full-size poodle. The sketches became a series, expanding like a rogues' gallery. As a preface, he'd written, What do these faces have in common?

After the eleventh had sold, in less than three months, Mark conceded that he owed Antonia a beer. That is, if he could afford it. He'd just gotten his car out of the shop, the eighteen-year-old TransAm he'd taken over from his uncle. Twelve hundred bucks on his credit card, not to mention the interest. The zeros on the bill haunted him. More out of desperation than hope, he decided to ask Mildred if she'd give him a show. His work was taking shape; it had some flashes here and there. If he could sell a few paintings. . . make a small debut. He went back over her responses as though he were counting credits. "Nice color going there." "The shapes in that one—very organic." Had anything impressed her?

He approached her at her desk cluttered with catalogs and brochures, the last Spanish still life emphatically occupying the wall just behind. She looked up from a catalog she was examining.

"An exhibit?" he asked.

"Old friend of mine from school," she said. He drew up to look over her shoulder, while she turned the pages. Mountains, cactus-studded landscapes, horses. Portraits of Hispanics. Nothing new, but genuinely well done. "She's got something," he said, leaning forward to read the name. Heather Duncan.

"A lot of talent. She used to do things like you'd see in a dream. I've got one in my bedroom. Went out to Santa Fe a few years back. Now they're selling everything she paints. Yeah," she said. "She's finally done it."

"Some great artists have gone out there to the New Mexico. Such a powerful landscape."

She didn't seem to hear him. "All she needs are a few cows' skulls."

"You going out for the opening?" he said, feeling some idiotic need to put off what he wanted to ask her.

"Too many things pressing," she said.

Then she said, "Sit down. There's something I've been thinking about. I just wanted to be sure it was the right moment."

His heart took a sudden leap, even as the Spanish still life met his eye and the orange bird seemed to stare right through him.

"Can you paint one of these?" she asked him, gesturing toward the painting.

You've got to be kidding, he almost blurted out. He was struck dumb. "Nobody's ever asked me," he said.

"I'm offering you a chance," she said. "There are lots of young artists around who could use the money."

Including himself. "Well, I . . ."

"Of course you can," she said, suddenly beaming at him. "I know you can—I've seen your work. Two hundred apiece," she said, "plus," she added indulgently, "an allowance for canvases and paints. I want another twelve of them."

Enough to get himself out of hock and have a little to float on. Would it be selling his soul? But then, maybe he could actually learn something, improve some of his techniques. Like the apprentices in the old days. The idea was beginning to appeal to him. "I'll give it a whirl," he said.

"Good boy," she said. "I knew you had it in you."

He spent the next Sunday stretching and gessoing canvases. He'd brought home the still life and hung it up on the wall, where, with the lights on it, it gave off an unholy garish sheen. He planted himself in front of it and tried to figure out the colors. Mix and match. When in doubt, lay on the cadmiums. Orange, red, yellow. After his initial drawing and painting classes, his struggling beginner's efforts, he hadn't done any close copying. But he figured he'd go about it the way he'd seen it done in the text books: make a grid, block out the forms, sketch in the details, set up some good background colors. Since this was a production job, he could try laying in the larger areas, moving from one canvas to another. He did the drape, the slab of building, the ambiguous mauve shape, then back to the first, working toward the more challenging objects. The flowers he found monstrously difficult—gaudy, truculent, but somehow elusive, innocent even in their vulgarity. He thought of Mildred. He had to keep the colors clean, pay attention to the parts but not neglect the whole. In its way, it all had to work—flowers, basket, grapes, apples, lobster, bird. As Antonia suggested, there was a certain genius in it. You had to find your way into that, on the terms it demanded. Harder than he thought—more time-consuming than he expected. For when he got through the first, the painting stood inert before his eyes. Still life indeed—nature morte. So what was wrong?

Every night he came home from work and after a quick supper—a sandwich, a can of soup heated up, or a frozen pizza he popped into the oven—he approached the painting with a certain dread, while the rest stood lined up against the wall. For two or three hours he tried to meet it on its own terms. He had to wipe away any trace of a smirk, humble himself; otherwise it wouldn't yield. Sometimes he wanted to weep with vexation—the damned thing wasn't worth the effort. Then one night when he'd almost despaired, it all came together. Just like that, as though something had sneaked in when he wasn't looking. He worked in a frenzy till four in the morning. Then it was finished, sweet Jesus—it was done. He collapsed into bed but couldn't sleep, fueled awake by a curious sort of excitement, even triumph. When he finally awoke from an exhausted sleep, he had to go immediately to look at the painting. It held, cohered, made a world, out of which the orange bird met his eye with a certain fierce partiality, seemed to follow him around the room, as though he'd somehow claimed it. He couldn't bear its gaze.

"Perfect," Mildred said, when he took it in. "Absolutely perfect. Look at this, will you," she said, calling over Antonia. "I think you've even improved on it. Those flowers have a certain subtlety." She considered. "Maybe with the rest you could give the bird just a few more touches." He didn't know whether to laugh or weep.

The subsequent paintings went more quickly. Mildred thought it best that he work from his own copy rather than the original. Let there be a few distinctive touches, so long as the painting had the same impact. He was learning quickly, discovering something from each one. Now that he'd got the colors down, he began to work up a kind of shorthand, laying in some of the areas almost without thinking. He'd got the flowers under control; the grapes had taken on a kind of fullness, as though they might explode into flavor on the palate. The apples, too, more and more appealing, were almost seductive. Now it was the bird that gave him fits. What was it doing there in its orangeness? Was there such a creature? Or a figment of dream caught in a landscape it too found unreal?

Now he painted in his dreams as well as his waking hours, painted endlessly in a kind of Sisyphean labor, so that he was more exhausted when he woke than when he went to sleep. Sometimes he was in an undersea realm, trying to paint a lobster as it disappeared in a mass of undulating bodies and snapping claws. Sometimes he found piles of wormy apples he had to sort through to find the two he needed to paint. And many a night he spent looking for the orange bird, who continually eluded him, at times leaving behind a single glowing feather. The bird challenged him in some uncanny way, and just when he'd given it up, it would appear for an instant, remote and formidable. On one occasion it landed on his shoulder, its voice in his ear, almost a human voice, but so gentle and caressing, it seemed more than human. When he woke, he felt he had gained something of incomparable value, though what he couldn't have said. When he looked at the painting, the bird confronted him as imperiously as ever, returning only his stare; and could it have uttered a sound, he would have expected a voice harsh as a crow's. From the finished canvas its eye followed him relentlessly around the room.

He wanted to be rid of its dismaying presence, wanted to be done with the whole ungodly mess. He worked as though under sentence, as though he'd entered a dimension where his dreams were part of the trial. Even as he brought in the canvases one by one, to Mildred's extravagant praise, he had no sense that he was emerging from his predicament. Then when he brought in the twelfth—they had been selling almost as quickly as he could paint them—she said, "I want a dozen more."

He broke into a sweat. *It's killing me*, he wanted to protest. His mind leapt into consequences and options. She might can him—and anything else he found had the prospect of being worse. "Let me think about it," he temporized.

"What's there to think?" she said. "You've got it down to a fine science. You don't have some foolish notion you're prostituting yourself?" She looked at him in amusement.

What could he say that she'd be willing to hear? That the job had been a stop-gap affair. That he was going stale with the repetition? That he had to give his energy to his own work. "Mildred," he said, "I've done twelve."

"So you want to bail out, eh? Sick of it—up to the gills with it, eh? Yeah, I've seen them, all the little boys and girls who want to do art. Do something *original*. Burn with a hard gemlike flame— I've even given a few of them house room." She gave a little sniff. "How many go on and do anything worth pissing on? Answer me. One in a thousand, when all's said and done—maybe one in ten-thousand. I know—the rest have their go at it. They paint their little canvases and write their little plays and audition for acting jobs, and scribble out their passionate prose. And you know what? I was among them. Can you feature that? I even won prizes." For a moment she seemed to dip down into the some memory of herself that brought her to a shrug and a small ironic dismissal.

She looked at him sharply. "And what do you think you've got that's so special? Even if you had the talent, you haven't got the moxy to . . . "

"Wait a minute," he said, blindsided by her attack. What was eating her? "I thought you liked what I was doing."

"Do you know how many are operating at that level of talent? Dozens. And not a drop more. No, you don't have it. And if you ever do, it'll surprise the hell out of both of us."

"So who the hell are you?"

"I'm trying to do you a favor," she said. "Save you some grief. Reputations are made in New York," she said. "How many have got what it takes to hack it there? You may as well paint still lifes. It'll get you farther than anything else you've done."

It was all he could do to keep from hitting her. Only there was no arguing, no proof to offer. Only the nagging suspicion that she might be right. "Okay," he said. "I'll just do that."

"Twelve more," she said.

The next week he was fueled by some sort of fever that turned days and nights into one continuous reel of shifting images in his head—all with the intensity of the Spanish still life, but of a reality heightened beyond it. He hardly knew what he was doing. He called in sick, went to bed and slept and sweated for hours. When he woke, wrung out, thirsty beyond belief, he didn't know day from night. He went to the sink and poured water down his throat until he felt bloated and mopped his face. For a time he sat staring at his hand, as though it were a strange attachment for which he had not yet discovered the use. He felt an overwhelming urge to paint.

He seized a canvas he had primed and set it on the easel. From the wall where the model hung the orange bird hunched as though it were shivering in its feathers. He hardly glanced at it. He could have painted the whole thing from memory. He had grown into habit and laid in the colors he'd used a dozen times before. No sweat. Then as he surveyed the pulsating blobs of color on his palette, he was seized by something equivalent to the fever that had taken him before, and from that point on he painted like a man possessed.

Whatever object he shaped with his brush took on a life its form could hardly contain. From the grapes, a bursting fullness— within each a small universe exploding into being. The apples rolled from their position lethal with temptation as the lobster moved in, straight from the sea, in its claw a wriggling frog with a human face. Beneath his hand, the drape and backdrop turned to rocks and trees, an original garden writhing with copulating human and animal forms. Monkeys swung from the vines. He struggled for order amid the riot of color and movement. Before he collapsed altogether, the eye of the orange bird caught his and wouldn't release his gaze, as though they had made some sort of pact. It looked ready to take off for some other dimension.

He woke early, for the first time in days breathing easily. It took him a while to remember where he was or to collect any of the pieces of the previous days. He had no idea how long the fever had engulfed him. His head was cool, and he felt as though a sweet breeze was playing around him. He remembered he'd been painting. It was only six, he saw from his watch, of whatever day was dawning. He slipped on his clothes, stepped outside to breathe the air. Then he went back in, turned on the lights and stood in front of the painting. He couldn't believe it. Someone else had painted it, not himself at all—taking inspiration from some source that lay beyond him. Well, he thought. Well. For all its madcap flourishes, it seemed more real than anything he'd painted before.

When Mildred arrived at the gallery, he was ready for her. As she walked in the door, he stood naked but for a hastily devised loin cloth, his hair matted and falling into his face—holding up the painting.

It required a moment for her to take him in. "What is this, some kind of joke? Look, I've got things to do. Are you out of your mind or what?"

"Number thirteen," he said. "The lucky number." He danced around the room with it. "I changed a few things."

Suddenly there were monkeys everywhere, cavorting through the gallery hanging from the fixtures, crapping on the floor, monkeys somersaulting, hanging by their tails. The orange bird had risen from immobility and was flapping around the room. He saw in the middle Mildred's face forming "The Scream," best painted by Munch, the clock melting down the wall, courtesy of Dali, the chair she stood in front of suddenly grabbing her and closing around her ankles, thanks to Remedios Varo. The copulating figures tumbled through the gallery, while the red and yellow flowers grew gigantic as cabbages. "Get out, get out," she yelled at him. Naked through the gallery he streaked, blowing her a kiss. Naked into the alley, monkeys clamoring around him.

The Darkness Hawk

The apartment was ridiculously cheap, even considering the fortunes of graduate students, and it was in one of those fine old houses with pillars and gingerbread across the porch that suggest perhaps a more gracious era when they were the domain of single families who could afford servants. The landlady had not yielded to the temptation of carving hers up into as many profitable fractions as possible, turning closets into bathrooms and slices of kitchen. She had only one apartment to let, perhaps enough to allow her to keep up the rest. Dana and Elizabeth had been walking by just as she put up the sign, after hours of frustrated search for a way out of their two cramped rooms they might possibly afford. "You're the first," the landlady said, scrutinizing them in a way that made them feel the discomfort of not being the last. She beckoned them inside.

They could scarcely believe it: hardwood floors and wainscotting that overflowed with grapes and foliage, real closets and a sizeable kitchen. The furniture was old but serviceable, with tables and bureaus of good wood. And to cap it off, a bay window that looked into a yard cool with grass and hydrangea bushes and locust trees offering shade. "How lovely," Elizabeth said, her hands floating outward.

"How much is it?" Dana said. They could never afford it.

She wished he hadn't spoken. He had already relinquished a space she wanted to hold onto as long as possible.

"We're students with a very limited income," Dana persisted, with the stiff justification that to Elizabeth's ear struck entirely the wrong chord. As though oblivious, the landlady hustled from here to there, opening cupboards, raising and lowering blinds. But Elizabeth kept the impression they were being narrowly observed, put to some sort of test.

"We'd take very good care of it," she ventured. "I enjoy taking care of lovely things."

The landlady gave her the merest smile.

"We have a very limited—" She gave Dana a little sharp jab. Whatever it cost—she'd find a second job if necessary—she had to have it.

"There's the porch," the old woman said with some emphasis, leading them back outside. "You've not seen the porch."

Though they had crossed it on the way inside, they recalled now that it not only swept along the front of the house, but curved around to the side. Just past the bend sat two large white rockers with wicker seats and backs, old-fashioned porch rockers.

"I'm afraid Jacob was convinced I'd run away with them," the landlady said to Elizabeth, then added in a low voice, "He was afraid everything would run away."

The chairs were chained to the porch with two great chains and heavy padlocks.

"I've been looking for the key," the landlady said, "to set them free—they won't work otherwise."

"You have to lock up everything around here," Dana assured her. "They'll steal anything that isn't nailed down."

Elizabeth nudged him again. "What happened to the key?" she asked.

"He always had it on him. Wouldn't let me touch it. When he—" she paused, "—passed on, I looked in his pockets, but it wasn't there. I always knew he'd make things hard for me."

Elizabeth refused to look at Dana, beckoned as they were toward denser thickets of peculiarity. He was not afflicted with her kind of curiosity.

"Sometimes he'd unlock the chain and sit and rock, just rock away. Only the chairs wouldn't take him anywhere."

"Where was he trying to go?" Elizabeth asked. Dana was a vessel of nervous impatience beside her.

The landlady looked vague. "I so want to find the key," she said. "I've dreamt about it. I used to dream of other things too. But he was afraid. Always afraid they'd take you somewhere beyond him." She gave them a piercing look. "All the dreams—" She shook her head. "Took every one out back where I couldn't see and wrung their necks."

"Terrible," Elizabeth murmured, struck at least by the old woman's passion. Dana was signaling her frenetically; he'd had enough.

"A true child of the Darkness Hawk," the old woman said.

"We'll take the apartment if you'll have us," Elizabeth said, surprised at her boldness. She wanted it, that was all there was to it.

The landlady patted her arm. "I was sure you would," she said. "Well, here's the front door key and the back door key," she said, reaching into her apron pocket. I'll just give you these and you can fetch your things."

"Wait a minute," Dana said. "There's a little matter of the rent." Elizabeth had quite forgotten: she had a tendency to overlook such matters.

The landlady stated a rent so low, they both gasped. Dana turned to Elizabeth with a little relenting shrug. For all his scholarly ambitions, he was a practical man, and if the old woman was as mad as a March hare, he still knew a bargain when he saw one.

•

It took only three trips in their friend Ivor's station wagon to transport all their worldly goods to their new domain: clothes, boxes of books, and their one luxury, a compact disc player. They did not own even a television. Too much distraction. So frugally had they lived the first three years of their married life most of their money had gone for books. Time enough for possessions once Dana got his degree. They made something of a virtue of their poverty, but their income was low enough and jobs hard enough to come by they couldn't do much else. And it was perhaps Elizabeth, even more than Dana, who looked toward the time when he would have his degree, a real job. She wanted a yard with a garden, and she could imagine a child playing in it.

They had the weekend to arrange their things, buy a new broom and shower curtain and a mat for the bathroom floor. By

Saturday evening Dana had been able to set up his files of note cards and was off Sunday afternoon to the library, while Elizabeth finished arranging the plants she had bought in a sudden burst of extravagance, along with a poster of the vale of Kashmir and another of the temples in Java. She spent the afternoon cooking chicken cacciatore by way of celebration. She'd splurged on a bottle of chianti.

They had just finished their dinner and were about to pour out the last of the wine when the landlady rapped on the door.

She appeared triumphant. "I've found the key," she announced and held it up for them to see.

"I'm so glad," Elizabeth said. " Would you like to celebrate with a glass of wine?"

"Oh, thank you, that's very kind. But I really must be under way. I came to tell you I'd be leaving."

"Where are you going?" Dana asked.

She held up her crossed fingers. "I'll tell you when I get back," she said. "We'll have a glass of sherry," she said, and nodded to confirm it. "Yes, some find old sherry. Just for special occasions. And I'll tell you all about it. Meanwhile, if you'll just look out for the chairs. They'll sit quietly. No one should bother them."

"Of course," Elizabeth said. "I take it you don't want them locked up."

"Oh no. Otherwise I couldn't get back."

"And how long will you be gone?" Dana wanted to know.

"It's hard to say," the landlady responded, "especially the first time. I'm guessing about a week." She turned to go.

"Bon voyage," Dana said. "I hope it's not a rough trip." When she'd left, he said, "I wonder what her game is. I'll bet she had that key all the time."

Later they heard the sound of a chair rocking, at first leisurely, as though the landlady were sitting on the porch enjoying the summer evening, then with a gathering momentum.

●

"I saw her, I'm certain of it," Dana told Elizabeth three days later.

A quick shadow flash across the front window and the sound of movement as he listened at the glass. She was in there, he was convinced of it. Hiding.

"Well, what if she is," Elizabeth found herself saying. The old woman seemed so intent on her journey it seemed wrong to disdain her.

"Absolutely off her rocker," Dana said, waiting for Elizabeth to appreciate the pun.

But Elizabeth was elsewhere. "You know, when we were kids, the porch swing would take us places. For some reason, we were always trying to get to Minneapolis. I guess we liked the sound of it. And we'd sit for hours in the abandoned cars in the back lot, shifting gears, traveling to all sorts of places."

"Only she's not six years old," Dana reminded her. "It's a small consideration."

"Oh, I know," Elizabeth said, smiling. She was bent on teasing him. "But after all, you go places."

"How's that?" he said, allowing her to waylay him from work he needed to do.

"You spend time fighting monsters, sacking cities, rescuing beautiful women—all in heroic company. You spend half your life in another age and time."

"But that's different," he said, riffling the pages of his book. "They've come down as artifacts to be studied. A matter of a cultural and social order—a reflection of the past. I'm studying a tradition."

"But first you read those stories," she insisted. "I loved the ones you told me—all those eddas and sagas when we used to walk along the river holding hands. It was like I was in another place and time. And didn't people believe them?"

"Ummn," he said, not listening. He was deep into a passage of Old High German.

She stood looking at the spot he'd left vacant. How she'd envied him the wings he sailed on—Old English, Old Norse and Old High German. They took him to those worlds she found so thrilling, and they'd end up taking him to the top of his profession. He was already considered something of an expert, the master of three highly inflected languages—on his way to a publishable book offering an original approach to the epic. He was much envied by the lesser lights, who could barely make it through one archaic tongue. Here was one to make a real contribution to knowledge— the rare soul. And the three years she'd been working at various jobs to get him there had seemed a small sacrifice.

A week later the landlady returned. Elizabeth first saw her in the back yard airing some of her things, shaking out the dust of travel, she supposed. She went out to meet her. "How was your trip?" she asked.

The landlady removed a couple of clothespins from between her lips. "Just wonderful," she said. Indeed there was color in her cheeks and a new light in her eyes. Even her stature seemed fuller. "I was there for the engagement of the princess and her prince," she said. Before Elizabeth could interrupt her with a question, she went on: "The prince had won her in a lying contest."

"You mean real lies?"

"Oh indeed. The princess had told her father, she'd only marry the man who could defeat her in a lying competition. A number tried, but they failed quite miserably."

Elizabeth considered this lack of talent. "She must have been good at it."

"Oh, supremely good."

Elizabeth was filled with delight. "And how did he win? He must have been clever."

"Exceedingly. She started off, of course. Her father, she said, had two hundred craftsmen and they were all engaged in fashioning a single cauldron that covered untold acres—"

"And the prince?"

"He said that in his father's garden grew a cabbage so huge an army could stand under each leaf. And so they went on for three days and nights—"

It was difficult for Elizabeth to take in the magnitude of such invention.

"But finally the prince said that the cabbage that grew in his father's garden would just exactly fit in the pot described by the princess, and she smiled and gave him her hand. The preparations for the wedding are underway, and in a month I shall go back for the festivities."

"How wonderful," Elizabeth said, almost ready to believe her.

"Oh, I nearly forgot. I brought you back one of the sweetmeats from the celebration of the betrothal."

It was a little cake with nuts and honey inside that Elizabeth found delicious. When Dana came home, she told him the story. She had saved him a bite of the little cake.

"An old story," he said. "North African. If I had time, I'd look it up."

"I didn't think of it as a matter for note cards," Elizabeth said, deflated.

"Hardly," he said, sitting down at his desk.

She looked for a moment at the back of his head and tried another approach, leaning down and nuzzling his ear. "Old stories can go on being beautiful stories," she said, slipping her hand past his collar.

But he had a meeting with his advisor the next morning.

•

On her next journey the landlady was not to be seen for nearly two weeks. Wherever she'd gone, she was not hiding in the house, for she'd asked Elizabeth to water her plants and to open the windows and let in some air. Elizabeth had wandered through the rooms admiring tables and dressers that been left oiled and shining, a brass lamp, a tapestry of giraffes and leopards and peacocks. But she kept returning to the portrait of a young girl on the wall just to the side of the fireplace, who appeared to be looking into the room for something she couldn't see there and seemed grieved not to find. The eyes had found a certain depth and looked into a certain distance. And whenever Elizabeth stood in front of her she found herself caught up in her yearning, though she had no idea why.

Indeed everything was going extremely well. Dana had finished the two most difficult chapters of his dissertation, and the rest would be, he said, a piece of cake. He had a found a wealth of materials, enough to keep him busy the rest of his life, and some days she scarcely saw him. There was the prospect of a teaching job for her in the fall. She would be able to leave her deadly job cataloguing periodicals in the serials department of the library, for which the only relief had been for her to sneak off to the stacks when no one was looking and read Boccaccio. Yet she was seized by a curious discontent. Once as she gazed at the portrait, she thought she heard sounds of feasting and music from behind the wall. She could almost see the landlady holding a goblet of wine, toasting the bride and groom. She wondered why she hadn't returned.

The next morning she found the landlady sitting in one of the rockers, looking rather dazed.

"I'm so glad to see you," Elizabeth said. "I was afraid something had happened."

"Sometimes things do," the landlady said in a weak voice. "The wedding had to be postponed."

"Oh, what happened?"

"It was the Darkness Hawk. I saw it. First the shadow— of the great wing of the Darkness Hawk herself. She'd come to interfere. And now the wedding's been put off. Could you bring me a little water, dear." She looked quite faint, and as she sipped the water, she admitted she'd eaten nothing for two days. "A terrible time," she said, shaking her head.

Elizabeth insisted she come in for breakfast. She called the library to say that she was ill and couldn't come in.

The landlady, still possessed by the experience, had to talk about it. "They're creatures of shadow," she went on, sitting at the table while Elizabeth busied herself over the stove. "They want everything for themselves and can't bear anyone else's happiness. They devour everything thinking it will feed them, but it's all shadows. I once saw one snatch up an ormolu clock from a room where the children were reading by the fire. Thought it must be valuable. As though it could steal time itself. But that's their way, spying in windows wherever there's warmth or light. . . ."

It appeared that as soon as the prince and princess had announced their engagement, ending an ancient quarrel between two royal houses, warring factions had sprung up to prevent the marriage, the very sort of plot the Hawk was pleased to inspire.

Now everyone was taking sides. There'd been a riot in the city, and at least one person killed. Meanwhile everyone was currying favor with the group they thought would win.

"The air stinks of corruption," the old woman said.

"What will happen now?"

The landlady shook her head. "They sent for an old wizard who lives in a cave," she said, "but he was too crippled with arthritis to come. So the king went himself. He told him to find the Flower of Dreaming Back. But no one had ever heard of it."

"Neither have I," Elizabeth said, buttering a piece of toast and setting a plate of eggs on the table.

"How kind of you," she said. "A terrible time," she murmured, still taken up with the recollection more than the food. "Well, they've all gone in search," the old woman said. "It's a flower that appears sometimes red and sometimes blue, but its true efficacy comes when the two colors join and it's purple. "

"Please eat while it's hot," Elizabeth encouraged her.

She took a bite of egg, a bit of toast. "Oh, yes," she said, putting down the fork. "I've brought you back a little chain," she said, reaching into her pocket, "with a stone. Green, you see—in the shape of a hawk."

"Why thank you," Elizabeth said. "It looks oriental. I'll wear it with pleasure."

"Don't think of it that way," the old woman said severely. "It's for protection—a reminder. Anyone can come under the shadow. Just a touch on the elbow and the cold goes all the way through. You always know when someone has been touched: the room goes heavy and the air is sucked away—the grief drips like poison. Oh, it's deadly I tell you."

When Dana came home, she showed him the chain and the stone. She refrained from distracting him with the details of landlady's trip.

●

She was in a quandary. When would be the best moment to break the news? Indeed she could hardly believe it herself, not only with

333

the precautions she'd taken but also considering how little they saw of one another. And more often than not, it was a quick goodnight and an exhausted sinking into sleep. She had put off going to the doctor for weeks, terrified of what she might find out. Now she had to be relieved; it had happened in spite of them. For they had agreed not start a family until Dana completed his degree. And what would be the effect? Dana had to finish his dissertation before he even thought of looking for a job, and it appeared now it would be at least another year. But they were going to want children sometime. They were simply getting an earlier start than they'd planned. She decided to celebrate the fact.

"A special occasion?" Dana said, looking at the lighted candle in the center of the table.

"Yes," she said, "the advent of a new era." One more story being set in motion, she thought. "But only you will be drinking the wine."

He looked at her questioningly.

"Sit down," she said. She'd made chicken tetrazini, a favorite of his. She put the plate in front of him and poured the wine, this time a light, pleasing chardonay. "We're having a baby," she said.

He laid down his fork. "Are you serious?"

It was going to be more difficult than she'd imagined.

"You've been taking your pills, haven't you? I don't see how it could have happened?"

"I don't know myself," she said humbly, " but it has."

He sat for a moment in further silence. "Try to think back," he said.

"I'd hoped you'd be pleased," she said. She remembered once his lifting a glass and toasting their future together. "It's an event," she said.

"Just surprised," he said.

"But not pleased?"

"Well, of course—now that it's happened. Of course, I'm delighted. A family. But it isn't logical," he said.

"Babies don't always come into the world by logic," she said. "Maybe neither of us would have gotten born if they did."

Apparently he was trying to think back as well.

"But you're not pleased . . . ."

"It isn't that," he said, considering. "When would you have had time to get pregnant?"

She rose from the table. "What are you trying to say?" she demanded. "—that in the absence of your attentions, I went looking for others?"

"Listen, calm down. It was—"

"Yes, I know your work—my work. Work more demanding than any mistress, let alone wife."

"Do you count it an infidelity? Do you think I'm doing it for myself?" He pulled his chair back, leaning into shadow.

Unaccountably, she gasped.

"What's the matter?" he said.

"It's me you think has been unfaithful. It's true, isn't it?"

"Don't be silly," he said. "I'm just thinking about our future."

"No, you're not," she said. "You don't know anything." At that very moment she had the impulse to rush out of the house and into the street, to fling herself into some dark unknown. Instead she rushed into the bedroom and locked the door. A moment later she could hear him trying the knob.

"Let me in," he demanded.

"I want to be alone," she yelled.

"Let me in." He was banging on the door.

"Why now? Haven't you left me alone long enough?"

"You can't just shut me out like this. It's my child too."

"It is not. Go away."

A pause. "What do you mean?"

She said nothing.

"I'm going to break in the door, and you're going to explain a few things."

"Like how I bent back over the library tables. Just think—you can conceive in any position. This child will be marked by books."

He was pounding on the door.

"Stop that. You can't break Mrs. Martin's door."

"She's turned you against me."

"Go away. You wouldn't do me any more good in here than

335

you do out there."

A stunned silence took over. But only briefly. Then he was banging on the door again, yelling for her to let him in. Her closing herself off clearly infuriated him. But she wasn't going to open up. He'd have to sleep on the couch. Tuck up all six feet of himself. Curl up his legs. Another interval of silence. Though she lay on the bed, she didn't turn out the light, but lay staring at the walls and ceiling. Suppose I painted them with cauldrons, she thought. Cauldrons and cabbages. Lavender cauldrons and blue-green cabbages. Yellow cauldrons and red cabbages. Dancing cauldrons and leaping cabbages.

"Go to hell," she heard him mutter, and then she heard his retreating footsteps. For the next few days they spoke even less than usual.

•

Though the landlady hadn't told her about going on another journey, Elizabeth had not seen her for several days. Finally, alarmed, she knocked at the door. She listened, heard nothing and knocked again. For a moment she stood uncertainly, then cautiously tried the knob. The door was unlocked—the old woman must be inside. She decided to venture farther, stepped inside and called, "Anybody home?" She listened inside the dim greenish light—the shades were drawn—and thought she heard a faint moan. Listening, she caught the sound again and moved toward the bedroom.

The old woman, lying in her bed, raised herself up slightly and extended her hand.

"Why, you're ill," Elizabeth said. "I wish I'd known."

"I'm very glad you've come," the old woman said faintly. "Sit by me."

Elizabeth pulled up a chair beside the bed. "Tell me the name of your doctor and I'll call immediately."

The old woman shook her head. "He'd only put me in the hospital and waste my time. I don't want to spoil the little I have left. I want to stay right here."

"But at least—"

"No," the old woman insisted, and paused to get her breath. "I don't want strangers interfering. Please . . . ." she said. It was in Elizabeth's power not to betray her. "There's another journey for me to take," she said, and paused for a long moment, as though awaiting the strength to continue. Then she said more firmly, "I dream of a great space, full of light, where the doors can be opened before they're closed, and everything lives in its own color."

"Yes," Elizabeth murmured.

The old woman gave a sigh. "You've been a great help," she said.

"I haven't done anything."

The old woman didn't argue, but continued, intent on what she was saying. "I want you to have the key," she said, indicating the dresser with two little drawers at the top. "It's in the bead box in that little drawer on the left." Elizabeth pulled it out, found the key, and showed the old woman that she had it.

"Good," she said. "Now everything's settled." She gave a little sigh.

•

They were going to have to move again. A son the old woman had never mentioned arrived to arrange the funeral and settle the estate, claiming the house as the next of kin—there had been no will. Now the house was up for sale, and several potential buyers had come to look at the property. Dana holed himself up in the library. After work and on weekends Elizabeth made the rounds to see if she could find another apartment for them—difficult in the middle of the semester. Dana was in a fury over the interruption moving would bring to his work, and Elizabeth knew he blamed her for the fix she'd gotten them into. She scarcely saw him: she was the one who'd have to come up with something. In truth, she was glad they had to move now that the old woman was gone.

Meanwhile doubt had riven the air between them. What she'd blurted out in anger, she made no move to retract and was almost ready to believe herself. Whenever Dana approached her in her maternity smock, she could see the question form that he didn't dare ask.

There was still the matter of the chairs. She had never told him, or anyone, that she had the key to the locks that held them. And what was she supposed to do about it? She found herself walking around the chairs, not wanting to look at them. But even so, she had a curious sense that they were waiting for her, quietly but insistently, refusing to be ignored.

Finally, one moonless night in November, not long after she thought she felt the first flutter inside her, she could resist no longer. Dana was off to the library and she was sitting alone wondering what the future would be like. On a sudden impulse she put on her jacket and went out onto the porch, where the chairs were two sets of angular shadows. "I'm sorry if I've neglected you," she said, as though she had to explain herself. "I know it's been a while." She stood for a moment trying to think what should come next. "But it just didn't seem like the right moment." When was there a right moment for anything? I loved him for his stories, she thought. The enthusiasm in his voice. The way he held her hand when they walked along the river. He'd been all caught up. And she supposed he was still, very likely would be for the rest of his life, every story spawning a possibility for research. But where was she to go? Was there nothing for her to do?

She unlocked the chains and set them quietly on the porch. Tentatively she sat down, vexed with questions. For a long moment she sat listening to the stillness, surrendering to the chill night. Perhaps she was trying merely to escape from everything she knew, giving way to a strangeness that not only Dana would scoff at. What would be the consequences? She didn't know whether she would depart for some unknown region or whether she was there waiting, at long last, for something to arrive. But if it did, she would embrace it, like someone given up for lost, returning now from a long absence, and say, "Welcome, stranger, it's been a long time." Slowly at first, Elizabeth began to rock.

Spirit Over Water

Now that Jade had embarked on her new venture, the house and porch had taken on the aspect of transition, that of people moving in or out. The porch was piled with furniture—bureaus and tables, chairs and chests, even an old wheelbarrow. On weekends and sometimes during the week, she drove off to estate sales and auctions, and returned in her battered truck with the treasures she'd acquired. From the beginning, Lavinia had her doubts. What did Jade know about refinishing furniture, and where would she sell it? She was convinced that her sister Maggie had allowed herself to be cajoled once again into another scheme that boded ill for the future.

Maggie, on the other hand, held her breath as she'd done each time Jade came back to gather her forces for a new foray into the world. How could she withhold her hope from her one chick, the next generation? This time it would be different, Jade assured her. She was through with men for one thing. Feckless and brutal and power hungry—walking egos with only their cocks to give them a sense of significance. And she was through with politics: the faction and delay, the meanness and self-interest. Let all that go too. Let the past be cut away like a bloody rag.

This time she'd put her faith, her muscle into a work of rescue, refinishing old furniture, restoring good wood to new life. Now she combed the newspapers for notices of auctions and yard sales. People had no idea what lay under the surface of old paint, ancient varnish. With a little imagination, think what could be done with chairs and tables with broken parts, marred surfaces. Just until she got back on her feet, Jade persuaded her, would Maggie give a little advance? Maggie juggled things as best she could. The house and yard would have to wait.

Two or three times a week Jade came home, exultant and eager. "See that table there—solid oak under that varnish. Just needs a little gluing and the leg replaced and those burn spots sanded off. I'll get triple for it. I paid only a hundred and a quarter."

A hundred and a quarter! How it all added up. Seventy-five here and fifty there. And God knows how much altogether. For Lavinia it was all nonsense. The girl should go out and get herself a job. Not that she'd ever held one for very long. At one point, Maggie said gently, "Don't you think you need to get some stuff in shape before you collect any more?"

That was not Jade's way of doing things. She had to reach a certain point of definition, a point that tipped from potential to actualization. The right moment, when promise could be shaped and materialized, sent winging into the world. Then she would be ready to turn her energies toward it with all the furious ecstasy of a hummingbird in motion. Get it all done at once. She needed inventory. Think of how much you could sell just with impulse buying.

Maggie sighed inwardly. It wasn't that Jade lacked talent or energy or intention— always she had been able to see the potential. But once again she was being called upon for patience.

•

Hurricane Katrina was gathering force out in the Gulf, headed toward New Orleans. Katrina. What a distinction, Maggie thought, as she laid down the newspaper, for the Katrinas of the world— named for a force of nature. She was pouring a second cup of coffee when the doorbell rang, and she opened the screen door to a young man, heavy-set, pink-cheeked, head carefully shaved. It gave off a shine like the peak of an innate cheerfulness. He was from the city. The yard had to be mowed, he told her—there had been complaints from the neighbors—and the stuff removed from the front porch. This was, in fact, the second complaint from the neighbors, and she was violating ordnance number 906A. The yard was not only unsightly, but it presented a health hazard. The grass was over four inches high.

"Ms. Mock," the young man said, "What are we going to go about this? We've got a problem here."

"Well, the grass just got out of hand. I've been out of commission for over a month now and . . ." She hardly knew how to explain. "My daughter has been collecting this furniture—it's her plan to refinish and sell it. We've got a garage in back. That's her workshop."

"You're not zoned for business. If she does the refinishing here and then sends it to a shop, that's something else."

"Yes, I see."

"But she'll have to get it off the porch and something will have to be done about the yard."

Already the grass was too high just to mow. She'd had to let it go after the accident that had left her with a broken wrist and neck injuries. She'd collected insurance money—the driver had been drunk, but now her settlement was about to run out. Soon she hoped to get back to her work as a potter. She had her work in a craft cooperative downtown, where she worked three days a week. She managed to eke out a living. The accident had set her back.

"Wouldn't you know it, my car got stolen about ten days ago, which I'd just got back from the shop. Some kids joyriding. They hot-wired it," she said, a new word for her vocabulary. "Only they ran it into a tree—didn't hurt anyone fortunately. Only it's back in the shop."

"Kids are wild these days," he sympathized. "No discipline. It's the parents' fault."

It was also youth, she wanted to tell him, the giddiness and wildness and sheer force of it. "It'll take us a while to get straightened out," she said as she followed him out the door and into the yard, trying to mollify him for the circumstances she found herself in. She hated it when she got pushed into the arena of officialdom. They walked round to the back, a tangle of weeds. He flicked through a notebook and extracted an envelope. "The city has given you thirty days." He paused to look at a path of mole mounds, small volcanoes. Life under the surface. Then he tripped into a hole Lavinia's dog, Siegfried, had created in search of a bone that was no doubt somewhere else. He had a poor memory for bones—no interest in moles.

She caught at the fellow's arm as he flailed to regain his balance. "It's all right," he insisted. "Good thing I didn't break a leg."

She agreed wholeheartedly.

"Are there snakes in that grass? The neighbor thought there were snakes."

And who could that have been? she wondered. The Jacksons on one side, the Filmores on the other? The people in back with the huge van? Someone across the street? "If there are," she said, "they've got a job to do on those moles."

He consulted his notebook again. "That would make it September 25th," he said. "You have till then. Have a good weekend," he said.

"You think that hurricane's going to hit New Orleans?" she said—it was on her mind.

"I'm glad it's not me down there," he said, before he turned away.

She contemplated the porch for a moment before she went inside. "Well, Jade, here it all is—what you've collected." She could hardly see into the pile to know what was there. The table with legs that needed gluing. The bureau that would bring big bucks once Jade found a marble top to replace the one missing and found new drawer handles. And the old trunk with flowers stamped into tin side panels and on the top that somebody in the throes of nostalgia was bound to shell out for. Ditto for the old wheel barrow. Must be over a hundred years old. The magic words. Destined to confer value. Broken tables, bottomless chairs—all that was stained, warped, disdained would be transformed into collectibles along with a new life for Jade, who, once and for all, would leave behind the trail of frustrated efforts and failures: colleges dropped out of, jobs abandoned, boyfriends sent packing, various projects come to grief, bills unpaid, two cats left to fend for themselves. All in the high winds of desperation.

Maggie had to be careful not put any doubts in the way, encouraging her till the flame flickered and caught, soothing her past discouragements; already there seemed a mountain to move.

•

There was activity on the front porch. The trunk with the stamped flowers had worked its appeal on Jade. She'd had a vision of what it could be and had bolted downtown for some acrylic paints. She was now painting all the flowers. Painstaking work. The rest of the trunk she had painted blue. Maggie stopped to admire it on her way to pick up her car from the shop. "Looking good," she said. And how much, she wondered, could Jade possibly charge to make up for the hours of her labor?

"You really like it?" Jade said. She stood up and eyed her work critically.

"I think it's splendid," Maggie said. No doubt about it. Jade's instinct for beauty was beyond reproach.

Inside, Lavinia was getting ready to entertain. Every Thursday, Myra Spears, a musician who sold Avon products, came for tea. That she'd played the flute for a small ensemble put her well above the rest of their acquaintance. Lavinia would be put in mind of things she loved, while Myra sat spellbound listening to her reminisce.

"You've had such an exciting life," she would say deferentially. "And such talent." Lavinia had played her one of her recordings.

"Just look at me now." Together they would bemoan her condition.

She had been part of the household for the past several years. Maggie had taken her in, her older sister, because she had nowhere to go. Her life, full of drama, had unrolled like one of the operas she'd starred in till her voice, as well as her manager, had betrayed her. He'd absconded with all her money, leaving her in shock, stripped of all she'd been accustomed to. Even though reduced to penury, she could never forget she was a diva, had sung in the major opera houses of Europe. Maggie's problems with the city and Jade's efforts on the porch were as far from her consciousness as the impending hurricane.

When Maggie stepped outdoors, choosing to walk the three

miles to the garage, the sky was clear. Still summery, a light breeze playing through the maples. For a moment she felt almost happy. After she'd driven her car off the lot, she stopped by the employment office to see if she could find a couple of men who could tackle the yard and help clear the porch. They could use Jade's truck to cart off the dead branches that had fallen from the trees. But she found only a couple of sad-looking women, one with a small girl, filing for unemployment compensation and an older man who was looking for a night clerk's job.

But her luck took a sudden shift as she was nearing home. Just down the street she spotted a man mowing the lawn, a yellow truck parked at the curb, whose side was painted with palm trees and birds of paradise. Letters formed of leaves and flowers spelled out *Dominique Desjardins. For your house and yard the gift of beauty.* And it was perhaps Dominique himself out in front doing the ordinary work of cutting grass—lithe and loose-limbed. His head, surrounded by a crown of curly dark hair, gave him the appearance of some wild bloom himself. His tawny skin caught the light.

She parked her Chevy, stepped out and waved to him as he approached behind his mower. He shut off the motor, stood up and gave her a smile and nod, followed by a little sweep of the hand as though she were an invited guest.

"Listen—" she said. No use beating around the bush. Either he'd do it or he wouldn't. "I've got a mess up at my place. Weeds like you wouldn't believe. Branches down all over the yard. Furniture piled up on the porch. The city's on my tail to get things cleaned up. And my money's just about . . ."

He held up his hand. "Oh, no hurry, ma'am," he said. "You fire like a machine gun. Just take your time." His voice caressed the words as though each sound was a gift to the ear. Not quite a song, but enough to carry her into a different rhythm. The man himself seemed not quite real, the way the sun played on his face and was given back in subtle lights. He stood at ease; he had all the time in the world. Or else he'd shed time, just passed right through it.

No wonder he had interrupted her. Suddenly overwhelmed, she could hardly speak. She wanted to lean her head against his chest and weep.

"I don't know what sort of work you do," she said in a low voice.

"I do all kind of things," he said, with a soft laugh and gestured toward the side of the truck. "I mow lawns and pull weeds and plant grass and flowers. And what's broken I can fix."

How about my life? she wanted to say. Just for starters. She was staring at the side of the truck, taking in something she had missed before. Or had it actually been there? *Spirit work*, she read.

"You mean my sign," he said, and laughed again, as at a joke they both shared. "If spirit don't help, it all comes to nothing. The yard don't prosper and the house ain't fit for living."

"You got it," she said, and stood dumbfounded. Here was the impasse that had confronted her.

He gave her a little pat on the shoulder. "Just tell me what you need—tell me slow."

She described the yard and reeled off what had to be done. She didn't ask the price. Like time, it didn't seem part of the consideration. Here was the man to help her, if anyone could.

"Why don't I just swing by when I get done here," he said. "I never know what the job requires till I plant myself right in the middle."

Encouraged, she wrote down her address and drove home to wait for him.

An hour or so later, his truck pulled up in front and he emerged. Jade was still working on the trunk when he arrived. "Hey, that's real nice," he said, pausing to look at Jade's flowers, as Maggie stepped out to meet him. "Looks like you got a heap of stuff here to do," he said.

Jade looked at him. "Looks like it," she said dryly.

"I'll show you what has to be done in the yard," Maggie said. "Jade's cut the grass in front, but the back yard's gotten out of hand. I've been laid up."

"Things can get away from you," he sympathized. He looked up and around. "Sun's good today," he said, extending his palms, feeling out the light. "Hot and lovely—good for flower beds once we get those weeds cleared out. You got some nice shade trees here."

Only they would shed their leaves again where she had let the others lie till they rotted into the ground. Good for the soil anyway—and the weeds. He followed her around the yard, where the grasshoppers, at their approach, shot up and out in all directions. "All this," she indicated.

"I see you got an apple tree over there. A couple of cherries."

"Just a few small wormy apples," she said. "The birds get the cherries."

"Needs some pruning and a little juice," he said. "Same for that lilac. Get rid of all those old canes and she'll bloom. You got irises—a sweet flower if ever there was one. Clean out those beds and separate those rhizomes and you'll see a difference." He made slow turns about the yard, Maggie following, being shown now here, now there, plants she had forgotten. Had let go of . . . So many things, it seemed. Slipping away into time.

"We can have it all in shape," he said. "I can see this place shooting out like fireworks. Flowers everywhere. Just takes a little doing."

Even as he lifted her into the cadence of his speech, the yard seemed to blossom around her. But she dared not let him seduce her with false hope.

"My daughter collected all that furniture on the porch," she explained. "Trying to start her own business. Only . . ."

"Well," Dominique said, "things slow down for me in another month. If she wants some help with the repairing and refinishing . . ."

"I think that would be terrific," Maggie said. They went back to the porch. Jade had gone somewhere meanwhile, leaving her paints and brushes. Her truck was gone as well. "I hope the two of you can work something out." Dominique went over to a bureau, pulled out the drawers, examined the interior, flipped away a loose scab of paint with a fingernail. "Some good wood here," he said.

"She has an eye for things. A way of imagining. Can see the possibility in them."

"That's a gift," Dominique said. "What keeps me going. Whenever I get in a tight spot, I picture gardens. Then I go round smelling the flowers just like they were there." He laughed.

A tropical mentality—she envied it.

346

"I tell you what—if she's willing. Every time I'm close I'll run by and take whatever I've got room for. I got a dolly I can bring. Just take it back to the shop and see what I can do. Maybe we can make a deal."

When he left, Maggie felt a rising excitement. Something new had entered the equation, and she allowed herself room to imagine beyond the present. Things could change? Was that too absurd a notion?

•

That Saturday Jade had gone to an estate sale out in the country. She returned followed by two men she'd hired to bring home her latest prize. It was an awkward and obviously heavy piece not to be left on the front porch, where it might attract the wrong sort of attention. She held the screen as they maneuvered it in. "There," Jade directed them. "In front of the couch." Marigold, the orange-striped cat, who'd been occupying a corner of it, left off washing a paw, leapt down and fled into the kitchen, where Maggie was cooking a chicken for supper. "Jade, is that you? What's all the commotion?"

"Come see," Jade said. Maggie emerged in time to see her counting out bills to two well-muscled young men. "Thanks, fellows," she said. "Hope you enjoy the table," the stockier of the two said, with what Maggie thought was a hint of irony.

"What is this?"

"Look, can't you see? It's a coffin. Look at that wood. Pine, but it's aged and see the grain—wonderful color. Must be a hundred years old. They've made it into a table. A coffin table. Isn't that wild?"

Maggie, stunned by visual proof that you could make a table out of anything, said, "What are you going to do with it?"

"Sell it, of course. Think of what it'll bring. Fortunately, the dealers weren't pushing up the prices at this sale. Rather a small affair. Otherwise I could never have gotten it. It's been out in the barn for God knows how long."

A coffin in the living room. What was she supposed to do

347

about this reorientation of space and mind? Coffin transformed into living room furniture—awaiting your teacup or wineglass. You'd have to protect the surface with coasters like any other. Yes, the pine, though rough, held some interest. To a great degree she shared Jade's passion for wood. Before she could determine how to take in this change of perspective, Lavinia appeared.

She'd just come in from a walk with her ancient poodle, and was stopped in her tracks. "What is this?" she demanded. It looks like . . ."

"It is," Jade assured her. "A coffin. A pine coffin. They weren't so tall in those days, so it's not a big one. Must have been a leftover. Somebody made it into a table."

"You're not going to bring that thing in here?"

Maggie was frowning, waving a hand, trying to fend her off.

But Lavinia ignored her. "We *live* here—didn't that occur to you? That is, we're *trying* to live here."

"It's temporary," Jade said. "Till I can sell it. You don't have to look at it."

"Are you mad? You think you can be in this room without knowing it's there?"

Jade shrugged. "It's my business—my way of earning a living. The shed's full."

"But perhaps we can make some space," Maggie suggested. "Move a few things around. It might not sell immediately . . ."

"You think you can do anything." Lavinia had been set in motion, and now she was carried forward by the momentum of a rage that was never fully banked—"You think you're always entitled. Look at your mother—just look at her. Doesn't have a mind of her own anymore. You say, 'Jump,' and she jumps."

"Oh, go sing in the church choir," Jade said, ready to take her on. "A bunch of yellow newspaper clippings—that's all you are."

"Both of you . . ."

"No," Lavinia said, drawing herself up. "That's not what I am. I had a talent, and I used it. I struggled and let it enter the world. Nobody can take that from me. What have you brought into this house but junk that ought to be thrown away?"

"And you still act like you're queen of the hive. Everybody

has to cater to you, walk around on egg shells because you're the great Lena Mock. Pardon me—Lavinia Tucker, transformed by celebrity. Who even remembers your name? Who comes to see you? You'd starve if . . ."

"Stop it!" Maggie yelled. "Both of you."

"I won't live with that thing in this house," Lavinia raged. "Throw me out in the street if you want to." Siegfied, dancing around among them, paused to piddle on the floor. Lavinia turned and fled to her room.

"The bitch," Jade said.

"Please," Maggie said.

"The way you cater to her," Jade said. "Taking her around to all the department stores to look at stuff she can't buy. So she can go to the dollar store and pick up a box of fake fancy crackers and a jar of cheese to entertain the Avon lady. The Avon lady, for God's sake. To impress her. And those costumes she brings out—her grand wardrobe. That ragged fox fur piece. She's got the same kind of little beady eyes. Disgusting."

"It's her only happiness," Maggie said. "She was Carmen; she was Desdemona. She had bouquets thrown at her feet. . ."

"Let her eat them," She turned away. "Why is she entitled to everything when I'm only trying . . ." Helplessly, Maggie held out her arms, took her in, smoothed her back, tried to reassure her. Jade pulled away. "You don't even know me," she said.

•

Now they were both looking at the aftermath, as though trying to assess the damage after a wind shear. Jade had packed up in the middle of the night, having rifled the little lacquered box with the lions painted on it, where Maggie kept the household money, and left the two women for the golden sheen of a future yet to be discovered. How often had it happened?

They stood looking past the open door of Jade's room, surveying a chaos beyond the typical mess she'd always lived in—drawers pulled open, clothes lying helter-skelter. Maggie picked up a necklace she'd given Jade for her birthday a month earlier and surveyed a shelf with various books, pictures, and keepsakes. When Jade packed up and moved on, the sheer force of motive thrust her past all possessions and distractions.

"I've said only what I've said long ago," Lavinia insisted. "She's abused you and you've let her. Always ready to lay yourself on the altar of sacrifice—believe everything she says, go along with whatever cockamamie scheme she comes up with, but I knew in my heart of hearts." The recitative. The tone gathering in the tragic irony, but with a hint of triumph, as Maggie kept to her silence, wiping her eyes.

Lavinia's talent had been noticed early, given full attention and all the family resources. Maggie's gift, conferred perhaps by the thirteenth fairy, had been the gift of uncertainty, a continual struggle to become anything at all. Then getting pregnant just out of high school she'd become a mother. Jade was her child in more ways than one.

Now among Lavinia's advantages was that she had at least the language of the stage to call upon. Large gestures, emphatic syllables. "I could see it coming." She could have launched into the aria, "I told you so," in the mezzo-soprano range, hitting the high notes of the resentment she felt toward Jade, who kept throwing away her chances, when her own had been reduced to nil and she'd been left to depend on Maggie's charity.

•

Wind and water. Destruction and chaos. The ruin of New Orleans. Maggie had watched the nightmare unfold on television and in the newspaper. People crammed into the Super Dome, where the forces of nature had taken over as well. Rape, murder, pillage, police brutality. She was haunted by the voices of those who'd lost the last vestige of shelter and the little treasures of their lives; by the faces of relatives searching for sisters and mothers, fathers and children, abandoned pets; by the images of dead bodies and alligators and dogs and cats floating in what had been streets

Moved to create some sort of order, she spent the morning in Jade's room putting things away. For a moment she was standing inside Jade herself following the urge for beauty that expressed itself in the prints on her walls, the rocks she collected, the little designs she made for stationery and bookmarks. Her childhood had been a passion of making things.

Afterwards she went to the grocery. They would have food on the table, water to drink. They still had a roof over their heads. That much at least—it was a great deal. That afternoon Dominique was supposed to come by. On her return she found Lavinia and Myra having tea at the dining room table. Their Thursday tête-à-tête. There'd been a sale on Earl Grey, Maggie remembered. And the cookies, too, had been marked down. They were sitting with their backs to the living room and apparently they hadn't heard Maggie enter.

"What I have suffered at her hands," Lavinia was saying. "Crazy, that's all you can say. You've seen that awful thing in the living room."

Maggie threw her packages onto the living room couch, and the two women looked up, startled.

"We didn't hear you come in," Lavinia said.

"I came on ghost feet," Maggie said. She was still standing in the living room, taking off her sun hat. No one used the living room any longer except as a passageway to somewhere else. Even the animals avoided it. Once Lavinia came to the piano to practice scales, first putting an afghan over the coffin-table. She tried one of her favorite arias till her voice went off key, and she shut the instrument with an impatient flourish. "It's the atmosphere in here," she complained. "That awful table exerts its influence even under cover. My voice has been like this ever since it entered the house."

Maggie, too, avoided the living room; it brought back the whole anguish of Jade's sojourn in the house, its fruitless conclusion, and the long history of abortive efforts that had gone before. In the evenings after supper she drank her tea and read in the kitchen, where the light seemed friendlier. There had been no word from Jade.

"Dominique's coming by," Maggie told Lavinia after Myra had left. "He's going to do some work in the yard.

"Well, the first thing he'd better do is take that table," Lavinia said. "I can't sleep with that thing in the house. It twists my dreams out of shape."

The world does that too, Maggie thought.

"I tell you, the thing scares me. This house . . . what will become of us—I think about it constantly."

"Don't remind me," Maggie said softly.

When Dominique arrived, she had him come into the house before he started work. "My daughter's gone," she said in a low voice. "Just took off," she said. "It's not the first time. I can't tell you how often I've tried. All kinds of things to get her on the right track. And always it turns wrong." Her hands went to her face. She couldn't stop talking. "If only I'd . . ."

"It was nothing you done," he said, putting his hands on her shoulders. "Nothing you done or didn't do. Maybe it's like she's got a cocoon wrapped around her and she's living inside, and the inside is different from the outside. Like a story she's done told herself and got to keep telling herself."

Is that how it is? she wondered. And do you ever break out? She brought herself back to purpose. "Now I have to do something with all the stuff out there. This is the last thing she bought," Maggie said, leading him past the cat-clawed armchair to the table.

"And it's the one thing I wish you'd take first," Lavinia said, emerging from the kitchen. "Supposed to be a coffee table," she said. "A coffin table. Great joke, isn't it?"

"Ever opened it?" Dominique said. The three of them stood gazing down at it.

"Heavens, no."

"Bet there's a spirit inside just waiting to get out."

"I thought spirits could walk through walls," Maggie said.

"Depends on the spirit. Some just get trapped and stay in one spot for years and centuries. Till somebody comes along and sets them free."

"Well, for my money, it can stay put," Lavinia said and left them to walk her dog.

"Yeah," he said to Maggie. "You never know what you might be in for." He shifted from one foot to the other. "Only I have to bring Jimmy around to help me with it. Next time I'm around."

"I just want you to take it away," she said, with a desperation that surprised her.

After he left, she felt unsettled, jumpy. A new breach had appeared in the state of her affairs with a chill wind ripping through it. The coffin table seemed to fill the house and consume her thought. Now her imagination was full of what might be in it, the unseen hazards she might be living with. The dead in the living room. Having it there one more day, one more hour. . . She felt again a passion that seemed peculiarly hers—a terrible longing that things might change.

She couldn't sleep. She woke up in the still hours to what she thought was the sound of groaning and got up and turned on all the lights. She tip-toed into the living room, where, except for the boards that creaked underfoot and the crepitations in the walls, all was as she'd left it. Perhaps Siegfried had had a bad dream. Suppose something was indeed trapped inside. Suppose she did lift the lid. It would take courage. And she wasn't strong enough. Weak and witless. When she went back to bed, she lay in the dark and once again thought she heard a sound—of moaning or mourning. She put a pillow over her head.

When Dominique appeared, with his helper in tow, Maggie could have thrown her arms around him. But as he stood in front of the table, he shook his head. "Can't take it away yet," he said. "Spirit don't like it."

She felt condemned. "Didn't we submit the proper forms?" she asked. "Do we need a special password?" She had never claimed ownership. It was there only because of Jade. It didn't belong to her, and she had no wish to claim it. Now it appeared spirit was in charge and she was somehow responsible. Dominique gave a little shrug. "Sometimes waiting's the best. See what it wants."

"Seems like I've waited all my life." She wanted to turn away from the day. But at least he and Jimmy did take action in the back yard, cutting down dead limbs, collecting fallen branches and chopping them up till they all formed a neat stack—wood for the fireplace. Then the two men started digging up plants and reviving an old circle with bricks around it to replant them.

They went over the yard with a roto-tiller and raked over the surface. That afternoon he came round to put in grass. He got a start on the other beds, cutting down saplings and clearing away vines. She could decide what she wanted to plant. He ended up by taking one of the bureaus and a table from the front porch in exchange for the work. The porch displayed a small cleared area.

The coffin-table remained where it was.

He came round the next morning so early she was still in her robe.

"Sorry to disturb you," he said, "but I got to take off."

"Take off? Why are you leaving Metairie? Where are you going?"

"New Orleans," he said. "I got to go back."

"Oh, but you can't leave," she protested.

"I got to go," he said. "I promised Sister Gertrude I'd be there if she ever needed help, and she's calling me back. I can hear her voice inside me."

"Oh," she said, devastated.

"Can't refuse," he said. "She's the one give me everything—made me what I am. She was a terror all right." He smiled over the memory. Said to me, 'Brother, you going come to your death in the gutter. And nobody to fetch you out. The bottle or the needle—that what you want?'

"Taught me planting—yeah, she's the one. Give me my name. Dominique." He smiled. "Garden Master. Instead of Tommy in the Ditch."

"When will you be back?" she ventured.

"Can't say for sure."

"Oh." Maybe never—she sank with the idea.

After Dominique left she walked around the yard, trying to look at what had been done—staring blankly. Bleakly. Abandoned there with everything yet to do.

●

In the house the coffin-table waited. Was there some sort of emanation that coalesced in all their troubled dreams and rose up like a miasma that moved even beyond the house? And what would clear it away? Something like the hurricane—ripping everything apart, bringing all to light: the hidden corruption revealed, the rickety structures built on the generations of poverty and neglect and entrapment? Everything swept upside down, turned inside out. Houses becoming coffins as the water rose in the living rooms up to the bedrooms, sending people to attics and roofs, where so many waited in vain. The stored-up agony throwing itself outward on the flood. Wind and water sweeping through, leaving behind the debris.

"Seems I'm stuck with you," she said. She could almost see something there inside, not just trapped—but struggling to get out. Herself? Jade? Both of them? Even Lavinia? But maybe something larger yet that took them in, the embodiment of struggle itself. Waiting to get out. She could feel its yearning as it joined her own.

It all had to come out—to be seen, everything in the light. It was there pushing forward, telling her what she had to do. Create something, as she'd always had to do, but this time with greater devotion, once again seizing upon the imperatives of the imagination as each moment required. And she could see herself in an emboldened moment opening the lid. Opening it up, letting out what?—oh, yes herself—and rising, oh yes, rising till she was there over the water—rising with whatever it was as it moved out over the water, over the troubled streets and the broken lives, facing the void—for what could she know with surety?—looking and searching, yes, until she could find Dominique dreaming of gardens.

The House on the Lake

When Isabelle came to take possession of the house she'd
inherited, she had the eerie feeling that it was already
inhabited. She kept waking in the middle of the night to sounds
that could have been the scraping of a chair, footsteps into the
hallway or across a room. Her heart pounding, she would get to
up to investigate, creeping along the wall outside her bedroom to
listen, afraid she might actually come upon an intruder. She found
no such evidence, but she was not appeased. Could someone have
crept in and kept hidden during the daylight hours and become an
elusive presence at night? Was the house pregnant with memories
that wouldn't sleep? Or was it simply her nerves?

Everything about the house seemed unreal, most of all
the way it had come to into her possession. She hadn't known of
its existence. She'd seen André, her step-father, in a hospital in
Lausanne just before he died, shrunken, skeletal, embittered over
the way life had treated him, as he'd knocked about from pillar to
post. Cheated, in other words. No mention of a house. Then a year
or so later, she'd been summoned to a lawyer's office in Geneva to
receive the deed to a house she'd inherited from her father. But it
wasn't André's name on the deed, nor that of her real father, whom
she hadn't seen in some years. She remembered the distant figure of
her youth who'd sent her money while she was at the Sorbonne. He
had helped her during a difficult period, and then there had been a
few intermittent phone calls and letters. They had rarely seen one
another. She stared at the signature of her benefactor and levied a
barrage of questions. But the lawyer patiently repeated that her
father had given instructions that she was to have the house. She
was handed a deed, keys, directions to the location, and the phone

number of the caretaker.

The moment she arrived, Isabelle experienced, first, astonishment: Who could have built such a dwelling? Could it be that André's mining ventures in Bolivia or Peru or Zimbabwe—wherever he'd been lured by the promise of instant wealth—had panned out? Was it his closely held secret—a wish to surprise and mystify her—in keeping with his sense of irony? But what would have been the purpose of disguise? He was too much of an egoist not to want to parade his largesse. When her astonishment had subsided, she felt something close to anguish. It was too much, far too much. More than she deserved, or perhaps more than she'd bargained for. She'd arrived to take possession—of what exactly? What sort of life could she live here, grafted onto what she saw as hopelessly twisted branches? The view of the lake, Lago Maggiori, near the Italian border—how could she quarrel with this sheer beauty? The house itself was a stunning marriage both of location and design, wealth and imagination. It would be all she could do to keep it up, pay the taxes.

She opened the gate to a garden at its peak. One bed held roses of every hue and description. In others were flowers that ranged from the palest blue to deepest purple, a vine of passion flowers clinging to the wall. Palm trees, so unexpected in that alpine region, as well as agaves, one in perfect bloom, rose above the color below. The granddaddy of prickly pears claimed both corners of the wall leading up to the doorway. Elephant ears and birds of paradise. It was not just variety and the explosion of color that took her eye, but the little walks and steps that took you to different prospects of lake and garden. Sculptures that you could walk through and around; columns and shapes, a little bridge that children would have delighted in. Not only a sense of beauty had been at work, but a kind of playfulness. Some of the forms had been left unfinished, as if they required further inspiration. A little maze led to the pond in the center, shaped like an eye, orange captured in a ring of lazily circling goldfish. When she drew nearer she saw that the center, the pupil, held water flowing over varying colors of glass. She stood mesmerized until finally she had to draw back or lose herself in its depths.

She caught her breath. What wizardry had created all this? Who was her father after all? She shook herself back into practicality and returned to the car for the groceries and the case of wine she'd bought in Lugano. She set them down to open the door. Her cat, Lily, followed her in.

In the entryway she met a towering, golden Buddha that looked down on her with a serenity that made her fidget. In its company was a dancing Shiva. Though she wanted to cling to the notion, it was difficult to think of André on any terms with these deities, unless something had figured into his last years. He had lived in the world on his own terms, insisting on his particular truth to the point of what madness? Oh, but she'd adored him when she was little! And she'd always had a soft spot for him, admired his sense of independence, his daring. She wanted to strike from the record that last vision of him as he lay dying.

She paused for a moment on the upper balcony past the entryway and glanced at the shelves of books that extended all along the balcony and took a brief survey: history, philosophy, plays, poetry, art. André had been well-educated, but she saw him as too much of a rolling stone to collect a library. She'd lost track of him during the unsettled period following their return to Europe and her mother's divorce. That era of ruined possibilities. They'd established contact after she was on her own, and would have dinner together when they were both in Paris—in his case, not often. But he had called for her during his last illness.

More books in the study, where the windows, she saw, were open. That gave her a start. But she herself had arranged with the caretaker to open up the house for her. He had removed the dust covers and prepared it to be lived in. Books and papers lay about the desk, as though someone had paused in the midst of his labors and would return to his work soon A clue perhaps that might lead her to the hidden genius of the house, that is, when she could take time from all the details that filled her day: getting telephone, gas and water connected, arranging for a new line for her computer, learning the domestic arrangements and finally meeting the caretaker, Paolo, who presented her with an African Grey Parrot. "A great friend of your father's," he said. "Cesario. He speaks very well—they used to have conversations. Only now he doesn't talk." He paused. "Grief—that is my impression. I have kept him since . . ."

"Do you think he'll speak again?" she asked. She could imagine André with a parrot, the first real suggestion that the house might have been his.

"When he is ready. I play music for him. He sways to the music. And he likes to survey the garden from this perch."

The parrot looked at her as though to size her up, tilted his head and took up residence on the perch.

"A great man, your father. He spent a lot of time here, together with Antonio, planting, installing the sculptures with the workmen. He was full of plans for that plot on the other side of the house."

•

In the days that followed, Isabelle tried to follow Paolo's instructions for taking care of the bird and to make sure there was no threat from Lily. She made some effort to coax it to speak, but, though it didn't appear unfriendly, it gave her no encouragement. She had the sense she had been led into absurdity and challenged by some standard impossible to meet. Outside influences seemed still to be at work shaping the space. Was she being watched? She was like her cat, ears cocked for the slightest sound, listening, pausing in the midst of whatever she was doing to catch a sound from upstairs that suggested a presence.

From the papers and books that littered the desk in the study she could imagine someone in the midst of a literary undertaking. She picked up fragments written on scraps of paper. *"But consider me in all this,"* she read. *"What is there but ruin and loss?"*

Whose voice was this? André's, her mother's, her father's? She considered a moment—or hers? On another: *"Is the notion of happiness itself an illusion? What is to be sought—is it worth the seeking?"* On the third evening of her tentative ownership, she could have sworn that a certain book lying on the desk had not been there before, or else had been open to a different page. *Lost Worlds*, she read in blue letters on the spine.

The writer spoke with passionate conviction about a vanished race lost thousands of years ago when a whole continent had blown apart and sunk to the depths of the Pacific. Home of the highest civilization known ever to have existed. He described a race of towering presences not yet materialized into human shape, who could communicate telepathically and whose sensibilities gave them an intimate entry into the inner lives of animals, trees and plants, down to the very stones. Consider the subjectivity of a flower or a stone, the writer suggested. Sentences were marked, underlined. Comments dotted the margins. *"How far beyond us,"* she read, after a description of their artistic and spiritual achievements. She bent to pick up a scrap of paper that had fallen to the floor. *"What the imagination once created—can it again come into being? Is it ever lost?"*

•

Imagination indeed. She'd never heard of such a place. Its remnants, she read, were still to be in found in the Hawaiian Islands, the fragments left behind from the great explosion that sent this civilization to the ocean's depths.

She was thunderstruck. Was this evidence of André's old passion—what had triggered his uprooting them all and taking them to Tahiti, supposedly to disprove Thor Heyderhal's theory that Oceania had originally been populated by the ancient Egyptians? The pretext for a quixotic search for a lost paradise? She closed the book. The room suddenly seemed to dissolve into an indeterminate space that could hold any possibility—as though what could be imagined could, with enough passion, take form. She could almost see the forest dwellings where this exalted race lived and schooled their young so that they would reach the highest levels of development in complete harmony with the universe.

Paradise. The golden time that lived in the common dream. Thanks to André she'd known such a time—that remarkable year of her childhood, when they'd sublet their apartment, left behind their friends and relatives in Paris, who thought they were out of their minds, and gone to Tahiti. There standing before her was Edwina Dawkins under her sun hat, her horsey face pale, with blotchy red skin, always in need of protection from the sun. "Now, my dears, she was saying, "tomorrow we'll go off to the Tuamutu Islands and do our hunting." With the parrot feathers on her straw hat together with her great beak of a nose, she was transformed into a giant predatory bird. "If only we could find a Gloriamaris or an Excelsus. Or even a Gaughini." Her great dream. Had she ever found any of those or other rarities? Isabelle wondered.

She and Martin, Dan and Maria, Tommy, and don't forget doll-like Nancy, were wild with enthusiasm for what the day promised. All of them in Miss Dawkins' charge. They were Isabelle's family, teasing, paying tag, racing one another into the waves, tumbling in the sand like puppies. The delicious freedom of it. The space around her became the beach and once again she was romping along the skirt of the ocean.

During the day they swam and explored. Come nightfall they took up kerosene lanterns and combed the beach. Their lamps drew up another life, otherwise hidden creatures emerging from the sand only to be popped into the sacks they carried. They took their treasure to Miss Dawkins, who put the creatures into slatted boxes and, with the help of the boys, buried them in the sand.

A month later they returned to dig them up. Carnivorous ants had eaten away the flesh of the creatures inside, and the shells, clean and shining, were ready for sale in the shops of Tahiti or back in England. "Hold them up to your ear for the sound of the sea inside," Miss Dawkins invited them. They all heard the subdued roar. She cherished a box of the shells Miss Dawkins had allowed her to keep. She had it with her still.

At the time she harbored a secret fear her mother might ask where they'd been or what they'd been up to during those days Miss Dawkins took them off to the islands 400 sea miles from Tahiti to search for what would become shells. What would her mother or André have thought of their sea baths among eels (since there was no fresh water)? Would they have been shocked to see their children covered in some tarry substance, a cleaning solution probably known only to the British? As far as she knew, none of the children under Miss Dawkins' care spoke to outsiders of their adventures. Perhaps even then they knew they had hold of something unique.

She needn't have worried—her mother had been much too absorbed in her painting to fret about what the children might be doing.

The buzzer from the front gate brought Isabelle back to more pressing matters, a letter she had to sign for. She expected some legal matter, but saw to her surprise it was from her daughter, Aimée. "I hear you've struck it rich," she read. How had she come by such nonsense? But waiting under the words was the giddy sense of opportunity to be snatched. "So I'm going to offer you an opportunity to be a real mother to me. I want to go into business." Business? When Aimée had no sense of money? What now? Isabelle wondered. "I have a chance to buy into a shop that sells body products. I want to create a new life." She then asked for a sum that made Isabelle gasp. Was she back on drugs? she wondered, and with something like despair tried to picture what state Aimée was in at the moment. Repeating, it seemed, her own troubled youth—trips to Amsterdam, flinging herself into the drug scene there and elsewhere, lost outside of memory. It was out of all this that Aimée had emerged into the world.

She put Aimée's letter aside, her mind a jumble of conflicting impulses about how she should respond, or whether she should respond at all. She was in need of distraction. She took a brief walk along the lake, then threw herself into a graphics project she had contracted for. She had set up her computer downstairs on a table in the kitchen, unable as yet to establish herself in the study. The sun was gone when she finally emerged, exhausted. She poured a glass of wine, then sat for a long time watching the mountains fade into the evening. The lake grew dark.

The darkness cut her off, created a wall, presenting her with her loneliness. She went into the kitchen to prepare pasta. She would be eating alone now and for how long? Mealtimes were always the most difficult—that pause when food and wine demanded the presence of others, the pleasure of conversation and company. She pushed aside the plate and went to phone her step-sister, Elise—a call long overdue. She would try to make it up to her for her neglect. She had to talk to her about the house, the father they had shared. The phone rang, but there was no answer. She left a message and turned away disappointed.

She had difficulty sleeping. But when she finally drifted off, she dreamt of a city of astonishing beauty. Its dwellings rose into crystal palaces and colors played within them. Better than Oz, more spectacular than Shanghai. Beyond compare. Occupied by presences continually revealing themselves in forms of thought, perhaps dreamers themselves in the midst of creating their own reality.

She woke to mist—the lake and sky merged into one, offering a disorienting sense of where she was. After her coffee and cigarette had returned her to the ordinary, she roamed the house adjusting a vase here, a throw rug there. Nothing of this belonged to her, but every item revealed a taste and appreciation that invited her to further discernment. She was avoiding the study, for fear she would be met by some new and unsettling offering. Finally she had to enter, and there she found André waiting for her.

He was running along the beach, a letter in his hand and shouting joyfully, "I'm ruined! I'm ruined!" They'd been getting a monthly stipend from Jacques, André's former brother-in-law, who had agreed to run the factory while André was away. Now here was the letter, no stipend enclosed, announcing that André was no longer owner of the factory. By some law peculiar to France, the business had become forfeit because André had been away for more than a year. It now belonged to Jacques, who had seized his opportunity.

Ironically, it was the escape André had been waiting for. He'd inherited the family business, manufacturing a brand of biscuits and butter cookies known throughout Europe. Though doing business was not in his temperament, he had greatly increased its sales. Perhaps one of the attractions he'd offered her mother was the living he provided. She had a taste for elegant surroundings and designer clothes, Lancôme perfumes and foie gras. But now that André was unleashed, free not to return, he was bursting with new ideas. He could build boats, hire out as captain for tourists. Her mother could continue to paint. "Think of the life we could build here. The mountains, the beach, life in the sun. The best champagne at the cheapest price. You could never starve here— wild fruits, fish . . . Paradise."

There began the first their many quarrels.

"Listen," her mother said, "even Gauguin had to invent his paradise. We'd already brought in the syphilis that killed him. I'm a European," she insisted, "for better or worse. I'm not here to repeat his efforts to escape civilization—it's already beaten us here. All right, so it's corrupt, but at least it's a corruption I understand. Money, I like it." She made a gesture of running bills through her fingers.

The air in the study was filled with accusation and outrage. Raw. Snakes hissing, dogs at each other's throats. André waving his arms, her mother screaming at him. Money. Money. She had a child to support. Isabelle stood before them offering up her little embroidered purse. Even now the field was darkened and rage poured through it. When had he ever denied either of them? Nothing but the best. What were pockets for but to empty so that you could fill them again—with pleasure, with new adventures. He could have lived on breadfruit and mangoes, waiting for the next best chance. Ah, that lover of possibility. Isabelle felt a longing in his direction. He could go with the flow—what did up or down matter?

Would it have mattered that the local culture was being turned into a spectacle for tourists, with its display of Polynesian beauties for them to gawk at? What would you have done, André, as more and more people poured in, pushing up the price of real estate, the cost of goods? "Even if he gets to the top of things one moment, he'll have lost it all in a poker game the next"—her mother's assessment. In the end he followed her mother back to Europe, then slipped away into gossip and legend while her mother resumed painting, made a place for herself in society, and married her third husband, a count, entranced with her beauty. Isabelle was sent to live with her grandmother.

She was left to puzzle over him, and the house. How could it possibly have been his?

"We had Paradise," he'd croaked at her from his deathbed, "and threw it away."

"I loved it all," she said. She could hardly tell him what it had meant to her, but the sense of it had shaped her, the sense of loss when they'd left. That space, original and unspoiled before complexity had set in. She could not tell him what it had induced of longing. But he already knew.

"Precious one," he said, holding out his hand. "We are joined like . . . " A cough interrupted him. "You have . . . the whole world." He fell back—the words had taken all his effort. His face became blank, as though he were looking off toward what had so long eluded him.

But what did she have? The whole world? She fretted over the ambiguity he'd left her with, quite certain he'd had nothing to do with where she found herself. Her mother had gone off to Argentina with the count. André was dead. That left only her father.

If there was a path to discovery, she had the uneasy sense that it lay within the study. In spite of herself she was drawn to it, intimidated by it, and yet when she reached a place where her work flagged, she was impelled to go upstairs and enter, tentatively, the way Lily, her cat, entered a room. But her cat never entered this one. Once again Isabelle was certain of a presence there. The book she had closed was lying open, this time to a page describing the mental life of the ancient race that had once existed. *Thought*— if that was what it should be called—quite beyond the mental experience of human beings. *Mind*—the five senses meeting and merging, finally leaping to a sixth, an antenna intuiting the whole fabric of existence.

•

Nothing of memory, just the forward pulsation of consciousness. Memory had come with man and his particular limitations. He was a creature of flesh after all. But those beings leapt into a reality that transcended mere form to become meaning. Isabelle seemed to stand on a chair looking through a keyhole into the realm of saints and mystics—quite beyond her.

Yet the vision didn't hold. The great crystal temples where the inhabitants entered to renew their creative lives and commune with the forces of the cosmos were there only for an instant. She was watching a sudden great explosion: the very planet shifted on its axis and, amid bubbling gases and shifting plates, the continent broke up, the temples blown to smithereens—as though some jealous force had been lying in wait, as indeed it had. Another race, eagerly vying for power, had plotted to seize control.

She looked around in panic as the nightmare unfolded on the page. Inwardly fragmented, she wondered if there could ever be a condition other than war. That night and those that followed it, she woke in a sweat, darkness boiling up and invading her dreams. Was there a doom built into the heart of things, life continually at war with itself? What if there had indeed been a civilization beyond anything the world had known, beings capable of dreaming to the essential, to the very heart of stillness, to the energies of the dancing Shiva. But man, the latest arrival, had taken the lightning bolts into his own hands and flung them about without mercy or reason. Ordinarily the newspaper accompanied her morning coffee and cigarette, however grim the news. Now she couldn't bear to look at it.

•

Though she hadn't followed her mother's path—her mother was beyond imitation—she had in secret shaped something of her mother's talent and made it her own. She'd done folders full of drawings, some of them with fanciful creatures on an island of her own invention. She'd carried these with her wherever she moved, neglecting them for long periods, then working on her drawings with feverish intensity. She hadn't touched them for a long time. In her troubled state she was impelled to take out her inks and colored pencils. On a weekend that stretched like a void in front of her, she unrolled a large sheet of drawing paper and began to draw, not knowing what would come. As she worked a vision opened up before her eyes of a great cataclysm—a gigantic flash, a progressive set of gaseous explosions in which the planet disintegrated, sending the seas into tsunamis and exploding mountains, rocketing men, women, children into space, heads and limbs torn apart and spewed out into the universe, where they might float forever. Caught up in her passion to set it down on paper, as if the premonition remained apart from the catastrophe. Was there no residue of consciousness?

Were all those eons of life creating itself totally extinguished? She worked late into the night, hardly conscious of what she was doing, until, numbed and exhausted, she threw herself into bed.

When she awakened to what she'd done, she couldn't bear to look at her creation. Quickly she rolled up the drawings and put them away. She knew what she had to do—sell the house and get out before she lost her mind. As soon as she had her coffee, she searched the telephone book for the names of realtors and called one for an appointment. What she would do once she wiped away the present, she had no clue. Suppose she simply set out by boat, train, plane, car, and spent the rest of her life hopping from one place to another, never looking back.

•

That morning she had a call from Elise. "Isabelle!" she said. "You're really back among the living?"

Isabelle wasn't certain.

"When I heard your voice. . . I've been so worried. The letters all came back . . ."

"I'm sorry," Isabelle said. "I went into hiding—Aimée, the divorce . . ."

"I thought you'd fallen off the edge. You know, of course, about Papa."

"No, " she said, knowing now.

"You didn't know," Elise said, in some confusion. "Not even with the house?"

"It wasn't in his name. I thought perhaps André was playing some sort of game."

"He changed it—legally. After he came back from India the last time."

"I don't understand."

"Something happened to him there. I can't tell you exactly, but it's like he woke up in a different skin. You can't imagine . . ."

"Do come," was all she could say.

"I can't leave the farm yet. My favorite horse—I may have to put him down."

"I'm sorry."

They spoke a bit longer. "I want to see you—and the house. It was astonishing the way he put his whole life into one idée fixe. So many sketches. Nearly all his money. His dream, his passion. His retreat. He went there to write."

"Write what?"

"Poems, stories, essays. Words poured out of him. I still have some of his travel journals. He never showed them to anyone."

How strange it was. Even while they were speaking, the question kept nagging at her. Why had he wanted her to have the house, his creation? Elise was more daughter to him than she had ever been. He'd settled her in Normandy on the farm she'd wanted. What Isabelle remembered of him was the awkward shyness between them. He'd tried to get her to talk about what interested her: what was she reading? Was she enjoying her lectures? Actually she never finished. He gave her a painting for her room. She was surprised later to discover it was valuable. She had given it to her roommate. Something of her mother's contempt for him had infected her, and he lacked André's appeal.

Now she had to take him on, confront what he'd left her with. It was dismaying to reassess her relation to him, especially now that he wasn't there—and yet he was. She had, in effect, chosen not to be his daughter. Now, it appeared, he was waiting for their reunion. Prompted by something more than curiosity, she was trying to prepare herself to relinquish what she'd held onto for so long. Hadn't she really wanted André to be her father, to take her father's place? Perhaps it all lay in that year André had given her, when the life force had rushed so joyfully through her entire being. When she hadn't had to give a thought to what Miss Dawkins was doing when she sent out her little band to do her business. Or how it was for the creatures that lived in the shells to be devoured by ants. The innocence of her delight. Now her father had shoved André aside and come back to stake his claims, to haunt her.

She was angry about it. And when she went past the study the next morning she was almost in a rage.

"I hate mystery," she told the room. "I hate not knowing. I hate the idea of caring about you and what you did or didn't do with your life." She stood for a moment listening to the throb of her ill feeling, and then to something like a sigh. Her own perhaps. Was there no escape?

●

She took a deep breath and stepped into the room. To her surprise, it was her mother who was waiting for her. She went to a rectangle she'd noticed between two bookshelves to see what lay behind the curtain that covered it. And there it was: the self-portrait of her mother that had struck like lightning into the midst of their lives. She studied it—it was not simply her own beauty her mother had captured, but something more fascinating, even fateful. No one could walk into a room without staring at her, being drawn to her. And yet it was a beauty too mercurial, too dazzling to hold onto. An enigma. Certainly André had been caught in the spell, as her father must have been.

The story had haunted her for years, how André on some business in her father's law office, where the portrait hung, had stood in front of it spellbound. "Who is this?" he demanded.

"My wife."

"But no longer," André murmured.

Had he heard, her father? Was there a response? Did he laugh and shrug it off? Tell the fellow he was an idiot? Didn't he have the balls to throw him out, or did he know he couldn't hold onto her? As for her mother, was she a mystery even to herself?

For it had happened exactly as André had spoken. To marry her, André had left behind a wife and three children.

Isabelle could remember nothing of their courtship. Perhaps it happened clandestinely. She'd been sent off to her grandmother's the day her parents had separated. When she returned, she remembered that the apartment was filled with flowers—from her father. He'd even left a meal for them. When he went to his bachelor digs, according to the story, there was a book of La Fontaine's fables open to one that applied directly to him, as well as a collection of poems by Bonnefoy, with certain lines marked:

Farewell, our destinies were not the same.

You must take this path and we the other,
And between them grows deeper and denser
That valley which the unknown looms over
With the quick cry of the swooping bird of prey.

He'd been stripped of his domestic life. But with what passivity! Though he'd remarried a young widow who came to him with her daughter, Elise, their days together had been short-lived. Three years later he'd lost her to encephalitis. He did not remarry.

She began sorting through his papers. Apparently his wanderings began long after Isabelle had had contact with him. She read descriptions of various islands of the South Pacific she'd never heard of, where he'd located ruins that had to have been the works of higher civilizations—great carved faces, massive blocks of stones, moved who knew how. No one he encountered could explain their origins. *"I lose myself in wandering,"* he wrote, *"since there is nothing left to bind me—very little to lose, even my life."*

Then on to India, Sikim, Nepal, Tibet. Looking for origins, perhaps, or relics.

She found a folder full of symbols that purported to describe the forces that once lay at the foundations of the lost world: trees and serpents, triangles and circles enclosed in a pair of triangles. She was unable to read the notes scribbled beside them. A name appeared farther on with various commentaries. Bits of conversation noted. A teacher or priest, it appeared, who claimed to be a descendent of those who survived the ancient catastrophe, those who'd fled to caves where they'd hidden, passing down their knowledge from one generation to the next.

These were notes apparently for a work in progress, and as she read them through, she did not know if her father had intended a work of fiction or whether this was a transcription of an actual experience. She could hardly believe it. He called it a construct of contemplation. *"I learned the sacred symbols of the creative energies that once belonged to us, how energy in its various particles is continually forming, reaching into infinity."* Beckoning her to another space and time. She heard her cat meowing to be fed.

Beckoning her. She couldn't give it up now, however difficult she found it to live there. She didn't know if the house would ever be hers or if she could enter her father's life enough to know where he had gone. She would have to start with what was there, just as when she first entered.. To reimagine its creation. She could envision the spot where he placed the house. The lake on one side and cliff on the other, its rocks jutting out. And he had accepted those rocks as a gift, incorporating them into the wall of the veranda—little vines growing in the cracks—that opened so expansively onto the lake. All part of the house now, but taking in water, mountains, sky. She had come to love sitting there in the evening looking out over the lake and the garden. Part of a Corinthian column stood at one side, with the figure of a youth beside it.

Her father had taken up those remnants of the past and reinstated them, those fragments of consciousness left from the explosions of time. Like a curator he had sought to preserve the sensual loveliness of things: in the colors of the furniture and drapes, the paintings and tapestries, and ceramic pieces that decorated walls and tables in his music library. As though having been stripped of everything, he'd put together for himself, not only a whole series of treasures but also his efforts to create something out of them. These he had left to her. She was beginning to gain a sense of her inheritance. Perhaps he'd chosen her, hoping to give her a platform from which something further might spring.

On the porch the parrot sat on its perch watching her. Would it ever speak? she wondered. Would she ever be able to commune with it? She imagined taking a feather with a strong quill, tapering delicately at the feathery tip and dipping it into a bottle of ink.

9659712R0024

Made in the USA
Charleston, SC
30 September 2011